I dedicate this book to my father.
He was a funny guy, and I miss his beaming smile.

TRIALS OF A MIDLIFE WITCH

J.C. YEAMANS

REED SHORE PRESS

Trials of a Midlife Witch

Published by Reed Shore Press under the Imprint Broomstick & Lace.

Lewes, DE 19958

ISBN: 979-8-88652-012-5

For content elements, visit the J.C. Yeamans website: https://jcyeamans.com/content-elements/. Please visit the link if you would like more information on the contents before reading this book. There are spoilers.

Cover: Charles W. Clark, Reed Shore Press.
The cover design uses Rosarivo font (designed by Pablo Ugerman) and Photoshop brushes by Brusheezy.com.

Content/Line Editor: Sarah Faeth Sanders

Proofreader: Reed Shore Press

PRONUNCIATION GUIDE

Gwynedd: GWYN-eth
Cockburn: CO-burn
Gorawen: GOHR-a-when
Shailagh: SHAY-la
Aonghas: ANG-us
Tuatha Dé Danann: TOO-a-day-DAN-ann
Cat sith: CAT shee
Dearg Due: DAH-ruhg DU-ah

CONTENTS

Chapter One

WHERE'S THE JURY?

The amber magic glitters as it swirls toward the ceiling and splinters the plaster upon contact, leaving a soot-stamped stain resembling a spider's web. Chunks of white fall onto the worktable and cover my concoction with a splatter of powdery dust. I cough as I wave at the haze in front of my face and stare into the wooden bowl at my failed protection spell. Did I add too much mugwort? I peek over my shoulder. My son Tyler Wolfe and his girlfriend Zoe Wu gape at me in silence.

"What? Like you've never fucked up a spell before?" I ask, spitting bits of plaster off my lips.

Uneven footsteps approach the magic room, and the door swings open with a bang. Agnes Pritchard, my hedge witch mentor, enters and eyes the damage to her dingy ceiling. She pushes back the strands of her salt and pepper hair and glowers at us. "OK. Who the fuck obliterated my ceiling?"

Zoe shakes her head, her short black hair flopping all around. "It wasn't me."

"And what about you?" she asks Tyler, adjusting her misshapen top.

"I didn't do it," he says, fiddling with the computer mouse. "I was setting up the desktop."

Agnes squints at me, her pale-gray eyes peeking through slits.

"I'm sorry." As I stare up at the hole above me, I brush off the white particles from my jeans. "I tried your techniques. You know...a pinch of this, a pinch of that." They all eye me like I'm a murderer ready to snap, questioning my every action, and the image of a mugshot with *Gwynedd Crowther* written underneath pops into my head.

"A pinch? Looks like you added the whole fucking jar!"

Tyler and Zoe snicker as Dr. Leslie Hughes, the Acting Chair of the Celtic Studies department, shuffles in wearing a short-sleeved blouse and cotton pants. She examines the damage while I pick up the larger pieces of plaster and dump them in a wastebasket. The laughing lightens my mood, but I've been walking on eggshells since Ostara—the night I murdered Dr. Nick Evans, the Tuatha Dé fairy who tried to win my love and whisk me away to the Otherworld.

"It's not like anyone will notice, Agnes," Leslie says wryly. "This will only complement the collection of blemishes on your walls."

Agnes squints at her girlfriend. "Are you deliberately trying to piss me off?"

We all chuckle, and Leslie walks to the table. An arrogant smile captures her mouth as she helps me dust off the table. I think these Saturday afternoon work sessions are snapping the hedge witch's last nerve.

"What were you trying to do, Gwyn?" Zoe asks, joining us at the worktable.

"I wanted to see if I could add potency to the protection spell I found in this old grimoire. If I'm gonna fight off a fae kingdom, I need a stronger pouch."

Agnes guffaws. "You'll need more than that."

"Well, it's a start," I say, shaking the debris out of my chestnut chair.

"You should have warned us, Mom." Tyler blows dust off the computer keyboard. "I finished setting up the desktop."

"I'll remember that the next time I screw up by accident," I say, frowning.

Leslie pats me on the arm. "Your mother is trying to be proactive. The portal remains open, and we have concerns about future beings crossing over, not only the Tuatha Dé Danann."

"Yeah, well, next time, ask me for help before you obliterate my house," Agnes whines.

"I can't believe the portal-closing spell failed." Zoe examines the contents of my bowl, picking out chunks of plaster. "Now we have to start over."

"No one is more disappointed than I am." I puff air at my wisp of bangs.

Agnes shuffles to a makeshift desk where Tyler and Zoe have created a workstation for all of us to enter spells into the online database he created. It took some convincing, but she finally acquiesced with some bribing.

"I don't know why I agreed to this." The hedge witch stares at the blank screen. "This is a terrible idea."

"I've encrypted everything," Tyler says. "We're good. You don't need to worry."

Zoe gestures at the walls and grins. "And now you'll get your house renovated. All the improvements we can do ourselves, anyway. I think we did great work on Gwyn's house."

"They did a fabulous job, including Spence and Tanner." I smile at Zoe and my son. They are twinning in their navy-blue Delaware University at Bearsden T-shirts and jeans.

"I may be old and not as technologically savvy," Leslie says, lifting her chin. "But I know criminals can hack files. That's disconcerting to us."

"I'll monitor the database regularly." Tyler turns on the computer and monitor. "You and Agnes don't need to enter anything. We'll take care of all the input."

"But we'll consult the two of you first to make sure we only enter incantations with accurate information and avoid duplication," I say, wiping off the last of the debris.

"You better." Agnes glances at the hole in the ceiling. "We'll have to live with that for now. What room do you want to start with?"

"You should start with the kitchen," Leslie says. "Paint the cabinets, replace the flooring and the countertops. You should buy new appliances, too."

Agnes scowls at her. "I don't have that kind of money, and you know it."

"Well, I can help with those, dear." Leslie smiles and rubs her girlfriend's back.

Agnes swipes gently at Leslie's silver bangs, exposing her copper eyes. "I suppose I could live with that, sweetheart."

What a difference a few months makes. I wasn't so sure the coven Elder and the hedge witch would find a way back to each other after Agnes discovered Leslie's secret of the Tuatha Dé's threat against me. But that's all water under the bridge now. Well, mostly…

"I only hope the renovations don't slow us down too much," I say, dumping the contents of the wooden bowl into the trash. "We still need to find another spell to close the portal."

"We will, Gwyn." Zoe straightens up a few piles of books next to the desktop computer and messes with Tyler's chestnut hair. "I'm ready to go."

Tyler turns off the computer and approaches me. "We better get going. The rest of the gang will have gotten a table for us at the Raven by now."

"OK." I slip on my hoodie and follow my son and Zoe to the door, snatching my purse as I leave. "Have a wonderful evening, you two."

"And you as well," Leslie says. "Enjoy your dinner."

Agnes flicks her hands like she's trying to rid them of debris. "Go on. Get out of here."

On the way to the Raven Pub, Tyler and Zoe rag each other about the Scotty dog mascots on their T-shirts. I chuckle at their banter and think of my Scottish lover, Archie Cockburn, who likes to joke with me. But I've had trouble laughing at the teasing since I killed his colleague. Well, the tension probably has more to do with the fact I slept with Nick the night before I eliminated him with Archie's family dirk.

The sun parts the clouds as we get out of Tyler's sedan, warming my pale skin. What a wonderful, temperate day for the second week of May. Too bad we had to spend the afternoon inside. I'm surprised my son found a parking spot on a Saturday night. The nearby railroad crossing on Manor Road dings as the gates fall. I cover my ears when the train rushes behind the restaurant, blaring its horns.

The Raven Pub looks grand with a fresh coat of paint on its two-story porch and turret as we approach the double-door entry. I'm looking forward to dinner with the young witches of our coven, the Fellowship of Associated Pagans to the "Unremarkables" of Bearsden. Archie isn't meeting up with us—too much grading to do. My best friend, Ronnie Baldwin, has to work.

Tyler, Zoe, and I make our way through the foyer, passing the wood steps to our right, and approach the hostess podium. But Spence Huxley, my old Celtic Studies classmate, shouts from our regular table in the room to the right of the entrance. His boyfriend, Tanner Jones, and Skye McGowen, my other former Celtic Studies classmate, wave to us. A young man in his 20s with a slender face and short, light brown hair sits next to her. He's wearing a T-shirt and jeans like the rest of us.

"Hi, Gwyn," Skye says in her husky voice. "This is Zachary Ward. He's finishing up a Master's in Chemistry."

He stands and shakes my hand. "Everyone calls me Zach."

"Nice to meet you, finally. DUB has an outstanding chemistry program. Skye has spoken about you a lot during our research at..." I bite my tongue.

"Oh, Zach knows about the Fellowship's secret," Skye says, chuckling. "He's *in the knowing*."

I raise my eyebrows. "That's good to know. I was going to say at our spell research sessions." I love the new coven rule that permits us to be open with our loved ones.

Spence runs around the wooden table to give me a tight squeeze while Zoe and Tyler find seats. He must be gardening, because he's got more color in his skin and lighter strands in his jet-black hair.

"So glad you came, sis. A shame Archie is stuck at home."

"Yeah. He has a lot of extra work after taking over...those extra classes." And that's my fault, too.

Tanner gestures to the chair next to him. "Why don't you sit here and tell us how the afternoon went at Agnes's house?"

"How did the old hedge witch take to the computer in her home?" Spence asks, sitting down.

"Eh. She's dealing with it." Tyler opens a menu. "Even Dr. Hughes acknowledges the efficiency of a spell database, but she's an academic."

Zoe adds, "We're fixing up her house in return for letting us do it, but we have to start all over. That sucks."

"You're entering spells into a database?" Zach asks, cocking his head. "Not a bad idea...unless someone hacks into it."

Skye points at my son. "Oh, Tyler took care of that. It's locked down tight."

Zach nods. "Gwyn, Skye says your boyfriend is a professor in the Celtic Studies department and took over the classes of that assistant professor who went missing. What was his name?"

The young witches goggle at me, and my gaze falls to my menu. Their judgmental eye beams burn through the laminated paper.

Skye twists strands of her wavy, fire-red hair. "Uh, no...he was our professor. His name was Dr. Nick Evans."

I sink into my chair and bury my face in my open menu.

"Right," he says. "I imagine you, Spence, and Zoe are pretty upset about his disappearance."

"Not really." Zoe rolls her eyes. Tyler elbows her, and she sits up straight. "I mean, it's sad, but he wasn't a friend." She pushes her menu up to cover her face.

Oh my gods, Zoe. I grind my teeth, and Spence interjects with a mouth full of lies.

"We're all shocked, for sure," he says as his hands move all about. "Who knows what happened to him?"

I know. He knows. And so do the others. I need to change the subject, so I peek over my menu and search for our waitress to get the orders started. The young DUB undergrad who brought our water glasses must be in the kitchen, but a skinny, young woman with dainty features and bleach-blond hair is clearing a table near the entrance to the room. She's shockingly pale and emaciated. Her Raven Pub T-shirt and black jeans hang loose on her body.

"That student over there doesn't look healthy," I say, gesturing with my head. "A stiff wind would push her to the ground."

Tanner turns his head in her direction. "Oh, she's not a student. Elijah found her wandering at night about a month ago, shortly after our failed you-know-what in the Celestial Gardens. Her clothes were baggy, and she appeared hungry. He took her back to the shelter, but she wouldn't eat much. She wouldn't talk either."

"Elijah Jackson?" Zach asks. "The city council member?"

"Yeah. He's the social worker who runs the Bearsden Shelter. The next day, he drove her to the clinic to get checked out." Skye leans over the table to lower her voice. "She wouldn't speak at first, but she answered yes and no questions. The doctors at the clinic said she has amnesia, probably the result of a traumatic event. A Bearsden Police officer interviewed her. They've checked all the missing person reports, and her picture didn't show up anywhere. She finally started talking about two weeks ago."

Tyler turns his head to grab a look-see. "Why is she bussing tables here, then?"

"The shelter psychologist said she needed to start doing shit," Spence says. "Get a routine going to prompt her memories to come back. But she doesn't have any ID. No social security card. All Elijah could do was get the manager of the Raven to pay her cash under the table. He helped her pick a name. She's going by Kate."

Zoe pouts. "She seems so sad, like she lost the love of her life."

I stare at the poor young woman as she knocks several glasses onto the floor. Good thing they're plastic. She throws them into the tub and walks toward the kitchen. I can't imagine what it's like to lose your memory. But recently, I've been thinking...wouldn't it be great to misplace some of them?

Tyler wraps an arm around Zoe. "That's why I love you so much. You're such a caring person."

"What happens now?" I ask. "Kate can't stay at the shelter forever. What if she never recovers?"

"Elijah asked me if I would take Kate in for a while," Skye says. "My roommate is moving out in a couple of weeks after graduation. I told him I could only do it for the summer."

"Can we order? My empty vessel is chanting 'feed me.'" Spence flags down our waitress.

"Hon, your stomach is never full," Tanner says, his midnight-blue eyes squinting. "Your constant fidgeting burns too many calories."

Spence grimaces at his love. "Go ahead. Mock me. See if you get any later."

We all burst out laughing, and our waitress arrives to take our order. A group of young male students sits down at the table near the entrance. Kate clears off the adjacent table and glances at the young men several times. How lonely she must be.

After dinner, Tyler and Zoe drop me off at Archie's cottage-style home. I've only stayed the night a couple of times since Ostara. Every time I plan to stay, I come up with a last-minute excuse to bail. It's been three weeks since the last time I slept over, and all we did was sleep. But I drag my feet to the rear door and enter.

I kick off my sneakers and amble into the living room where Archie is sitting on the leather loveseat. Grading, I assume. His head is hanging, his eyelids twitching. His fingertips rest on the keys of his laptop. I sit down carefully next to him, admiring his gorgeous, chiseled face, and glance at the screen. He was in the middle of writing an email, and a finger was stuck on F, creating a line of the infamous letter. I swipe wavy ash-blond strands off his forehead, and he stirs. He lifts his head and rubs the nape of his neck as he focuses on the screen.

"Fawk." He presses the backspace key several times and clicks send.

"How long have you been asleep?" I ask.

He turns his head and smiles. "Who knows? I'm so far behind, it doesn't matter. How was dinner?"

"It was fun to hang with the young ones. I met Skye's new boyfriend, Zach Ward. He seems nice. He mentioned the missing professor when I said you were too busy covering extra classes to meet up for dinner. When he asked what his name was, I cringed. The young witches gawked at me. Zoe and Tyler did the same thing at Agnes's when I screwed up an incantation. They're afraid of my every movement."

Archie grimaces and replies in a thicker Scottish brogue. "I'm sure they aren't. You're paranoid."

"I'm not. You look at me in the same way."

He caresses my arm. "Oh, Gwynedd, that's not true. You're..."

"Imagining all of it? They all stare at me as if I'm ready to pull out a knife and go on a murderous rampage at any minute. You do, too."

Archie chuckles. "To be fair, you could have done that before you killed Nick."

I gape at him. "That's not funny."

"No. It's not. I'm sorry. I was trying to lighten the mood." He closes his laptop and places it on the steamer trunk in front of the loveseat. "You have to admit you've been on edge since that night, and you have every reason to be."

"I've tried to put the entire incident out of my head, but how?"

"You don't. But you have to recognize your feelings, Gwyn. You've tried to move on as if nothing happened."

"Talking about the incident only winds me up more. I'm so tight, a spring may pop." I fling my fingers at his face for emphasis.

Archie laughs, and the crow's feet around his icy-blue eyes fan out. "Exactly." He moves his face close to me, inching his lips toward mine, but holds back. "Is this OK?"

"Yeah." I brush my fingers across his cheek.

He kisses me tenderly and pulls back an inch. "I've not pressed the issue, but we haven't made love since..."

"I know. Give me more time. I don't feel very sexy after what transpired."

"Because I slept with Laura?" A crease forms between his eyes.

"No. That wasn't your fault. It's all me. I can't reconcile how I let myself fall into Nick's trap...his glamouring."

"Oh, Gwynedd. I've told you over and over to purge that guilt. He was as cunning as your Aunt Gorawen said he would be. He fooled all of us." Archie lays his forehead against mine. "I love you. You're not on trial here."

Aren't I? I think the jury is still out. "Can we go to bed early? I'm exhausted."

"That's a wonderful idea. My body was sending me an obvious signal, anyway."

He stands and offers me his hand, and we go upstairs. While I'm lying in bed, I stare out the window at the moon, nearly full tonight. I'm comforted by the arms of my lover, but I can't shake the guilt that's erected a fortress inside me. My mind floats back to poor Amnesia Kate from the Raven Pub. How lucky she is.

Chapter Two

FRIEND OR FOE?

Archie enters the Celestial Gardens through the gate. Ribbons of fog stretch across the yard, filtering the light from the moonbeams. He heads toward the mound, turning his head to scan the right side of the backyard, as if he heard a noise. His brow furrows...

My eyelids lift. What a strange dream. Archie is dead to the world, so I slide out of bed and sneak into the bathroom to clean up and get dressed. After I put my breakfast dishes into the sink, I go into the mudroom to put on my sneakers. Footsteps echo in the hallway. When I raise my head, Archie is leaning against the doorway and messing with his disheveled ash-blond waves.

"I'm on my way to work," I say, while tying my shoelaces.

"I was so knackered I didn't notice when you got out of bed. Did you eat breakfast?"

"Yeah. The pan should still be hot." I stand and zip up my DUB hoodie. "I wish I could have slept in with you, but Shane needs me to work today and for the rest of the week. This last stretch of the semester is going to be brutal for Jeff. He has a few projects to complete for graduation, so he can't work. I only have one left." My heart aches for my co-worker Jeff Williams, still grieving over the death of his cousin.

"How has he been getting on? Does he bring up Audrey much?"

"He gets teary-eyed occasionally, but he's focusing on graduation. I think that's helped immensely. But losing your cousin, the only person who really cared about you...that will stick with him for years. I'm glad he's seeing a therapist."

Archie shifts closer and hugs me. "Speaking of therapy. I was thinking. Maybe we should look for a therapist."

"You're kidding. Right?" I chuckle, but he isn't smiling. "You're serious. I'm not saying it's a bad idea, but how would those sessions go exactly? 'So, we're having trouble with intimacy, because I slept with a Tuatha Dé fairy who I thought was trying to kill me but actually just wanted to take me to the Otherworld and procreate. And Archie slept with a former witch lover who was obsessed with him and cast a love spell.' If we tell that to a professional, they'll be requesting psych evaluations on the both of us."

His shoulders fall. "We don't have to tell the therapist what actually happened, Gwyn."

"Then what do we share? Do I confess I murdered Nick Evans? Because that's what gnaws at me."

"Point made. By the way, that detective from the Bearsden Police Department is stopping by Stewart Hall tomorrow to talk with me. Seamus as well."

I hold my breath for a moment. "Why does he want to talk to you again?"

"He must want to clear up loose ends, as they say."

I bite my lower lip and stare at the tile floor.

"Don't worry. Only the witches in our coven know what happened. The Bearsden Police have no reason to come knocking on your door...well, maybe Leslie's door. Just stay in your bedroom."

"If only I could be as confident as you." I pick up my backpack and small purse. "I really need to get going or I'll be late."

"When will you stay over again?" he asks, gazing longingly into my hazel eyes.

"My time is so booked with these extra shifts at Mystic Sage and a research paper to turn in. I promise I'm not avoiding you. In fact,

I'm going for a hike with Ronnie after dinner to help clear my head and work off some of this stress." I push up on my toes to kiss him. "Thank you for being so patient with me. I love you."

Archie brushes my chin with a finger. "My heart is yours, my love."

The walk to Mystic Sage is on the cool side under gray, overcast skies, and an occasional breeze plays with my wisp of bangs. When I hit Main Street, I glance across the street at the apartment window above Roots of the Earth. A vision of Nick Evans standing in the window shirtless flashes in my head. A gust of wind blows my hair back, and I shudder. I shove my hands into the pockets of my hoodie and continue down the paver sidewalk.

When I arrive at Mystic Sage, I wave to my best friend, Ronnie Baldwin, across the street. Ringlets of crimson hair fall to the side of her face as she's cleaning off the tables outside her restaurant, the Sunshine Garden Café. She waves back and opens the umbrellas to provide shade. I enter with only a few minutes to spare and turn on the lights and the fuchsia neon sign displaying the words CRYSTALS, TAROT, MAGIC in the window. As I tap the power button to turn on the cash register, I pinch my nose to stop a sneeze from the attack of the herbal scents permeating the front room.

I meander around the store to tidy up the shelves a bit, but they're mostly organized thanks to my boss and witch friend, Shane Murphy. But there's always one curious Unremarkable who dumps out a bag of mixed crystals and leaves them in a pile. Probably a curious child. While I'm placing them in their storage pouch, the glass entry door dings and closes with a clank of the bamboo chimes. As I rush to put the bag on the shelf, a repeated clicking sound travels back to the crystals room, and my heart skips a beat.

As the clicking continues, I amble to the front of the store. Dr. Seamus Duffy, the visiting professor from Northern Ireland, is filling a basket with dried herbs as he leans on his cane with its unique cat head. He's wearing a navy-blue blazer over a white shirt and matching slacks, and his long black hair is gathered behind his head. The last time I saw him, a vision of the Tuatha Dé fairy flashed in my brain, and I ran to Archie's house—only to find him in bed with that skank, Laura Lovelace, now an expelled witch of the Hockessin Coven.

I shuffle past him and sit on the stool behind the sales counter, planning what I should say. Thinking of how rude I acted toward him, believing he was my foe. A pleasant expression adorns his oblong face as he brings the herbs to his nose and inhales. Shane should really charge for huffing the dried plants.

Seamus finishes filling his basket and turns around, smiling as he approaches the counter. "Good morning, Gwynedd Crowther. I haven't seen you for a few weeks."

"I've been busy," I say as I ring up his herbs and bag them. "But then, so have you."

"Ah, yes. Dr. Cockburn and I had to take over coverage of Dr. Evans's classes when..." He stops and stares at me, his eerie sea-green eyes shining like glass under the lights. "When he went missing."

I avert my eyes and finish bagging his items. "Yeah. Archie told me."

"Of course, he did," he replies in a softer Irish brogue. "It's quite a mystery what happened to the young professor, isn't it? He was a wonderful lecturer with a vibrant career ahead of him. We miss him in the department."

Are you sure about that? Now your job is more secure. "Yeah. It's sad he disappeared. We became friends when he translated a tome I inherited from my mother." I stare down at the counter and fidget with the skull mug holding the pens. "Well, it was nice seeing you, Dr. Duffy."

"And you as well. Please, call me Seamus." He picks up his eco bag and limps toward the door. But then he turns his head around. "Gwynedd, I'm glad to see you're doing well. I was concerned about you after you ran out of the store the night before the spring equinox. I thought something ominous was afoot."

"Everything is fine." I swallow and force a smile. "Thank you for your concern."

"Have a good day." The door dings as he exits the store.

Air hisses through my lips, and I wipe my face. Does he know something? Did I actually see him in the parking lot the night I killed Nick Evans? And what about that buzzing I felt when he touched me the night he followed me on campus? I chew on a thumbnail as my heart rate increases, and a hot flash erupts. With a quick pull, I unzip my hoodie and stuff it under the counter. I snatch an old pagan magazine from Shane's stash and fan myself.

The rest of the afternoon allows for plenty of time to proofread my final research paper. Only an occasional shopper drops in and browses the witchy wares and games in the store, typical for the last week in the Spring Semester. Around a quarter to six, the ringtone on my cell phone plays *Don't Stop Believin'*.

"Hi, Shane. Everything is fine. Just a little slow."

"As expected for a Sunday," he replies in his North Carolinian accent. "No sense in keeping the store open until seven. Why don't you shut down at five and go to dinner early, darling?"

"Thank you so much. I'm eating dinner with Ronnie at her café, and we're going for a hike afterward."

"That sounds like fun. How are you doing? You seem to be preoccupied lately. Please, don't let what happened engulf your life. You did what was necessary."

"I know. But that doesn't erase the obvious." That I committed murder—in an Unremarkable's eyes, anyway.

"I reckon your emotions are all jumbled up and ready to pop. A walk through the spring forest will do you some good. Give Ronnie my best."

"Thanks. I will. Enjoy your evening, Boss." I swipe the red icon on my phone screen and stuff my cell in the back pocket of my jeans. As I'm on the floor packing up my computer in my backpack, the door dings. Great. A last-minute customer, apparently someone in spiked heels.

When I stand, I jump at the presence of an attractive, shapely older woman waiting at the counter, dressed in a vibrant red dress. It's difficult to pinpoint her age, because the snow-white skin on her long face only has a few wrinkles. She has butt-length black hair with bluish undertones, brought out by her deep blue eyes. The blood-red lipstick does nothing to complement her complexion. Staying out of the sun probably saved her skin, but now she resembles a vampire—a day-tolerant version.

My eyes wander to an unusual black leather choker hanging around her neck. A teardrop glass amulet full of blue, glittering liquid dangles from it. I don't sense it, but is she a witch?

"May I help you find something?" I ask, smiling.

"I certainly hope you're able," the woman says in a thick southern accent. "Is the owner of the store around?"

"No. I'm sorry. He took the day off. Are you upset about something you purchased?" I've never come across her in the store, but she could have bought items on a day I wasn't here.

"No." She turns her head and examines the products on the shelves. "This is the first time I've visited Mystic Sage. I'm looking for Shane Murphy, the owner."

"Oh, he should be back tomorrow. The store opens at ten. Would you like me to take a message?"

She taps her polished red nails on the counter. "No, but thank you kindly. I'll stop by tomorrow sometime and surprise him. Have a pleasant evening."

The mystery woman exits, and I rush to the door to snoop at her through the glass window, but she's gone.

I return behind the counter to gather my belongings. After setting the security alarm, I turn the sign to CLOSED and lock up the store. The walk to Ronnie's café would be short if I ran across Main Street, but I don't want to take the chance of getting run over in rush hour traffic. So, I use a crosswalk to the west. We inhale our food and hop into her car to drive to North Basin Creek Park.

Clouds of gray blanket the sky, but we zip up our hoodies and accept the risk of a drizzle. A hike in the woods is exactly what I need, a connection to the natural world to remind me more important things exist than my minuscule problems. I inhale the petrichor from the damp earth below and soak in the brown and green hues of the forest. Ferns curving gracefully. Ornate mushrooms crowding together. Moss hugging tree roots. Branches intertwining over our heads to create a protective roof.

Ronnie skips over a muddy area in the trail, and her crimson curls bounce on her shoulders. The white strip of hair that starts at her forehead has grown about eight inches now and resembles a stick of peppermint as it swirls around the red strands. It complements her freckled, heart-shaped face with bow-shaped lips, and her azure blue eyes gleam with an endless zest for life. With the body of a sexy model, my best friend is a beautiful woman from head to toe, even wearing baggy sweatpants and an oversized hoodie.

"Don't get me wrong," she says. "I love hiking after a light rain, but this trail has so many muddy spots."

"Thanks for coming with me," I say. "I really needed this. Archie and I usually get over here once a week, but the extra class load has taken up all his free time, even with Seamus Duffy agreeing to help. Leslie took over one class, too."

"I didn't want to bring up the topic at the café, in case of eavesdroppers. How are you doing? And don't try to color your feelings with pink roses. I'm your friend."

"I'm OK. But you know me. No matter what I do, the reality of what I did gnaws at me like flesh-eating bacteria."

She cackles and crow's feet splay around her azure-blue eyes. "You're so descriptive. Have you and Archie..."

"No. I just can't get in the mood. My brain says it doesn't matter if he slept with Laura. He was under her influence. Unfortunately, my heart reacts on its own. I forgave him for obvious reasons, but I can't forgive myself for being duped by Nick—Nuada—despite knowing he glamoured me. Archie said he doesn't need to forgive me for anything. I stayed at his place last night. Small steps."

"No. He doesn't, and you must stop blaming yourself. Keep moving forward. You'll get there together." She jumps over a large rock. "How is the investigation going? Have you heard anything new?"

"The detective assigned to the case is talking to Archie and Seamus tomorrow, hopefully for the last time." I swerve around another mud puddle, ignoring the urge to jump in headfirst.

"I'm so relieved. This will blow over eventually, and you can put the entire drama behind you."

"I wish I were as sure as you are."

As we approach a section of the trail with an S shape, the Earl Grey tea I drank at the café kicks in. Good thing I grabbed a handful of tissues from Ronnie's car.

"I knew I shouldn't have drunk that tea at dinner. I've gotta pee."

"Tell me something new." She cackles loudly, and her voice reverberates throughout the treetops.

"Watch out for hikers at the bend in the trail. Or they'll get a free show." I laugh and start walking toward an opening in the woods.

"You're a riot. Do you need TP?"

I raise my hand bearing tissues as I continue into the thicket. When I find an area to hide behind, I scan for poison ivy or oak. The last thing I need is a rash on my dimpled butt. Or chiggers. I push my jeans and panties down to my knees and squat, hoping I don't lose my balance and end up on the twig pile below. A foul odor passes through my nostrils while I tinkle, and I wave my hand in front of my face. Twigs snap to the right of me.

"Ronnie?" I yell as my heart skips a few beats. "Ronnie?"

I shrug and wipe myself with the tissues. A soft growl reverberates behind me, and I pull my panties and jeans up, zipping them so fast I catch the material in the metal teeth. In hiking books, they tell you to turn around slowly when you encounter animals. But all I see is a puddle of brownish-red sludge near my feet. I hop over the wet substance, thinking it's my pee. The animal must have fled.

"What are you looking at?" Ronnie says from behind in her usual boisterous voice.

I yelp, and my heart takes off like a horse right out of the gate in the Kentucky Derby. "For fuck's sake. You scared the shit out of me."

"Sorry. I heard you call my name, so I thought you needed me. For what? I couldn't imagine." She peers over my shoulder. "But when a friend calls, you..." Her face turns white as her voice trails off, as if someone pulled a shade over the sun. She gapes at something behind me and emits a spine-chilling scream.

"What's wrong? Are you hurt?!"

I snap my head around to find a male body lying on the ground, his arms and legs bloodied. My gaze travels up the torso, but I can't get a good view of his face. I shift a bit and shriek at the sight. Our voices resound throughout the park, like blaring sirens.

The young man's neck is ripped open, the skin falling in flaps to the side like shredded paper. His veins are protruding. A small pool of blood collects next to the body and trickles into the reddish-brown puddle I stepped over.

Has the evil Sluagh returned?

Chapter Three
MEOW?

I PACE BACK AND forth on the trail, stopping to check the bottom of my hiking boots for blood. "What's taking them so long?"

"Stop pacing. You're making me jumpy," Ronnie says. "The police have to hike up here like we did. We're probably a thirty-minute walk from the closest parking."

"Well, I hoped Archie and Derek would be here by now. And I'm not making you nervous. It's the dead body in the woods."

"What do you think happened to him? Did an animal rip his neck open?"

I stop and stare at my friend. "Do you think the Sluagh crossed over again? We know anything can come through that portal now."

"Nah," Ronnie replies. "The Host of the Unforgiven Dead plucked eyeballs. That guy may not have much of a neck left, but his eyeballs are still intact—bugging out like he saw what was coming." She shudders.

In the distance, faint footsteps kick up stones. Archie, Derek, and Elijah run around the bend in the trail, wearing polo shirts and jeans. Upon seeing us, they increase their speed. I imagine our coven leader, Trinity Johnson, isn't far behind them. Ronnie's boyfriend darts to her.

"Are you OK, babe?" he asks, hugging her with his burly arms.

"Yeah. We're fine. Just shaken a bit."

Archie hugs me. "Trinity should be here soon. She couldn't keep up with us on the trail in her spike heels. Where's the body? Elijah and I should examine the wounds before the police get here."

"It's through the opening there. Behind the laurel shrub. Elijah, why are you here?"

Elijah towers over all of us like a gentle giant, the dark-brown skin around his eyes crinkling in concern. His deep bass voice fills the clearing as he speaks. "I thought I should check out the body. See if it's one of our patrons from the shelter."

"Ohhh. You think the Sluagh has returned. Ronnie doesn't think so." I rub my palm as I recall the murders of the town's homeless by the Host of the Unforgiven Dead.

"We'll make our own assessment." Archie waves Elijah toward him. "Let's take a look."

Elijah nods. "I sure hope Ronnie is right."

Me too. While Archie and Elijah enter the gap in the trees to examine the body, Trinity arrives, holding her footwear in her hands. She's huffing and puffing as her burgundy hair blows with the wind. The curvy woman grimaces as drips of sweat trickle down her velvety dark skin.

"I'm getting too old for this shit," she says, slipping her feet back into her high-heeled shoes. "Hi, Derek. Thanks for coming."

"No problem," he replies.

She flips her jade-green eyes between Ronnie and me. "Well? Who's gonna fill me in? We don't have much time."

We share what happened with Trinity and Derek, interrupting each other every few words. Our coven leader puts a hand on her hip and directs her gaze toward the woods.

"Elijah and Archie are in there, I assume?"

"Yeah. They're checking out the wounds," I say.

Derek scratches his head through his dark-brown locks. "Did you hear anything?"

"No. Nothing," Ronnie replies. "But I was waiting on the trail. How about you, Gwyn?"

I recall the growling behind me while I was relieving myself. "Actually…"

Archie rushes out of the thicket of woods and joins us on the trail, creases forming between his eyes.

"What do you think?" Derek asks him. "Is that Sluagh being back? That evil fairy almost killed Ronnie."

Archie rubs his goatee. "I don't think so. Different wounds, but the culprit is something with claws or sharp teeth."

"What say you, Elijah?" Trinity asks. "Could the victim be someone from the shelter?"

"Nah. Hard to tell for sure, but I think he's a young man, probably a DUB student."

Several people march toward us, moving at a brisk pace. Officers Braddock Wilson and Quinn O'Connor, both street cops, are present along with four others. Two men and a woman are wearing Bearsden Police jackets over polo shirts and slacks, carrying backpacks and cases—forensic kits, I assume. A short, stocky man dressed in a blue blazer over a white collared shirt and khaki pants leads them. He waves at the group to wait and walks over to us, flashing his badge.

"Hello again, Dr. Cockburn," the man says. "I didn't expect to run into you here." His neck is so short, his balding head appears to sit on his shoulders. A prominent brow ridge protrudes over his dark eyes.

"Everyone, this is Detective Jonathan Schmidt from the Bearsden Police Department." Archie's eyes twitch. "He's investigating the disappearance of Dr. Nicholas Evans."

"I go by Jack. Who made the 911 call?" he asks, scanning our faces.

"I did. My name is Ronnie Baldwin. My friend Gwynedd Crowther and I found the body." She gestures toward me. "We were hiking. When we discovered the body, we called the emergency number and then our boyfriends."

"I'm Elijah Jackson. I serve on the Bearsden City Council. When Archie called me, I contacted Trinity Johnson and asked her to meet me here. She's the director of Family for All and a good friend of the ladies. I worried the victim might be a man from the shelter or a homeless LGBTQ student in her group. I'd like to view the victim if it's OK with you."

Way to cover up you've already seen the body, councilman.

"I recognized you, Mr. Jackson. You, too, Ms. Johnson. I imagine you're both worried the serial killer that was never caught is responsible. I'll allow the councilman to view the victim." Detective Schmidt glances at me and back at my friend. "Where is the body?"

"It's through that opening into the woods," I say, pointing. "Behind the large shrub."

He squints at me. "What were you doing in there? If I may ask."

"I had to pee," I say, cringing. "I know we're not supposed to go into the woods, but I have a weak bladder. Menopause."

Archie smiles. "I can confirm that."

"You carry a watermelon and birth it after nine months and see if your bladder survives," Trinity says, scowling.

I frown at Archie but peer back at Detective Schmidt. "Would you like me to take you there?"

"No," he replies. "Everyone needs to steer clear of the area now. We'll investigate." He motions to the forensic team to enter the woods at the opening. "Mr. Jackson, follow me carefully and try not to disturb the area. Wilson and O'Connor, take their statements and place yellow tape to block off the trail."

"Will do," Officer O'Conner says, her voice squeaking like a mouse. "Braddock, why don't you talk with the men, and I'll take statements from the women."

Pushing seven feet, Officer Wilson towers over O'Connor's almost five-foot frame. He nods and replies in a bass voice, "Gentleman, if you'll follow me to that old oak tree."

Derek and Archie follow him a few steps up the trail, and Office O'Connor removes a notebook from her backpack. Loose strands of her light brown hair fall from her ponytail to the sides of her face. She pulls out a pen and flips open the notebook.

"Ms. Crowther, I'll start with you," she says, swatting at a fly. "Start from the moment you entered the woods to relieve yourself."

I glance in the direction of the woods where the forensic team examines the body and collects evidence, hopefully not including a sample of my pee. "When I went in there, I searched for a shrub to hide behind. I didn't notice the body. Not until Ronnie showed up and started screaming. I turned my head and screamed, too."

"Ms. Baldwin, why did you walk in there?" Officer O'Connor asks, squinting. "Did you have to go, too?"

"Oh, no. Gwyn shouted my name." Ronnie stares at me. "Why did you call for me?"

Officer O'Connor tilts her head. "I'd like to know that, too."

Should I mention the growling to the officer? I don't have a choice. "While I was—you know—I heard something growl behind me."

"For the love of all the gods, Gwyn," Trinity exclaims. "Why didn't you mention that?"

Ronnie slaps my arm. "You didn't tell me either?"

"I was a little busy shrieking at the top of my lungs," I say, frowning. "I was about to share what I heard when the police showed up."

"Did you see the animal, Ms. Crowther?" Officer O'Connor asks.

"No." I didn't say it was an animal. Who the hell knows what it was?

Officer Wilson, Archie, and Derek approach us, and we chat about the gloomy weather. Not long after, Elijah and Detective Schmidt emerge from the woods, their faces sullen. Not surprising. The shredded neck of the young man and the puddle of garnet-colored blood are horrifying.

"We found tracks of an enormous cat not too far from the body," he says. "Must be that cougar roaming through here again."

Archie nods. "I remember sightings of a mountain lion when I first moved to Bearsden."

"Detective, you think an animal has done this and not some deranged person?" Derek asks, scratching his stubbled chin.

"I can't comment on an investigation officially, but I'd be surprised if a person created those wounds," he replies. "They'd have to be out of their minds on meth or crack."

Trinity eyes the detective. "We should let you all do your job. Once you've done your initial investigation, let us know what to say. We'll get the word out to our communities."

"Are you finished with us?" Ronnie asks, nervously tapping her fingers on her arm. "I'd like to get as far away from here as possible."

Detective Schmidt turns his head toward the woods. "We have your statements. O'Connor and Wilson, make sure you get their contact information before they go."

When the officers have finished with us, we head south on the path to the parking lot. I walk briskly, leaving the others trailing me.

"Do you have to be somewhere, my love?" Archie asks, running to catch up.

My best friend shouts from behind, "Slow down, Gwyn. You're gonna pop a vein!"

"Ditto!" Trinity shouts. "I can't walk fast in these heels."

"Sorry." I stop and wait for them to reach me. "I'm anxious, I guess. And I walk fast when I'm thinking."

"What about?" Derek asks. "The death of the young man back there?"

"What else? Detective Schmidt seems to think it's a big cat like a cougar," I say. "What if it's another supernatural being that crossed over through the portal in the mound?"

Archie clasps my hand. "You're talking about the big black cat you thought you saw."

"For fuck's sake, Gwyn," Ronnie says. "You're bringing that up again?"

Derek peers in my direction. "What black cat?"

"Oh, Gwyn thinks she saw an enormous cat the size of a Doberman." Trinity rolls her eyes. "Probably WAS a Doberman."

"I didn't imagine it twice, and it wasn't a dog." I scowl and pound the gravel with my hiking boots. "That cat knocked me down near the castle in Buckley, Wales, *and* it showed up in you-know-who's bedroom on Ostara. Both areas have portals."

Archie squeezes my hand. "I believe you, Gwyn. But no one else has seen evidence of a black cat that size. Are you suggesting this being might have murdered the young man back there? If so, why didn't it kill you? There were two prior opportunities to do so, and now a third."

"I don't know," I say, grimacing. "It seems like an unlikely coincidence, and you always say you don't believe in coincidences."

He raises a corner of his mouth. "I don't."

Ronnie interjects. "You're putting two and two together and coming up with five. Makes more sense the cougar killed the guy. He was probably a student trying to de-stress from finals. I'd hate to be the person to break the news to his parents."

"You'd drizzle tears of empathy all over them, babe." Derek kisses her on the cheek.

"Thanks, handsome," Ronnie replies, batting her eyes.

Our coven leader chuckles. "Get a room, you two."

"I've had to deliver such sad tidings too many times," Elijah adds. "I feel for the police officer who has to make that phone call."

We arrive at the trailhead parking lot, and the setting sun colors the sky in streaks of pink and gray as the clouds dissipate. If the violent death of a young man hadn't just occurred, one might say the night had become dream-like.

"Goodnight," Ronnie says, hugging me. "I'm gonna need melatonin to sleep tonight. That or sex." She winks at Derek.

He snickers. "Goodnight, everyone. And be careful."

"Same to you both," Archie says, winking.

I wave to them both. "Night."

While they walk to Derek's car, Trinity taps her foot. "We should discuss this at the next Fellowship meeting."

"So, you think my theory about the black cat may have some teeth to it?" I ask.

Trinity smirks at me. "Hell no. But we should warn everyone the cougar may be prowling again. I'm not gonna wait for the Bearsden Police Department to get the word out."

"I don't know what you saw, Gwyn," Elijah says. "But it's odd you're the only one who has observed such a creature."

Hmph. No one really believes me.

"Elijah, can you drop me off at Mitchell Hall?" Trinity asks. "I can't believe they finally finished the renovations. I just got the key to the office, and I want to make sure it works before the building closes at nine."

"No problem," he replies. "I'll be setting up a satellite for the shelter there soon. It's gonna be fantastic to have a space close to campus. Would be great to take a peek at it. Night, all."

"Goodnight," Archie and I reply in unison.

On the way back home, the hum of Archie's Tesla calms my jitters a bit. But I wish I had proof of the oversized cat's existence. When we arrive at Leslie's house, he lays a hand on mine before I exit the car.

"Will you be all right?" he asks in a thicker Scottish brogue. "I wish you were staying with me tonight."

"Yeah. It's not like I haven't seen a few bloodied bodies before. I've even seen a mummified one."

What does it say about my life now? I've experienced so much death, it's become the norm. Archie leans over and kisses my cheek.

"Please, don't hesitate to call me if you need to talk. Sleep well, my love."

I stroke his goatee. "You, too, honey."

When I enter the house, I find Leslie has gone to bed early, and her ginger and black chimera cat familiar has, too. Mr. Yeats is curled up on a rug near the fireplace hearth, purring. I'm determined to put the death of the young man in the park out of my mind as I roll on my left side and curl my legs into a fetal position. But when I close my eyes, the dead man's frozen, fearful eyes stare back at me like golf balls with dilated pupils.

Chapter Four

A Woman with a Past

"Aghhh!" I scream, opening my bedroom door and nearly smashing into Mr. Yeats. "Please don't wait outside my door. It's creepy."

Dr. Hughes's chimera cat familiar blinks his yellow and powder-blue eyes. "I am most certainly NOT a creep," he replies in his Irish brogue.

"I said you're being cree-*py*, not a creep. Why are you skulking out here, anyway?"

He adjusts his spectacles and straightens his gray suit jacket. "Dr. Hughes left early this Monday morning for campus and asked me to relay a message to you. She asks that you stop by Mitchell Hall this evening and check on the Seelie Fae children, assuming there's no one visiting, of course."

"OK. Got it. Anything else?"

"Only a reminder that we have a divination conference with your parents scheduled later this week."

"Fine. Can I pee now? Or am I gonna let loose right on this floor?"

He squishes his face like a prune. "You can be so crass, Ms. Crowther."

"So I've been told," I say, rushing to the bathroom.

I spend my morning cleaning up Leslie's magic room with Mr. Yeats's assistance, if you count standing around and giving directions as help. The week before, I had to squeeze in divination and spell-casting practice between school assignments. The older, experienced witches in the coven can go without, but I'm too new to chance skipping practice, and I'd left quite a mess on the worktable.

After lunch, I zip up my thin hoodie and walk to Mystic Sage following the maze of paver walkways on the Green down the center of the Bearsden campus. Patches of gray clouds stretch across the sky, allowing a sliver of sun to peek through. I pass the red-brick Georgian buildings and manicured hedges, relieved that classes have ended. Maybe I can finally relax, and my libido will return. Who am I kidding? My mind will just have more time to obsess over what happened now.

When I enter Mystic Sage, the front of the store is empty. It's not like Shane to leave the merchandise unattended. I drop my purse behind the counter as voices travel from the back. My boss and a woman are having a heated discussion, judging by the tone of their speech. But it's none of my business, so I log into the cash register and prepare for the day.

After a few minutes, they amble in from the crystals room, speaking more amicably. The woman in the red dress who came by on Sunday walks through the doorway first, chuckling. Today, she's wearing a black pencil dress and high heels, the same amulet hanging around her neck. Shane twists his white beard as he follows her. His eyes catch my inquisitive gaze, and he smiles.

"Gwyn, I'd like you to meet Cordelia Davenport. I knew her when I was a young man living in North Carolina. Cordelia, this is my good friend Gwynedd Crowther. She's the ancestral witch I told you about. Came into her powers recently, but she's powerful—when she wants to be." He has a twinkle in his emerald-green eyes.

Cordelia smiles cordially at me. "We actually met yesterday. I stopped by, but you weren't here. I asked her to keep a little secret, so I could surprise you."

"Well, I'm glad you did, despite my original reaction," he says.

"I better get going. Nice to meet you again, Gwynedd Crowther. Shane, I'll see you tomorrow evening." Cordelia bats her eyelashes at him and exits the store.

My boss clears his throat. "I'll be in the back emptying boxes." He turns toward the doorway.

"Oh, no you don't," I say, squinting. "You can tell me it's none of my business, but I have to ask. Who was that woman? Her name sounds familiar."

"I told you about her. Remember?" He shoves his hands in his back pockets.

"The only woman you mentioned to me was a woman with jet-black hair and…" My lips part. "Holy crystals. That's the woman who dumped you."

Shane chuckles. "Like a sack of potatoes. Apparently, I left a lasting impression on her. She searched for me online until she found my store and took a chance I was the right Shane Murphy. She sent me an email after Ostara, but I told her I wasn't interested."

"But she came, anyway. She must really have fond memories of your time together." I recall him receiving that email.

"And if she hadn't, I'd not have given her another thought. But when she walked in here today, all the memories flooded in like a dam breaking. She's at least eight years older than I am, but she's as beautiful as I remember. Must be partaking in youth enhancing spells—would explain her extremely pale skin."

"Does that bother you?"

"It bothers me a smidgeon she would go to the trouble. Unfortunately, she always had a vain side. But that didn't matter to a young man in love."

"Well, she may have worried you would reject her if she had more wrinkles. She must still have deep feelings for you if she went through the series of spells required to change her appearance. I wouldn't be too hard on her. Society puts pressure on women to be youthful—witches, too."

A slight grin peeks through his beard. "I appreciate your opinion, being a woman and all. I better get back to the inventory. The board games aren't gonna jump out of the boxes themselves. Holler if you need me, darling."

"I will," I say, returning behind the counter.

A steady stream of customers flows in and out of the store all afternoon. Ring, open. Ring, shut. Stuff the eco bags with merchandise. Dust the shelves. Straighten the games. I take a break for dinner in the back while Shane monitors the front, and he leaves for dinner when I've swallowed the last of my hummus wrap. When I finally have time to sit down, I realize the clock reads five before eight. So, I set the alarm, lock up, and head toward Mitchell Hall.

The moon peels away the clouds and shines on my face as I stroll into the Celestial Gardens. It's open to the public, lampposts dotting the area to make it accessible at night. But now there is danger of the Seelie Fae children being seen. The Bearsden Coven witches have been taking turns checking on the pranksters, reminding them to only cross over at the darkest part of the night. They don't always listen. So far, we've been lucky, but who knows when their mischievous side will pop out?

I stop for a moment and absorb the wonder of the refurbishment. The landscaper's attempt at returning the gardens to its former grandeur deserves accolades from the city. Short, manicured boxwood hedges guard rose bushes of many colors: red, yellow, white, pink, and orange. And the infamous black ones—in reality, a deep burgundy trained to turn mostly black. Rose Mitchell had an unusual taste, and her husband, Alistair, acquiesced. He only wanted her to be happy.

As I stare at the young hawthorn tree in the back right corner, I understand Rose's desire to attract more fairies. Little did she know the tree would become the host of the evil Sluagh fairy. I sure wish the landscapers hadn't replaced the one that blew up when I stabbed the Sluagh occupying it. *Sigh.*

I glance back at the entrance to make sure no visitors loiter nearby and call on Shailagh and Aonghas. The portal lights up, and they appear through the swirl of light. I kneel as they run to me.

"Aunt Gwyn!" they shout. "Have you come to play?"

"No. It's still early, and the gardens are open to Unremarkables. Remember, I told you they don't understand fairies are real."

The children giggle. "We should meet them, and they will!"

"No, that's not a good—"

The children skip to the right side of the gardens, and my back pinches when I try to stand. That muscle I strained when I fell on the pavement in front of the old city parking building when it imploded returns every so often and always at the wrong time. As I straighten, a faint growl travels with the breeze toward me—the animalistic kind. But this is different. The sound is distorted, as if someone is stretching it apart. I glance at the hawthorn tree where the Seelie Fae are playing, but it stands majestically with its thorny branches and glossy green leaves, no sign of evil beings amidst its boughs.

Rubbing my lower back, I inspect the well-lit gardens. Only the giggles of the children disturb the silence.

"Shailagh. Aonghas. Come here, please?" I ask.

The pranksters skip to me. "Are you leaving us?"

"I have to go home. You need to go back through the portal and return later when the city locks the entry gate. But always peek first before coming out to play. Please do this for Aunt Gwyn?"

"We will," they say, waving to me before crossing over.

When I check the time on my phone, I discover it's almost nine. I rush through the gate toward the paver walkway, texting, and

SMACK. I knock into someone. No. I've knocked them to the ground.

"Oh, my god. I'm so sorry," I say, rubbing my forehead. "Are you OK?"

The skinny, young woman with nearly white hair whimpers on the sidewalk, her hands scuffed. I bend down to help her up. It's Amnesia Kate from the Raven Pub.

"I shouldn't have been staring at my phone. I'm as bad as you young people. Your hands are bleeding. We should clean them."

"I'll be all right," Kate says, staring at the blood on her hands. "I'm on the way to the Raven to work."

"Kate...that's your name, right?" I ask. Her blue eyes are so pale, one shade lighter, and they'd be white as paper.

"Well, I don't know what my name is."

"Oh, right. Elijah helped you pick the name."

"Yes." Her stomach growls, and she lays a forearm on it. "I'm hungry, but I didn't have time to eat."

"You should tell the manager you haven't eaten. He'll feed you."

"I will ask him. I have to go." She walks away slowly.

"Kate? Are you OK?"

She turns around and smiles. "I will be soon."

As Amnesia Kate drags her pitiful body to the Raven Pub, I ponder how sad it must be for her. Has amnesia and is probably anorexic or bulimic, too. But she has no memory of her behavior before. What was so traumatic that caused her to blank out her entire life?

On the stroll back home through the Green, I remember Archie was supposed to speak with Detective Jack Schmidt again. So, I stop by his house first. I enter through the back of his cottage home into the mudroom and kick off my sneakers. He's not in the living room, but the basement door is ajar. As I descend the stairs, the musty air fills my nostrils, and the hum of the dehumidifier echoes from his magic room.

He's standing over the table, his hand raised over a metal bowl, chanting softly. When he's finished, I wrap my arms around his torso, and he yelps.

"Gwynedd?" He turns around and laughs. "You scared the bollocks off me."

"I hope not. That wouldn't do much for our future love life."

He squints at me. "Are you saying we'll have one?"

I sigh and release my grasp. "Of course, I'll get my libido back, but I'm too preoccupied right now. I came by to find out what Detective Schmidt had to say to you and Seamus."

"Ahhh. I should have known there was another reason for your surprise visit." He extinguishes the incense and cleans up the table.

"What were you working on?"

He stares at me for a moment and presses his lips together. "A spell of confusion."

"Directed at whom?" I ask, my eyes narrowing.

He smiles and pulls me to him, hugging me tightly. "Not you, my love. You don't need any help on that front recently."

I frown and pinch his arm. "Who is your target, then?"

"The detective. He had a new list of questions for me to answer, and I had to lie...well, stretch the truth a bit on a few. He spoke with Leslie again as well, but she couldn't add anything more than what she'd told him before. She told him Nick's references checked out at the collegiate level. He's not closing the missing person's case on Nick Evans."

"Shit. What did he say?" I ask as I bite my thumbnail.

"He's befuddled why there is no record of him anywhere in the US. No matching fingerprints. No pictures of him anywhere online, other than the DUB Celtic Studies faculty web page. His birth certificate turned out to be fake. No surprise to us, of course. I told him all of his references seemed to check out. All of Nick's diplomas were valid. He attended those colleges, but there's no evidence of him before he started school. His high school records were fake. Detective Schmidt won't stop until he finds more answers, I'm afraid. I decided sending a bit of confusion his way could help our situation."

Suddenly, I'm nauseous. "What if he figures out I dated him? He'll come after me, especially since I didn't divulge the fact. I'm sure my fingerprints are all over his apartment."

Archie strokes my cheek. "Worrying about it won't change the possibility."

"What about Seamus? Did you talk to him?"

"I did. He told Detective Schmidt he had nothing further to add. That he worked with him, thought highly of his academic work, and enjoyed his company. He said the detective asked questions regarding his Northern Ireland origins, if he was returning anytime soon. Of course, DUB has offered him another year to stay on while there's a search for a replacement for Nick. And he seems agreeable to the prospect. Why are you worried about Seamus?"

"I've told you I still have weird vibes about him. I don't know why I experienced a buzzing sensation when he touched me on the Green...and there's something else I never told you. The night of Ostara when I—you know. I'm sure I saw him standing in the shadows of the parking lot. Only for a split second. I blinked once, and he was gone. I thought I'd imagined it. But now..."

"That is disconcerting. If he was there, he observed everything. But he wouldn't know what happened. That—"

"I'd killed him." I grind my teeth. "Archie, if he was there, he knows. He came into the store yesterday and acted kind of strange. I mean, I know he's a little odd, but he said something to me about the night before, when the vision of the fairy appeared in my head as he was talking to me. He said he hoped I was OK, since I ran off. He seemed authentically concerned, but it left me with an unsettled feeling."

"We should tell the coven on Thursday night, but if I were you, I'd tell Leslie beforehand. He works with us, and she's known him in academic circles for years."

"I'll tell her tonight. By the way, I ran into that young woman with amnesia tonight...literally. I was reading the time on my phone exiting the gardens and bumped into her. She fell on the pavement. I felt awful. She said she was OK, but she scuffed her hands."

"I've not met her. She's living at the shelter, no?"

"Yeah. Elijah got her some part-time work at the Raven Pub. The police interviewed her and made a report. Elijah and Trinity have searched online and contacted missing persons organizations, but they haven't found any leads. She's barely got any meat on her bones. Something traumatic happened to her."

"No doubt. She's probably disoriented, not knowing who she is."

"I suppose. Well, it's getting late. I better get home before Leslie goes to bed."

I kiss him, and he pulls me tight against his torso. The bulge in his pants presses hard into me, but I'm still numb.

"Don't go. You can talk to Leslie in the morning," he says, stroking the small of my back.

"I know you want to make love, but my libido left town. I don't know when the sizzle will return."

He lays his forehead on mine. "I won't pressure you, Gwynedd. But you won't know unless you try. I'm worried I'm losing you."

"You're not. I love you," I say, passing my fingers through his wavy locks.

"At least sleep with me tonight. I promise I won't attempt anything lascivious." He winks at me.

"OK. But I'll have to sleep in my undies. Will you be able to restrain yourself?"

"Aye. I accept the challenge."

He breaks away from me and puts the spell bowl back on the shelf, and we head upstairs to sleep. While I lie in bed, I ogle his chiseled face in the dark, wishing I could summon the horny tendencies that overwhelmed me before Ostara. The image of Nick's face flashes before me, and my heart takes off like a jet. Fuck you, Nuada of the Tuatha Dé Danann.

Chapter Five

WITNESSES FOR THE DEFENSE

THE BEARSDEN COVEN, ALL thirteen witches, gather in our circle on Thursday evening at the Pumpkin House, the renovated DUB Victorian with orange siding and gingerbread molding. This may be the last time we're all together until the fall. With three taps of her staff, Leslie starts the coven meeting.

"Good evening, everyone. Because of the ongoing work on the witchcraft database and the continuing search for a portal-closing spell, I will only visit the UK for two weeks this summer." She smiles at her lover. "Agnes will travel with me."

The hedge witch shakes her head. "I can't believe you convinced me to get on a fucking plane. I'd rather fly across the fucking Atlantic on my broom!"

Everyone chuckles, and Leslie continues. "We have a few items on our agenda, so I'll turn the meeting over to our leader posthaste."

"Before I begin, Gwyn has something she needs to share with you," Trinity says as she stands.

"I've already informed Leslie, Trinity, and Tyler, but I wanted everyone to know that there's a chance Dr. Seamus Duffy may have been in the Roots of the Earth parking lot on the night of

Ostara. Although I'm not sure it was the professor. I was pretty upset after...you know."

My fellow witches mumble among themselves, and my son fidgets in his seat. I sit down, and Archie adds a few words.

"Gwyn is very hazy in her recollections of that night, but we wanted you to know. Because all of you were involved."

Agnes throws her hands in the air. "Fucking fantastic. We're all accomplices. But I don't fucking care. It had to be done." She glares at me, shaking a finger. "And don't you forget that, Gwyn."

Everyone stamps their feet, and the floor rumbles with the sign of their support. A faint smile graces my face, and Archie squeezes my hand. Tyler nods at me.

"Now, for the most pressing item on our agenda," Trinity says. "Most of you have heard about the death of the DUB student by now. The Bearsden Police are still investigating the incident, but they're fairly certain a cougar has returned to the area. He was hiking alone, which is never a good idea."

Spence shoots his hand up, stretching it high in the air and shaking it frantically. Trinity sighs and gestures to him. He jumps out of his chair.

"How do we know it's a cougar? Just because some detective says it is. He's an Unremarkable and doesn't know about the other possibilities." He wiggles his eyebrows.

"I'm with Spence," Tyler says. "That Sluagh almost killed Ms. Baldwin and was after Mom. It could have returned. The portal remains open."

Archie chimes in. "Elijah and I examined the victim. He'll confirm the wounds don't match the injuries of the Sluagh's victims. But we can't rule out the possibility of a Sluagh's return."

"The young man's neck was shredded," Elijah replies. "But there were no other similarities."

Zoe blurts out, "You mean he had his eyeballs?" Everyone goggles at the young witch, and she slides down her chair. "Only making sure we didn't forget that M.O."

"I didn't forget," Elijah replies. "I was trying not to be graphic."

A brief silence occurs, and I use it as my opportunity to offer my theory to the entire coven. "You know, I think we should consider another supernatural being has crossed over."

The older witches and my son shake their heads at me while the other young witches raise their eyebrows. Skye breaks the silence.

"You mean another fairy from the kingdom of the Tuatha Dé Danann?" she asks.

Tanner leans forward in his seat. "Do you think they could have found you this fast?"

"I hope not. I think it may be a cat sith. It's a black cat as big as a Doberman. I've seen it twice. Once in Wales and then on the night I..."

The rest of the words get stuck on my tongue. My fellow witches stare at me as if I'm going to snap and go on a murderous rampage any minute. Beads of sweat sprout on my upper lip, and an aura builds inside. Archie grasps my hand as my face flushes, but I combust and rush out of the house. My chest tightens as if I'm having a heart attack.

When I step onto the front porch, I wipe the perspiration from my face and neck and relish in the chilly evening air. Students rush past the porch toward the Green, and I remember standing on the porch on Samhain two years ago—the night I discovered I was a witch. For a moment, I imagine what my life would be like if I'd never taken that first graduate class and met Archie. Would I have been better off living the quiet life of a widow with a dead, cheating husband? The wooden screen door creaks open and slams shut. When I turn around, I expect Archie to lecture me, but Skye is standing there instead.

"I expected Archie." I lift my hair off my neck to enjoy the cool breeze.

"No. Everyone voted on who was coming to get you. I lost." She crosses her arms and chuckles. "They knew I wouldn't take any shit from you. And Ronnie had to run to puke in the toilet. She's not feeling well."

I frown and pull on my damp shirt. "I see how you all look at me—even my son. Ever since I killed you-know-who, everyone thinks I've got this killer instinct or something."

Skye cracks up and her light-blue eyes twinkle with the laughter. "We're worried about you, but not like you think. We rejoiced when you killed Nick Evans. Frankly, I feel a lot safer knowing you won't hold back when push comes to shove. And you may have to do it again. We all have to live with the threat of Nick's entire fairy family coming through that portal. I, for one, don't stress about it. Why? Because I know you'll do whatever you have to do to save us all."

"You've been talking about me behind my back?" I squint at her.

"Oh, for fuck's sake, Gwyn. Of course, we have. Anytime you talk about the night of Ostara, you clam up like you did tonight. Tyler was so worried about you he asked us for advice. Don't be mad at him. We're family now. And that's what family is for. To support each other through the best of times and the shitty ones, too."

I chuckle. "Yes. And I'm glad I have all of you."

"We're not worried you'll snap and kill somebody. We're afraid of what the guilt is doing to you. Are you ready to face them? Because you know Spence is gonna laugh like a hyena when you walk back into the parlor."

"OK. But they better not give me shit about the black cat. I know what I saw."

"We believe you, but the next time you see the damn thing, how about taking a picture with your phone?"

"Sure. If a Tuatha Dé fairy tries to mate with me and snatch me away to the Otherworld, I'll pull out my cell and snap a pic."

Skye snickers. "That's the Gwyn I know."

I enter the parlor, and Spence covers his mouth. But the chuckle sneaks through. Everyone smiles as I take my seat between Archie and Ronnie. She elbows me while rubbing her stomach, and Archie squeezes my hand. Trinity addresses me.

"Gwyn, I know we've been snarky about your big cat sightings. It's not that we don't believe you, but you were being glamoured the entire time. Without proof, we have to assume Nuada could have influenced your recollections. I think the rest of the coven will agree we should keep an open mind, especially with the recent death in the woods. That being said, let's remember not all things lead to a supernatural explanation. Sometimes shit happens."

"Thank you for humoring me these past few weeks," I say, scanning the circle. "I got the impression you all thought I'd turned into a killing fiend."

Agnes snorts. "Not yet, but I'd welcome a dirk-wielding woman at my side if Nuada's family shows up. We're proud of you for what you did, Gwyn. It's time you accept your badassery, too."

My fellow witches stand and raise their hands, summoning an amber glow in my honor. I'm overwhelmed with emotion, and my face flushes again. Archie offers a hand to help me stand with him, and I call on my magic to join them. Leslie lifts her chin and grins. This is what she wanted from me since the beginning—a powerful witch who wouldn't run from danger. It's time I accept my destiny fully.

Trinity gestures for us to sit down. "Enough of the sappy support magic. We need to move on. The semester will end soon and our regular meetings will convene as needed. As Leslie said, she's shortening her time in Britain this summer to concentrate on the database. Tyler, would you update the coven on the progress? Elijah, you can share your discussions with the council members after he's finished."

My son makes his report from his chair. "First, I want to say something to my mother. I don't want to embarrass you, but I figure this is my payback, right? You've gone through so much. I'm proud of you, Mom."

I tear up and mouth the words, "I love you."

"Now about the database." He clears his throat. "I set up a desktop computer in the magic room at Agnes's house. Since all incantations and spell ingredients need to be entered, we have to start over. We'll go through the books we already sifted through and then move on to the others. This will be tedious and could take a couple of years. Thank you, Ms. Pritchard and Dr. Hughes, for agreeing to it. You won't be sorry."

Agnes scowls at him. "Yeah, yeah. Tell me that after some nefarious witch, or worse, hacks it. And stop calling me Ms. Pritchard."

Tyler flinches and sits down as Elijah stands to give us news about his private meeting with our allies on the city council. Leslie glares at her partner.

"Jessica Devine and the others are concerned about our timeline to close the portal in the mound. I've reiterated we have no idea when we'll find a spell. They're distraught at the possibility of other Unremarkables discovering the evidence of the Seelie Fae children."

Trinity crosses her arms. "Hmph. They'll have to deal. We're doing our best to monitor them every night."

"They have a point," Spence says. "Going in there late at night is getting old. I need my beauty sleep." He bats his eyelashes, and we chuckle.

Leslie chimes in. "The responsibility falls on us, my friends. We must keep the little ones in check."

"One more thing," Elijah says. "I want to thank Skye publicly for taking in the young woman who lost her memory. She'll recover much better in a normal environment."

My fellow witches respond with overlapping comments of "what a friendly gesture" and "you're the best."

"I don't mind," Skye replies. "Kate, that's the name she chose. Seems like she's had some major trauma in her life, but she's very sweet and tries so hard to please everyone."

Elijah nods. "Well, I can't thank you enough. It's risky taking in a total stranger who has no history."

"As the leader of this coven, I commend you," Trinity adds. "Just be careful not to use any magic around her."

Skye sends a thumbs up. "Understood."

"Is there anything else for the good of the coven?" Leslie asks.

Shane glances at me and raises his hand. "I'd like to make you aware of a new witch in town. She's an old friend from my younger days and is considering moving to Bearsden. I wanted you to be aware in case you sensed new magic in the air."

"How do we know we can trust this friend of yours?" Agnes asks. "We know nothing about her."

"I agree we should vet her, and it appears we'll have plenty of time to do that. She's renting an apartment for a few months to see if she takes a liking to the town. I'll be sure to keep an eye on her."

Zoe snickers. "I bet you will."

"Zoe," Tyler says, nudging her.

Shane chuckles. "It's all right. I can swallow some ribbing. Certainly, Zoe has endured her share in our circle."

Leslie stands and taps her staff. "With that, I adjourn this meeting. Stay safe, everyone. And enjoy your summer."

She meant that bit of well-wishing for everyone but Archie. With the "disappearance" of Nick Evans, he and Seamus have to teach summer school. Considering his summer class schedule and my low libido, we may not have sex for months. Damn you, menopause...and Nuada. I exhale slowly.

We stack the chairs, and a few of us gather on the porch. I wave goodbye to Tyler and Zoe as they leave with Elijah, Skye, and Trinity. A gentle wind displaces my bangs, and I zip up my hoodie.

"I'm sorry I burst out of the parlor," I say, eating crow. "You are truly family to put up with me." As I lower my gaze, Archie brushes my arm.

Shane approaches and gives me a fatherly hug. "We all heal at our own pace, darling. See you tomorrow at the store." He descends the steps toward his home on Elm Street.

"Gwyn, we'll see you at Agnes's on Saturday." Tanner pulls on his sport coat. "I'm going to assess her kitchen."

"I can come by as well if you like," Archie says.

"You'll be busy with grading, but we could use your help during the reno."

Archie curls up a corner of his mouth. "Absolutely."

Spence taps the hedge witch's shoulder. "Are you excited to get your kitchen redone?"

"I'm still not keen on you doing the renovations while I'm in Britain with Leslie," she replies, twisting her face into a knot of wrinkles. "What if I don't like what you're doing?"

Ronnie stuffs her hands in the pockets of her Virgo constellation hoodie. "We'll send you pictures. I'm heading back to the café. I have to close up. Goodnight, all."

Leslie buttons her floral cardigan and reaches for Agnes's hand. "I'm sure they'll do fine work, dear. You need to trust people more."

Agnes snickers as she grasps her lover's fingers. "That's funny coming from you, sweetheart."

The Elder frowns at her, and the rest of us crack up. There was a time when she would have turned her back on the hedge witch and marched away for such a clap back.

"Oh, come on, sweetheart," Agnes says, puckering her lips. "Let's go to my house and get to bed."

Leslie glares at her as they leave. "May you have a restful sleep, everyone."

"Let's go as well, Gwyn," Archie says, yawning. "I'm pure done in. Tanner, text me if you change your mind."

Tanner flashes a thumbs-up as he and Spence head to their car. On the stroll through campus, Archie clasps my hand, and I grip his tightly. As a phantom zephyr plays with his wavy locks, I ogle his chiseled profile. How lucky I am to have this man's unconditional love. I grin widely, and he catches my gaze.

"What? Do I have a snotter on my nose?"

I laugh and lean into his upper arm. "No. I gaze at your gorgeous face and am so grateful to the otherworldly powers for bringing you to me."

He lifts my hand to his mouth and kisses it. "Stay with me tonight. Perhaps the magic will flow to our otherworldly nether regions."

"I appreciate you trying, but I have to work tomorrow. And you have grading."

"You'll be alone with the familiar, you realize."

"Oh, shit. I'll have to deal. I don't have any clothes. By the time I pick out what to wear and stuff my backpack, I'll fall on the mattress and collapse. Tomorrow night?"

We arrive at the bottom of the driveway, and he pulls me close to him. His icy blues shimmer under the moonlight, and I sense the thirst in them. He swipes a finger down my cheek and kisses me. I part my lips, inviting him in, and he accepts fervently. He pulls away, adjusting his bulge, and cups my face.

"I'm sorry. I want you so badly, I ache."

"Skye's lecture made me reevaluate how I've been perceiving everyone's concern. Moving forward, I know what to do to get my mojo back."

"And I'll be waiting for you. Sleep well, my love."

"You too, honey."

Archie ambles up the street, and I push the red side door open with my hip and enter. When I tiptoe through the living room, Mr. Yeats is fast asleep in front of the fireplace hearth on his favorite rug in chimera cat form. After washing up, I hop into bed and pull my linens to my neck. I'm so thankful for this family full of witches who defend my murderous actions. But all this worry about the detective finding out I murdered Nick Evans has chomped away at my sanity and libido bit by bit. What do you know, Dr. Seamus Duffy? Well, I'm going to find out.

Chapter Six

HAUNTING MEMORY

Archie ambles into the Celestial Gardens, shutting the gate behind him. A distorted sound prompts him to scan the area. Moonlight scatters through the threads of fog and mist, obscuring his search, and lines form in his brow. He spins around. Suddenly, he's lying on the ground.

"Aghhh!" I yell when I open my eyes to discover yellow and blue eyeballs staring into mine, only an inch away.

Mr. Yeats's meow morphs into a high-pitched scream as he transforms into his human presentation. I shove him off the bed.

"What the fuck are you doing in my room? On my bed?!"

He searches the floor for his spectacles and places them back on the ridge of his nose. "I was only being proactive. Dr. Hughes said you had to work on this Friday morning, and you weren't up at your usual time. I was checking your nostrils."

"My nostrils?" I grimace, but my face relaxes immediately. "You were checking if I was breathing."

Mr. Yeats brushes off his gray suit jacket as he stands and fluffs up his bow tie. "Yes. I wanted to make sure you were...still of this world."

How can I grumble over his concern for my life? "OK. But can you leave now? I have to get cleaned up and dressed for work."

"Of course. I am terribly sorry for frightening you. I will take my leave." He walks through the doorway but turns around. "Don't forget the appointment you have with your parents this week. They'll be expecting you for a divination conference."

"I won't forget, but thank you for the reminder. I have been more forgetful than usual for the last few weeks. But now you have to move. I gotta pee."

"Of course," he says, stepping aside. "I'll be in the magic room if you need me. Have a wonderful day, Ms. Crowther."

"You, too, Mr. Yeats."

I recall the dream. It's the same as before, but longer. Does it mean something?

After a quick breakfast of granola, oat milk, and Earl Grey tea, I throw on my tree-of-life T-shirt and a pair of jeans and head to Mystic Sage to open the store. Thankfully, Jeff returns tomorrow to work for a couple of weeks until he graduates, and I can go back to part-time hours. I have a long to-do list, and Seamus Duffy sits in the number one spot.

The morning drags on with a sprinkle of shoppers stopping in to browse, buying trinkets of tiny crystals and mini tarot card decks. The students are stuck in their dorms and apartments, cramming for finals. Soon, most of them will leave for the summer, and the townies will experience a breather. Two young boys walk in, and they wave to their mother as she points to the store across the street. Is she really going to leave them in here to wreak havoc?

I lock the cash register and amble over to the puzzles and games where the unaccompanied children are sampling the wares. They're well-behaved, but how irresponsible of their mother to let them enter a store alone. The glass entry door dings, and I turn around expecting to see the woman, but I'm taken aback when I discover it's Dr. Seamus Duffy.

He passes by me wearing a DUB polo shirt and black slacks, smiling as he nods, and limps toward the herbs using his cane. I continue monitoring the miniature shoppers until they notice their mom is tapping on the window glass. They scuttle and giggle as they exit, and I exhale. I'd hoped to give her a lecture on allowing her young children to roam freely in a store. Right after, Shane enters with a ding.

"Hi, darling. Slow morning?"

"Yeah," I say, returning to the cash register. "A few browsers, including those boys. Their mother let them loose in the store without supervision. We're in different times."

"We certainly are." Shane hangs his moon phases hoodie on a hook behind the counter. "Why don't you take a break and get some lunch?"

Seamus approaches the cash register with a full basket and sets it on the counter. He places an eco-bag on the surface.

"OK," I say. "As soon as I ring up Dr. Duffy's items."

"How are you both faring?" Seamus asks. "I'm deep in grading. So much to finish before the finals."

"I'm getting along just fine," Shane replies. "Did you find everything you need?"

"Oh, yes. You have the best dried herbs and flowers. It's why I make a special trip to your store."

"Well, I appreciate your support."

"And how about you, Ms. Crowther?" the professor asks. "Archie mentioned you found the body in the park. It must have been dreadful."

I'm silent for a moment, taken aback that Archie would have told him. "Yes. My friend Ronnie and I were hiking. We screamed so loud, it probably echoed throughout the entire North Basin Park." I continue to bag his merchandise, and a tremor appears in my hand.

"Was it the first time you chanced to view a dead body?" he asks, his sea-green eyes capturing mine.

I swallow and hand him his bag. Shane interrupts before I can answer.

"I hope the end of the semester isn't too stressful, Seamus. Will you head back to Northern Ireland when you're finished with classes?"

"No," he replies. "Since the department is short-staffed, Dr. Hughes asked me to remain for next year. Possibly apply for a permanent position. They are trying to work something out since I'm not qualified for the chair position."

My breathing stops, and I avert my eyes. "How wonderful for you."

Shane shakes his hand. "Well, congratulations, professor. I'm sure DUB is as happy as a lark you're willing to stay on."

"Thank you. I better be on my way," Seamus says. "The research papers won't grade themselves."

Shane smiles. "Have a good day."

As Seamus exits, I snatch my purse from under the register and dash to the front of the store. My boss walks behind the counter.

"I'll be back in an hour, boss!" I yell as I open the door.

"Take as much time as you need, Gwyn. I'm not going anywhere."

I run out and scan the east side of Main Street, then the west. Seamus appears to be walking back to campus. I push through the crowds littering the sidewalk but lose track of him. When I arrive at the opening where the Green intersects with Main Street, I scour the maze of paver walkways. There he is! I turn toward the steps as a hand taps my shoulder.

"Hello! Gwynedd Crowther, right?" says a woman with a Southern accent.

I turn my head and find Cordelia Davenport standing next to me dressed in a short-sleeved blouse, a tight skirt, and black high-heeled shoes. "Hi. I'd love to talk but..." I glance back at the Green. Seamus has disappeared.

"I was on my way to eat at that adorable pub up the road," she says. "Shane took me there for dinner. I've not got any food in my fridge yet. Only moved into the apartment I leased over Roots of the Earth this week. Have you eaten yet? I'd love to buy you lunch and get to know one of Shane's friends without him around. Girl talk can't flourish with a man slipping in his opinions. Am I right?"

Holy crystals. She rented Nick's apartment. I guess they finished cleaning it out. She better never invite me for dinner. Seamus must be back at the department by now, and what was I going to find out following him there, anyway? And I do need to eat.

I glance at the Green once more, considering her offer. "Sure. Why not? The Raven has an awesome lunch menu." But she's a little overdressed for a tavern. I notice she's wearing that tear-drop glass amulet again. The blue essence inside swirls mysteriously, sparkling when a sun ray reflects off the glass.

"Fabulous. We'll have to stroll at a snail's pace. My heels get caught in the cracks of these pavers. Why can't they have concrete like every other city?"

Isn't she critical? "They used to have concrete, but they renovated Main Street by adding paver walkways when the city council and the local businesses worked together to improve the downtown. They even won an award."

"Well, sometimes what you see on the surface is only covering up the shit beneath. I say better to keep things practical."

As we stroll to the Raven Pub a block away, Cordelia prattles on about getting her nails done at the local salon, complaining the nail technician splattered dots of polish on her cuticles.

"Just look at this mess. If she was expecting a tip, she had a rude awakening coming."

Oh, my gods. I don't know what Shane ever saw in this woman.

"Here we are," she says. "I'm gonna ask the hostess for that table for two under the glass case displaying the stuffed raven."

Can you not? I can't stop her. She's paying for lunch. The hostess with blue hair and facial piercings shows us to the table. I glare at the raven as the waitress hands us menus.

"I read in the menu the restaurant got its name from the poem by Edgar Allan Poe. Because he slept here when he was lecturing at Delaware University at Bearsden's English department. Rumor says he put a curse on this establishment. Do you believe that story?"

"Well, they say he stayed at the hotel that occupied this space before they built the Raven Pub. That one burned down to the ground."

Cordelia lets out the most ear-scraping laugh. "Well, butter my butt and call me a biscuit."

That's a phrase you don't hear every day. "I should get something easy to make, like a kale salad with goat cheese. Shane needs me back in forty-five minutes."

Cordelia pushes her long black hair onto her back. "Oh, sweetie, he won't mind if your lunch goes over a bit."

"That's not the point," I say. "I don't like to take advantage of my friendship with my boss." *But apparently, you wouldn't have a problem doing that.*

"Sweetie, that's a woman's prerogative. The gods gave us tools only women can use wisely. You're wasting energy if you don't use them."

What a cauldron full of bunk. While she laments about a floral dress she wished she had purchased at Roots of the Earth, Amnesia Kate ambles in carrying a bus tub. While she clears a table on the other side of the room, I catch her staring at us. I wave, and she snaps her head down, continuing to collect the dirty plates and glasses. She peers up through strands of pale-blond hair at us again. When I turn back toward my lunch date, she's spying on the frail young woman.

"Do you know Kate?" I ask, perusing the salad section of the menu.

Cordelia casts her gaze onto the menu in her hands. "Who, pray tell?"

"The young woman bussing the table. You were looking at her. Do you recognize her face?"

She glances at Kate briefly and continues to read the menu. "Can't say that I've made her acquaintance."

"I was only asking because you looked at her as if you might. She has amnesia and can't remember who she is."

"Poor thing," Cordelia says. "The salads look absolutely scrumptious. I believe I'll order one too, and you can make it back to Mystic Sage on time."

Kate peers at us one more time and leaves the room, holding the tub of dishes and glasses. She's probably confused every time she sees a new face. I can't imagine what she's going through.

We chat about Cordelia's younger days when she was dating Shane, and her face lights up recalling their time together. But she asks a lot of personal questions about him I can't answer. Has he dated anyone since his wife died? Did he ever search for her on the internet? How are his magic skills using crystals since they parted ways? Parted ways? He said she dumped him. Sounds like her recollections don't align with his.

When we finish our meal, she insists on picking up the tab, and I let her. I'm a poor grad student now. As we're getting up from our table, I grimace at the dead raven behind the glass. How nauseating. Who came up with the bright idea of stuffing a dead animal? As we're meandering toward the exit, Detective Jack Schmidt wanders into the main room and approaches the hostess. I lower my head as we pass and dart to the door.

"Why are you in such a rush, Gwyn?" Cordelia asks when she catches up with me. "You've got plenty of time."

"No reason. Eager to get back. The store gets busy during lunch." I step onto the porch, holding my breath, and exhale when the door shuts behind me.

"Thank you so much for joining me for lunch. I can see why Shane speaks so highly of you. He said you came into your powers only a couple of years ago and practice magic with an amazing skill level."

I blush. "Well, Shane exaggerates. I still have much to learn about the craft. Thank you for lunch."

"You're most welcome, sweetie. And tell Shane I'll call him later after he's closed up shop. Bye now."

I wave as she struts toward her apartment above Roots of the Earth, and I cross the street to make my way back to work. She's not what I imagined when my boss first shared the story about his past love.

Mystic Sage has a line at the register when I enter, and I dash behind the counter.

"You got here at the right time," Shane says, ringing up a customer. "Can you take over the register while I help customers in the crystals room?"

"Sure." I address the next customer. "Give me a minute to log into the computer, and I'll be right with you."

"Where did you eat for lunch?" my boss asks as he walks away.

"At the Raven. I ran into Cordelia, and she took me to lunch."

Shane turns around and grins. "Well, wasn't that sweet of her? I'll be in the back."

Was it? I'm not so sure. But how I feel about Cordelia doesn't matter. If he wants to give this woman a second chance, it's not my business.

When I enter through the back door of Archie's cottage home, the intoxicating aroma of freshly baked bread overwhelms me. I kick off my sneakers and peek in the oven to discover he's cooked Mushroom Wellington. I amble through the short hallway to the foyer. The dimmed alabaster ceiling light in the living room casts eerie shadows on the weapons display of flintlock pistols and Scottish dirks.

"How was work?" Archie asks in a soft Scottish brogue. He appears relaxed in a black T-shirt and jeans—must have finished a lot of grading.

"Fine. The morning was pretty chill. But when I returned from lunch, there was a throng of shoppers packing the store. Unusual for study week."

I shuffle into the dining room. He's lighting candles, and the chandelier emits a faint glow. His Scottish tartan china rests on the table, and a bowl of salad waits to be served. He pours white wine into our glasses.

"What's this? My birthday isn't until May 20th. What are we celebrating?"

He saunters over and kisses me. "That we're here. Together. Do we need any other reason?"

"No." I stroke his arm. "We don't."

"Good. Then sit down, witch. I need to get the Wellington out of the oven before it burns."

I chuckle and sit in one of the heavy oak chairs while Archie darts into the kitchen. He returns with the main dish and sets it on the table. As I'm filling my bowl with salad, an aura warms my torso. I pass the bowl of greens to him and smile coyly.

"Do you have a lot of grading to complete tonight?"

"Naw. I closed my laptop for the day, so I'm all yours this evening."

"I know what you're doing. You cooked this meal on our first date."

"Aye. First time I ever cooked a Wellington. But I wanted to impress you."

I stab my romaine lettuce. "You could have served me anything. I'd have come back again."

"I'm so glad you did." He slices the Mushroom Wellington and sets a slice on both our plates. "Anything else happen at work?"

"Seamus Duffy came by the store. He still sends a chill down my spine. There's something about him. Why don't you sense it?"

"I don't know, Gwyn. I mean, his social skills are lacking, sure. What did he say to you?"

"He asked how I was doing after discovering the body in the woods. You told him it was me?"

"Yes. I told him you were quite upset. Is there a reason I shouldn't have?"

I chew hard on a piece of Wellington and swallow. "I guess not, but I told you he may have seen us in the parking lot the night of Ostara. He asked me if that was the first time I viewed a dead body. Shane interrupted us, so I didn't get to answer."

His brow creases. "That's an odd question to ask, but it may mean nothing. He hasn't said anything to Leslie or me."

"Let's not worry about it tonight. I don't want to ruin the wonderful dinner you made. I went out to eat and ran into Shane's old flame, Cordelia Davenport. She offered to buy me lunch. We ate at the Raven. She appears to be a very superficial person. Odd for a witch. But they say it takes all kinds. I am a little puzzled why Shane is attracted to her."

Archie raises a corner of his mouth. "He was young and following the desires of his groin. Don't worry about Shane. He's a seasoned witch and has a lifetime of experience."

"I know. By the way, Detective Schmidt walked into the Raven while Cordelia and I were leaving. He walked to the hostess...alone. Do you think he was investigating?"

"No way to know. More likely he was, since no one was with him. But he could have been meeting someone, too."

I finish my Wellington and stand to collect our plates.

"Don't bother, Gwyn. I'm going to stuff everything in the fridge." He points a finger at me. "And if you follow me into the kitchen like the last time, you'll earn a good spanking."

I chuckle. "Promise?"

"You're a tease, witch." He fills my glass with a bit more. "Why don't you take your wine into the living room? It's too warm for a fire, but we can relax in front of the hearth."

"Don't take too long. I'll be waiting."

While I lie on the plush beige rug, I remove my socks to let my toes breathe. Soon after, Archie saunters into the room, grabbing his wine glass along the way, and lies down next to me. I suck on my lower lip, anticipating his next move. My stomach churns, and I gulp some wine.

"Gwynedd, please don't feel pressured. I hoped a pleasant romantic dinner would help us rekindle our feelings. But I'm chuffed to lie here next to you and sip our wine." He brushes a finger along my jawline.

"You've been so patient. I love you, Archie Cockburn."

I lean over and kiss him, recalling how ardent he was on our first date. He cups the back of my head and presses harder, parting his lips. Our tongues intertwine, and a warmth emerges between my legs—a yearning I'd missed.

"Sit up," I ask, licking my upper lip. "I want to take your shirt off."

He chuckles. "I do as I'm told."

I laugh and remove his shirt, tossing it aside. As I caress his shoulders, he fondles my breasts through my blouse. But he's tentative, sliding his hand to my back.

"If you need to stop, just say so. I don't want to make things worse."

"You could never do that. I always feel safe in your arms."

As I pass my hands over his nipples, I kiss him, longing for the arousal to keep building. He pulls away, and a mischievous smile erupts as he pulls my shirt over my head. As always, he unclasps my bra deftly and slips it off. He traces a circle around an areola, never taking his eyes off mine.

"There's nothing sexier than a topless woman in blue jeans."

"Except one wearing nothing?"

I unbutton the top of his jeans and tug the zipper down slowly. The bulge in his pants causes the denim to flap open, and I massage his groin through the material.

"Ahhh...that's much better," he moans. "I missed your touch so much. I love you, stubborn woman."

When I bend my head and kiss him passionately, he pulls me against his chest, wrapping his arms tightly around my torso. The touch of his skin against my breasts sends all the negative thoughts away. *I can do this.* I can finally make love to him after the awful mistake I made sleeping with Nick. The guilt flees like a dove escaping captivity in a tower, and my body fires up with desire.

"Stay still," I say, panting. "I want to shower you with kisses."

I place my warm lips on his neck and work my way down to his pecs, kneading his nipples as I go. All the while, I'm rubbing his manhood through his pants. I'm so excited to give him pleasure after he's been so patient with me.

"Oh, Gwyn," he moans, stroking the back of my head. "Your lips titillate my skin when you plaster me in kisses, but let me pleasure you first."

I peer up at his clear-blue eyes. "No. I want to."

"Well, if you insist, I'll not argue with you, witch," he says in a thicker Scottish brogue.

"You should know better after all this time."

I chuckle as I graze his abdomen with my tongue. When I reach the top of his underwear, I lean back and hook my fingers around the banding. As I pull them down, I glance up at this man I love so much, only to find Nuada's face staring back at me! An urge to vomit takes hold, and I run to the powder room off the kitchen. Archie dashes after me.

"Gwyn! What's wrong?" he asks, banging on the door.

I try to hold back, but I throw up a little in the toilet and tears roll down my cheeks. I slam the toilet lid down and wipe the wetness from my face. That bastard will not ruin my life from his mummified state. I open the door, and Archie's standing there, his jeans zipper pulled up and his bulge gone.

"Are you all right, my love?"

"No. But I'm gonna be. I appreciate all you went through tonight. It almost worked."

He hugs me and caresses my bare back. "We'll try again when you're ready. Why don't you go up to bed? I'll join you after I've taken the dishes to the kitchen."

"OK. Can you bring my bra and shirt when you come?"

"Of course." He kisses my forehead. "Save a spot for me."

I go upstairs to get ready for sleep. Archie's steps echo in the stairway a few minutes later. While he's washing up in the bathroom, I stare at his family's ancestral dirk in the glass case, recalling the moment I inserted the blade into Nuada's torso. You're not going to win from the grave, Nuada.

Chapter Seven

GIRL TALK

THE NEXT MORNING, RONNIE sets a cup of Earl Grey tea on the table for me and sits down with her mug of death coffee—black and thick as molasses. I don't know how she drinks the stuff. It's not like she needs the extra caffeine to wind her up more than she already is. The pale blue kitchen walls create a serene atmosphere, like a relaxing day at the beach with my toes in the sand and an ocean breeze cooling my face. I drop in a teaspoon of stevia and pass a hand over my cup. The spoon twirls with a swirl of amber magic.

"Look at you. Flaunting your magic," Ronnie says, cackling. "Derek left for the gym early, so we could be alone to have a girlfriend chat. I'm sorry you're having such a hard time coping. But I'm glad you're trying to face the problem head-on. Archie loves you. He waited for you before. He'll do it again."

"I have no doubts about him. Nuada is dead, and I'm glad I killed him. It doesn't change the fact his entire fairy kingdom could cross through that portal any day."

"We sent his remains across the country via the national connections of covens. His family won't find you."

I sip my tea and savor the calming effect of its aroma. "I sure hope you're right. Meanwhile, we can work on that witchcraft database. Working toward a solution to close the portal keeps me focused on what matters. But I'm concerned about the ongoing investigation into his disappearance."

"I'm sure you are. How can the detective connect the death to you, though? Only the coven knows what happened." Ronnie gets up from her chair and goes to the counter to pour another cup of coffee.

"Because Dr. Seamus Duffy may have been there that night." I drop my cup with a clink.

"*May have*," Ronnie emphasizes. "From what Archie said, it seems like your memory of seeing him that night is fuzzy. I don't understand why you didn't tell me about him before the meeting."

"When I saw Seamus standing on the far side of the parking lot, I blinked, and then he wasn't there. After killing Nick, I figured I was traumatized and seeing things."

"You were," she says, returning with her coffee. "What are you going to do?"

I peer up at her through my wisp of bangs. "I'm gonna start a teensy investigation of my own."

"For fuck's sake, Gwyn," she cackles. "You're gonna stalk him?"

I snicker. "I didn't say that. Maybe I'll get to know him better. That's all."

Ronnie fills the kitchen with laughter. "You go, girl. But be careful, because he's an academic. He could suspect what you're doing and report you to the detective. Then where will you be? Have you heard anything more about the mauling of that college student? Nothing in the news."

"No. I must have been wrong about a supernatural being causing his demise. It was a cougar, and the animal must have moved on."

"Maybe, but I believe you. Who knows what's crossing through that portal? The Seelie Fae children may not be the only ones." Ronnie hugs me as she sits down. "OK, I'm intentionally changing this morbid subject. What did you think of Shane's old girlfriend, Cordelia?"

I shrug. "Not the type of woman I expected Shane to find attractive, but he was young. She appears to care more about her nail polish and clothes than a quality friendship. It doesn't surprise me she left him. He had nothing to offer her at the time, I suppose."

"Hmph. She better not hurt him, or she'll have us to deal with." She shimmies in her seat.

I chuckle. "I'm sure Shane can handle himself at his age. But I'm right there with you."

My friend picks up a magazine from the table and fans herself, and my eyebrows jump.

"Are you having a hot flash?" I ask.

She frowns and pulls at her short-sleeved blouse. "I think so. My periods stopped a couple of months ago, and I am forty-five. Mom hit menopause early at forty-eight."

My brow crinkles. "Could you be pregnant?"

"No, sadly. Derek and I have been trying for a year. I kept quiet, because we didn't want to get our hopes up. He's OK with not being parents, but I really wanted to have a baby with him." She drops her mug on the table and points a finger at me. "And before you get the brilliant idea of using magic, remember what happened when Leslie, Agnes, and your mom tried to help Rose Mitchell?"

"We could give it a tiny push." I grin at her and gesture toward the magic room. "Or go to a fertility clinic?"

"Nah. Getting pregnant at my age was a long shot. We've made peace with it."

"I'm sorry, Ronnie." A quick glance at my cell phone reminds me it's time to go, and I push up from my chair. "Thanks for making time to talk, but you need to get to work."

"Yeah. The café is my baby." She slaps the magazine on the table and stands.

She grabs her purse and keys, and I follow her outside. The passing shower has cleared, and the sun shines a bright yellow, drying the damp blacktop and heating my face. I imagine the garnet-red azaleas at my old house are blooming. Spence and Tanner get to enjoy them now.

"Have a good day at work," I say. "I'll wave from across the street."

She chuckles. "Gwyn, if you're right about Seamus Duffy, he may have a nefarious reason for not going to the authorities and telling them what he knows. Watch yourself."

"Don't worry. I won't do anything to bring attention to myself."

She cackles loudly. "'Cause that *never* happens."

"Thanks, friend," I say, frowning.

I get into my blue metallic Prius and head home. When I arrive, I park my car and decide to take a stroll on campus to surprise Archie for lunch. It's the perfect spring day—upper 60s and warm under the heat of the sun. In the distance, the Old Men Oak trees are in full bloom and resemble scruffy men badly in need of a haircut. In contrast, the dark blue-green grass appears clean-cut, separated by the red paver walkways.

As I approach Stewart Hall, Seamus Duffy is exiting the building. He's wearing the same DUB polo shirt and black slacks he always wears to work. By the time he makes it to the bottom of the steps, I've arrived. The visiting professor smiles.

"Good day, Gwynedd. Are you here to visit Archie? I believe he's with a student at the moment."

"Oh, I expected he would be free. Should I go home?" I ask.

"I'm sure he'll finish the meeting soon. How are you?" He leans on his cat head cane and stares at me. Those sea-green eyes never budge.

"Great. My semester work is done. I don't have any finals, and I finished my final project last week."

"Wonderful. You must feel a sense of relief, then."

"Mostly." I glance at the enormous double-door entry to Stewart Hall. "Well, I better go see if Archie has finished his meeting. Enjoy the rest of your afternoon."

"And you as well, Gwynedd."

Seamus continues on down the paver walkway toward Main Street, and I hurry up the steps to the enormous double-door entry. I grab the doorknob and glance back. The visiting professor turns and cuts through an alleyway farther up the Green that leads to the far end of Douglas Street, the road I cross to get to Drummond and Duncan. Curiosity itches at my brain, so I abandon my plans and rush back down the steps.

By the time I run through the alleyway leading to Douglas Street, I'm gasping for air. I scan up and down the street, listening for the click of his cane. I turn my head left and glimpse the long black ponytail on the back of Seamus's head as he turns right onto Kent Way. The other intersecting street is Sussex. I always said it was like the English to cut through the Scots.

I pull my hood up to shield my face and follow the visiting professor, trailing him by at least a block. He turns right onto Drummond Lane. The streets are empty, so I tiptoe in my sneakers to the corner and immediately jump back after peering around. Seamus is entering the front door of a two-bedroom bungalow. He's renting a house up the street from where I live?

I grind my teeth as I walk nonchalantly to the side of the house. Standing on my tippy toes, I peek in through the bottom of the window. He passes by and limps into the back. My heart skips a few beats and takes off like a racehorse as I drop below the window. There's a wooden fence surrounding the backyard, so I rush to the gate in the back. I grab the latch and pull up, but hesitate.

What the fuck am I doing? This is an intrusion. What if he catches me? He'll call the cops, and they'll arrest me—exactly what I'm trying to avoid. Getting cuffed for trespassing is a better charge than murder, though. I pull on the gate and enter. The backyard is sparse except for a few shrubs lining the back of the property. The fence only exists to provide privacy from the side facing the street. There's a window right off the corner of the house, but I'm not tall enough to see in over the open rain barrel. So, I pull myself up and squat on the rim.

Through a sliver of opening in the curtains, I'm able to see Seamus. He's sitting on the edge of his bed and pulling off his pants. This is wrong. Now I'm going to get arrested for being a "peeping Tom"—more like a "peeping Thomasina." I shift a little to get down, but stop when he lifts his left leg. The muscle and skin are a mangled mess of scars. It's no wonder he limps. His entire calf area is half the size it should be. What was it he said to me that day he escorted me home? "I stepped into a private matter I shouldn't have."

Seamus stands up and limps toward the hallway. I need to get out of here. But I can't feel my legs after squatting this long. I lean to place a leg down and...SPLASH! My ass ends up in the rain barrel! I manage to pull my butt out and fall to the ground with a thud. My legs have pins and needles, but I dart to the back of the lot and push through the neighbor's thick shrubs, hoping they're not home. I peek back at the house through the greenery while my heart does jumping jacks. The visiting professor has pulled back the curtain. He glances to the left and right, then closes the curtain.

I run down Douglas Street and turn left at Sussex Way, not stopping until I crash through the side door of Leslie's house and remove my sneakers. My jeans are dripping as I shuffle to my bedroom. Mr. Yeats hisses at me and transforms into his human persona. He eyes my wet derriere.

"Ms. Crowther, what happened to you? Your, uh, bottom is wet. Did you have an accident?"

I scowl at him. "Yes. And if you tell Leslie, I'll never ask you for help with divination again."

"Well, that's rather harsh," he says, adjusting his gray suit jacket.

"Too bad. Get out of my way."

I enter my bedroom and strip out of my clothes. While I put on new blue jeans for my shift at Mystic Sage, I recall Seamus's mangled leg. What is his story? And why isn't he telling the police I was at Nick's apartment the night he disappeared?

At 8:58 p.m., I lock the cash register while Jeff Williams flips the store sign to the CLOSED side and turns the key to the glass entry door. He waits for me, holding two books under his arm while I grab my small crossbody bag. I set the alarm, and we stroll west on Main Street. Clouds have rolled in and a misty haze lingers in the air, inviting the imminent rain.

"So, are you done?" I ask, smiling.

A gigantic grin lights up his face. "Yes! I can't believe it. Except for graduation, of course. I wish Audrey could have been here to attend."

"I'm sure she will be, in her own way." It hurts to watch him grieve over his cousin's death, but that wound will take a long time to heal. We are his only family now. "Have you decided what you're doing following graduation? Have you applied for jobs yet?"

"I did. I received three offers, but the last one is the most appealing for now."

"That's fabulous, Jeff. Starting your career will help you to... I don't want to say move on. You never get over the death of a loved one." I'm still processing my husband's passing and his cheating on me. "Where is the job?"

He chuckles. "In Bearsden. We just left the place."

I stop and stare at him. "I'm confused."

"Let's keep walking," he says, grinning. "Shane asked me to become a partner in the store. I would take on a lot of management duties and work more hours. Give him a break now that he's older. He's always wanted to sell online but didn't have the skills or the money to pursue it. I only have access to some of the money while it's in a trust. Once the courts declare my aunt and uncle dead in a few years, I'll get everything. And everyone I care about lives in Bearsden."

"Well then, it sounds like a wonderful arrangement for the both of you. I know you lived in the dorm this semester. Will you move back in with Shane or find an apartment?"

He snickers. "Shane has been entertaining a lady friend recently. I don't think he needs me cramping his style."

"You mean Cordelia Davenport," I say. "What do you think of her?"

"I only met her briefly today when she came to the store to meet Shane for lunch. She must like him a lot, because she had an arm locked around his as they left the store."

"She appears to," I say, arriving at the steps to the Green.

"Jeff, I don't wanna come back when it's raining to check on the Seelie Fae children. With the gloomy weather, I doubt anyone is on an evening stroll in the Celestial Gardens. I'm gonna get it out of the way now. You have a great evening."

"You, too, Gwyn. Be careful. That cougar could be on the prowl. Should I go with you?"

"No. I have to go. It's my turn to monitor the pranksters. I think the attack was an isolated incident."

"OK. Goodnight. See you at the store next week."

"Goodnight to you, too."

I jaywalk across the street, because getting arrested for not using the crosswalk is the least of my worries right now. It's after nine, so the gate is locked. A quick wave of amber magic takes care of that. I enter the gardens and walk along the side of Mitchell Hall until I've almost reached the back of the house. When I catch sight of the mound, I stop and hide against the mansion's exterior wall.

Cordelia Davenport stands in the misty haze with her hands stretched out, facing the portal mound. She clasps her amulet with one hand and reaches toward the sky with the other. I survey the gardens, but Shailagh and Aonghas haven't crossed over for the evening. Shane's old flame chants, but she speaks too softly for me to discern what she's saying. Solitary witches perform rituals like this all the time, but it's odd she chose the gardens for her private ceremony. Shane should probably warn her about the Seelie Fae.

In the distance, sirens blare, increasing in volume. I'll have to come back later. Interrupting her ritual would be rude. I exit the gardens, locking the gate with a swipe of magic as I pass, and dart across Main Street.

As I descend the steps to the Green, the flashing red and blue lights of police cars catch my attention. Bearsden PD and DUB Campus units are parked along University Avenue. Probably drunk students letting loose before finals. A few officers are conversing to the left, so I cross the street on the right side of Central Campus.

When I get closer, I find a crowd of students has gathered, and officers are taping off the area in front of an alleyway. Others are questioning a couple of young women off to the side. Through a break in the group, I glimpse the legs of a young man. Panicking, I dash to the gathering and push through the students to get a closer look, but the police are blocking the body. My chest tightens, and my hands shake uncontrollably.

"Do you know what happened?" I ask the undergrad next to me.

"No. But there's blood everywhere," the young man says. "The guy's neck looks like someone took a cheese grater to it."

As I push up on my toes to get a better view of the body, someone taps me on the shoulder. I snap my head left and discover Jeff. I wrap my arms around him and squeeze.

"Geez, Gwyn. What's this all about?" he asks, pushing me back.

"Oh, my gods. I worried it was you, but I'm so relieved it's not." I pat my upper chest.

He presses his lips together. "Me, too. It appears that cougar is preying on students on campus now. Good thing the semester is nearly done."

"Yeah. Well, now that I know you're OK, I'm gonna head home. Or maybe to Archie's. I'm a little shaken."

"Would you like me to walk you back?"

"No. I should be OK. All the sirens and the flashing lights probably spooked the animal. I'll see you next week."

I push through the horde that's accumulated so I can use the other alleyway shortcut to get home.

"Ma'am, you shouldn't walk through here. We're still investigating." The officer tilts her head. "Ms. Crowther? You found that body in the woods."

"Yeah. That's right. I live only two streets over on Drummond Lane. If I walk around all of this, it will take me longer to get home."

She glances back at the other officers examining the body. "I suppose you'd be safer walking through there, then." She gestures with her head.

"Thank you, officer," I say, forcing a smile.

As I amble by, I get a view of the victim at the entrance to the alleyway. Flaps of skin hang down and veins protrude from the neck like electrical wiring. A small amount of blood puddles onto the pavement. I hurry by, flinching at the sight, but stop abruptly when I discover Seamus Duffy leaning on his cane under the hazy glow of a lamppost. Holy crystals.

CHAPTER EIGHT

A WOMAN WITH NO PAST

WALKING THROUGH A HAZE of white under scattered beams of moonlight, Archie enters the Celestial Gardens. He closes the gate behind him. A sound in the gardens distracts him, and he frowns as he looks around. Like a quick cut in a TV show, he's lying on the ground unconscious. A warped growl builds in volume nearby.

Beep, beep, beep, beep. My eyes snap open to a racing heart. The same dream again. Has to be stress. Waking up at the crack of dawn isn't how I usually plan my Sundays, and it blows. But we have to keep to a schedule if we're ever going to get through the spell books in Agnes's library and find another incantation to close the portal in the mound. Because of the incident on the Green last night, I didn't get to check on the Seelie Fae to keep them occupied. I hope they aren't miffed and planning on shenanigans.

After a quick shower, I join Archie in the kitchen. He places one of his magical veggie omelets on the kitchen table in front of me. I inhale the enticing aroma. His cooking is rounding out my hips again. Why do all the extra calories have to land there when I need them to fill out my boobs? I put a tasty morsel in my mouth.

"Now that I have time, I need to increase my days at the fitness center. Your yummy meals are taking up lodging on my backside."

He sets his plate on the table and smacks me on the side of my butt. "Just more of you to enjoy, my love."

"Sure. That's what all men say, and the next thing you know, they're sleeping with a colleague."

Archie sits down and slices off a piece of omelet. "How many times do I have to tell you I'm not Richard?"

"Zero," I reply, smiling. "How about the second mauling? Do you think it's the cougar?"

"The Bearsden Police appear to think so. It's disconcerting the animal is wandering through campus. I know you believe it's a supernatural being, but the evidence seems to confirm it's a cougar."

"Yeah, it does." I'm still not so sure. But if I never see it again, I'll never know.

I need to bring up the topic of Seamus living down the street from Leslie's house. But how can I do that without telling Archie I followed the visiting professor home? "I didn't mention it last night, since we were occupied with the death of another student. But I saw Seamus standing nearby. Why would he be on campus on a Saturday night so late? Or was he walking through on the way home? Did he move?"

Archie sips his tea and sets the cup down. "Actually, he did recently. He's living up the street from Leslie's on Drummond."

"What? Don't you think that's odd he moved to a house so close to me?" When was he going to tell me?

"No. DUB owns a few small homes on this side to rent out to new faculty. Seamus wanted to be closer to campus because of his limp. But I knew you'd be a wee bit concerned, considering your worries about him."

I chew hard on my egg. "It's weird. He always seems to be around."

"Most likely a coincidence," he says, taking his plate to the sink. "Like I said before, if he was there that night, he would have gone to the police by now. Shouldn't you get moving?"

"Yeah. We're only working a couple of hours this morning. You have more grading?"

"Aye. We all have a heavy load except Leslie, since she's the acting chair. Only one more week, and we're finished with Spring Semester."

"How many classes do you have to teach this summer? Only one I hope."

He sighs. "Aye, unfortunately. Seamus offered to teach one as well."

"That was nice of him. He had plans to return to Northern Ireland this summer." I may be wrong about the visiting professor, but that's not a reason to stop snooping.

"We should be able to visit Scotland and Wales in August as planned, though. The family is excited to have us visit for Lughnasadh. They've already made arrangements for Aunt Gorawen to visit while we're there."

"Yeah. She told me during a video chat on Friday. But her magic butler will have to remain at the house." I laugh, thinking about her flying helping hand, and shimmy to him. "I'm sorry about last night. We were supposed to...try again."

Archie strokes my cheek. "We have the rest of our lives, my love. Although, I'd rather not wait *that* long."

"I'll see you sometime this week." I kiss him. "Oh, I almost forgot. I never got to check on the pranksters."

Creases form between his eyes. "I thought you stopped there?"

"I did, but the Seelie Fae hadn't crossed over yet. And Cordelia Davenport was in there, doing a ritual."

He cocks his head. "That's odd. I would expect her to perform rituals in her apartment. She moved in recently and probably doesn't have an altar set up yet. But an Unremarkable might see her. Did anything seem unusual?"

"No. But I didn't stay long. I was intruding. And then the sirens distracted me." I grab my purse and car keys. "I'm going to say something to Shane tomorrow. He'll need to talk to her. See you sometime this week, honey."

"Bye, my love." He puckers up and blows a kiss.

Spence talks with his hands in the air. "Not to be morbid, but death follows you around like a puppy dog—the ghost of one, anyway."

He's typing incantations into the witchcraft database while Skye, Trinity, Agnes, and I sift through the books to mark repetitious spells. We've covered page after page with sticky notes. Leslie is in her office on campus, grading.

"You know what? I was fine before I met all of you," I say, frowning. "No evil Sluagh. No greedy, murderous ancestral witches. No stalking...you know who. Believe me. Do you think I'm trying to attract the macabre?"

"Like flies to shit." Agnes laughs and drops a stack of books on the table.

Trinity bursts out laughing as she carries a grimoire to the waiting-to-be-entered pile. "You can't argue with any of that."

I smirk and slam a book shut. "I suppose I should be happy you're not walking on eggshells around me."

"You're better like this." Skye chuckles as she presses a purple tab on a page. "Because we know you're OK."

"I'll second that." Agnes flips a page and places a sticky note at the top.

I turn another page. Am I? I don't think I'll be able to move on completely until the missing person case is officially closed.

Trinity addresses Spence and Skye. "Are you two looking forward to graduation?"

"Yeah, but it's not like we're really done," Skye replies. "We still have to finish our doctorates."

"Speak for yourself. I'm the first person in my family to earn a master's degree." Spence shimmies in his seat. "I'm gonna par-taaay."

"Well, I'm proud of you both," I say. "It took me thirty years to work on mine."

"And we'll have the biggest party ever when you finish, too, sis. You'll deserve one after all you've gone through."

"Thanks, Spence. You both helped me a lot with that first class."

"Enough of the admiration society. When is Tanner coming by to discuss the renovations to my kitchen?" Agnes asks. "I don't want the summer to get away from me. But I am looking forward to a couple of weeks away with Leslie. The end of the semester has kept her busy as a witch with a hex list. She's grading on a Sunday, for fuck's sake!"

"Yeah. Archie is, too." I cross my arms and huff. "Maybe I should have waited until the semester ended to off Nick."

They sit up straight and gape at me, their eyes frozen wide.

"It was a joke." I roll my eyes and rip off another sticky note. "Apparently, a bad one."

Spence slaps the table and guffaws. "That was fire, sis. Warped but lit."

Everyone cracks up, and Agnes pats me on the back.

"We all deal with our trauma in our own way," she says. "You do you, Gwyn."

We work for another hour and leave our piles for another weekend. The continued search for a portal-closing spell has become part of our normal routine. It may take a couple of years, and we will either find a spell or we won't. But in the end, we'll have a searchable witchcraft database to share with our fellow covens throughout Delaware when we're finished. While we're gathered in the foyer, Skye fills us in on her new roommate.

"Listen, you know Kate, the young woman with amnesia, moved in with me. She keeps to herself way too much, so I'm trying to schedule a few meetups to get her to socialize more. Elijah thinks the more she interacts with people, the sooner her memories will start emerging."

"That's a fantastic idea," Trinity says. "Would you like me to send a text to the whole Fellowship?"

Skye slips on her hoodie. "Yeah, but I should probably ease her into a smaller group first."

"You tell me when, and I'll make a reservation at the Raven Pub." Trinity enters a reminder into her cell phone.

"We should get the young witches together," Spence says. "Kate doesn't need the old farts putting her under a microscope."

Agnes grimaces. "Well, fuck you, too."

"I don't think he means it in a bad way," I say. "Being with people her own age will make her feel more comfortable. That's all."

"Yeah, yeah. Well, fuck you, anyway." She sticks her tongue out at Spence.

Spence hugs the hedge witch. "Oh, you know I love you, Agnes."

She pushes him away and waves a hand. "You smell."

"It's my new aftershave. Do you like it?" he asks.

Agnes holds her nose. "No. It stinks like bad cedar incense."

Spence crosses his arms and scowls at her.

"OK. I think we need to let Agnes get on with her day," Trinity says. "Thank you all for your dedication."

The hedge witch pushes us toward the front door. "Now get the fuck out of here and let me relax. I earned it. Shoo."

"Goodbye, Agnes!" we yell as she shoves us onto the porch.

Skye follows me to my Prius. "Gwyn, what are you doing for lunch?"

"I'm going home. I was gonna offer to make sandwiches for Leslie and me. She's really feeling the stress at her age."

"I was hoping you might come with me to the Raven. Kate is supposed to meet me there for lunch before she starts her shift. Zach is coming, too. Spence was mostly kidding when he talked about the older witches being too judgy. Personally, I think it would be great if she had a mother figure. I know if I was recovering from some kind of trauma, I'd want my mom. Could you help with that?"

"You know how that worked out the last time I tried to play the mom role? Now Audrey's dead." I press my lips together.

"That was different, and her death isn't your fault. Her own mother killed her."

"I know." She's right, but I have a lump in my throat. "OK. Meet you there?"

A grin brightens her face. "Awesome. Thanks, Gwyn. You won't be sorry."

That's what I thought the last time.

Skye gets to the Raven Pub before me, because I get stuck at the railroad tracks that run behind the restaurant. I park in the last spot. Their Sunday buffet brunches fill the place. When I enter, there's a long line waiting to be seated, but Skye and her boyfriend Zach Ward wave to me from a table for four in our usual room. I meander around the packed tables toward them. Amnesia Kate is waiting with them, sitting motionless and her hands folded on the table.

Zach passes a menu to me. "Hey. I'm so glad you could eat with us."

"Well, thank you for inviting me. It's great to see you again," I say.

Skye gestures to me to sit down. "This is my new roommate. Kate, this is Gwynedd Crowther, but we call her Gwyn. I met her in a class at DUB almost two years ago."

"Hi, Kate." I glance at Skye. "We already met informally. I wasn't looking where I was going and knocked her onto the paver sidewalk. Again, I'm so sorry. How are your hands?"

"They're all right," she says in a barely audible voice.

Kate shows her palms to us. There are a few noticeable scrapes. She still appears frail, but her cheeks are as pink as a rose—a healthier glow. I grasp the underside of her hands. They're cold as ice.

"They should heal soon. But your skin is so chilly. I don't know why they have to turn on the air-conditioning this early in the month. Would you like my hoodie?"

"No," she says, pulling her hands to her lap. "I'm fine."

"Are you accident prone, Gwyn?" Zach asks.

Skye chuckles as she reads her menu. "You could say that."

"Don't mind them, Kate. Skye has known me for a while and is joking around. I've earned that title."

Kate smiles and lifts her menu.

"We should order," Zach says. "I need to get back to studying. Skye may be ready to dance on her diploma, but I've still got a semester to go. I'll graduate in December."

Skye waves at our waiter, and he arrives to take our orders. Zach and Skye order burgers. I order a salad, because my hips don't need more lodgers. Kate orders French fries and slides off the booth seat.

"I need to go to the...Ladies' Room." She glances at the doorway. "I'll be back."

When Kate is out of sight, we shift in our seats. Skye leans over the table, and we join her, lending an ear.

"She acts like this all the time," she says, her brow crinkling. "And you watch. She'll only nibble at those fries she ordered. It's like she doesn't know how to eat."

Zach slides his glass out of the way. "When I ate dinner with them on Friday night, she barely touched her dinner. She got up and carried her plate into her bedroom."

"That doesn't sound good at all," I say. "Did she eat the food in there? Or did you find it in the garbage?"

Skye shrugs. "I don't know. Her plate was clean, but I couldn't inspect the trash. She took it out before I could check. Sometimes she talks funny, too, like she's trying too hard to get the words out. And the cell phone Elijah gave her? She doesn't know how to use it. It's like she's never seen one before. That doesn't bode well. I bet someone held her captive in their basement, and she escaped."

"Hmph. I don't know what to say about the speech or the cell phone, but that behavior sounds like an eating disorder, doesn't it?" I ask. "Did you mention it to Elijah? He'll want to tell her counselor."

"I haven't yet, but I will. Shh. Here she comes."

I turn around to welcome Kate back to the table and glimpse a man speaking with the hostess at the podium in the main dining room. She points in my direction, and he glances our way. It's Detective Schmidt. I swivel in my seat as my heart palpitates like a car with a bad carburetor.

"Skye, please tell me that man isn't looking at us." My hands shake, and I grab the side of the wooden table.

Kate sits down, and her eyes flip back and forth. "What's going on?"

"He isn't looking at us," Skye says, widening her eyes. "But I'm lying."

"Oh, shit." I peer over my shoulder into the main room.

Detective Schmidt nods to the hostess and walks through the hallway to the exit.

"Someone going to explain to Kate and me what that was about?" Zach asks, sipping his water.

"I'll explain later," Skye says, goggling at me. "It may mean nothing, Gwyn. After all, you found that body in the woods."

Kate folds her hands and lowers her eyes to the table. "You mean the boy...that got hurt?"

"Yeah," I say. "Don't worry about this, Kate. You have enough on your plate trying to regain your memory." I lay my hand over hers and squeeze. "It will return eventually."

She peers up at me through strands of pale-blond hair. "Thank you, Ms. Crowther. I hope so. I don't know how I'll survive if I don't figure out—"

"Even if you don't recall any of your prior life. Know that you have friends here who care what happens to you," I say, smiling.

Skye and Zach nod and grin, prompting Kate to laugh softly under her breath.

We chat about the most recent attack by the cougar, and Kate averts her eyes. This is NOT a pleasant conversation to bring her out of her shell, so I change the subject. As Skye mentioned, Kate picks at her plate of fries during lunch. But thanks to the detective's appearance, I barely shove down a few forks full of greens and goat cheese either. That doesn't make me an anorexic. The trauma of losing her memory must stress her out twenty-four-seven. Poor thing.

When we finish lunch, I enter my cell phone number into Kate's phone, and she thanks me. Such a sweet young woman. I hope her memories return. She starts her shift bussing tables, and the rest of us amble to the exit. On the way out, I glance back at the hostess as my heart continues to flutter. What the fuck was that about? Please, karma. Be on my side.

I rush into the house shouting, "Archie! Archie!" as I kick off my sneakers.

A tremor appears in my hand, and I make a fist as I dash to the living room. He's not in there.

His warm baritone voice travels down the stairs. "I'm in my office, Gwyn!"

I run upstairs and find him deep into grading. His laptop is open, and he has it connected to a large monitor. I stand in the doorway, trying to catch my breath. My fist hangs next to my side. He peers up at me.

"You said you weren't coming back today." His gaze drops to my hand, and he arches an eyebrow. "Planning to hit me, my love?"

As I glance down at my fist, I shake it out and chuckle. "No. It was to stop the tremor in my fingers."

"Something happened. Are you going to tell me, or do I have to drag it out of you?"

"I ate lunch at the Raven with Skye and her boyfriend, Zach. And Amnesia Kate. Skye said it might be nice if I befriended her since she has no memory and might be missing her mom." I grimace and amble toward him. "She's got some issues. But I'll tell you about her later. Detective Schmidt stopped by to talk with the hostess again. She pointed at our table, and he stared at us. I couldn't see him. Skye faced that direction. But she said he looked really hard at us and appeared to thank the hostess and left."

Archie stands and hugs me. "Gwyn, you don't know what transpired. They could have been discussing Kate."

"Do you think so? I mean, he's probably still investigating her, too."

He places a finger under my chin and angles my head up. "You worry too much. I've cast two spells of confusion his way. Hopefully, he's grabbing at straws."

"What do I say if he comes asking questions? You know I'm a terrible liar. He'll figure out I'm hiding something. And then, bam! Before you can say 'burn the witch,' I'll be in the slammer wearing an orange suit."

He chuckles. "You would look damn sexy in orange. Come to think of it. Why don't you wear orange?"

"Because I don't like it. It clashes with my hazel eyes. Stop joking around. I'm petrified he's found out I was friends with Nick. People would have seen us together at the Raven. Although, we never exhibited PDA."

"You don't have to lie to the detective. If he calls you and asks about Nick, answer the questions truthfully, but don't be specific. Unless he comes right out and asks if you killed him, he won't have a reason to arrest you. There is no corpse. No evidence of kidnapping or murder. We were careful to remove any proof. Elijah made sure of that."

He cups my cheek. "Eventually, Detective Schmidt will hit a dead end, and they'll close the case. With no hint of foul play, they won't bother the FBI. Especially since they can't find next of kin."

"And he never will, I hope. Nuada's family could show up searching for him, passing as Unremarkables. And then they'd come after me."

He kisses me on the forehead. "Stop thinking the worst, my love. That body is long gone."

"But there's still Seamus. I'm certain he was there that night. My witch sense says so. I don't know why he's not reporting me—us—to the police. But I'm gonna find out." I'm not telling him about my trespassing at the visiting professor's house. My actions would only worry him.

He cocks his head. "Do I want to know how you're going to achieve this discovery?"

"No," I say with a chuckle. "The less you know, the better. You need to enter grades. I'm sorry I freaked out. I panicked. You're probably right. He was following up on Kate. He must have wanted to speak with her, but didn't want to interrupt our lunch." I kiss him and fondle his chest. "For sure, I'll stay over sometime this week. I promise."

He pats me on the butt. "I look forward to it, my love."

Chapter Nine

A RELUCTANT WITNESS

By Tuesday morning, a rainstorm has passed through, leaving Bearsden with a partly sunny day and cooler temperatures. I can sense the heat of summer lurking around the corner, and I anticipate donning shorts and flip-flops—and our August trip to visit family in Wales and Scotland.

When I enter the kitchen, Leslie is sitting at the tiny table for two under the window, drinking coffee. Her long silver bangs drape across her face, covering one of her copper eyes. She's dressed in a blouse, skirt, and a heavy button-down sweater. Mr. Yeats is curled up at her feet in his chimera cat form, his tail swishing back and forth.

"Good morning, Gwynedd. I trust you slept well?"

"Yeah. Better than the night before, thanks." I get a cup from the cabinet and warm up water in the microwave. "Thought you'd be on campus by now."

"I'm leaving soon. The department has a meeting this afternoon, and I need to prepare."

When the microwave beeps, I remove my cup and drop a tea bag in. "Will Seamus attend?"

"Of course. He's walking with me to campus this morning. He moved into a bungalow up the road." She gestures toward his house with her knobby fingers.

"Archie told me." I bite my lower lip. "So, will he be free in the morning? I had a few questions about some lore I've been reading."

Leslie finishes her coffee and takes her dishes to the sink. "I imagine he has grading to complete after yesterday's finals. Are you still concerned he was in the parking lot on the night of Ostara?"

"A little. But Archie believes he would have gone to the police by now if he'd been there."

"I wholeheartedly agree." She raises her chin and pats my hand. "I hesitate to mention his name, but I must if I'm going to state my opinion on the matter. Nuada glamoured Archie, you, and me. His magic clouded our recollections and thoughts throughout those months. There is no way to know how that affected your perception of that night. And there could be lingering effects. What I can verify is that the Seamus Duffy I know would never harm a soul. My witch's intuition tells me not to worry about the professor."

"Thank you, Leslie. I appreciate your opinion." But I still don't trust him. Although they're still developing, I have witch instincts, too.

The Elder averts her eyes for a second. "I wasn't sure how to broach the subject. It can be embarrassing for an older woman. But I saw your damp jeans hanging in the bathroom to dry. When I asked Mr. Yeats about it, he said you had an accident."

I glare at Mr. Yeats, and he scuttles out of the kitchen. Never trust someone else's familiar. What the fuck did he tell her?

"Don't be upset with him. I had to pull it out of him like taffy. I, too, am incontinent occasionally and keep adult diapers in the closet if I'm leaking. You're welcome to use a pair if you have the need."

I gape at her and press my lips together to dam the laughter trying to break free. "Thank you. I'll remember if I have issues in the future."

"Splendid. Seamus is most likely waiting at the corner for me. Have a wonderful day, Gwynedd."

"You, too. I'm sensing today will turn out to be one of the best."

She grabs her leather satchel and heads out to meet Seamus. I immediately stomp toward the magic room where the turncoat familiar must be hiding. He hisses at me and transforms into his human form.

"I...I'm sorry, Ms. Crowther. My loyalty is to Dr. Hughes, but I don't think she suspects anything."

I scowl at the traitor. "How can she? I didn't tell you what happened. My insurance."

"You won't be needing my assistance at the next divination conference with your parents now, will you?"

"Oh, you can help. But keep your trap shut. I'll only be updating my parents about my emotional state. It's a little weird they worry from the Otherworld, but whatever."

"Thank you, Ms. Crowther. You know I meant no harm."

"No, you never do, but that doesn't stop you. You're a scuttling disaster that trips over its own tail." I cross my arms and squint at him.

Mr. Yeats purses his lips like a prune. "You don't have to insult me."

As I stroll along the paver walkways on the Green, regret clouds my head. I shouldn't have been so hard on the familiar. He's duty-bound to Leslie, not me. Good thing I didn't confide in him and spill the beans about stalking Seamus. I stop in my tracks. Yes.

That's the only description for it, and I was so wrong. Better to snoop out in the open. He'll never suspect.

I descend the stairs to the musty basement of Stewart Hall and pass by Leslie and Archie's offices, stopping at Seamus's door. His name placard was removed and placed on the office next to his—Nick Evans's old room. I suck in the moldy air and knock. After a moment or two, the door opens. The visiting professor cocks his head and smiles awkwardly.

"Gwynedd. What a pleasant surprise. What can I do for you?"

"I've been reading a book on Scottish and Irish folklore, and questions keep popping up. I had a few minutes to burn before work and stopped by. But I can come another time if you're busy." Please don't be busy. *Please don't be busy.*

"I would welcome a break from the tedious task of grading finals. Please, come in."

He moves aside, and I enter, snatching a breath of relief when I discover all of Nick's belongings are gone.

"Thank you. I won't be long, because my shift at Mystic Sage starts soon."

Seamus limps to his desk chair and sits as I drop my purse to the floor and plop into the seat next to his desk. My stomach does somersaults as I glance around the office until my eyes arrive at the painting hanging on the wall with his diplomas. A large cat, resembling a panther, dances upright on a patch of grass. A white star shines with rays of magic from its chest. I point at the picture.

"What an interesting painting. Is that a cat sith?"

He contorts his body to view the painting as if he doesn't already know it's hanging there. "Oh, yes. I forgot I'd hung it there. This office is much larger, so I'm able to display more of my artwork. Do you like it? A friend of mine painted the canvas and gifted it to me. Wasn't that kind of her?"

"Yes, it was." I roll my lips inward while I determine my next question. "The reference I read mentioned the cat sith. What can you tell me about the tale?"

He folds his hands and leans forward on his desk. "That is quite a lot of information to pass on in a single answer. But I'll give you the abridged explanation. Cat siths appear in Irish folklore, so I do research on those stories, but you'll find more tales in Scottish lore as well. The stories tell of large black cats that haunt the Highlands and steal the souls of the dead. The people believed the legends and would keep cats out of the room during wakes."

"That's what Archie's brother Quinn told me when I visited over the Yule holiday. The family had a figurine of one sitting on a table in their family room."

"Not surprising. Other tales speak of a demonic cat sith called Big Ears that would grant wishes to those who would burn the bodies of cats in a ceremony lasting a few days."

I cringe. "That's disturbing. Those poor cats."

"People were superstitious in those days. I'm sure the odor kept away more than soul-eating cats." A slight smile breaks his flat demeanor.

"Quinn also mentioned a cat sith witch? What you can tell me about that lore?"

Seamus stares at me, his glassy sea-green eyes piercing my comfort zone. "In folklore, this type of witch can transform into a feline nine times before succumbing to its cat presentation permanently."

"Why would a witch want to do that? Witches are supposed to be powerful through the use of magic. What could they gain by presenting as a cat?"

He leans back in his desk chair and rests his hands in his lap. "Maybe the witch needs a bath?"

My mouth falls open as I stare back at the professor. And I laugh. "You must kill your students with jokes during your lectures."

"Unfortunately, no," he says, grinning widely. "But I'm working on my delivery."

My cell phone screen reads 11:45 a.m. "I need to get to work, but thank you so much for making time for me."

I grab my purse and amble toward the door. But a question has been burning in my brain since I entered his office, so I turn around and ask him.

"Does it feel strange occupying his office?" I lower my eyes to the floor.

"When Leslie suggested I move into it last week, I was completely against the idea. Not even two months have passed since he went missing. But she insisted. She said if he were to return, DUB would fire him for abandoning his contractual obligations."

"Oh, I didn't think about that." Of course, the university would let him go. He disappeared in the middle of the semester.

"Gwynedd, I sense the young professor will never return to us, and we may never learn what became of him. I miss his youthful presence and humor. And his academic knowledge of Welsh folklore."

"Yes. I'll miss that about him, too."

"It was obvious he cared for you very much. I'm certain he would want you to move on and not let his disappearance consume you."

Did Nick tell him we dated? If so, did he tell Detective Schmidt when he questioned him? Was he in the parking lot that night? If so, why isn't he asking me? I peer up at Seamus and swallow the lump of guilt in my throat.

"Enjoy the rest of your day, Seamus."

"And you as well, Gwynedd."

I exit his office and shut the door. Archie is probably in his office by now, but I don't have time to see him. A visit with him will have to wait until later.

On the brisk walk to Mystic Sage, the questions repeat on a loop in my head. As hard as I'm trying to put Nick's murder behind me, the memory is following me like a bad ex-boyfriend—terrible analogy.

I enter Mystic Sage with a ding of the bell and a clank of the bamboo chimes. Jeff is ringing up a customer. I don't see my boss.

"Hi, Jeff. Where is Shane? I need to talk to him before I start my shift."

"He's in the back checking in deliveries," he replies. "You seem flustered. Are you OK?"

I stuff my purse under the counter and laugh nervously. "Yeah. Don't worry about me. Same old, same old."

I rush to the rear of the store where Shane is signing off on deliveries. He's full of smiles and hugs.

"Hi, darling. Enjoy your day off?" He releases me from his grasp and moves a couple of boxes.

"Yeah, but you know me. I get antsy if I don't have something to do."

He laughs. "Well, I've got plenty for you here. You're gonna be as busy as a bee restocking shelves this afternoon."

"I don't know whether to thank you or cuss under my breath." I grin and open a box to find jars full of dried herbs. "Jeff told me he's going to buy into the business. I think that's fantastic. For you and him."

"I'm getting old and would like to enjoy life a little more, you know?"

"Yeah. I do. And I still have another year of grad school to finish. I don't know why I thought getting a master's degree at my age was a good idea."

"Oh, darling. No education or training is ever a waste of time. You have plenty of life left. And I'm far from having a foot in the Otherworld yet. I plan on enjoying my time while I'm healthy."

"Does Cordelia have something to do with this renewed vigor of yours?"

A smile peeks through his beard. "She just might, Gwyn. I never imagined I could feel this alive again. I would like you and the others to spend time with her. We should all have dinner at the Raven some evening, so you all can get to know her better. She would love that."

"That's a great idea. And it would be a wonderful opportunity for Amnesia Kate to socialize with a larger group. I'll stop at Mitchell Hall and ask Trinity about it." I scan the room, searching for a segue to mention Cordelia's lapse in judgment the other night.

Shane rips open a box. "Something on your mind?"

"Actually, yeah. I'm sure she didn't think it was a problem at all, and it was dark. But I caught Cordelia performing a ritual in the Celestial Gardens when I went by to check on Shailagh and Aonghas right after work. The iron gate was locked, but..."

He pulls on his beard as he rocks his head. "She shouldn't be going in there at all. Quite a risky thing with the portal mound there. I'll have a talk with her. Don't you worry. You have enough to keep you up at night."

"Even more. I came from a meeting with Dr. Seamus Duffy. I was hoping to get a sense of whether he was in the parking lot on the night of Ostara. But after talking with him, I have more doubts than answers."

"Did you ever think of coming out and asking the man directly, Gwyn?"

"No. If he wasn't there, he'd start asking questions. I'm thinking I imagined it like Leslie suggested—influenced by the glamouring."

But there's still something off about the visiting professor, and I plan to find out. The door dings, and my shift has officially started.

"Back to work. You're not paying me for conversation."

"No, I'm not. But if I did, I don't think I could afford you." Shane fills the backroom with hearty laughter.

"Very funny," I say, frowning. "I better get out front."

As I stroll to the front of the store, Shane continues to chuckle, and I laugh at myself. I discover the recent shopper is Amnesia Kate. She's dressed for work in her Raven Pub T-shirt, jeans, and sneakers. Her navy-blue DUB hoodie hangs on her like it's one size too big. She meanders around the store as if she's going through the motions, searching for an item, but not sure what. Jeff doesn't take his eyes off of her. The young woman is frail, but arguably has one of the most beautiful faces I've ever encountered. You can tell he's smitten. I walk behind the counter.

"Hi, Jeff. Busy this morning?"

"No. I spent most of it dusting off everything." He glances at me but returns his attention to Kate. "I like to stay busy."

"I'm right there with you. It's a curse. I wish I could force myself to relax." And that's difficult to do being *in the knowing*.

He whispers next to my ear. "I've never seen her in here before? She's wearing a DUB hoodie, but I haven't run into her on campus either."

"That young woman isn't a student," I whisper back. "She chose the name Kate until her memory returns. Elijah Jackson found her on the street recently. She's living with Skye McGowen temporarily. To help her out, the manager of the Raven gave her a job bussing tables."

"That's sad. I should offer to buy her a coffee sometime."

I smile and log into the cash register. "Why don't you go talk to her? Strike up a conversation. But don't hit on her. I have a better idea. I'm going to chat with Trinity Johnson about meeting at the Raven Pub for dinner some night. It's mostly so we can all meet Shane's friend Cordelia, but you could come. And I could invite Kate, too. How does that sound?"

An enormous grin erupts on his face. "Awesome."

Jeff hurries around the counter and walks over to the puzzles section where Kate is fiddling with a sample. He talks with her, introducing himself and shaking her hand, and attempts to solve the puzzle but fails. She chuckles, and he laughs, too. This match could be the best thing to happen to both of them. Or it could be the worst.

CHAPTER TEN

THE GATHERING

WHAT A DIFFERENCE A couple of days make in the weather. By Thursday, the temperatures are in the mid-70s, and the meteorologists on the news are forecasting mid-80s by Sunday. I'm so excited about the gift of unexpected summer heat, even if it's only for a brief time.

While I primp in front of the mirror on my bedroom closet door, I admire my figure in my V-neck teal tee and skinny jeans—amazing considering I had to squeeze a few extra pounds into them. Time to get back to the fitness center and take back my life. Out of the corner of my eye, I catch Mr. Yeats staring at me—always a busybody.

"Do you need something?"

The familiar adjusts his spectacles. "No, Ms. Crowther. I wanted to remind you we haven't had a divination conference with your parents as planned. You should really inform them of your,"—he drops his voice to a whisper—"extracurricular activities."

"I haven't had time," I whisper back. "Shhh. Dr. Hughes could hear you. And my extracurricular activities are none of your business."

Leslie opens her bedroom door. She's dressed in a floral blouse and pink skirt—bold colors for her. She's also applied eyebrow pencil and pink lipstick. Mr. Yeats attempts to appear uninterested as he stands in the hallway fluffing his bow tie.

"You look very springy, Leslie," I say. "The colors bring out the copper in your eyes."

"Thank you, Gwynedd. I'm off to pick up Agnes. The engine in her 1957 Chevy won't turn over, and her incantations no longer work to spark life into it. I offered to buy her a new car, but she refuses. Too much pride."

That's rich, coming from her. I suppress a snicker. "So, I'll see you both at the Raven. The Fellowship hasn't had a group dinner like this in a long time. It'll be fun."

"It should be. Mr. Yeats, I have no errands for you to complete. Enjoy your evening of solitude."

He smiles as he straightens his back. "Thank you, Dr. Hughes." He transforms into his black and ginger fur and scuttles into the office.

"Shall we go?" Leslie asks, walking toward the mudroom.

"I only need to grab my purse."

While Leslie drives to the farm to pick up Agnes, I stroll over to Archie's via Sussex Way. When I arrive at the corner, I stare at Seamus's house a block away. Talking to him directly didn't get me anywhere. Would I be stupid to add breaking and entering to my jaywalking and murder criminal activities?

Archie is waiting on the stoop of his house for me, dressed in a navy-blue Henley short-sleeved shirt and worn jeans. He's engrossed in his phone.

"Hey, gorgeous. What's so interesting on your cell you didn't see me coming?"

He raises his head and grins widely as he stands. "Reading the Bearsden local news."

"Anything worth sharing?" I push up on my toes and kiss him tenderly.

"Mmm. Nothing as worthy as your kisses." He grasps my hand. "We should start walking. The young witches reserved the entire room for us."

"What were you reading about?"

"You're in such a good mood. I should tell you later."

I nudge him. "Tell me. Is the news you're reading that bad?"

"Aye. Quite disturbing and sad, actually. The article was a wee bit too descriptive of the wounds found on the mauled student on campus, and the first one they found in the woods."

"That's awful. What else did the article say?"

"They released the names of the young men, and the parents aren't happy with the paper for divulging so much personal information so soon. But their need to glorify death and sell papers will always take precedence over the mental state of the victim's family."

I grimace. "I can't imagine what they're going through. Did the police release any of the information in the forensic reports?"

He shrugs. "No. I imagine they're not releasing everything while they investigate further. The parents are devastated by their violent deaths and have demanded the city pay for a search to find the cougar. That cat has eluded capture for years. They're not likely to find it now either."

"Don't you think it's odd they haven't released the results of the forensic reports?"

"No." He squints at me. "What are you thinking? You still believe it's a cat sith fairy?"

"I don't know. I spoke to Seamus on Tuesday. You were busy, so I didn't stop by your office. He confirmed what Quinn told me about them. That they eat the souls of the dead. What if one crossed over and is killing those young men so it could eat their souls?"

"Oh, Gwynedd. What a macabre idea. But a cougar is a simpler explanation."

"Let's enjoy the rest of our walk to the pub. All this talk about the maulings is ruining my appetite."

"I told you I should wait."

We stroll along the paver walkways of the Green, soaking in the late afternoon sun. Pink, red, and white azaleas color the foundations of the red-brick Georgian buildings. As we pass the alleyway where the second student was attacked, I recall the pool of blood next to his lifeless body. My mind drifts to the recent dreams I've had of Archie. Could they be visions of future danger involving the cougar?

When Archie first ignited my magic, I had dreams that came to fruition. There was the Sluagh attack, and then Nick's transformation into Nuada. Perhaps I could enhance my abilities by using crystals and further the visions, if that's truly what they are. Archie and Leslie wouldn't want me to. I'm inexperienced. The vision that ended with Archie's oral prowess flashes in my head. I chuckle under my breath.

"What's tickling your fancy, my love?"

"I was remembering one of my premonitions I thought was only a dream. The vision of the first time you made love to me...with your tongue."

A devilish smile emerges on his face. "Aye. You screamed so loud the entire neighborhood must have thought I was committing murder."

"Ha. Ha. Ha. It had been so long since I'd had an orgasm, I fell into another dimension. Anyway, I never told you when the dream occurred."

"Does it matter? I'm chuffed it happened."

"Do you remember the second class you monitored for Leslie? I came late, but you didn't appear to notice when I entered the classroom."

"Ah, yes. I heard you enter, but I didn't want to embarrass you."

"I had a terrible nightmare about finding out Richard had cheated on me. And then, out of nowhere, a sexy man appeared in the dream. I woke up to my alarm when you were about to..."

Archie bursts out laughing. "Is that why you yelled stop when I was almost at your sweet spot that evening?"

"Yes." I chuckle and pull him close to me. "It scared me, but I didn't want you to stop."

"I'm so glad you let me continue." He kisses me deeply while students dash past us, laughing. "Sleep with me tonight, Gwynedd. Let me show you it can be like that again."

"But your grades are due tomorrow." I clasp his hand and begin walking.

"I'll finish them. They aren't due until midnight."

The corners of my mouth slowly curl up. "OK. You convinced me."

We arrive at the Raven Rub, entering through the double doors to the foyer. The aroma of freshly popped popcorn permeates the air, and my stomach growls. We meander around the tables into our regular room to the right of the entrance.

It appears all of the Fellowship has arrived except for Leslie, Agnes, Shane, and Cordelia Davenport. Trinity's wife, Charlie, has joined us, along with Elijah's girlfriend, Jasmine. And Derek is here with Ronnie. We've become quite an extended family of witches and Unremarkables who are *in the knowing*. The young witches sit at one end of the table, congregating away from us older folk. They shout at Archie and me as we sit down.

"Hey, Gwyn! Hey, Archie! What took you so long?"

"You know, Mom," Tyler says. "She had to pick between her jeans and....her other jeans."

I scowl at my offspring. "Very funny."

"Don't give your mom a hard time," Zoe says. "She's had it rough recently."

"Thank you, Zoe. I can always depend on you." I frown at my son.

Elijah chimes in. "But she's doing just fine now."

Amnesia Kate walks by carrying a full bus tub. Skye gets up from the table and darts to her. They talk for a minute, and Kate smiles, nodding. Skye returns to her seat.

"Kate is going to join us in a minute," she says. "I imagined this would be too many people, but she seems excited. She's gotten to know Zach, me, and Gwyn."

"She's still quiet," Zach adds. "So, don't overwhelm her with questions."

Tanner grabs a menu. "I think it's awesome you allowed her to crash at your place. It was a risk to put up a total stranger."

"Pfft," Spence says. "Who else could take her in and make her feel comfortable and stable? Could you see her staying with me and Tanner? Or Zoe?"

Zoe sits up straight. "Hey, that's not fair. I told Elijah I have to attend Summer Session, and I don't have an extra room."

"I'm only messing with you, sis." He blows her a kiss.

We all chuckle at their banter but let them go back to their babble about Skye and Spence's upcoming graduation. Zoe has one more semester like Zach. I'd hoped Jeff would come, but it appears he may have gotten stuck at Mystic Sage. Now that he's part owner of the store, he's been spending long hours there. I'm disappointed, because he took a liking to Kate. Trinity bends over our end of the table and motions us to do the same.

"Before Kate gets here, I wanted to confirm our dates for checking on the Seelie Fae nightly. I know it's a royal pain in the ass, but our allies on the council asked us to keep them occupied so they won't carry on. And we agreed."

Archie replies, "For now, I think we can handle the commitment. But eventually, even going every other week will become tedious."

"I know I'm not in your group and shouldn't comment," Charlie says. "But I wonder how long all of you can keep this up? Weeks? Months? Years?"

"It's tiring me out, too." Ronnie yawns. "I've still not caught up on the late night from last week."

Derek wraps an arm around her and rubs her back. "You should go to bed early tonight, babe."

My shoulders fall. "Well, I'm the only one who has to go every Saturday. It's already wearing me down."

"They favor you, Gwyn," Trinity says. "I worry they will tear up the place if they don't see you at least once a week. You created a special relationship with them. As they say, 'You reap what you sow.'"

Elijah lets out a deep, resounding laugh. "You sure did, Gwyn."

"Oh, Elijah," Jasmine scolds. "I feel for you, Gwyn. I wish I could help, but I've never even met the...children."

"Thanks, Jasmine." I chuckle at the gentle giant and sigh.

Soon after, Leslie and Agnes arrive and sit down with us. The hedge witch is in rare form. The young witches yell, "Hello!" She responds by giving them the bird, and they crack up.

"This place is too swanky now," she grumbles. "When I worked here, the Raven didn't have a big, fancy porch. And we certainly didn't wear those ridiculous T-shirts."

Leslie rolls her eyes. "Oh, Agnes. When you worked here, the place smelled of pot and bad whisky. My shoes stuck to the floor, and the Heathens biker gang were patrons. Atrocious."

Agnes laughs and slaps a hand on the wooden table. "Fuck yeah. Those were the days."

When I glance up from my menu, Jeff walks in and takes a seat next to Skye. He grins when Kate shows up at the table and sits down next to him, dropping her backpack to the floor. She's changed out of her Raven Pub T-shirt into a loose pink tee and smiles sweetly as Skye introduces her to everyone. The backpack never leaves her side.

Shortly after, Shane enters with Cordelia, who is hanging on his left arm. She's wearing a tight-fitting red dress and so much makeup, you could peel it off. He's grinning from ear to ear. The young crowd gets quiet as he introduces her.

"Good evening, everyone. I'd like to introduce you to Cordelia Davenport, the friend I told you about at the last meeting. Cordelia, these are my beloved friends of Bearsden. I'll let them introduce themselves."

Cordelia smiles as we take turns spewing our names at random. Shane pulls out a chair for her, and they sit down at the end of the table.

"Well, I declare," she says in her thick Southern accent. "You all are so friendly. But I'm not surprised. Shane spoke so highly of you."

Archie smiles and hands Cordelia a menu. "It's wonderful to meet you finally. Gwyn had wonderful things to say about your lunch together."

No, I didn't, liar. I said she was a superficial witch.

Cordelia peers at me, a slight smirk present on her mouth. "Yes. We had a fabulous meal right here at the Raven."

She's acting strange. What is her angle?

Agnes eyes her up and down. "How old are you?"

"Don't ask her that," Leslie chides. "It's rude."

Cordelia laughs as she squeezes Shane's arm. "Honey, a lady never tells."

"Riiight," Agnes says, squinting. "And a bunny doesn't fuck."

We all burst out laughing, and Trinity motions to our waiter. "Since we're such a large party, we'll have to split up the bill at the end. But Kate, we'll take care of your meal. Order whatever you want."

"Thank you, everyone," she says in an angelic voice. "You have been so nice to me. Given me a place to stay. Helped me find a job. I'll never be able to repay you."

Cordelia interjects, "I'm sure you'll find a way."

What an odd thing to say to a woman you just met. Kate lowers her head and sinks into her seat. Jeff glares at Cordelia and whispers something into Kate's ear. She giggles and sits up.

"Archie, can you order for me?" I ask, standing up. "I have to go to the Ladies' Room."

Cordelia jumps up from her seat. "Wait for me, Gwyn. That afternoon tea has shot right through my kidneys."

We make our way to the restroom, and she prattles on about the bad hairdresser at the local salon. I only half listen until we enter the bathroom, and she turns the lock on the door.

"What are you doing?" I ask, my brow creasing.

Her heels echo on the tile floor as she approaches and thrusts her face into mine. "We need to have a teensy private talk, you and I. Shane reprimanded me for using the Celestial Gardens at Mitchell Hall for my solitary ritual. He said you saw me in there."

"I doubt he reprimanded you. That's not his way. I had to tell him I caught you in the gardens. As he probably told you, there is an open portal in that mound, and fae children cross over occasionally. But more important than that—Unremarkables could have seen you. It's dangerous."

Cordelia scowls at me and shoves her finger into my chest. "It was none of your concern. From now on, stay out of my business. And if you ever tell Shane anything again, karma will have its way with you."

I grab her finger and push back on her hand. "Are you threatening me, Cordelia? Because I don't think Shane would approve."

"Just you mind your own beeswax. Shane is an experienced adult and doesn't need you ruining his life."

She walks to the door, unlocks it, and leaves. I stand there, fuming. Droplets sprout on my chest, and I break out in a hot flash. I wet a paper towel to place on my neck while I pee. How am I going to sit through dinner with her and act like nothing happened? I want to strangle that woman. There goes my killer instinct again. My hands are shaking, I'm so angry. Calm down,

Gwyn. Cool off before you go back out there. This time, I really could snap."

While I chillax on the porcelain throne, the door bangs open. A young woman is crying as she locks the door. She runs water as if she's washing her face. When she finishes, she darts to the stall next to me and drops a backpack on the floor. It resembles Kate's bag. I pull up my pants and exit the stall to wash my hands. She takes little gasps of air, a poor attempt to stop the crying. There's blood smeared on the sink she used.

"Kate? It's Gwyn Crowther. Are you OK?"

She whimpers. "No. I got blood on my clothes."

"What happened? Can I help you?" Blood? Did she cut herself?

"I...the courses came...from my..."

A light bulb clicks on. "Do you mean you got your period?" Courses? Who the hell calls it that now?

"Yes. Yes. My monthly. I found a rag at the apartment, but there's too much blood. I can't remember for sure, because of my memory loss, but I think I haven't had them for a long, long time."

She used a rag? "Kate, put the used material into the paper bag inside the bin on the wall. Then put it in the metal container on the floor. I have something you can use. It's a pad. I'm passing it under the door to you. I carried some with me in case I spotted, and they're still in my purse. That can happen when you first hit menopause and aren't sure you'll not bleed again."

"How does it work?" What the fuck? How does she not know how to use a sanitary napkin? "Pull off that strip of paper on the back and press it into your underwear. It will stick." It's like I'm talking to a young teen getting her first menses.

"Thanks, Gwyn. But I have another problem." She walks out of the stall with her Raven Pub T-shirt in her hand, splattered in blood. "I used it to clean the blood off. I wasn't thinking. What am I going to do?"

"Why don't you wipe your face and pat it dry? I'll wash it out, so it won't stain. You can throw your clothes in the washing machine when you return to the apartment. And ask Skye for more pads. She can also show you how to use another hygiene product called tampons."

I get most of the blood out—enough to keep it from setting in. Kate stuffs it into her backpack, and we go back to the table. Our food is waiting for us when we arrive. Archie leans into my ear.

"What took you so long? I almost came in after you?"

When I glance at Kate, she mouths, "Thank you." I nod subtly to her and whisper back to him, "I'll tell you on the way home."

I pick at my dinner and so does Kate. Two peas in a pod, we are. I can barely swallow my food because I'm so angry. Everyone laughs at Cordelia's boisterous story about Shane's early mishaps when learning magic. He doesn't appear to mind, but I'm sure he wouldn't say if he did. I force a grin, stretching my cheeks as far as humanly possible, but refuse to laugh at her insulting jokes.

Archie whispers in my ear, "What's the matter with you? Are you angry with me?"

"No," I whisper back. "I'll tell you later."

Suddenly, there's a woman screaming in the back bar area where the restrooms are. "There's a dead body behind the dumpster out back! Call an ambulance!"

Elijah jumps up. "You all stay here. I'll go check."

"I'll go with you," Archie says, throwing his napkin on the table. "Gwyn, I'll be back."

"If you think I'm staying here, you don't know me as well as you thought."

He frowns. "Suit yourself, but haven't you've seen enough dead bodies?"

"You go, friend," Ronnie says, dropping her fork on the plate. "I'm having enough trouble eating already."

She's not alone. Everyone in the restaurant has lost their appetite—except for Cordelia. She continues to stuff her mouth full of Brussels sprouts, chewing to her heart's content. Does this woman even have a heart?

As I get up from the table, Trinity says, "Report back to me."

When we get outside, the manager of the Raven is corralling people back. After pushing through the throng of onlookers, we observe the body of a young man wearing a DUB T-shirt. He was probably celebrating the end of his finals. Something shredded his neck like the other two victims—veins, tendons, and pieces of muscle protrude from the area like globs of jelly. What does it say about me that these wounds no longer turn my stomach? The three of us huddle together.

"Nothing we can do here," Archie says. "The manager and his staff are keeping the patrons at bay."

Elijah rubs his jaw. "I agree. We didn't find the body, so no reason to hang around."

"Let's go back and tell the others to pay the bill, and we'll be on our way. Come on, Gwyn."

I stare at the mauled corpse and the small puddle of blood. Why are the wounds always on the neck? Does the cougar sense it's a weak spot? I follow the men back into the Raven, and we tell the others what we observed. The Bearsden Police arrive with sirens screeching and clear the bar, but many people hang around like vultures, wondering about the prey. What started as a joyful gathering has ended in an evening of despair.

As the Fellowship disbands, I wave goodbye to Tyler and Zoe. I glare at Cordelia as she struts up Main Street, hanging on Shane's arm. What a cold-hearted woman. How does he not see that? A slight smile erupts when I catch Jeff chatting with Kate. He waves to her as she and Skye leave for their apartment. Ronnie and Derek remain behind.

"Were the wounds on the young man the same as the other victims?" Derek asks.

"Aye," Archie replies. "Exactly the same. Evidence of a struggle. A broken beer bottle in his hand."

An image of his wounds flash in my head. "His neck was destroyed. His skin resembled strips of torn paper."

Ronnie covers her mouth. "I think I'm gonna be sick."

"Let's go home, babe." Derek wraps an arm around her and kisses her on the top of her head. "She's still trying to shake this stomach bug."

"I hope you feel better," I say, stroking her arm.

"We should go, too, Gwyn," Archie says, grasping my hand.

On the sullen walk back to his house, I tell him about Cordelia accosting me in the Ladies' Room at the Raven.

"That explains your foul mood through dinner. Are you going to tell Shane?"

"I can't. She's an experienced witch, and I don't want to piss her off any more than I have."

"I doubt she is more powerful than you. You have developed your skills well."

"But I still have so much more to learn." Like using crystals to enhance my visions.

When we hit the intersection of Sussex and Drummond, I stop. "I think I'm going to head home. Cordelia zapped my mood into smithereens."

"I expected as much," he says, caressing my arm. "Better I get a good night's rest and finish my grading early tomorrow. Come by for dinner and...recreation?"

"Sure. I'll come by after work."

He escorts me home and says goodbye at the side porch door. I wrap my arms around his torso, and he kisses me fervently, offering his tongue. A twinge of arousal sparks between my legs, and I rub them together. My libido is still there.

"Sleep well, my love," he says, panting.

I fiddle with his goatee. "You too, honey."

As he ambles up Drummond Lane, I recall the wounds of the student lying behind the dumpster. Cougar, my ass. Where are you, kitty-kitty?

Chapter Eleven

PUFF, THE MAGIC POISON

Early the next morning, Mr. Yeats grinds the mugwort, and I set fire to the star anise incense I bought at Mystic Sage. My Great-Aunt Gorawen prefers to use it, so I figure, why not burn both? My familiar assistant sits in the corner chair and opens a book while I set the photo of my mom in front of me. I focus on her image, raising my hand with amber magic radiating from my fingertips. Her face appears as a golden, glowing image, wavering like a reflection in the water.

"Hello, daughter. It's so good to conference with you. Your father is busy today. How are you feeling?"

"I'm better. Not as stressed about what happened. For now, everything is fine. The coven has been incredibly supportive. But Archie and I have experienced some bumps in our...love life."

Mom chuckles. "You can spare me the details, Gwynedd."

"I know TMI. The missing person case on Nick Evans remains open, so that's unsettling. And since I conferenced with you last, three young male students were killed, one last night."

"Oh Gwyn, murders in Bearsden?" Her image intensifies.

"Not murders. Do you remember the cougar that someone let loose and was killing dogs and cats back before you passed?"

"Yes. It was very irresponsible. So many people lost beloved pets."

"It showed up after you were gone, too. Then it disappeared for a few years. The police think it's back. The wounds resemble those of a wild animal, so they believe the cougar has returned."

"You don't sound convinced. Do you think it's a supernatural being? The enormous cat you saw on the night of Ostara?"

"I don't know what to think. The first time I encountered it, I'm sure I was being lured by Nuada toward the portal near that castle in Buckley. The second time was when I...you know. I never saw it again."

"We now know Dr. Seamus Duffy wasn't the fairy who was stalking me, but there's something strange about him. But enough about all that. I wanted to conference with you to ask about using crystals to enhance visions. I told you I've had a few. Some were frightening. Others were..." I snicker when I think of the sexy dream starring Archie. "Anyway, did you ever try to enhance premonitions? I assume you had some since I did."

"Oh, I had many as a child, and they increased in adulthood. But Aunt Gorawen said I should wait until I was older and more experienced to increase the intensity of them, because they can overpower your mind and affect your emotional state badly. You've only practiced witchcraft for a couple of years, dear. Perhaps when you are—"

"Older?" I roll my eyes. "Mom, I'm fifty-four. Am I supposed to wait until I'm in my 70s?"

She laughs, and her golden face shimmers in and out. "You're not ready, Gwynedd. I may have stopped practicing the craft in my youth, but I know enough to respect what Aunt Gorawen told me. She knew of witches who attempted to enhance their visions when they were entirely too young. And they went mad. Please heed my warning, daughter."

"All right. It really sucks you get to tell me what to do, and you're dead."

Mom snorts, and her image breaks into sparkling golden flecks. "Your father sends his love. I hope to conference with you again in a few weeks. Meanwhile, you should contact Aunt Gorawen if you have more questions."

"I will. Thanks, Mom. Tell Dad I love him."

Her vision fades until the last gold fleck disappears. I extinguish the incense in a bowl of water. Mr. Yeats comes to the worktable to help me clean up.

"You have become quite adept at divination conferencing, Ms. Crowther. I disagree with your mother that you aren't ready to move on to more difficult layers of magic. I've seen you develop from a neophyte to a level three. And you conference with no hesitation."

I cross my arms and squint. "Why are you being so...supportive? Do you want something?"

He fiddles with the buttons on his vest. "I've always been rooting for you, Ms. Crowther. I am hurt that you would think otherwise."

"Suuure," I say, wiping off the table. "Thanks for your help."

"Anytime, Ms. Crowther. I am at your service." He skips out of the magic room, transforming into his cat presentation, and scuttles up the hallway.

I lean against the worktable and consider my options. Leslie can't help. She doesn't have visions. Archie wouldn't train me. He'd agree with my mom and Aunt Gorawen's assessment. Trinity hasn't ever mentioned having premonitions and would be hesitant for the same reasons. There's only one witch who would ever say 'fuck it' and take this kind of risk. A wicked grin curls my mouth.

I drive up the gravel road, and the stones crunch as my tires roll over them. I don't even know if Agnes has visions. But she's amassed pieces of witchcraft from all kinds of witches in her lifetime. Agnes collects spells like other 80-some year-olds accumulate bells, ceramic figurines, or vintage plates. Not the hedge witch. She hoarded grimoires.

Tanner and Spence are meeting with her on Saturday to plan the renovations to her kitchen—an economical one. The house needs painting on the outside, too. Paint chips fall off the siding every day. A project for the fall.

I bang on the front door and shout, "Agnes? It's Gwyn. Can I talk to you for a few minutes?"

The door creaks open, and she tilts her head. "What the fuck are you doing here? You're getting your days mixed up. We're not meeting until tomorrow."

"Oh, I know that. I'm not here for the kitchen reno meeting. I need some witchcraft advice."

"Why didn't you ask Leslie? She was a neophyte when I met her, but she's more than experienced enough to give advice, unless..." She pushes her salt and pepper hair aside.

I press my lips together and raise my eyebrows. "Exactly. I'd rather you not tell her about this."

"We're together now, you know. You're asking a lot for me to keep secrets from her, especially after the years she hid stuff from me. And I held it against her the whole time. I'd be a hypocrite."

I stare at the open fields of wildflowers, realizing she's right. It's too much to ask. Yet...

"Fuck it," she says. "Come on in."

I follow her into her outdated kitchen with the mismatched '20s cabinets and mod geometric-patterned linoleum floors. But it's a wonderful old space. Tanner and Spence did a fantastic job on the renovation of their kitchen in my old home.

"Want some iced tea? I made a fresh batch."

"Sure," I say. "But I only have a few hours. I'm eating dinner with Archie and..."

"Frolicking after?" She chuckles as she pours the black tea over my ice-filled glass and sits.

"You always make the best tea. I should watch you sometime."

"Nothing to it. I let the tea bags soak in a huge glass container and remove the bags. You're procrastinating. What the fuck do you want, Gwyn?"

"Questions hang in my brain about Seamus Duffy. Leslie probably told you he moved up the street from us. She thinks Nuada's glamouring distorted my perception—an after-effect. I actually snooped on him. Followed him to his house. Don't think poorly of me, but I snuck into his backyard and peeked in a window at him."

Agnes laughs and slaps the table. "Pervert."

"I'm not a pervert," I say, scowling. "I wanted to see if he was hiding something."

She leans over the table and snickers. "Well? How big is it?"

"What? For fuck's sake, Agnes. I didn't see his...junk."

"What did you find out, then?" she asks, gulping down her iced tea.

"Nothing." I sigh and take a drink. "But I observed an old injury on his lower left leg. He's missing part of the muscle and has a huge scar. Almost like he was..."

"Mauled?" she asks. "That begs a huge question, doesn't it?"

"It sure does. And there are the deaths of those three young students. The police think it's that cougar roaming around, but no one has actually sighted it this time."

"What do you want from me?"

"In the past, visions popped into my head or appeared in my dreams, warning me of things to come. A new one has appeared over and over, but it never progresses." I can't tell her what it is, fearing it could affect the outcome. "I've read I can use crystals to enhance my abilities, but my mom says I've not practiced witchcraft long enough because of my late start. She said Aunt Gorawen spoke of ancestors who became mentally ill when they tried too soon."

Agnes rocks her head back and forth. "It's a risk. Why didn't you go to Archie? He can help you better than I can."

"He'd say no, because of Aunt Gorawen's warnings. Can you help me? Have you ever had premonitions?"

"Sure, I have. More when I was younger. Now, I have them every so often. But I don't use crystals." She gets up from the kitchen table, hobbles to her pot cabinet, and grabs a jar. "I use a potent blend from my garden. I save it for special occasions. This is reason enough to pull out the old Bearsden Poison."

I sit straight up in my chair. "I'm not going to smoke pot with you. That's never been my thing, and my allergies would run amok. I may have inhaled some at the Raven one night, but it did nothing but give me a headache. And anything called Poison doesn't sound like something I should try."

"It's not actual poison, Gwyn. I only gave this particular blend the name because of its potent effect. At best, you'll experience an increase in your visions. At the least, the most euphoric state will capture you. With the PTSD you have from...you know...you've been a little depressed. Don't tell me you're all better. You'd be lying to yourself."

She's absolutely correct. And it's affected every area of my life, including frolicking under the sheets with Archie. Should I consider it? I tap my fingernails on the kitchen table and stare at her.

"Oh, for fuck's sake. What do you have to lose? Try it once. If the THC doesn't help to intensify your visions, then we can try the use of crystals. I've got a grimoire we haven't gotten to yet that has specific directions for increasing premonitions. But I'd feel more comfortable if you tried something safer first."

I bite my lower lip. "Oh, all right. I'll try one puff and test it first."

Agnes slaps my arm and grins widely. "Attagirl. I'll roll the joint."

"So, when did Leslie first smoke pot? I was shocked to find her partaking when I walked in on you two after the Pagan Conference in Lewes."

"I coaxed her one night. Only wanted her to loosen up a little. One drag was all she needed." She snickers as she runs her tongue along the paper. "After that, she was all over me."

"You mean it made her horny?"

"Like a bunny rabbit." She guffaws and passes me the joint. "Here, hold this while I get my lighter."

I hold the freshly rolled joint between my thumb and index finger, examining the preciseness of the point. Am I really going to do this? My parents would put me in a corner. Or would they?

Agnes sits down next to me and takes the *funny cigarette* back. She puts the tip in her mouth, lights the other end, and inhales, holding the smoke for a few seconds until it passes through her lips in a small stream. I cough and wave my hand.

"Your turn. I recommend only a teensy bit for your first try."

She passes the lit joint to me, and I place the tip on my lips. I inhale the tiniest amount, and she laughs at me.

"You'll need more than that. Try again but inhale more deeply."

"OK. Remember, this is my first time. And I've never smoked."

This time, I try to emulate her, sucking in as far as I can. My face becomes flush, and I expel the smoke, hacking and coughing uncontrollably. Agnes guffaws and pats me on the back.

"That's more like it. Now give it a chance to work."

"It's doing nothing. No visions. No euphoric feeling." A hot flash overwhelms me, and I grab a piece of mail from the table and fan myself as sweat rolls down my face and neck. "Shit. If this is all I'm gonna get from it, you can keep your pot."

Agnes chuckles. "Sometimes you have to wait a few minutes, Gwyn. Be patient."

"Fuck patience. Give me the joint." I inhale one more time, coughing less, and pass the joint back to her. "Maybe it won't affect me. I hear some people don't react at all."

"That may be true of weaker strains, but my Bearsden Poison?"

"Well, I'm an ancestral witch," I say in a cocky tone. "I may need more." I snatch the joint out of her knobby fingers and inhale again.

"Damn, Gwyn!" she yells. "You're gonna regret this. Give it back."

She grabs at my hand, and I yank the joint back to take another hit...and another. When there's barely any left, I hand her the end. Sweat trickles down my neck into my boobs, and I pull at my T-shirt, desperate for air.

"You're too cocky for your own good." She grimaces and puts out the joint in an old ashtray.

"I want it to work, Agnes, or I'll have to use crystals."

"But now you probably overdid it. Leslie will lecture me for sure."

"Nah. Your weed hasn't affected me. I appreciate you trying, though." I grab the keys out of my purse and stand. The room pivots around me like a merry-go-round, and I plop back into my chair.

Agnes snickers. "No effect, huh? Tell me what's happening."

"I'm light-headed, and the room is swerving back and forth." I try to focus on her face, which is morphing into a more youthful version. "Have I told you what a beautiful woman you are? It's no wonder Leslie fell in love with you."

"Yeah. You inhaled too much." She bursts out laughing. "How do you feel?"

"Everything is so colorful and shiny." I stare at the geometric patterns on her floor, and they become three-dimensional. "Woah." I grab the table.

Agnes pats my back again. "Why don't you focus on the vision you've been having? See where it goes."

"OK. I'll try, but all I want to do is laugh."

I giggle and close my eyes, recalling the image of Archie walking into the Celestial Gardens in my dreams. Nope. Nothing. Nada.

Then a vision of Archie's muscular, naked body appears, and an aura works its way toward my pelvis.

"Well, I've been smoking for years and know how to imbibe. We can try again."

I grin and snicker. "But I feel great!" A tingling emerges between my legs.

"I bet you do," she says. "You should probably sleep this off a bit before you try to drive."

"No," I say, standing. "I'm not dizzy anymore." But I sure am horny! "I think I'm gonna go."

I grab my keys and purse and drag myself to the front door. Agnes follows behind me, rubbing her back.

"Are you sure you're OK to drive?"

"Yeah. I'm going straight home." I rub my legs together. "Actually, I'm going to Archie's. So Leslie doesn't suspect anything." I wink at her and chuckle.

"Riiight. I'm sure he can help you come down off your high." She laughs and slaps my arm. "Attagirl. Go give him a time he won't forget."

CHAPTER TWELVE

LIBIDO UNLEASHED

ON THE WAY TO Archie's house, laughter overcomes me, and I have to pull over twice to stop my hyena fits. When I finally roll in front of his house, my hysterics calm to a soft chuckle. I'm so full of energy. It's as if I slept twelve hours last night. I lock my Prius with a beep-beep, then do it again for good measure.

I walk around the house and enter through the back door. Archie is probably in the kitchen, preparing dinner. But it's not food I want to consume. I snicker as I kick off my sneakers and amble through the doorway. He's investigating options in the fridge. Little does he know, I'm going to inspect him like he's eyeing those fresh veggies.

"Gwyn," he says, smiling widely. "I didn't expect you this early, but I'm elated to see you."

I slink over to him, sporting a naughty smile, and caress his chest. "Did you miss me?"

"Of course. I always want you here," he says in a breathy voice.

I stroke his goatee. "Good to know."

When I slide my hand down and fondle his package, he rises to my touch. I wrap my hand around the nape of his neck and pull him toward me, kissing him ardently. He cups a butt cheek and presses me against his bulge, and our tongues intermingle. He comes up for a breather and raises a corner of his mouth.

"This is promising. At least you're making a laudable effort. I appreciate you trying so hard."

"No. You're the one who's hard." I giggle and rub his groin again.

He adjusts his bulge and sniffs. Cocking his head, he leans into me and inhales a teensy closer. "Gwynedd, have you been smoking pot?"

"Maybe? If I'd known it would make me feel this good, I would have tried it in college." I look away, frowning. "But Richard was a goody-two-shoes."

Folds form in his brow. "Where did you smoke pot on a Friday afternoon?"

"At Agnes's house. She hoped it would…" I can't tell him why I really went. "Lighten my mood. Does it matter? I want you so badly." I kiss him again and slip my fingers underneath his T-shirt, relishing the firmness of his abs under my touch.

Archie pushes me back. "As much as I desire you, we should wait until you've come down from the high a wee bit. What was that old hedge witch thinking? I'll cook dinner and make you some black tea, strong."

He moves toward the fridge, but I grab a belt loop of his jeans and tug. As I inch toward him, the desire increases between my legs.

"I'm not hungry for dinner." I suck on my lower lip and wiggle my eyebrows.

He chuckles. "You're so high. We shouldn't make love in the state you're in. You might regret it in the morning, and you'll be pissed. Then we would have made no progress at all."

"I don't know how things would have gone if I weren't high, but I came here to do more than eat dinner, Archie. You're not taking advantage of me." I unbutton the top of his jeans and pull down the zipper. "Maybe I'm ravishing you."

I slip my hand into his boxer briefs and clasp his manhood, and he moans. He swipes a finger across my lips and kisses me lovingly.

"Gwynedd, you're making this very difficult for me to stop you. I long for your touch, but I don't want you to be sorry later."

I lead him over to a kitchen chair, chuckling along the way. "Sit down."

"I'm not going to win this time, am I?"

"Do you ever win?" I laugh and pull on his jeans, catching his underwear as I tug.

"Fair enough. But be gentle, my love."

He laughs while I slither up his legs, separating them as I get closer. Nuada's face flashes before my eyes, and I flinch. He stole the intimacy between Archie and me, and I refuse to let him invade my thoughts anymore. I push his image from my mind. Then I peer up at Archie's icy-blue eyes and take him in my mouth.

He moans. "Oh Gwynedd, how much I've missed your tender touch. Come here."

I release his manhood and remove my T-shirt as I stand. He bends down and kisses my abdomen while I run my fingers through his wavy locks. I unclasp my bra and toss it to the floor, and he moves his tongue toward my left breast. He stops and kisses the red dragon tattoo above my left nipple. His fingers brush my skin, sending a wave of heat through my body. When he circles his tongue around my areola, I dig my nails into his shoulders.

"Don't stop. I'm on fire." A hot flash overwhelms me, and droplets appear all over my skin.

"I'm only getting started, my love."

Archie stares up at me, holding me captive with his eyes. I undo my jeans and push them down to the floor, and he hooks his fingers onto the top of my panties, slipping them down my legs. I kick them off to the side, chuckling, and straddle him. When he enters me, an aura overtakes my body. I glance at my hands, but there's no amber glow. He kisses me, and I savor his tongue in my mouth, wanting to devour him whole.

The room spins, and I lose track of how long we've been making love. The arousal increases as the kitchen swirls around me, and when I'm about to reach my peak, the vision of Archie entering the gardens pops into my head. There's a distorted growl, and he turns his head. Something leaps at him. Then he's lying on the ground. The image disappears.

I reach the peak of my arousal and grip his back. My body shakes and quivers, but I don't know if it's from the excitement or the vision. I hold on to him tightly, not wanting to let go. What does it mean?

"Gwyn?" Archie says, panting. "Are you all right?"

I stroke his goatee. "Yeah. I'm here with you. I'm always OK when you're with me."

"As much as I love screwing in a kitchen chair, can we take this amorous love-making to the bed?" He chuckles and kisses my cheek.

"Sure." I get up and dart to the doorway, laughing. "Meet you upstairs."

He removes his T-shirt while he runs after me, chuckling along the way. When I get to his room, I flip the linens back and hop onto the bed. He jumps over the footboard and crawls up the bed until he's on top of me.

"I sure hope you're as happy about tonight when the morning sun rises. But if you're not, I won't regret it. I worried so much he took you from me."

"No. He could never do that. I love you."

Archie kisses me deeply and enters me, making us one again. Time stands still and moves past me all at once as objects in the room bend and melt. The aqua gem on the dirk in the glass case radiates, splaying rays of light. He grunts in my ear with his release, and I wrap my arms around his torso. I'd missed this connection so much.

My mind wanders, and the image of him lying unresponsive on the grounds of the Celestial Gardens appears in a misty haze. I press my hands into his back.

I don't want to let go.

My skull throbs like someone stuck needles in it. Lifting the bricks weighing my eyelids down proves a challenge, because they're sticking to my corneas. I reach for Archie, but his spot next to me in bed is cool. When I try to lift my head from the pillow, the room twirls, and I fall back. My mouth is dry. I struggle to swallow, and I have to pee badly. So, I roll out of bed and drag my throbbing head to the bathroom. What the hell was I thinking? Using crystals can't be half this bad, and if I lost my marbles, I wouldn't know, anyway.

My hair is a disaster—stringy bangs and frizz all over. I wash my hands and make a futile attempt to smooth the strands down. Only a shower can remedy this mop. The bloodshot eyes and dark circles aren't attractive either. What a mistake that was.

Or was it? The pot allowed me to see a little more of the vision, but unfortunately, not enough. I grab Archie's robe from the back of the door and stagger with lead feet down the stairs toward the kitchen.

Archie's seated at the table for two, sipping tea and perusing his social media feed. I lean my head against the doorway as a chuckle tries desperately to surface. The floor creaks, and he peers up at me, grinning.

"Good morning, my love. You seemed fatigued after last night, so I let you sleep in. We were up late. How do you feel?"

"Like utter shit. If I'd known the hangover for pot was this bad, I wouldn't have tried it."

He offers his hand. "Come here."

"I can't move. If I lift my head, it's gonna fall to the floor."

I put my hands on my noggin and shuffle over to him in my bare feet. He chuckles and wraps his arms around my lower torso, holding me steady.

"You should have spoken to me before you tried marijuana for the first time. I would have told you not to overdo it."

"Oh, Agnes warned me, but I wanted it to work faster. To enhance my..." I stop mid-sentence when I realize I almost let the real reason slip.

"To enhance your what?" He grins and pats me on the butt. "Your libido? Aye, it did."

"Yeah. That's what I meant." It wasn't my original objective, but I was elated at the side effects. Now? Not so much.

"I worried about us making love while you were high. You weren't in control of your behavior."

The chuckle finally escapes. "I was more in control than you think. But you said we were up half the night?"

"Aye," he says, frowning. "You don't remember any of it, I bet. It was wrong of me to let things continue."

"You're wrong," I say, smiling coyly. "I remember everything that happened in the kitchen." And the vision after.

"You were a vixen." He laughs and caresses my backside.

My tongue sticks to the roof of my mouth when I attempt to swallow saliva that's nonexistent. "I need water."

"I'm sure you do. Sit down, and I'll get you a glass with some ice. You may not be hungry, but you should eat some breakfast before you go to Agnes's."

I wipe my face. "Oh, shit. I forgot about the renovation meeting."

"You shouldn't drive in your condition. I'll take you over in my Tesla. Since I've completed a few renovations myself, I'm sure I can help."

I gulp down half my glass of water. "No more pot for this woman. I like to remember what I was doing. We had sex half the night, and I only remember the first part. Did I enjoy it?"

"Aye," he says, grinning like a Cheshire cat. "And I did as well."

"I bet you did. But I'm glad I went through with it."

"I am, too." He smiles and bends down to kiss me, then waves his hand in front of his face. "Holy shite. Your breath smells like a sewer."

"Noted." I smirk at him and drink more water. "I'm going to take a quick shower and brush my teeth while you get breakfast started."

"A shower should help. Get a move on, or we'll be late. And Agnes will chop your head off."

I move toward the hallway. "Right now, I'd welcome the axe."

Archie helps Tanner measure the floor while I sit in a chair, writing the length and width on the paper graph of the kitchen. It's all I can handle. Spence, Tyler, and Zoe pull out food from Agnes's dirty cabinets while Agnes and Leslie remove dishes. Skye and Zach have a bucket of sudsy water and some sponges ready to clean them out.

"Thirteen feet eight inches," Tanner says. "Did you get that, Gwyn?"

"Yes." Does he have to talk like he's shouting through a megaphone?

Spence shouts in a high-pitched voice. "Holy shit. The expiration on these saltines is a year ago."

"Oh, my gods," Zoe yells. "They're probably stale as day-old bread—only a lot older."

"Ms. Pritchard, I mean, Agnes. You shouldn't eat saltine crackers past eight months." Tyler throws the dated box into the trash.

"Don't throw that box out," Agnes says, bitching and moaning. "Those are the only crackers I have. And I put them in my soup, so it doesn't matter if they're stale or not."

Leslie snickers and passes her three plates. "I tried to throw them out once before. She removed the box from the trash and put them back."

"Ewww," Spence says, grimacing. "You ate from the trash?"

"It's my garbage, and for your information, not everyone grows up without wanting. I picked through my share of dumpsters when I was young. You wouldn't know about that, growing up in a middle-class family in your California surfer-dude city."

"Can you all not shout?" My head continues to throb, and the arguing increases the pounding exponentially.

"No offense, Gwyn," Skye says. "But your face looks like someone trampled over it in your sleep."

Zach chuckles. "I can't believe the way you guys talk to each other. It's not like any religious group I ever belonged to."

"Seventeen feet four inches, Gwyn," Tanner says. "Make sure you write that down."

"I got it." Their words stab me in the brain, and I want to throw the graph pad at them. "Welcome to the Fellowship, Zach. You'll learn witches don't hold back, and they can hold a grudge."

He glances at Skye and chuckles. "So I'm learning."

"You love the fact I'm so blunt," Skye says, giving him a kiss.

Agnes puts a cup of black tea in front of me. "Here. Drink this, Gwyn. And when you're done with that cup, I'll get you another. Go on, drink up."

Tyler glances in my direction. "What is wrong with you, Mom? You look ill."

"I wasn't gonna say anything, but he's right," Zoe says, her brow crinkling. "Did you catch Ronnie's bug?"

Agnes snorts. "She's not sick. She's got a pot hangover."

The others snap their heads around and gape at me. I ignore them and continue to write the measurements down.

Spence chuckles. "Oh, my gods, Agnes. Did you give her one of your joints?"

"My best stuff," she replies. "My special strain, Bearsden Poison."

"Ma-ahm, was that your first time?" Tyler asks, snickering.

Tanner smiles and moves to the doorway to measure. "You should let up on your mom for now. Ask her twenty questions when she feels more human."

Archie remains quiet but fails at hiding his inaudible laughing as he joins Tanner to measure the opening. I glare at him, squinting.

"Yes, it was my first time," I reply, frowning at my son. "And it's gonna be my last. I never want to feel this way again."

My son laughs. "You could have asked me, you know."

"I prefer to pretend you're still my innocent little boy."

Zoe snorts and throws out several expired spice jars.

A faint smile forms on Leslie's mouth. "The same thing happened to me, Gwynedd. You have to take it slowly. It won't happen in your subsequent attempts."

"Not happening ever again. It's not for me." I can't believe I'm getting pot advice from the Acting Chair of the Celtic Studies department.

Zoe cocks her head. "It's so not like you. Why did you smoke it?"

I stare at her, speechless, but Agnes comes to my defense.

"Gwyn's been a little depressed, and I hoped it would brighten her spirits. And it did. It's not my fault she nearly smoked the whole joint."

"Wow, sis. Way to hog the weed," Spence chides, crossing his arms. "Why wasn't I invited?"

Agnes scowls at him. "Because I wouldn't have any left, and you know it."

Tanner laughs. "Dude, give it up. You know she's right."

Spence mocks his boyfriend as he pulls the pasta from the cabinets.

"Whenever I smoke too much weed, it makes me horny," Zoe says, snorting.

Skye chimes in. "Sometimes it can be worth the excess. Right, Zach?"

"I'm not commenting," he says, grinning. "I just met you people."

Everyone cracks up and continues with their chores while I rub my temples and doodle on the graph paper.

Zoe picks up a couple of cans and stares at me. "Wait, is that why you..."

Spence gawks at Archie and chuckles. "I see it on your face. You had some fun last night."

Holy crystals. How did this conversation end up on a discussion of my sexual antics when that's not even why I smoked pot in the first place? But Agnes is keeping my secret tucked away in her witchy head, so I'm grateful.

"I'm not commenting," Archie replies, smiling at me. "But I can report I slept like a baby."

I glare at him, fire blazing in my hazel eyes, and press my lips together.

The hedge witch cracks up and impersonates Archie in a baritone voice. "Thank you, Agnes." She answers herself, "You're welcome."

Everyone bursts out laughing, including me, and invisible spears poke my ears. I peer at Agnes and mouth the words thank you. She winks at me.

Leslie clears her throat. "Dr. Seamus Duffy asked me to make an announcement to all Fellowship members and their loved ones. He invites you to a housewarming at his new address after the graduation ceremonies."

Well, that's convenient, isn't it? The wheels turn in my head.

"That's fabulous," Spence says. "All of you can meet my fam. They're flying in from SoCal."

Agnes grimaces. "Fuck me. Do I have to go? I hate parties. I have to get all gussied up."

"Of course you'll go," Leslie replies. "It would be rude not to. Skye, how is Kate getting on? Is she acclimated to your apartment yet?"

"Yeah, but she has some strange habits." She steps up on a stool and wipes out a cabinet. "Like she always eats in her bedroom. She won't shower—washes up at a sink. Cleans the dishes by hand. She didn't know how to use a cell phone. It took me an entire week to teach her. Zach can tell you the weirdest shit."

Zach wrings out a sponge and looks up. "Kate asked for a bucket to keep in her bedroom. I shouldn't be sharing this, but it's questionable behavior. The reason she wanted it? So she could pee in the bucket overnight."

"I had to tell her it wasn't sanitary," Skye says. "To go to the bathroom and use the toilet."

Agnes scoffs at them. "I think it's brilliant. In fact, I should get a bucket for my bedroom. I hate getting up in the middle of the night to take a piss. It's what commodes were for."

Leslie raises her head. "You do that, and I won't be sleeping in your bed."

We have a hearty laugh and spend the next hour emptying the cabinets. When we've finished cleaning and the men have completed measuring for the floor tile, we head toward the front door, all except Leslie. Agnes tugs at my T-shirt and motions with her head toward the magic room. I follow her in, and she hands me a thin grimoire with frayed edges.

"I hesitate to give you this, but I want you to have it. It has instructions on using crystals to increase visions during the sleep state." She clasps my hand. "I care about you, Gwynedd. Promise me you'll not jump into the cauldron while the flames are burning. If you get my point."

"I do. You didn't want to give this to me, did you?"

"If your Aunt Gorawen warned Lowri about its dangers, I'm inclined to believe her. So, I'm giving you the grimoire against my better judgment, which we all know is for shit, anyway."

I chuckle and hug her. "Thank you, Agnes."

CHAPTER THIRTEEN
UNUSUAL SUSPECT

I TAKE A DETOUR through campus on the way to my shift at Mystic Sage, wearing a comfy loose V-neck blouse, jeans, and sneakers. The sun shines brightly in a cobalt-blue sky without a cloud in sight, and the temperature hovers in the mid-70s. Nothing can ruin this perfect spring day.

You can't beat a stroll on the tree-lined Green on a Sunday morning. Undergraduate students are snug in their beds, some awaiting the last of their finals in the coming week. Most of the dorms will empty for the summer, and the townies will relish in the reduced bustle on Main Street.

As I walk under the shade of the old elm trees, I recall my antics on Friday night and chuckle. I'm back to normal today after a good night's sleep in my own bed at Leslie's, thanks to Spence switching Seelie Fae check-in nights with me. Despite the positive effects marijuana had on me, I'm never trying it again. Maybe the grimoire Agnes gave me will have some instructions for easing into the use of crystals without stripping my brain of its faculties. I need to know if the dream is a premonition or only junk in my head. I've brought the spell book with me to work, so I can research during slow periods.

When I enter the store, Jeff is chatting with Amnesia Kate at the counter. You can't deny the flirting between the two of them. At least something positive could come out of her predicament.

"Good morning, you two. A beautiful day, isn't it?" I ask.

"Hi, Gwyn," they reply in unison.

"Kate, you have your Raven Pub T-shirt on. Do you have to work today?"

"Yeah." She peers up at Jeff and smiles. "But Jeff is going to meet me for an early lunch."

Jeff fiddles with the pens in the skull mug. "I hope that's all right."

"Well, you and Shane are both my bosses now. Should you be asking me?" I raise my eyebrows.

"I don't want to be that kind of boss, Gwyn. It will leave you in the store alone."

"Thanks for asking, then. And yes, I'll be fine. I'll go to lunch at Ronnie's when you get back."

Kate glances at me and back at Jeff. "I better get to the Raven. Have a nice day, Gwyn."

"You, too," I say, nodding.

Jeff stares at Kate, a budding love growing in his brown eyes. "See you at noon, Kate."

She exits the store, and Jeff's gaze follows her until she's out of sight. I amble around the counter to store my purse.

"You really like her, don't you?"

He grins as he logs out of the cash register. "Is it that obvious?"

"Only to everyone with a brain and a heart. She seems to like you, too. Am I being too intrusive if I ask how things are going?"

"I have to talk to someone, and unfortunately, Shane is occupied with Cordelia. We've gone out once since the Fellowship dinner, but she doesn't want to be alone with me. And I get that. We just met."

"She has no memory of her prior life, but I believe she experienced some trauma."

"Yeah. I get that vibe, too. She's so jumpy. For instance, Thursday night when we all met for dinner, she was all bubbly and sweet. And then she went to the restroom. She was gone for such a long time. When she returned, her hands were shaking, and she kept scanning the restaurant. And then there's the comment Cordelia made to her. So rude. I know Shane likes her, but she rubs me wrong."

I exhale. "You and me both, Jeff. But we can't dictate to others who to love."

"Yeah," he says, messing with his taffy-brown hair. "I'll be in the back emptying boxes. Shout if you need me."

"OK, boss," I say in a sarcastic tone.

He laughs and meanders into the back of the store. I grab a duster and clean off the shelves until the door dings. I turn around to discover Cordelia in a black knee-length dress. In an effort to be civil, I smile at her.

"Good morning. Shane isn't here, but I can help you."

"I doubt that." She narrows her eyes. "Shane said he has a new shipment of smoky quartz, and I should help myself."

What a bitch. She sways her hips dramatically as she walks back to the crystals room. I hate to admit she's right, but I don't know much about crystals since I've spent most of my time training with herbs and ancestral magic. I pull out the spell book from my purse and flip through the pages. Why don't witches organize their spells? The database will be a lifesaver when it's complete. After a few more turns, I find a list of recommendations and slide my finger down the page. Smoky quartz is great for reaching out to fairy spirits, tree spirits, and—ghosts. Interesting.

As I lay the book down on the counter, Cordelia ambles into the front of the store, ignoring me, and heads straight for the exit.

"Wait," I say. "I need to ring that up."

She purses her lips. "I told you Shane told me to pick whatever I want."

"Sure, but I have to ring it up to keep track of inventory."

"Fiiine. Do it quickly. I'm in a hurry."

Since when is a crystal purchase an emergency? She hands the special cut quartz to me, and I scan the UPC, passing it back to her when I'm done.

"Have a wonderful day," I say, grinding my teeth.

She glances down at the open grimoire, and I close the book.

"You should mind your own house, Gwynedd. I warned you once, and I'll not say it again."

The bitch from North Carolina drops the smoky quartz in her purse and exits the store with a clank of the bamboo chimes. She's up to something, and I'm going to find out what it is. As soon as I'm done snooping on Seamus Duffy, of course.

I stuff the grimoire back into my purse and bend down to shove it back under the counter. The door dings. I'm in no mood to be friendly to customers now. When I stand, I flinch at the face of Detective Jack Schmidt.

"I'm sorry. Did I scare you, Ms. Crowther?" He's dressed in a button-down shirt and khaki pants, as if he's working. Do detectives work on Sundays?

My heart leaps toward my ribcage. "I wasn't expecting you to be standing there. Can I help you, officer?"

"As a matter of fact, you can," he says, flashing his badge. "Since the store is empty, do you mind answering some questions?"

The tiny fairies hammering under my ribcage urge me to say no. Don't panic, Gwyn. The door opens with a ding, and Seamus Duffy walks in, leaning on his cane. Could this day get any worse?

"Sure, detective. Ask away." I glance out of the corner of my eye at Seamus as he picks up a shopping basket and limps toward the herbs.

"Were you at the Raven Pub the night that student was found dead behind the restaurant?"

My shoulders relax, and I take a cleansing breath. "Yeah, I was. The Fellowship, the local community pagan group I belong to, met for dinner."

"Did you notice anything unusual while you were there?"

"I—we—heard a woman scream. One of the waitresses, I think. She had taken trash to the dumpster and found the poor soul. We left when the police arrived and started clearing the restaurant out. That's it."

I'm not telling him that Archie, Elijah, and I saw the body. What's the point?

Seamus turns his head, as if he's listening intently to the detective's questioning.

"Do you know what time you heard the scream?" He takes out a pen and pad from his back pocket.

"I didn't check my phone, but I'd say around 8:30 p.m. It was already dark out."

He writes on his pad and peers up at me. "Thank you for your time. I'm checking with anyone who was there that night who may have got a glimpse of the cougar."

"Sorry. I didn't see any kind of cat." I glance back at Seamus, and he's placing herbs in his basket.

"Thank you again. Have a nice day." Detective Schmidt walks toward the door but stops and turns around. "One more question. Did you know Dr. Nick Evans, the professor who went missing?"

I gulp my saliva, and the tachycardia in my chest takes off like a speeding train. "Yeah. He translated a Welsh tome for me, a family heirloom."

"So, is it possible you met with him at the Raven?" He cocks his head.

Holy crystals. Keep calm, Gwyn. "Yeah. We met there to discuss the translations a few times."

He rubs his jaw. "And when was the last time you were with Dr. Evans?"

I freeze and perspiration blossoms on my upper lip and chest. I grab a mail flyer from under the counter and fan myself. Seamus limps toward us while I melt behind the counter.

"What were you saying? I'm sorry. When a hot flash occurs, I lose my train of thought." I swallow.

"I asked if you can recall the last time you saw Dr. Evans?"

"Uhh...I'm not sure." How the fuck do I answer without lying?

Seamus interrupts, placing his basket on the counter. "Hello, Detective Schmidt. I'm sorry I was rude and overheard the conversation. Gwynedd, I believe that would have been the same evening I saw the assistant professor."

My eyes widen as Seamus continues.

"And when was that, Dr. Duffy?" Detective Schmidt asks.

"We attended the same concert together at the School of Music. Do you remember, Gwynedd?"

Why is he speaking up for me? "Yeah. It was a Celtic music concert."

Detective Schmidt writes on his pad and shoves it in his back pocket. "Thank you, Ms. Crowther. I'll leave you to your work. Dr. Duffy, you have a nice day as well."

"Good day to you, detective," Seamus replies.

Detective Schmidt exits the store, and I ring up Seamus's herbs. He places his credit card into the machine as I bag his items.

"The detective was being inordinately intrusive. Don't you think?"

I peer up at his shiny sea-green eyes. "Well, it is his job to investigate." I hand him his eco bag.

"Sometimes things are better left alone. Wouldn't you agree?"

My lips part, but I've got nothing to say.

"Enjoy the remainder of this exquisite Sunday, Gwynedd."

Seamus limps out, and I stand there in a frozen state. Jeff ambles into the front of the store.

"Well, Shane won't have that to do when he comes in tomorrow. I'm going to leave for lunch now. Sounds like you were busy. Any sales?"

I shake my head. "Only a few herbs and a crystal." I fall onto the stool and fold my hands to stop the trembling.

Jeff's brow wrinkles. "Are you OK? Did something happen while I was in the back?"

"That was one fucked up morning," Ronnie says. "What are you going to do about the detective?" She passes me a menu with artwork of the sun, the moon, and a constellation on the front—a wonderful addition to the Sunshine Garden Café.

"Nothing. I hope he's done with me after what Seamus said. I sent a few texts to Archie about the detective's questions. He says he'll cast another spell of confusion, but I don't think it helped the last time. The new menus have your cosmic witchy vibe."

She grins. "Thanks. I ordered them after I changed the lighting. So, Seamus's last words to you sound like he knows what really happened to Nick. Are you going to confront him?"

"You think he's gonna come clean he was in the parking lot that night? I don't think so. Besides, I guess we'll all be going to his house. He's throwing a combination housewarming and graduation party for Spence and Skye. And I have a better idea, anyway."

She cackles. "Please, don't tell me. Better I'm in the dark. So, Archie's cooking you a special birthday dinner. I'm kind of sad we won't be celebrating together like we always do, but I understand. He'll have an extra special gift for you in bed, too, I bet. After your pot-infused sex, he's counting the minutes and seconds until then."

"I imagine so," I say, my face flushing. "I only wish I remembered more of that night."

"Yeah, it's why I stopped using pot. I want to remember every spicy moment with Derek."

"I'm sure they're on instant replay in your head."

"You know it. But damn, I wish I'd been there with you and Agnes. I would have some serious blackmail videos of you." She laughs, but her expression goes flat. "You should tell Shane about Cordelia's threats, though. She's using him, Gwyn. He deserves to hear the truth about her."

"Jeff agrees with you, but I can't do that to him. He really likes her." A crease forms between my eyes. "Are you feeling better?"

"Yeah, but since I entered early menopause, my entire GI system has revolted. I'll spare you the details. I see my GYN in June, so I'll deal with it until then."

"We better order, or I'll be late getting back to work. Not that Jeff would be angry. I'm so happy for him. Starting a new life here in Bearsden. And he and Kate seem to get along well."

"That's awesome, but it must be weird dating a woman who doesn't know who she is or where she came from. And, let's face it. She's a tad weird. To not know what menstrual pads are? Do you get the feeling someone kept her captive all her life?"

I grimace. "That would explain a lot of her quirks and why she can't remember her past. She blocked out her horrific memories. But Jeff had a horrible life with the Kenilworths. If anyone can support her through this, he can."

"He's a sensitive young man…and rich," she cackles. "She hit the jackpot with him."

I chuckle. "And she has no idea."

Archie kisses me at the front door. "I wish you could stay tonight. This time we could have sex and you'd remember."

"Very funny. It's enticing, but I had an awful day. Well, a terrible morning. But lunch with Ronnie was fun."

"She always raises your spirits. A devoted friend. Don't worry about Detective Schmidt. I'll cast a stronger spell of confusion.

And I'll see what I can find out about Seamus. What he said is peculiar, for sure. But if he knows about Nick, he must support you for some reason. Be thankful he's on your side."

"Do you think we should confront him?" I ask, slipping on my hoodie for the cool night stroll.

"What if he doesn't know, and you're misreading him? Then you've let the cat out of the bag, no?"

"You're right. I have to go check on Shailagh and Aonghas now. They haven't seen me for over a week and get mischievous without my regular visits."

"Please be aware of your surroundings when you go into the gardens. The Mitchell's mansion isn't far from the Raven, where the last student was killed. Should I go with you?"

The dream of him walking in there and lying on the ground lifeless pops into my brain. "No. It's unnecessary. I'll be careful. When is your turn to check on the pranksters?"

"Not until next week, and they always ask for you when I go."

I sigh. "Trinity was right. I should have never formed an attachment with them. Too late now. I better go. I'll text when I get home."

"Goodnight." He brushes my chin and winks.

I kiss him one more time. "You, too, honey."

When I arrive at Mitchell Hall, I quickly scan the area for passersby and dart to the iron gate entrance to the Celestial Gardens. The lock is hanging open. I enter, tiptoeing on the brick walkway until I reach the back of the mansion. Cordelia is in here again. My blood boils, realizing she has defied both Shane and me. Unremarkables could sneak back here and catch her performing these outdoor rituals. Why can't she perform them in her apartment? Is Nuada haunting it? I laugh silently. My humor has become so morbid.

I don't see Shailagh and Aonghas playing, so I'll have to come back later when the wicked witch is gone. I turn around, but stop. If she's going to break our rules, she can't complain when someone watches her. I tiptoe further into the gardens and get down on my hands and knees, crawling below the trimmed hedge until I can view her profile. I'm going to pay for this later with a sore back.

When I peek over the hedge, she's got one hand in the air and another on the necklace hanging around her neck. The amulet glows—a halo of blue spreading out from the swirling essence inside its glass. The magic disappears instantly with the snap of her fingers, and she struts out of the gardens while I hide behind the evergreen shrubs. Shit. I only caught the end of her secret ritual.

I wait for a few minutes and stand, stretching my aching back and wiping my palms on my jeans. A distorted growl emerges behind me, and I swivel on my sneaker to inspect the hawthorn tree. Nothing. I scan the gardens, searching for the cat sith. It must be here. The snarl almost sounds human-like as it echoes throughout the space. I dart from one side to the next, searching for the culprit. The portal lights, and the Seelie Fae children run to me, giggling.

"Aunt Gwyn. Aunt Gwyn. You finally came to visit with us."

I hug their tiny fae bodies and continue to survey the gardens. "I missed you, too, Shailagh and Aonghas. My life has had some bumps in it, but I'm here now." The morphed growls have disappeared, but what I heard was real. "Before we play, I need to ask you a question. Have you seen a woman with long black hair in here?"

"Oh, yes," they say. "She was mean to us, so we don't come out when she's here anymore."

"OK. Have you heard anything growling in here? Like a big cat or something else?"

"No, Aunt Gwyn," Shailagh says.

Aonghas continues. "But sometimes we hear a noise that doesn't sound like an animal."

Well, that's certainly weird. "Thank you. We can play for a little while, but then I need to get some sleep. Let's go!"

After I check the gate to make sure it's locked, the children chase me around the hedges, playing tag and giggling when they catch me. I imagine my mom running around with them in the '60s, and my heart swells. The Seelie Fae whine when I say it's time to go home, but they skip back to the portal and cross over.

On my way out, I recall the end of the ritual Cordelia performed. I've never seen a ceremony like that. What the fuck was she doing?

Chapter Fourteen

Happy Birthday to Me?

MONDAY TEMPS WILL REACH into the upper 80s, hinting at summer. I can barely contain my excitement as I slip on a loose V-neck tee and my first pair of shorts for the season. What a fabulous gift from Mother Nature on this 20th of May. I check my cell and find a slew of texts from my witch family, wishing me a happy birthday. I only reply to three.

Ronnie: *Happy birthday, friend! Stop by tomorrow for a free bday lunch.*

Me: *Thanks!*

Tyler: *Happy birthday! Have a wonderful time at Archie's.*

Me: *Thanks. See you on Saturday at Seamus's house.*

Tyler: *Sounds like fun!*

Archie sent me a message with a gif of a birthday cake on fire.

Me: *You think you're funny.*

Archie: *LOL. Happy birthday, my love. See you for dinner.*

Me: *I can't wait.*

Leslie already left for campus, but she left me a card on the kitchen table from her and Agnes—old school. Mr. Yeats sits on the kitchen floor, observing my every move while his tail sways back and forth.

"Have a good day. I'll be back tonight after dinner."

I shove my phone in my purse, grab my sunglasses, and head out the door toward the Green. When I reach the crosswalk at University Avenue, the pedestrian traffic clogs the road as I cross. Not surprising with the last of the finals taking place over the next two days. Shoppers and workers on the way to their jobs pack the paver sidewalks.

When I approach the area where the Green intersects Main Street, I peer at Mitchell Hall in the distance. Trinity should be in her office today. That's my hope. I cross the busy road and walk briskly to the mansion, realizing I've not had a reason to enter the building since the city completed the renovations.

As I enter through the front door, I can't get past the feeling I'm underdressed in my T-shirt, shorts, and sneakers. The aroma of fresh paint and polyurethane still permeates the building, giving the interior an impression of newness. The foyer alone is magnificent. Extra high ceilings adorned with wide molding and a crystal chandelier welcome me, and I imagine Alistair and Rose Mitchell greeting guests here. How I wish I had met them.

The enormous living and dining rooms have the same wide moldings around the ceilings and grand marble fireplaces. Palladian windows have floor-length drapes, and period furniture decorates the spaces to allow for mingling, like at cocktail parties. The walls are painted a shade of dull yellow, the color of straw. At least a dozen vases full of pink carnations and bunches of pale-purple lilacs adorn the tables. The fragrance tickles my nostrils, and when I sneeze, a shriek travels up the ornate wooden staircase.

"Who's down there?" a familiar female voice yells from upstairs. "I don't like people creeping in here when I'm the only one in the mansion." Clicking sounds reverberate above, increasing in volume until Trinity is standing at the top of the stairs. She's dressed in a purple dress and spike heels, her long burgundy hair cascading on her shoulders. "Oh, hey, Gwyn. Whatcha doing here? Not coming to the engagement party, are you?"

"What? Is that why all these flowers are everywhere?" I ask. "No. I came to talk to you about something. If you have a few minutes."

"Sure. Come up, and I'll take you to my new abode. And happy birthday, lady."

"Thanks. I got your text."

I run up the stairs, squeaking in my sneakers on the wooden steps, and follow her into her spacious office that used to be a bedroom. There are two desks set up on one wall and a shelf on another. A small conference table sits on one side of the room. I grab a padded chair and slide it to her desk.

"Is this the first time you've been inside the mansion since the completed renovations?" she asks.

"Yeah. I didn't have a reason to come in here before now. The city did a fabulous job refurbishing the interior. Rose and Alistair would be pleased, don't you think?"

Trinity leans back in her high-back leather desk chair, smiling. "I believe they would love it. The city brought in an interior designer who tried to remain true to the period, even down to the light mustard yellow on the walls. Wouldn't have been my choice, but no one asked me. I'm elated they gave Elijah and me such a large space for our organizations. But I don't think you came here to talk about Family For All."

"No. I didn't. I'm going to tell you something, and I haven't even told Archie about the latest incident. A while back, I caught Cordelia Davenport performing a ritual in the Celestial Gardens. I told Archie, and he said I should tell Shane. So, I did. Then Shane mentioned to her I caught her in there, and..."

Trinity tilts her head. "And what? I promise to keep this between us, which would piss off the Elder and the hedge witch, but so be it."

"The other night at the Raven when Cordelia said she had to use the restroom? She only went with me to chew me out. She threatened me and told me not to stick my nose in her business again. Then last night, I went to check on the Seele Fae, and she was in there again. Even after Shane warned her about performing rituals in there, because an Unremarkable could have seen her. Except last night, what she was doing seemed to be more than a typical ceremony. I only caught the end of her incantation, but it differed from any magic spell I've ever observed. Her amulet that she wears around her neck was glowing a bright blue and appeared to be sucking some kind of essence from the portal."

"That's alarming. She isn't a member of our coven, so she doesn't owe us any explanation. But she shouldn't be messing with the portal. I'm in a tough spot here. If I admonish her, she'll likely know who told me. We don't know if her threats are just that...or more serious. If I tell Leslie and Agnes, they'll confront her, and that could make things much worse. If she's only talking, which she's exceptional at, then it wouldn't be fair to Shane to have made the accusations." She taps her purple polished nails on the desk. "If you catch her in the gardens again, let me know. And I'll decide how we should proceed."

"Can I tell Archie about last night? He'd keep it under wraps. Also, I need to share something else with you. I've been having dreams—visions? Sometimes it's during the day. Archie is always entering the gardens, but I don't know what he's doing there. He checks on the Seelie Fae every couple of weeks when it's his turn, so it could be for that. I smoked Agnes's weed, Bearsden Poison, and the vision lengthened the next time. He was lying unconscious on the ground. At least I hope that's all."

Trinity grabs my hand. "Did you smoke her pot hoping to further your visions? What were you thinking, girl? You don't know what that shit could have done. The last time I smoked that stuff was years ago. Fucked me up. Didn't remember half of what I did the night before."

"I must enhance these dreams, Trinity. I need to know what's happening, so I can help Archie avoid this future. And no, I haven't told him. I'm afraid to. I didn't even tell Ronnie."

"So, what will you do? Smoke that Bearsden Poison again?" She snickers and leans forward. "The last time I tried that strain, I was so horny, I kept Charlie awake until the sun came up."

"Yeaaah. So I found out." I chuckle, and my face flushes. I grab a pamphlet off the desk and fan my face. "No. I'm never smoking that again. I woke up with the worst hangover. My family used crystals to enhance their visions in the past. You're supposed to have years of practicing the craft under your belt, or it could turn your brain into jello. Agnes knows about the dream and gave me a grimoire to help me, but she didn't tell Leslie. The Elder would try to talk me out of it."

She leans back in her desk chair. "You haven't told Archie you're doing this either, I assume?"

I shake my head and exhale.

"Gwyn, I don't know what to tell you to do. As your coven leader, I'd advise you not to dance with the unknown. But as your friend? If I knew of a way to save Charlie from pain or death, even if it might be risky to me personally, I'd do it in a heartbeat. Sometimes a witch has to do what she must. But go slow at first to be extra careful. And I'm OK with you telling Archie about what Cordelia did in the gardens, but I wouldn't tell anyone else."

"Thanks, Trinity," I say, standing. "Archie was right."

"About what?" she asks as she meanders around her desk.

"When he stepped down as coven leader, he said you should have always been the one to guide us."

"Well, he had his good leadership points, too. But I appreciate the sentiment. I guess I'll see you at this shindig Dr. Seamus Duffy is throwing at his home?"

"Of course. I wouldn't miss Spence and Skye's graduation celebration. It was nice of him to offer to host it."

And I certainly don't want to miss a chance to snoop at Seamus's house—a prime time to inspect the premises while filled to the brim with witches and their loved ones. I amble toward the door but turn around.

"You know, I occasionally have flashes of memories playing with you when I was little. One where I fell off the bed and hit my head. You came running and picked me up to check my skull for injuries. You were there for me, protecting me when my parents couldn't. Just like now."

Trinity's jade eyes well up with tears. "I miss your parents, Rhys and Lowri, terribly. They were good witches."

"Except they turned their backs on the coven and magic, denying me the opportunity to be the best witch I could be." I pause in thought, then shake my head. "See you at Seamus's."

"Gwyn." Archie's voice is distant. "Gwynedd," he says in an elevated voice.

"What? I'm sorry. My mind is preoccupied." With questions about your potential demise.

He takes a sip of white wine and sets his glass down on the dining room table. "I'd hoped you could enjoy your birthday dinner at least. Didn't you like it?"

"Oh, it was scrumptious, as usual. I'm still tired from the other night."

"Are you upset about turning fifty-five? You're still a sexy woman." He winks at me.

"I don't feel any older than yesterday or the day before that. In fact, it's the best I've felt in a few years. As long as you discount the hot flashes, forgetful moments, backaches, pinched bicep muscles, fatigue... Should I go on?"

He chuckles while I play footsy with him under the table. He's so sexy in his black tee and soft denim jeans. I even wore a low-cut dress for the occasion and put on some lipstick. Despite my cleavage deficit, I caught him eyeing my small stack throughout dinner. I believe him.

"I'm knackered as well," he says. "As much as I wanted you to stay, maybe you should get a good night's sleep in your own bed." He clasps my hand and caresses my fingers with a thumb.

"I probably should." And I'm eager to search through that grimoire on crystals when I get home. "I'm preoccupied with what Cordelia was doing in the gardens, too."

"It's concerning. But we can't confront her until we know more about what ritual she was performing. Trinity has the right to keep this from Leslie, but I'm uncomfortable with it. The Elder will blow the top off her cranium."

"True, and I don't want to be there when it happens. Would you be upset if I didn't stay to clean up? I'm waning now." I can't stand lying to him, but I don't know how it might affect his future to share the visions with him.

Archie follows me to the front door, wraps his arms around me, and kisses me passionately. "I can give you your other birthday gift another time, when you don't have a high probability of falling asleep."

"I can't wait." His woodsy cologne fills my nostrils as I slide my hand to his butt and squeeze.

He adjusts the bulge in his pants. "You better go, or I'll carry you upstairs and have my way with you."

"You wish." I chuckle and pat his butt.

"Very much so." He kisses me again and opens the door. "Should I walk you home?"

"Nah. There haven't been any more sightings of the cougar."

"Aye, but to be factual, there weren't any sightings—only evidence of its victims."

"True. But I'm only one street over. I'll text you when I arrive home." The image of him lying on the ground pops into my head again. "Promise me you'll be as careful as you're asking me to be. Especially when you go to the gardens to check on the Seelie Fae children."

"Aye. But remember, we're ancestral witches. We can handle a small cougar. Sleep well, my love."

"Thanks. I hope so, honey."

On my stroll home, the dream about Archie replays in my head, and I know what my next step must be. I enter the house and send Archie a text. Mr. Yeats, in his ginger and black cat form, scuttles into the kitchen. He stares up at me, his yellow and blue eyes reflecting the ceiling light, and meows.

"You can't help me with this, I'm afraid," I whisper. "And you can't tell Dr. Hughes I'm doing anything in secret behind closed doors. Understood?"

He hisses and runs into the living room. Leslie is engrossed in a book as I pass through and enter my bedroom. After I shut the door, I take out the grimoire on crystal use and flip through the pages at breakneck speed, searching for instructions to enhance dreams. Shane could have probably advised me, but I didn't want him to know about them. Besides, he's preoccupied with Miss don't-fuck-with-me-witch from North Carolina.

I come upon a page recommending fluorite to encourage a night of more restful sleep, enriching your dreams and allowing them to thrive. The general introduction recommends starting with only one crystal and focusing on the vision as you fall into sleep mode. When I enter the living room, Leslie is still reading a book in her usual comfy chair next to the fireplace. Mr. Yeats curls up on a rug at her feet.

"I'm so tired from the weekend, it bled into Monday," I say, yawning. "I should turn in early tonight."

She smiles faintly. "No wonder. I imagine you lost a lot of sleep the other night. Did you enjoy dinner with Archie?"

"Yes. He's such an outstanding cook. Thank you for the birthday card."

"You're most welcome. A long rest will leave you ready to tackle the day tomorrow. Goodnight, Gwynedd."

"Goodnight to you, Leslie."

I wash up, change into my PJs, and hop into bed with the fluorite crystal in my hand. I place it on the nightstand, thinking I shouldn't have it so close the first time I try. My hands tremble at the unknown reaction I may have, but I have to pursue this. Archie's life could be at stake. On second thought, I snatch the fluorite and shove it under my pillow. Closer proximity should increase its effectiveness and, unfortunately, the chance of unwelcome side effects.

At 10:00 p.m., I'm wide awake, staring at the ceiling and wishing I hadn't drunk that afternoon tea. My lower back hurts from lying there so long, so I roll over and tuck my legs against my chest. My eyes become droopy, giving way to slumber.

Through a haze of misty white and moonbeams, Archie strolls into the Celestial Gardens. The warped call of an animal distracts him. He scans the area and frowns. Abruptly, he's lying on the ground, just as I remembered before. I call out his name, "Archie!" An enormous black cat stands next to him on its hind legs. The sound escaping its open mouth is like a mix between a deep meow and the roar of a panther. When I glance back at Archie, his neck is bleeding.

I sit up, gasping for air, and flip my pillow. The room is dark except for the glow of the fluorite. My PJs are soaked as well as the bottom sheet. I pull my knees to my chest and wrap my arms around my legs, shaking.

The cat sith is going to kill Archie.

CHAPTER FIFTEEN

THE FRIENDLY PROFESSOR

ALMOST TWO WEEKS HAVE passed, and I haven't increased the length of my dreams by even a nanosecond. Any attempts to influence my visions in the waking state fail miserably as well. And Archie thinks I'm avoiding sex with him again. The truth is, I can't increase the intensity of my dreams with the fluorite if I'm spending nights at his place.

Further investigations in the grimoire recommended meditating with the crystal right before bed, but that didn't work either. The last on the list suggests using a combination of crystals together in a grid. My mother had an old one in the steamer trunk. But should I chance it? I don't know how I will react to them. Aunt Gorawen could be right. I could lose my marbles. Or in this case, my crystals.

While I'm in the bathroom applying makeup, there's a knock on the door. Mr. Yeats scuttles by and Leslie follows.

"I'll get the door, Gwynedd," she says. "You finish primping."

She opens the front door, and Archie's baritone voice echoes down the hallway to the bathroom. "Good afternoon, Dr. Hughes. That floral blouse is becoming on you."

"Thank you. Gwynedd suggested I try to brighten my wardrobe. But I always say there's nothing wrong with basic black. It goes with everything."

I enter the living room wearing my favorite teal dress and approach them where they're standing in front of the screen door. Outside, a car parks, and a door slams.

"It does," I say. "But people who only wear black when they dress up look like they're going to a funeral or are performing in a classical music concert. Or they're witches."

Archie smiles. "You're beautiful, Gwyn. I love that dress on you."

"Aww, thank you, honey." I kiss his cheek.

"Get a fucking room," Agnes grumbles as she approaches the screen door. "What a waste of a Saturday. Let's get this the fuck over with. The sooner we go, the sooner I can go home and strip off these ridiculous clothes."

She's wearing a royal blue tunic top over a pair of black cotton pants. A pentacle charm hangs on a leather choker around her neck, and her salt and pepper hair appears styled. As we exit the house, Leslie rolls her eyes at her girlfriend.

"You didn't own appropriate clothing for a graduation party, Agnes." She addresses Archie and me. "I took her to the store and purchased this outfit for her last week. Don't they make her appear—"

"Fucking normal. And you know I'm far from it." Agnes pulls on her shirt. "Don't expect me to curtail my language. I won't pretend to be something I'm not."

"You look fabulous, Agnes, and no one expects you to," I say. "Besides, the only people you won't know are Spence and Skye's parents and Spence's brother. He's a witch, but remember, their parents are Unremarkables and aren't *in the knowing*. No witchy talk."

Agnes scowls at all of us. "Yeah. Fuck that, too."

"Oh, Agnes," Leslie chides. "Could you put the F word in your back pocket for two hours?"

She makes a face at the Elder. "These fucking pants have no pockets...DEAR."

"Touché, Agnes," Archie says, laughing.

I love listening to their banter. You'd think they hated each other, but we know better. It took fifty-some years for them to rekindle their love. Nothing will ever separate them now.

We arrive at Seamus's house, and the front door is open. So, we walk right in. The compact bungalow has a large living area. An archway on the left leads to a dining room, and further on, to a kitchen. A doorway in the living area must lead to the bedrooms. We walk through to the dining room and find Seamus in the kitchen, retrieving a platter of cheese cubes from the fridge. He lifts his head and sees us.

"Welcome," he says in his soft Irish brogue. "Everyone is out back. More room in the backyard than in my diminutive living area. Could you help me carry out these food trays? I paid for a caterer, but I have difficulty limping down the porch stairs with them in my hands."

"We'd be happy to help," Leslie says, picking up a tray. "Seamus, I'd like you to meet my partner, Agnes Pritchard."

"Lovely meeting you. Leslie has spoken of you in high regard."

The hedge witch snorts. "I'm not sure I believe that."

"Oh, Agnes." Leslie shakes her head.

"I would never lie about such a thing," Seamus replies. "You're as lovely as she described you."

He butters them up with compliments. But would he lie about other matters?

Archie grabs another tray. "You should ask a couple of the young witches to help."

"Except for Spence and Skye," I say, getting the back door. "They're the guests of honor."

Seamus nods once. "And it's well-deserved."

I smile as he passes me, stepping onto the porch. Members of the Fellowship and their guests, including Unremarkables, fill the yard. Everyone is wearing nice but casual clothes for the occasion. Unfortunately, that includes Cordelia Davenport, who is hanging on Shane's arm like always. Jeff and Kate wave to me from a corner where the young witches are huddled in a group. Tyler and Zoe are with them. They wave, too. Leslie and Agnes walk over to join them.

"Archie, I'm going to join Ronnie, Derek, and the others," I say.

"I'll follow you in a minute. I need to talk to Seamus about Summer Session."

"Ugh. Spring Semester is barely over, and you're talking about the summer."

"Aye, but it begins the second week of June. He won't have much time to prepare."

"OK. See ya over there when you're done with your chat."

As I approach Ronnie, Derek, and a few other witches in our coven, Cordelia's annoying laugh dominates the chatter. It's a forceful, fake laugh that grates at the ears. Her skin is as white as a sheet. She'd probably appear healthier with a touch of sun, but she must have renewed one of her aging spells only this morning. The blood-red lipstick only accentuates her baby-smooth porcelain skin. Trinity, Charlie, Elijah, and Jasmine have joined the group.

"Hi, everyone. What are you laughing about?" I ask.

Ronnie chuckles. "Cordelia was telling us a story about Shane."

"About the time I fell into a swamp," he says. "Came out with leeches all over me."

You've still got one sucking the life out of you now, boss.

Derek winces. "That doesn't sound good. What did you do?"

"Well, I can't exactly say how I really removed them," he whispers. "Unremarkables abound."

Cordelia kisses him on the cheek and speaks in her loud, grating voice. "Nonsense, Shane. He summoned his witch energy, and they all blew off." She laughs at the top of her lungs, prompting the partygoers on the other side of the yard to glance in our direction.

"Shhh," I whisper in a scolding tone of voice. "You can't talk about magic here."

"She's right, darling," Shane says. "You have to be selective in your conversation around Unremarkables."

Trinity stares her down. "We have rules in Bearsden. It's important that you abide by them."

Cordelia purses her lips and sends me a side eye, and I fear a hex may come my way soon. But I'm elated Shane admonished her in public. It's about time.

"Hey, Gwyn," Elijah says. "When do you plan on volunteering again?"

"I knew you'd get that invite in first thing. I'll have time over the summer," I say, grinning.

He chuckles in his deep voice. "Thanks. Gotta stay staffed. You remember Jasmine?" He gestures to the woman at his side.

"Oh, yes. How are you doing?" I ask.

"Just fine. I hope to start a new nursing job soon at a local doctor's practice. I want more time with Elijah."

Trinity snickers. "Girl, you picked the wrong man if you want more time."

"Oh, don't listen to her, Jasmine," Charlie says, slapping Trinity's arm. "He's a good man. You'll not find a better one out there than Elijah."

Cordelia purses her lips. "Oh, I don't know about that. Shane could give him a run for his money."

"True dat," Elijah says. "If I ever need someone to back me up, I can count on you, bro."

"Well, I certainly appreciate the compliment, friend." Shane fist-bumps Elijah. "I haven't seen you recently, Gwyn. Now that Jeff has taken over half the management of the store. You seem well."

"I am," I say. "Although I miss working with you as much. But now you have more time for a social life."

Shane lays his hand on Cordelia's arm, which is wrapped around his like a boa constrictor. "And I can't thank him—and you—enough."

Leslie and Agnes are chatting with Seamus near the back porch, and Archie is shaking hands with unfamiliar guests hanging with the young crowd. I decide I need a break from the witch bitch.

"If you'll excuse me, I'm going to join Archie and say hello to my son. I'll talk more later."

I meander around the refreshment tables toward the others, grabbing a bottle of water from the cooler on the way. Archie smiles as I approach.

"Here's my better half now," he says warmly. "Come meet Spence and Skye's parents and his brother. They're wonderful people."

Spence interjects. "Let me do the introductions, professor. They're my fam. Gwyn, my parents, Garrison and Arden. And this is my little brother Cameron. We call him Cam. This is Gwynedd Crowther. We met in one of my Celtic Studies classes first year."

They are all lanky like Spence and have dark hair and brown eyes. Arden shakes my hand.

"Oh, you're the prior owner of Spencer and Tanner's beautiful, quaint home."

"It's hardly quaint, dear. It's nearly 2800 square feet," Garrison says, offering his hand. "A pleasure to meet you."

I grip his hand firmly. "Likewise. And the house was a disaster when I owned it. Spence, Tanner, and the other young Fellowship members helped me fix it up. After they moved in, they did more."

"Helping Gwyn made me realize it was time to stop renting and put down roots," Tanner says. "A place Spence and I can call home."

"Now you need to make it official." Arden taps her wedding ring. "You're both dressed up today. You could march to town hall while we're visiting."

"Time to change the subject," Spence says, frowning.

We all have a little chuckle, and Tanner rubs his partner's back.

I come to his rescue. "Do you attend college, Cameron?"

"You bet," he replies. "I got into UCLA, but I chose UC Irvine so I could keep surfing."

Spence sighs. "Rub it in, Cam. I miss those waves."

Skye introduces her two moms to me—Lucy and Willow. Lucy has her coloring—fire-red hair and sky-blue eyes.

"Gwyn, Spence, and I took the same class together," Skye says. "We've been friends since."

"Skye says you're working on a master's, too?" Willow asks.

I nod. "Yeah, but I've got another year to finish."

"Well, I think it's a tremendous accomplishment to go back to college at your age," Lucy says. "Kudos to you. And thanks for being such an awesome support to Skye."

I chuckle. "In that first class, I think it was the other way around."

Leslie, Agnes, and Seamus mingle with Shane, Cordelia, and the others. The witch-bitch snatches my gaze and sends a hate-filled glare that could burn a town down—or is she looking at Kate just behind me? I choose to ignore it, turning round to chat with Tyler and the rest of the young people when Archie joins us.

I hug my son. "How are you, dear? Anything new happening?"

"Not since this morning when you reminded me about the party, which I didn't need a reminder of."

"Well, that's my job. Right, guys?" I ask, elbowing him.

Archie takes a sip of his iced tea. "He's a grown man, Gwyn. And he has a cell phone."

Jeff adds his two cents. "I'd love to have a mom to call me once in a while. Be happy you have her to do that."

"I wish I knew who my mom was," Kate says in a meek tone of voice. "Or my dad."

Tyler sighs. "You're right. I'm sorry, Mom. Between you and Zoe, I won't ever forget anything again."

"You know you love it," Zoe says, hugging him.

Kate appears run down again—so pale and thin. Even the rosy color has disappeared from her cheeks. Maybe Jeff can encourage her to eat more. The food spread for this small shindig is amazing. It was so nice of Seamus to hire a caterer for this party. I don't know whether to question his motives. But for now, he's trying to be friendly. I could be wrong about the visiting professor.

We continue mingling into the evening while we fill our plates and stuff our mouths with some of the most delicious food I've ever eaten. It rivals Ronnie's chef at the Sunshine Garden Café. Lucky for her, this business only caters, or she might have competition. Whenever my eyes cross paths with Cordelia, she appears to cast a spell of I'm-gonna-get-you-witch. But I don't fear her. I'm an ancestral witch. She'll never be a match for me.

My bladder is about to explode from all the water and iced tea, so I run into the house, searching for the sole bathroom. I meander through the living room and enter the doorway leading to the bedrooms. I spot a sink at the end of the hallway and head in that direction, peeking into the first room as I pass. Inside, there's only a desk and some unopened boxes. The next room has a full-size bed and a single chest. Seamus massaged his leg on the bed in there. I take two steps past the entrance, stop, and peer over my shoulder. This is my chance.

I tiptoe back into the living area. Awesome. The house is empty. I rush back into his bedroom and go to his dresser. I hesitate. What the hell is the matter with me? I shouldn't be snooping in his underwear drawer. But... I pull the top drawer out—yup, boxers. The next one contains neatly folded shirts like you see on display at a department store. He could teach Archie a thing or two, and that's saying something. The last two contain shorts and sleepwear. I check the nightstand. Nothing.

There are two closet doors. A quick search of the first reveals dress clothes and shoes. I clasp the doorknob of the other closet and pull, except it's locked. I check above the door for a key. Nope. I jiggle the knob again.

"Can I help you, Gwynedd?" a familiar Irish voice asks.

I freeze, clenching my teeth. Shit. I turn my head to discover Seamus leaning against the bedroom doorway, smiling. Fuck.

"Hi. I was looking for a bathroom and figured the larger bedroom would have one?" I am lying like Pinocchio.

"No. This house is a bungalow. It only has one bathroom." He points down the hallway. "You can view the sink from the hallway."

Way to call me out without calling me out. I swallow and walk toward him. "Oh, I must have missed it in my rush." I shake my leg. "I really have to go."

"By all means. I won't keep you from your business."

He steps aside, and I dart to the bathroom and slam the door. I turn around and shriek at the painting hanging to the left of the doorway—only seen when the door is closed. I shove my panties down and examine the creepy artwork while I relieve myself. On a gray, stormy background, the distorted figure of a woman kneels over a man lying on the ground. His clothes are ripped and bloodied. Who the hell puts a morbid picture like that in their bathroom?

While I wash and dry my hands, I rethink my theory about Seamus. Maybe he doesn't know what happened on Ostara. He certainly doesn't act like he's aware I'm a killer. When I open the door, I yelp when I see Seamus leaning against the wall, waiting for me.

"I'm sorry for hogging the bathroom. I was just, um...admiring...your painting here," I say, gesturing at the grotesque artwork.

He stares at me, and an awkward silence ensues. I swallow. Damn. He's suspicious of me now. Why wouldn't he be, after seeing me jiggle his closet doorknob?

"So, what does the painting depict? Are you a Twilight fan?" I chuckle nervously and avert my eyes.

"No. Only a fan of folklore."

"Well, I moved faster with it hanging on the wall."

He chuckles. "Why do you think I put it in there? With only one bathroom, I want visitors to be quick about their bodily functions."

"Oh, I get it," I say, laughing at his odd solution to being bathroom challenged.

"The friend I spoke about—the one who gave me the artwork in my school office—painted this one as well. I didn't have any visuals for this Celtic legend, so she created one for me to use in my lectures. My tiny office at DUB had no room, and I didn't think it would be appropriate for the living area. The placement is perfect, don't you think?"

"Worked for me," I say, inspecting the painting. The strokes on the cloud formations seem familiar, but I can't make out the artist's name—smudged and hidden under a glob of oil paint.

Seamus enters the bathroom and closes the door a little to view the painting. "It's a Dearg Due. She was a vengeful woman who drank the blood of young men after being separated from her true love."

"Like a vampire?"

"Not according to the definition of the word. More like a ghostly demon."

"Now if you don't mind, I really must ask you to leave the bathroom or you'll be viewing my bodily functions."

"I'm sorry." I exit through the doorway, and he shuts the door behind me.

When I get outside, I search for Cordelia Davenport, because I want to inspect that amulet around her neck, but I can't find her anywhere in the yard. Archie ambles over to me.

"Where have you been? You don't usually take that long in the loo. Are you feeling all right?"

"Yeah. I'm fine. I was chatting with Seamus in the bathroom."

His eyebrows fall. "In the loo? A rather peculiar place to have a chat."

"He has a really macabre oil painting in there. He was telling me about the folktale that influenced it." I scan the party guests. "Where is Cordelia Davenport? I don't see her anywhere."

"She and Shane left right after you went into the house. Spence and Skye's parents and his brother left as well. They have early flights in the morning. Kate was overwhelmed by the amount of people here, so Jeff took her home."

Police sirens blare in the distance, but not too far away. Another follows. And one more. We all dart out to Kent Way to investigate. Police cars are lined up along Douglas Street, and officers have gathered near the alleyway. A compact sedan drives up, and Detective Jack Schmidt gets out of the driver's side. He rushes to the alleyway in his usual attire—a blue suit jacket and khaki pants.

I peer at Archie. "Do you think it's another attack?"

"No doubt. But there's only one way to know. Gwyn and I are going to check things out," he tells the others. "We'll be back."

Spence crosses his arms. "If you think we're gonna stay back here while you poke your noses where they don't belong, you'd be wrong."

"Let's go," Trinity says, waving. "Can a few of you stay back to help Seamus clean up, at least?"

Tyler nods. "Sure. Zoe and I don't mind."

"Charlie, why don't you and Jasmine remain here? I'd rather you not see this."

They walk back into Seamus's yard with Tyler and Zoe. The rest of us walk across Douglas Street and approach the police.

Neighbors have seeped into the road. As we get closer, Officer Wilson puts his hands up.

"You all need to stay back. It's a pretty gruesome sight."

"More than the others? Because they were bad," I say, grimacing.

"Yes. No one should view the body." He raises his voice. "Please, everyone, go on back home and let us do our jobs."

I motion to Archie to step back. "Can you distract him while I sneak around to get a peek?"

"Gwyn," he says, frowning. "You don't need to see the body. Take his word. We can glean from his description that it's more severe. That's enough."

"I'm gonna go whether you help me or not."

"You stubborn woman. All right. But I warned you. You'd think you've seen enough gore for one lifetime."

"Thanks, honey. Give me about two minutes to get to the other side of the hedge."

I squeeze his hand and push through the members of the Fellowship and a crowd of students who have arrived. The police are right there, blocking my view, so I climb behind the foundation shrubs to get a better view. Unfortunately, I'm too far away to inspect the injuries. I pull out my phone and zoom in, snapping a couple of pictures before they notice me. When I've got a few pics, I rush back to Archie.

"What did you see?" he asks.

"I don't know. I took pictures but haven't looked at them yet."

When I open the gallery on my cell and bring up the first picture, I cover my mouth, holding back the urge to vomit. Officer Wilson's assessment was correct. Something ripped open the body of the young man in several places, including the neck. The internal organs, arteries, and veins are protruding like they would in a slasher movie. Only small pools of blood puddle next to the bloodied corpse. I scan the crowd, searching for any hint of clues.

"Who are you looking for, Gwyn?" Archie asks.

"Not only who, but what?"

No sign of Cordelia or the cat sith. If it's the soul-eating fairy, it's still greedy, eating up the souls of the dead young men. If Cordelia is involved, I don't know what she's doing. But I'm going to find out.

Chapter Sixteen

BLOSSOMING LOVE

The sun's rays beam through the curtains, burning my eyelids. I squint as I pull up my pillow but find the fluorite has no glow. Meditating with the crystal before I went to sleep did shit. I may have to pull out that grid after all. Four killings have occurred now.

I grab my cell phone from the nightstand and check the local online Sunday newspaper. The Bearsden Police report the cougar is still on the loose, and Animal Control continues to search the surrounding areas. There were no visual sightings, and the police found no evidence of paw prints near the body or around the perimeter. I drop my cell. *Strange.*

I have to figure out how to lengthen this recurring dream before it happens to Archie. It's been almost two weeks since I slept with him, and if I had balls, they'd be navy blue by now and ready to burst. Leslie slept at Agnes's last night, so the feline busybody is probably waiting on the other side of my bedroom door. I squeeze my legs together, but my menopausal bladder can't wait. I rush to the door and swing it open.

"Aghhh!" Mr. Yeats screams. "You scared me."

"Good. Serves you right for standing right here. Move. I gotta pee."

"You seem to do that a lot, Ms. Crowther," he says as I shut the bathroom door. "Maybe you should get that checked out."

"You know, you're awfully clingy for a cat!"

"You don't have to insult me," he replies in a muffled voice.

When I open the door, he's scuttling down the hallway. "I'm sorry, Mr. Yeats. I'm frustrated about something, and it has nothing to do with you."

It's all about me and my lack of crystal skills. Mr. Yeats misses Leslie, too. She's been spending a lot of time at Agnes's farmhouse, sifting through years of junk. Last night, she helped Agnes pack for their two-week trip to Great Britain. How will he act when she's gone?

My cell phone vibrates. It's a text from Archie.

Archie: *Missed you last night. How did you sleep?*

Me: *Like usual. Woke up once.*

Archie: *Better than the norm then. It's been two weeks.*

I set my phone down, sighing. He's going to suspect something if I don't make time for him. But not tonight. I have to try the grid.

The phone rings, and I swipe the green icon. "I've been working on a project here, and I'm almost finished."

"What project?" he asks, a hint of frustration in his voice. "You're avoiding me again."

"No, I'm not. Give me a few more days."

"You said that nearly a week ago." He's right. I didn't think it would take me this long to decipher the vision.

"Soon. I promise. Did you read the news report this morning?"

"Yes, but you're changing the subject."

"There were no paw prints. Don't you think that's strange?"

"Aye. But there's probably an explanation. Will you stop by tonight after work?"

"I have to check on the Seelie Fae. Because of the ruckus last night, I never made it there. Shailagh and Aonghas are getting restless. I'm worried they'll commit mischief if we don't tire them out every night."

He sighs into the phone. "I understand. Be careful tonight, my love. Your magic is stronger than a cougar, but it could still hurt you."

"Don't worry about me." And I still don't think it's that kind of cat. "Love you. Bye, honey."

"Stay safe. I love you, too."

I swipe the red icon and jump into the shower. When I'm dressed and ready for work, I flip through the pages of Agnes's grimoire, searching for instructions on using a crystal grid. I find a detailed list. My mom's old grid rests on the tray of the steamer trunk. But should I heed her and Aunt Gorawen's warnings?

After lunch, I leave for work. As I walk toward Main Street, I pass our new neighbor. Seamus is watering flowers he planted out front—Black-Eyed Susans and yellow marigolds. He's transformed the drab, brown bungalow into a bright and cheery residence, if you discount the morbid painting in his bathroom. I wave to the professor as I pass, and he raises his hand. Could everyone be right about him? The glamouring from Nick left my brain in a deep fog. I might have only imagined I glimpsed him in the parking lot that night.

When I arrive at Mystic Sage, Jeff is unpacking new shipments of T-shirts for the upcoming summer solstice. They display cartoon images of the sun and the crescent moon.

"Do you want any help?" I ask, placing my purse under the counter.

"Sure. If you want to help me fold."

"OK. As soon as I log into the cash register." When I finish, I join him at the tarot table. "I hate folding. Almost hoped you'd say no."

He chuckles. "You don't have to."

"Jeff, you have to stop doing that. Treating me like I'm a guest here. I mean, employers can be abusive, but you're almost the opposite. Apologizing for asking me to fulfill my expected work obligations. I despise arranging clothes because I was a mom with a husband who never helped me with the laundry. You're paying me to fold."

"True. But I've felt uncomfortable giving you job assignments when not too long ago, I was working alongside you. It feels weird."

"You'll have to get over that. I'm your employee. When I say I don't enjoy doing something, I'm only venting my dislikes. That doesn't give me an excuse not to do my job." I tilt my head. "Hmmm. But it's an awesome reason to ask for a raise."

He laughs. "Yeah, no. Even though I bought into the ownership of the store, I'm still not taking home much more than I pay you. We need to get the store online to increase sales."

"Oh, that's right. And it's a fabulous idea."

The door dings, and Kate skips in, appearing refreshed. Today, her skin tone is peachy, and her cheeks have a rosy glow. Her full lips shine in a vibrant shade of dark pink. Even her pale-blond hair seems fuller. Skye must have insisted on a makeover this morning before they left the apartment.

"Hi," she says, smiling coyly at her new beau. "I'm on the way to work, so I thought I'd stop by. Skye dropped me off."

Jeff grins widely. "I'm glad you did. I wish we'd had more time to talk last night after the graduation celebration."

She lowers her gaze to the floor. "I'm sorry. But thanks for dropping me at the Raven."

"Gwyn, can you watch the store for a couple of minutes?"

"Sure. It's dead right now, anyway."

"Thanks. Kate, we can talk in the back."

She follows Jeff to the rear of the store, and they chat for a bit while I continue folding the shirts and piling them according to size. After a few minutes, the young lovers walk back into the front, holding hands. How sweet.

"How are you doing, Kate?" I ask. "You must have gotten a good night's rest. Your face is glowing today. Or did Skye give you a makeover?"

She smiles timidly. "Yes. She was so kind to buy some makeup for me. I slept for a long time, too. I'm not used to eating so much for supper."

"Have you acclimated to living with Skye? You know we're all here to help you...if you end up staying in Bearsden."

"She has been wonderful. And that would be grand. Everyone is so nice to me. I don't know what I would have done without all of your support, especially Skye...and Jeff." She peers at him and her face flushes.

"We'd love to have you, Kate," I say, touching her arm briefly. "Think of us as your new family."

"Thank you, Ms. Crowther. I can't remember anything about my past family, but I sense they weren't as loving as all of you."

How sad. "You can call me Gwyn. Well, I better get to work, or my boss will yell at me." I grin and return to the T-shirt piles.

"Kate, I'll call you later tonight," Jeff says, smiling.

She averts her eyes. "I may have to work late tonight. Wait until after ten?"

"OK. I don't open the store early on Mondays, anyway."

She smiles demurely. "Thank you, Jeff." She tilts her head and kisses him lightly on the cheek. "Bye."

Kate exits the store, skipping like a teenager. I peer out of the corner of my eye at Jeff, and he's blushing.

"Why did you have to drop Kate off at the Raven after the party? I didn't think she'd go to work that late?"

"She said she left something there. I think she's afraid to be alone with me. I tried to get her to go for a short stroll in the Celestial Gardens in the moonlight. But she wouldn't go in there with me."

How odd. Something dark and traumatic happened to that girl. If she could remember who she was and what happened, we could help her cope better.

"Well, I better get back to those T-shirts," he says.

We finish folding and separating the cotton shirts according to size, stacking them on the shelves when we're done. Jeff goes to the back to open more boxes. A few DUB students come in and rush to the new clothes display. Soon after, Shane walks in.

"Well, look who decided to come to work for a change," I say, ringing up a customer. "Miss us?"

He chuckles. "I've only been enjoying my personal time, darling."

"I know you are. Don't mind me. I'm only razzing you. It's great to see you so happy. I mean, more than your usual jolly self."

I finish bagging, and the last customer exits the store. Should I talk to him about Cordelia? No. What can I say? I don't know what I observed her doing in the gardens. Shane scratches his head as he stares at me.

"What? Do you need to tell me something? We're friends, Shane. You can share anything with me."

"The way you spoke to Cordelia at the party last night…"

Here comes the backlash. "I'm sorry I was so curt. She doesn't seem to understand she needs to follow our rules. But she's a strong-willed woman. And that's probably what you find attractive in her. I get it."

"She's not unlike another headstrong woman I know." He tilts his head and smiles. "Someone I also care deeply about."

I chuckle. "You don't say."

"I do, darling. I do." He takes a breath. "I think you two got off on the wrong foot. Would you and Archie like to have dinner with us some evening this week?"

Holy crystals. The last thing I want to do is eat another meal with that bitch. But do I have a choice?

"Can I suggest Ronnie and Derek join us, too? Cordelia enjoyed talking with her last night." I am so lying. My friend was tolerating her, just like I was.

"That sounds wonderful. She would enjoy getting to know you all better. A large gathering hardly allows for that. I'll talk with her and send you a couple of nights to consider."

"Sure. I'll tell Archie and let Ronnie know," I say, gritting my teeth.

"Now I better get to work. Holler if you need anything."

There's no way I could make it through dinner without Ronnie. She'll keep me from leaping across the table and strangling the woman. I may be right about my killer instinct.

The rest of my shift passes quickly as shoppers come and go. I decide to buy myself one of the new Summer Solstice T-shirts in a small. Jeff left for the day at dinnertime, leaving Shane and me to lock up the store.

"Will you be seeing Cordelia tonight?" I ask, being nosy.

"No, sadly. She said she needs to *rejuvenate* her beauty. Which I assume means she's taking a long, hot bubble bath." A mischievous grin erupts on his face. "She likes those a lot. And then she'll slather on a tub of moisturizer. That's the part I love to help with."

I laugh at my boss. "Please, don't get specific."

He turns the sign to CLOSED and opens the door for me. "Keep your wits about you as you walk. That cougar has killed four young men. So sad."

"Yeah. It is." But I'm believing more and more it's not a cougar.

"Have a blessed night, darling."

"You, too, boss."

As I stroll down the paver walkway of Main Street toward the mansion, I growl at the idea of having another meal with that Southern Wicked Witch. I know hexes are bad, but...

Chapter Seventeen

BLUER THAN THE MIDNIGHT SKIES

When I arrive at Mitchell Hall for my check-in, I catch Amnesia Kate darting from the Celestial Gardens gate and running toward the Raven Pub. She was too scared to go in there with Jeff, but she went in by herself? Or perhaps she wasn't alone. I enter through the gate and inspect the grounds, but find no one around, only the sounds of crickets. The portal lights up and the Seelie Fae children skip toward me.

"Aunt Gwyn," they shout. "We missed you last night."

"Yes. Something came up. Before we play, I need to ask you a question. Have you ever seen a big cat run through the gardens? It's brown and dangerous."

"No," Shailagh replies. "That would be scary."

"Yes. It would. How about a big black cat?"

"We never saw one of those either, Aunt Gwyn," Aonghas says.

"If you ever do, please tell me. I'm worried the animal will hurt Archie, and then he couldn't come and play with you."

"We will. Now let's go play." They tap me and run away, yelling, "Your turn to catch us!"

I run after them, and we take turns chasing each other back and forth, darting around the manicured shrubs and blooming rose bushes. After thirty minutes of this, I've clocked my cardio for the day. I convince them to cross over, and I wait for the brightness of the portal to dissipate. As I amble toward the gate, light flashes from behind me, and I spin around.

"Aonghas? Shailagh?" I yell. No response.

I scan the gardens. The Seelie Fae are either hiding or only crossed back over for a millisecond. A sudden whoosh of air blows past me, displacing my bangs. I sense a presence and turn around. The gardens appear frozen in time except for the sliver of moonlight highlighting the hawthorn tree in the far-right corner. A gust of wind blows my hair back again, and a distorted growl travels with it. It's almost human-like. Immediately, a mini cyclone engulfs me, lifting me off the ground and tossing me onto the gravel walkway. As I push myself up, the portal lights up and closes with another blast. *What the fuck was that?*

A notification vibrates my phone.

Archie: *You have to come here right away. Help!*

Me: *I'm on my way! Are you OK?*

Archie: *No. I desperately need you!*

Me: *Hold on! I'm coming!*

The vision of him lying on the ground unconscious flashes in my head, the cat sith roaring on its hind legs next to his lifeless body. Perhaps the vision was wrong about the location of his demise. I run as fast as I can through the Green, taking the detour through the alleyway to Douglas Street and cutting through neighborhood yards to get to Duncan. Palpitations seize my heart as a hot flash overcomes me, causing my shirt to stick to my chest. The living room curtains are drawn when I arrive. I gasp for breath as I push on the door.

"Archie! Where are you?" I shout in a hoarse, scratchy voice.

The house is dark except for sparse light flickering and spilling into the foyer. A whiff of roses passes my nose.

A faint Scottish voice responds. "I'm in here."

I rush through the archway, catching my breath. "Are you OK?" I stop abruptly, panting. "Fuck."

He's standing in front of the fireplace, his muscles glistening under the flicker of several candles, holding a single scarlet-red rose. Several vases of them fill the room with their fragrance.

"You're naked! You said you needed my help desperately."

"Aye," he says, cupping his package. "They're bluer than the midnight skies."

I laugh uncontrollably and amble toward him, kicking my sneakers off as I go. "Oh, my gods. You scared the shit out of me. I imagined the worst."

"Only aching for you, my love."

Archie offers me the rose, and I take it, inhaling its enticing scent.

"I'm so sorry. If I had any idea you were this miserable, I'd at least have recommended online porn."

He chuckles and replies in a thicker Scottish brogue, "As appealing as repetitious, loveless sex sounds, I'd much rather have you, my love."

He wraps his arms around my torso, pressing his waking bulge against me. Surprisingly, I find myself aroused and kiss him.

"Mmm...I missed your mouth," he says, lowering his hand to my bottom. "I'm sorry I tricked you into coming here. I hoped you would have a difficult time saying no if I were ready for the moment."

"You know me way too well, professor." I run my hands across his firm chest.

"Will you stay? I don't know what this project is that has kept you from me for so long, but I won't be angry if you walk out the door."

I wrap my hand around his manhood. "It can wait a night."

"You just made me an *extremely* happy witch." His lips curl up, and an impish twinkle captures his eyes. "You have entirely too many clothes on. Let me remedy that."

Archie removes my shirt, unhooks my bra, and slips it off. Clasping my hand, he leads me to the quilt he's laid on the floor in front of the fireplace.

"It's too warm for a fire, so I lit large candles in the hearth instead. I love ogling your body in the candlelight."

I chuckle. "Because it hides all my flaws. The wrinkles. The bumps. The rolling cellulite."

"I love every one of your imperfections, Gwynedd. They only add to your beauty. And it's you I love, not your shell of a body. But I don't mind partaking of its offerings."

As he bends down to kiss my neck, he unbuttons my jeans, working his way down to the red dragon tattoo on my left breast. He hooks his fingers around the waistband and pulls them to the floor as he kneels. I step out of my pants and kick them off. He kisses the inside of my thighs tenderly, his fingertips caressing my legs.

He offers his hand. "Come down and join me."

I kneel in front of him and press my body against his, laying my head against his chest. His heart beats wildly into my ear, and I hug him tightly, relieved that he wasn't hurt. I can't keep the secret of my dreams from him, even if it affects my future visions. But for now, I will enjoy his love. Because one never knows if there will be another time. I gaze up at his handsome, chiseled face, and he runs a finger along my jawline.

"Lie down and relax. I have so much work to do." He winks at me as I lie back on the quilt.

"You have a devilish glint in your eyes. Like you've been planning something."

"Aye. I've been fantasizing about this night for a while."

He climbs over me and kisses me deeply, offering his tongue, and the warm spot between my legs becomes wet. For the moment, I don't care if the vision ever returns. The dream should never have come between us. He grazes my neck with his lips, planting soft kisses as he moves toward a nipple. I moan when he takes it into his mouth.

"Oh, Archie. This is why I put you off. Once you touch me, I'm yours."

He lifts his head and kisses me between my breasts. "And you have my heart, Gwynedd. I plan to show you how much."

His hands work their magic as he moves down my abdomen toward my belly button, planting kisses and titillating my skin with his tongue. The whiskers of his goatee tickle me, and goosebumps rise. A wicked grin emerges on his face as he spreads my legs.

"Do you remember the first time?" he asks, smiling.

"Of course," I say, panting. "I hadn't made love in years. I was so scared of how I might respond...or not respond."

He kisses me on my inner thighs, spreading my legs further, and a fire ignites inside me. Sweat slinks down my face and neck while he continues to tease me, inching closer and closer to the origin of the blaze.

"Aye. You surprised me, but I had a wee bit of suspicion there was more than a witchy past hiding inside of you. I was determined to bring your passion to the surface. Like I'm doing now."

He lowers his head, and my hips rise when he finds me. I moan and squirm while he feasts on me, running my fingers through his wavy hair to encourage him. Except this time, I don't squeeze my eyes shut. I stare into his icy blues as my arousal reaches new heights. He intertwines his fingers with mine and summons his magic, sparking mine to radiate from my hand and up my arm. The amber glow overtakes my entire body, and I scream in ecstasy when my body gives way to the pleasure. Archie continues to kiss and nibble while I quiver under his touch.

"I want you," I say, catching my breath. "Make me scream again."

"My pleasure, love," he says as he crawls over me. "As many times as you want."

He kisses me as I guide him in, and he makes love to me slowly, as if this is the last time we'll be together. I cup his face and get a whiff of my scent, kissing him deeply. He increases his thrusts until he can't hold back any longer. My fingers dig into his back, and he grunts with his release, collapsing on me. I stroke his back lightly with my fingers and realize I have to reveal the vision to him.

"Archie, I need to tell you something. It's about my project."

He lifts his head, panting. "Now? In our afterglow?"

"Yes. Or I may change my mind."

"Sure, but can I lean on an arm and stay here? I don't want to leave you yet."

"Yes," I say, stroking his goatee. "But it may kill the mood."

His brow crinkles. "I doubt it, but give it a go. What's the project?"

"I've been having dreams...premonitions. I think something terrible is going to happen to you."

He arches an eyebrow. "I'm intrigued. Go on."

"You walk into the Celestial Gardens and suddenly, you're lying on the ground." I lay my hand on his cheek. "I think you're dead in the dream."

"Oh, Gwynedd," he says, leaning his forehead against mine. "When did these visions start?"

"Weeks ago. And to lengthen the dreams, I've been attempting to use crystals to enhance them."

Archie's eyes widen, and he slides off of me onto his side. "Gwyn, crystal use can be dangerous if you haven't become skilled in the practice."

"I know. My mom warned me. Aunt Gorawen told her past family members went insane when they tried to enhance their visions using crystals without years of training. But I've been careful. And they haven't worked well."

He cocks his head. "Is that why you smoked pot with Agnes?"

I chuckle. "Yeah. I asked her for help, and she suggested I try her Bearsden Poison first."

"Bloody hell, Gwyn. I mean, I was elated with the results, but I wish you had told me about the visions."

"I worried that talking about the dreams might stunt them. But the last time it lengthened the vision, I discovered one more thing. You were lying on the ground, and a cat sith was standing on its hind legs next to you, roaring. I think there is a soul-eating fairy hiding in Bearsden. It's killing these young men and eating their souls, and it's going to eat yours, too."

He strokes my arm. "Did it ever occur to you they are merely dreams influenced by the stress over everything that's happened to you? The cat sith could represent the cougar running rampant."

"Sure. But Archie, my witch sense tells me they're like the others I had after you first ignited my magic. I also realize Nick's glamouring could have embedded these into my brain somehow. Humor me. Don't check on the Seelie Fae children until I can enhance my visions further."

He cups my face with a hand. "You're going to try again, then?"

"Yes. I have to. I can't bear the thought of losing you."

"All right. Do you want me to help? I've never used crystals to intensify my dream state, though. I preferred not knowing about the future."

"You're in my visions, so I have to do this alone. Agnes gave me a grimoire with instructions, and I've been taking baby steps. But I'll let you know when I'm trying, so you can check on me afterwards. OK?"

He sighs. "Do I have a choice?"

"No." I kiss him. "Promise me you won't go in the gardens?"

He swipes a finger across my lips. "I promise."

"Thank you, honey. I worry about what's going on in there." I recall the incident that occurred right before he texted me. "Holy crystals...I almost forgot." I sit up straight as my heart skips a few beats. "Something weird happened right before you sent me a text. An unusual gust of wind blew past me, twice, and I heard the warped call of an animal except it was...human-sounding. Could have been the air rushing past my ear, though. And then a swirl of wind lifted me off the ground, and I fell on the gravel. And here's the strangest part. The mound lit up for a split second and went dark. Was it only the portal opening and closing on its own?"

Archie sits up and leans on an arm. "Hmmm...disconcerting, for sure. But it could be the mound releasing energy. You didn't see anything?"

"No. If that whoosh of air was some kind of entity, it moved way too fast for me to catch a glimpse. But I didn't imagine being lifted off the ground." I show him the minor abrasions on my hands and forearms. "I have the wounds to prove it happened. Should we report the incident to Leslie and Trinity?"

He scratches his goatee. "We'll have to sleep on that. We're taking Leslie and Agnes to the airport tomorrow to catch an overnight flight to the UK. Bad timing."

"Oh, there's one more thing," I say, rolling my eyes. "Shane wants us to go to dinner with him and the Wicked Witch. I told him we would. What else could I say? But I'm inviting Derek and Ronnie to go, too. Ronnie will keep me from jumping across the table and strangling the woman."

Archie chuckles. "I see you've accepted your newly acquired murderous ways."

I slap him playfully. "That's not funny."

"You're the one spewing violent threats against a witch who's only asking you to stay out of her business. No?"

"Point made," I say, frowning. "Whose side are you on?"

He kisses me tenderly. "Yours, my love. But I don't want to see you lose your friendship with Shane over Cordelia. What if Tyler hadn't liked me? Would you have stopped seeing me?"

"That's different, because you wouldn't have threatened him. You would have just walked away." I rub my nose on his. "Instead, Tyler liked you so much he tried to get us back together."

"It hurt so much to leave you that day at the house. I thought I'd lost you forever."

"Never. I'm not going anywhere."

I kiss him again, and he pushes me back on the quilt.

"Ready for round two?" he asks, sliding his hand between my legs. "I don't have school tomorrow."

"Ohhh...then school me, professor."

Chapter Eighteen

ONE DEGREE OF SEPARATION

Standing on the sidewalk at the Newark Airport in New Jersey on Monday evening, Agnes bats at her salt and pepper hair and clutches her quilt carry-on bag against her body. I've never seen her so nervous. Nothing frightens this rough and tough hedge witch. Archie consoles her.

"Agnes, you have nothing to worry about. The airlines you're flying on have the best reputation. The odds of you crashing are infinitesimal."

"But knowing my luck, I'll hit the jackpot of plane crashes," she replies.

"Oh, Agnes," Leslie says, sighing. "You've cast thousands of spells with nary a care. Why are you so anxious about the flight to the UK?"

I hug my former mentor. "You'll be fine. Eat your dinner on the plane and then try to sleep."

"I don't have control over the plane. That's why. And I plan on sleeping like a baby. I ate an edible before I left the house." She winks at us.

"That may not have been the best option," Archie chides. "You could become unruly."

Agnes snickers and punches his arm. "I'm not fucking stupid. I didn't consume my Bearsden Poison, only a mild strain that makes me pass out."

"We better head in and check our bags," Leslie says, rubbing her knobby fingers. "Keep us informed on the progress of finding the cougar. I certainly hope Animal Control is successful. Losing four young men to the beast, two on campus alone, is a monumental tragedy."

Archie's brow furrows. "DUB's administration is none too happy with the city. They say it's tarnishing their reputation."

"Because their reputation is way more important than the death of four of their students," I say, scowling. "Their parents must be threatening to sue by now."

"For what?" Agnes asks. "They were told to be careful and not walk alone at night. It's not the university's fault those boys ignored the police warnings. It's a fucking shame, though."

Leslie gives Archie and me an awkward hug. "Be careful, my friends. We'll message you when we arrive."

The Elder and the hedge witch drag their bags into the airport, and we begin the long drive back to Delaware. The Tesla whirs down the interstate, absorbing the bumps in the road while I stare out the window, contemplating our decision.

"Leslie and Agnes will blow their witch hats off when they discover we didn't tell them about the phenomenon in the gardens. They'll accuse us of withholding information from the coven."

Archie lays his hand on mine. "Aye. But you know Leslie would have canceled the trip. And Agnes would have welcomed any excuse to avoid getting on a plane."

"You're right. But I can feel uncomfortable about the decision."

He squeezes my hand. "They'll be back in two short weeks to attend the Summer Solstice Celebration. What can happen in that amount of time?"

"I suppose you're right."

He smiles. "Thank you for indulging me last night. I truly expected you would throw a shoe at me."

"I considered it," I say, squinting. "But when I saw you standing there in all your bountifulness, I lost myself."

He chuckles. "That was my plan. But I prepared for both. Will you sleep at home tonight?"

"I think I should. Mr. Yeats feels abandoned, I'm sure. He paced back and forth in his cat presentation all afternoon. If I sleep a couple of nights there, he should be OK after that."

"If not, I could always sleep there. And we'll make such a racket making love all night, he'll kick you out the door."

"That would probably do it. Better yet, see how he reacts if we invite him in."

Archie snorts.

The night of Leslie's departure brings no solace for crystal work, with Mr. Yeats racing from one room to the next. To avoid his whining all night, I take the risk of leaving my door open for him to wander in. Better he rest at the bottom of my bed sleeping than me waking several times to his meows of despair. But when I wake the next morning, the area at the footboard remains empty, save my Welsh dragon throw I bought in Wales. I rush to the bathroom for my morning routine, and he's absent when I step out into the hallway. Where is the busybody feline?

Leslie's bedroom door is ajar, so I peek inside. Mr. Yeats is curled up on her antique spindle-post bed. He lifts his head and stares at me, his glassy yellow and powder-blue eyes blinking. I shuffle to the footboard and stroke his back.

"You miss her already, don't you?" I ask.

He hops off the bed onto the wooden floor and transforms into his human persona, pulling out a handkerchief from his gray suit jacket and dabbing the corners of his wet eyes.

"I always worry when Dr. Hughes leaves. I was so lonely when she took me in. Now that she has Ms. Pritchard to occupy her life, I'm less important for her needs. And someday, her human body will succumb to the inevitable. And then what becomes of me?"

"Unfortunately, as much as we want our loved ones to live forever, crossing into the Otherworld will happen to all of us." I gaze into the forlorn eyes of the feline and make a monumental decision I may regret forever. "I can promise you this, Mr. Yeats. When Dr. Hughes leaves this world, I won't leave you alone. You can become my familiar...*if* you want."

His lower lip quivers, and he straightens his suit vest. "I would be honored, Ms. Crowther, to accompany you in your future endeavors."

"Well, I think we both hope that time arrives far into the future. We want Dr. Hughes and Ms. Pritchard around for as long as possible."

"Most definitely." Mr. Yeats approaches me and wraps me in a stiff hug. "I'll be in the magic room if you need my assistance for anything. Even your dangerous crystal use."

He rolls his eyes at me and transforms into his chimera cat presentation as he scuttles down the hallway. He's not wrong. And now I'm increasing that danger by using a grid. I hope skipping last night doesn't cause a regression. I'll find out tonight.

After getting dressed and finishing my usual breakfast of eggs and veggies with a cup of Earl Grey tea, I load the dishwasher and head into my bedroom to reread the grimoire's instructions on the use of a crystal grid. Filling it would probably give me the extra boost I need to see the entire dream sequence. But will my mind survive the extra charge? I flip through more pages, searching for further advice, but the doorbell rings.

I rush to the front door and pull on the knob. Detective Jack Schmidt is waiting on the front stoop. I flinch, and microscopic fairies do somersaults in my stomach.

"Detective Schmidt?" Perspiration sprouts on my upper lip.

"Did I scare you?" he asks, flashing his badge. "That wasn't my intention."

"No. I wasn't expecting you. May I help you? Are you here about the cougar victim?" I bet he caught me taking pictures. So much for trying to sneak a few snaps with my phone camera.

"You sure can. I have a few questions to ask. May I?" He gestures toward the door.

I open the screen to let him in. "Sure. Come in." Leslie's house has no foyer, so I usher him into the living room.

The detective removes his pad and pencil from his pocket, and I wait impatiently for a lecture on "invading the area of the young man's demise." He flips the pages of his notepad back a few and stops to read his handwritten notes.

"When I spoke to you at Mystic Sage, you said you and Dr. Nicholas Evans were friends. Correct?"

"Yes. I told you I met him when I asked for his help in translating an old family tome I inherited, and we became friends." He's not here to reprimand me for snapping photos at the scene of the last victim?

"How often did you meet with him at the Raven Pub?"

WHY is he asking me about Nick Evans again? "I don't know. I didn't count. A few times."

Mr. Yeats ambles in and circles around my feet. He stares up at me and blinks several times. I wave down at him to sit.

"According to one waitress, you met with him more than that." He reads from his notepad. "She said you ate breakfast with Dr. Evans nearly every Sunday morning."

Shit. My heart takes off like a rocket, and Mr. Yeats slinks against my leg—an attempt to soothe my nerves, I guess.

"Yes. I told you we were good friends. We had a lot in common. He studied Welsh culture, and my parents were from Wales. We met regularly to share our love of the country." And to keep him from divulging his knowledge of knowing about the coven to Leslie. Little did we know the professor was hiding his own secret.

His eyes narrow. "When you say good friends, how close would you say you were?"

I swallow. What is he hinting at?

"Close enough to have each other's cell phone numbers?"

"Of course. People usually have their friends' contact information."

"Or that of their lover's," he says, smiling. "Certainly a lot closer than your standard six degrees of separation, wouldn't you say?"

I freeze while Mr. Yeats shifts in front of me, resting at my feet.

Detective Schmidt bends down to pet the feline. "What an unusual cat you have. Hey there."

Mr. Yeats opens his mouth and hisses at the detective. Jack Schmidt must not understand a cat's warning, because he continues to pet him. The familiar responds by taking a chomp on the side of his hand.

"Aghhh!" The detective's hand springs back, and he inspects the wound. "What a nasty cat you have, Ms. Crowther."

"I'm sorry." But I'm absolutely not. "Mr. Yeats is not my cat. He belongs to Dr. Hughes, but he usually takes to strangers. He must sense something about you." Like you trying to dig into things you shouldn't.

"Damn." He closes his notepad and slips it back into his pocket with his left hand. "I have more questions, but we'll have to continue this discussion another time."

I shouldn't offer, but I want to appear cooperative. "Would you like me to get my first aid kit out? To clean the bite?"

He frowns. "Don't bother. I should get to an urgent care. I assume he doesn't have rabies?"

"Of course not. He's a house cat. He never goes outside."

"I hope not. Ms. Crowther, I'll be in touch."

I nod as he exits the house. The screen closes with a clap, and I slam the front door closed. I break out in a hot flash and run to the basket of magazines in the living room. I grab one to fan myself and collapse into the chair. Mr. Yeats transforms into his human presentation, picks up a loose newspaper, and fans me with it. I'm as drenched as if I jumped into the neighborhood pool.

"What an inquisitive busybody," the familiar says. "Sticking his nose into your business."

I tap my upper chest, an ill attempt to calm my nerves. "It is his job. But I hoped he wouldn't find out I dated Nick Evans for a short time. His next line of questions will ask me about it, I know. But thank you, Mr. Yeats."

"My pleasure, Ms. Crowther." He continues to fan me, moving the newspaper up and down. "I knew where the questions were headed, and I couldn't allow it."

"Well, you only delayed the inevitable. He's going to come back. But it bought me a few days. I need to tell Dr. Cockburn."

Mr. Yeats nods and ambles toward the magic room while I send Archie a text.

Me: *Det. Schmidt stopped by. Thought he was going to ask about the photos I snapped.*

It seems like an hour before he responds.

Archie: *He didn't? Then what did he want?*

Me: *He asked about Nick again! Wanted to know if I had his phone number in my cell.*

Archie: *What did you say?*

Me: *Yes. What choice did I have? We were friends, so it shouldn't matter. But...*

Archie: *But what?*

Me: *He asked if lovers have that info, too.*

Archie: *Shite. What did you answer?*

Me: *I didn't. Mr. Yeats bit his hand, and he left.*

Archie: *LOL. Good for him. It gives us time for you to think of a good story.*

Me: *I can't lie to him. You know I'm a terrible liar.*

Archie: *Don't panic, my love. We'll figure it out. Do you want me to come over?*

Me: *No. I have something to do tonight. Please, don't ask.*

Archie: *I know I can't stop you. Please be careful, Gwyn.*

Me: *I will. I love you.*

Archie: *My heart is yours.*

I don't have time to deal with this now, so I have to put it on the back burner. First on the list is figuring out how Archie is supposed to die. I text Ronnie.

Me: *That nosy detective stopped by the house. I think he knows I dated Nick.*

Ronnie: *Fuck. What are you gonna do?*

Me: *I can't worry about it right now. I told Archie about the dreams.*

Ronnie: *I'm so glad. What does he think?*

Me: *He believes the dreams are stress induced, but he's going to stay out of the gardens.*

Ronnie: *Good. Safety first. Now what?*

Me: *I'm using the crystal grid tonight.*

Ronnie: *Double fuck. Why tell me?*

Me: *If I don't wake up, the two of you will have to bring me back.*

Ronnie: *Triple fuck. You'll be fine. I'll see you tomorrow night at the Raven.*

Me: *Yes. Thank you for going. That woman makes my magic bubble.*

Ronnie: *You crack me up. Be careful, friend.*

Me: *I will. You're the best.*

I shove my phone in the back pocket of my jeans. "Mr. Yeats, I need your help," I holler in the direction of the magic room.

He appears in seconds. "Anything, Ms. Crowther. I am at your service."

I walk to my bedroom, dig out my crystal collection from my family steamer trunk, and place the grid on my nightstand. What if Mom and Aunt Gorawen were right? May the gods save my marbles.

CHAPTER NINETEEN

WICKED WITCH OF THE SOUTH

THROUGH A MOONLIT, MISTY haze, Archie strolls into the Celestial Gardens, pulling the gate closed behind him. He turns his head toward the garbled call of an animal, but the threads of fog obscure his vision. Suddenly, he falls to the ground, struggling to fight off the attack. I can't make out the offender. The vision flashes forward to Archie's still body lying on the grass, the cat sith roaring next to him.

I gasp, my heart pounding against my ribcage, and sit up in bed. I'm dripping—a night sweat. My mind reels with images of Archie's future demise as I clutch my chest.

It has to be the cat sith. But where is it hiding? Is it the presence that passed by me in the gardens? Eyeing the crystal grid, only partially filled, I realize I may need to add more of them in future attempts. I'll do it one by one. It's the only safe choice. At least the increase in the crystals doesn't appear to have affected me in any other way. *Phew.*

When I hop onto the floor to dash to the bathroom, my legs collapse underneath me, and bam! I fall on my left side with a thud, shaking the house. Mr. Yeats comes scuttling into the room and changes into his human form. He darts to me.

"Ms. Crowther, are you harmed?" He checks me over, touching my arms and legs.

I push him away. "Stop! I'm OK...I think?" I wiggle my toes. "Well, my legs still work, but they're a little numb. Help me up."

He grabs my elbow, and I stand, but my lower body is still precarious. I sway into him, and he catches me.

"Can you help me to the bathroom?" I ask. "Because I really have to go."

"I'm at your service. Hold on," he replies.

Mr. Yeats waves his hand with a sprinkle of magic, and we slide down the hallway and into the bathroom. "Would you like me to assist you further?"

I grimace. "I'm not an invalid. My bodily functions are intact." I grab the side of the toilet, shaking my leg. "Shoo!"

"I'm sorry. I'll leave you to your..."

The familiar clears his throat and closes the door as he exits. I push down my PJs and plop onto the porcelain throne. I summon my magic and place my hands on my thighs, casting a healing intention. Please work. I really dread having the feline lift me off the toilet. The amber glow spreads throughout my lower extremities, and my legs tingle from the top to my toes.

After a few minutes, my magic dissipates, and I grab the edge of the sink to pull myself up. I can stand. What a relief. I clean up and return to my room to dress. The familiar is pacing back and forth in his human presentation. He darts at me and gives me a hug.

"Oh, Ms. Crowther, I'm so relieved you are better. Perhaps you shouldn't use the crystal grid again. It left you impaired."

"I'm fine." But is he right? How severe will the side effects be next time?

He crosses his arms. "You're being obstinate."

"Too bad. Mr. Yeats, Dr. Cockburn's life may depend on me deciphering this dream. I'll add more crystals to the grid slowly. Will that satisfy your concerns?"

He purses his lips. "I suppose. Dr. Hughes might never forgive me if I allowed anything detrimental to happen to you."

"Did you promise her you'd watch over me?"

He fiddles with his bow tie. "I can't answer that question without incriminating myself."

"Right. Well, I have to get moving. Dr. Cockburn is meeting me at the Bearsden Shelter, and the traffic can be bad on Wednesdays. We're discussing what happened at Mitchell Hall with Ms. Johnson and Councilman Jackson." I point at the doorway. "I'd like to get dressed."

He flinches. "Forgive me. I'll let you get to it." He transforms into a cat as he slinks into the hallway.

Leslie told him to watch after me. A smile curls my mouth. The Elder is becoming a softie.

Archie and I enter Elijah's office at the shelter, and Trinity follows us in. Elijah closes the door and leans on his desk. Even though I put on a tank top and shorts, I'm sweating bullets. The temperature jumped ten degrees from yesterday and is supposed to hit 82. I grab a piece of mail off the desk and fan myself as I spill the tea on the phenomenon I witnessed in the Celestial Gardens. The shelter must have the AC set high to conserve energy.

Trinity grimaces and taps the heel of her stiletto on the floor. "And you didn't see this entity?"

"No. I only felt its presence." I throw my hands in the air. "Or I was paranoid, and it was only the wind. But the feeling was strong."

Archie wraps an arm around my shoulder. "I think we need to trust Gwyn's witch sense."

"True dat," Elijah says. "Gwyn's perceptions were right on the money in the past, even before she discovered she was a witch and knew what they meant."

"What did Leslie and Agnes have to say about the occurrence?" Trinity asks.

Archie and I glance at each other but say nothing.

"Oh, for the love of all the gods," she says, placing a fist on her hip. "You didn't tell them before they left for the UK?"

Elijah bellows in laughter. "There will be some hell to pay when they return. I can promise you that. The Elder and the hedge witch won't appreciate being left out of the loop."

"I told Gwyn we shouldn't tell them," Archie says. "Agnes would have used it as an excuse to not get on the plane, and Leslie would have canceled the trip. We don't know what this phenomenon is. For all we know, it's the mound releasing energy."

"Should we poke around in there some night?" I ask.

Trinity scratches her head. "We've been taking turns checking on the Seelie Fae as it is, and no one else has noticed anything."

"I'll check tonight when I go," Elijah says. "But I've not noticed anything unusual. Only the pranksters trying to stretch out their playtime every time I go."

I exhale. "They have to stop that. I'll go later after you've worn them out. Have another chat with them."

"Sounds like a plan," he replies.

"Gwyn told me about the visions she's been having," Archie says. "Something was attacking me in the gardens, but the dream didn't reveal the culprit, only that I was lying on the ground unconscious."

Elijah pushes his lower lip up. "That's disturbing. Do you think it's a cougar attack?"

"No," Trinity interjects. "Gwyn told me about the dreams. She believes it's a cat sith."

"I'm seeing the fairy in the dreams, but Archie thinks it's a representation of the cougar. He could be right. I'm still recovering from what happened that night."

"While we're on the subject," Elijah says. "I need to share what a member of the Bearsden PD told me about those young men. Apparently, every victim has been nearly drained of all their blood."

Archie scratches his goatee. "That's quite odd. Now that you mention it, every one of them had only a small pool of blood nearby."

"Shit," Trinity says. "Do they have an explanation?"

"No." Elijah scratches the back of his head. "It's the strangest thing about the attacks."

"So, their blood was missing." My mind drifts back to the grotesque painting in Seamus's bathroom. "Seamus shared a legend with me about a vengeful woman who drains the blood of young men. I saw a picture of it in his bathroom. He called it a Dearg Due." And I know of a hateful woman who fits the bill.

Archie cocks his head. "Yes. I've heard of the lore."

"Oh, for fuck's sake, Gwyn," Trinity says. "First, you think it's a cat sith fairy and now you think we've got a vampire in town?"

"Well, more like a ghostly demon who drinks blood. I believe Cordelia is involved."

Elijah rubs his jaw. "Do you have any proof?"

"Well, no..." Other than her snow-white, smooth skin and nasty disposition.

Trinity shakes her head. "I know you don't like her, and she's got questionable magic rituals going on in the gardens, but we can't go accusing her of anything without evidence. Right now, she's only a superficial crystal witch with a penchant for control. As much as I don't like her, I think you're grasping at straws."

"But there is something up with her. My ancestral witch sense keeps itching me."

She snickers. "Maybe you just need to scratch."

"Very funny," I say, frowning.

"I'll let you know if I hear anything else," Elijah says. "I think we should consider all the possibilities."

Trinity nods. "I agree. I'm just kidding with you, Gwyn."

"Before we go, Gwyn has a small request, and I'm inclined to play it safe," Archie says. "She wants me to stay out of the Celestial Gardens until she's able to increase the clarity of her visions, if that's what they are. Could someone take over my slots for the time being?"

Elijah lays a hand on his shoulder. "I got you, Archie. We can't take a chance of losing you."

"Thank you, councilman. I owe you a few more shifts at the shelter."

He laughs and pats Archie on the back. "Damn straight."

"One more thing," Trinity says. "I told Elijah about Cordelia, in case we have to confront her about her behavior in the gardens. I don't want to bother the young witches about this. It's gonna be awkward enough if we have to discuss the issue with Shane. We don't need an outside witch causing a rift in our coven, but...if she's performing unacceptable rituals using the portal, that could trigger who knows what. For now, let's just keep it between the four of us."

Archie nods. "Sounds like a good idea."

"Will do, Trinity." Elijah opens a scheduling app on his phone. "Now, Archie, about those extra shifts..."

Archie and I sit in the booth with Ronnie and Derek, waiting for Shane and the Wicked Witch of the South to arrive. Freshly made popcorn permeates the back room as we nibble. The Raven has a few empty tables, not surprising for a Wednesday night. Shane wanted to eat on a less crowded evening rather than shout over a packed room. Personally, I'd welcome the chatter, so I can pretend not to hear her grating voice.

As my boss would say, "We're all gussied up for dinner." My best friend suggested putting on a dress and a little makeup to gain Cordelia's respect, since she's always dressed to the nines. But I'd rather wear yoga pants and ditch the mascara. That bitch is the last person I care to impress. Archie and Derek are wearing button-down shirts and casual pants.

"I wonder what's taking them so long?" Ronnie asks, picking a kernel out of her teeth.

I chuckle. "And you say I'm uncouth."

"There is no worse pain than a popcorn bit stuck between your teeth," Archie says. "Pick away, Ronnie."

Derek wraps an arm around her shoulders and squeezes. "One of the many reasons I love you, babe."

"Liar. You're just here for the kinky sex." She cackles and throws a popped kernel in her mouth. "I'm a great shot, too."

"You seem to feel better," I say. "Did you finally shake that virus?"

"Oh, yeah. Now I'm eating like a pig. I guess I'm making up for the weeks I didn't eat too well. And gods, I'm so bloated. Menopause sucks." Ronnie leans over the table. "Before Cordelia gets here, have you caught her doing rituals in the gardens again?"

I glance at Archie. "Nothing new." I hate lying to my best friend, but Trinity asked us not to tell anyone else. Ronnie hid her secret from me about being a witch in a hidden coven back when I wasn't *in the knowing,* and I was none too happy about it. How will she react when she finds out I kept this from her?

Shane strolls in wearing a Hawaiian shirt and cargo pants. That's as formal as his hippie style allows. Cordelia is wearing a ruffled white shirt over a bright red pencil skirt with matching pumps, and she's hanging onto my boss's arm like the leech she is. You could peel the makeup off her face. As she approaches the table, I see why. Her skin appears more wrinkled than usual, and there are faint dark circles beneath her eyes—likely a sign her magic anti-aging routine is in need of an update. Either that, or she must have slept with her face squished into the pillow all night. No wonder she layered on the goo.

Stop it, Gwyn.

This is not like me. I don't judge people for their looks. Ronnie's right. We should give Cordelia a fresh start. Shane appears to adore her, and we owe it to him, despite my suspicions about her. He approaches us with a euphoric grin.

"Hello, friends. What a beautiful day to meet for dinner. Thank you for joining us."

"Hey, y'all," Cordelia says, grinning. "I'm ecstatic you could dine with us. I had such a fabulous time talking with you at the party last weekend."

Ronnie stands, and Cordelia gives her a peck on the cheek, leaving a red lipstick smudge. The rest of us get up as well and shake her hand, but no kiss for me. She purses her lips and pulls her hand back.

Smile, Gwyn. Do it for Shane.

"We have menus for you both," I say. "Their veggie burgers are amazing and come with sweet potato fries, but they don't beat Ronnie's at the café."

"I won't argue with you." My best friend passes the menus to Shane and Cordelia. "I've got the best chef in town."

Cordelia taps Ronnie's hand. "I'll have to come by and sample your offerings, sweetie. I know we can become great friends."

What a crock of horseshit. She's trying to schmooze my bestie. I force a grin.

"How are you settling into your new apartment?" Archie asks.

"Oh, it's smaller than I'm used to, but I love the layout. It's my understanding the prior occupant disappeared, a young professor in your department, I believe. When I performed a cleansing..." She stops and peers at me. "Do I have your permission to speak about such things here? Is everyone *in the knowing* at this table?"

My eyebrows jump. She's actually asking me?

Derek nods. "Yes. I'm the only Unremarkable, but I am *in the knowing*."

"He's been aware of us for a long time now," Shane says. "Good thing, too. He's not a member of the Fellowship, but he was an immense help when we fought off the Kenilworths."

"I can't imagine how helpful an Unremarkable could be," she says, shrugging. "They have no skills to fight supernatural beings. Personally, I don't socialize with anyone but my kind." She addresses Ronnie. "But I'm sure Derek has his strengths, dear."

Holy crystals. My friend's eyes narrow. "Damn straight. You don't have to have magic skills to be worthy, Cordelia. I'd put my man up against any witch."

"Except maybe Archie," Derek says. "Ancestral witches pack a punch. A humongous amber one."

Archie chuckles. "You flatter me, friend."

"Aww, get a room, you two." Ronnie cackles and nudges Derek.

I laugh at my friend's teasing and turn my attention to Cordelia. "To answer your question. Yes. You have my permission to continue." I don't care if my impertinence pisses her off.

"Fabulous," she says, squinting at me. "Where was I? Oh, yes. I performed a cleansing, but I sensed the young man who had lived in the space had suffered his demise there." She glances at me and smirks. "In the bedroom, in fact. It makes me wonder why the police aren't calling it a homicide."

My eyes widen until the whites must show. Fuck. My witch sense tells me she knows. Everyone at the table becomes eerily quiet, and Archie clasps my hand under the table.

"They never found a body, but let's leave that to the Bearsden Police, buttercup," Shane says.

My boss glares at his love, and she averts her gaze. There's no way he told her what really happened to Nick Evans, but she sure got her dig in. It's a shame she's such a bitch. She's supposed to have impeccable crystal use skills. I could have asked her for help. If I ask her now, she'd probably tell me to load the damn grid just to fry my brain.

"I suggest we flag down our waiter and order," Ronnie says, raising her hand. "I'm starving."

Archie leans into me and whispers, "Don't take her bait, my love. She's testing you."

"Well, I think I failed," I say, sighing.

He raises a corner of his mouth. "Shane came to your defense. Don't let her get to you."

Dinner passes as Shane shares more stories about his time in North Carolina when they were together, and we discuss the most recent updates on the search for the cougar. But there's so much tension, you couldn't hack through it with a machete. I can't keep pretending I like this woman. The fake front gnaws away at me like a rat. Eventually, I'm going to lose my cool and scream at her in front of Shane, and I'll lose our friendship. Better to tell him directly—but not now.

I scan the rooms around us and search for Amnesia Kate when I go to the bathroom, but she isn't working. I hope she's out with Jeff. Their blossoming romance warms my heart, and it seems to have helped her heal.

After the tense but cordial meal, we gather on the porch in the cooler evening temps and say our goodbyes. I slip on my sweater and wait for Shane and Cordelia to leave before losing my shit.

"Aghh! I was about to tear my hair out. There is nothing appealing about that witch. What does Shane see in her? What did he *ever* see in her?"

"Calm down, Gwyn," Ronnie says, putting on her hoodie. "Before you burst capillaries in your face. She has her strengths."

I grimace. "Name one?"

Archie chuckles. "She's a pro at setting you off."

"That's not funny," I say, scowling.

Derek chuckles. "Oh, come on. We all know why he's with her. She's an attractive older woman he had an affair with years ago, and

I bet the time between the sheets with her was hot. He's reliving those days. Can you blame him?"

"I sure don't hold it against him," Ronnie says. "Shane's wife Judith passed away ten years ago. He had us, yeah. But he was lonely. He deserves companionship, even if we don't particularly care for her demeanor."

Or her secretive rituals, which defy the coven's rules. But I can't tell her yet. "Well, I'm tired, and I still have to give the Seelie Fae a lecture about procrastinating. Elijah should have tuckered them out by now."

We make our way down the steps of the Raven Pub's porch, and I turn toward Mitchell Hall. Ronnie stops me.

"Shouldn't Archie go with you? With the cougar still on the loose?"

"No. I'm still having premonitions," I say. "I asked him not to go into the gardens, at least not until I decipher more of the dreams."

"Be careful, Gwyn."

"I can handle a cougar." I splay the fingers on my right hand.

Derek chuckles. "Those amber fireballs are powerful, babe. She'll be fine."

"OK. I'm acting like a mother hen...as if I have any idea how that feels." She hugs me. "Goodnight. And don't lose your marbles tonight, if you know what I mean."

"I won't. I'm going slowly. That's why it's taking so long. I'll see you at Agnes's on Saturday. Goodnight."

Ronnie and Derek stroll to the parking lot while Archie and I chat a bit more.

"Everything Ronnie said? Ditto," Archie says, squeezing my hand. "Your magic skills have increased in potency over the last couple of years, but you can only defend yourself if you sense the danger is coming. A cougar could surprise you. A cat sith as well."

"Thank you for not doubting me. I agree the cat sith in my dreams could be a representation of the cougar, but every part of my being tells me it's real. I can't explain why I haven't seen it other than those two instances and why it only shows up now in my premonitions. But I trust my gut, my witchy innards."

Archie shakes his head. "You have a way with words, my love." He kisses me. "Text me when you arrive home. And that's a command."

"Yes, professor. I do what I'm told."

He chuckles. "No. You fawking don't."

"I love you." I kiss him. "Goodnight, honey."

"Sleep well, my love." He pats my butt as I leave and turns toward the Green.

I walk briskly to Mitchell Hall, eager to get this over with. When I arrive at the gate to the Celestial Gardens, it's ajar. Did Elijah forget to lock it when he finished playing with the pranksters? I tiptoe carefully back and stop at the edge of the house. The partial moon breaks through the strings of gray clouds, spotlighting the mound—and Cordelia.

That bitch is performing another ritual at the mound. While she chants unfamiliar phrases, amber magic radiates from her raised hand, and the portal lights up. That's it. I'm gonna give her my two cents, whether she reports me to Shane or not. She's violating Bearsden Coven rules, and we gave her a warning.

I take a step forward but stop when a blue haze appears, morphing into an unrecognizable figure that reminds me of the night I viewed my dead husband's spirit on Samhain. The amulet glows, appearing to suck the essence from the wavering blue phenomenon. Then snap! The connection breaks when Cordelia waves her hand, and the blob disappears into the portal. Is that the entity that whizzed around me the other night? And what the fuck is she doing with it?

Cordelia touches her face lightly and grins. She straightens her dress and turns around. I scramble to find a place to hide, but there isn't a shrub big enough to hide me. So, I sprint out on my toes to the paver walkway and run around the front iron fencing in my high heels to the other side of the house. I wait for her to walk by.

I grab my chest and pant, relieved I avoided a confrontation. This is bigger than merely violating our coven rules. She's into some serious shit.

CHAPTER TWENTY

SNEAKING SUSPICIONS

THURSDAY MORNING, I AMBLE into Archie's living room wearing my PJs, and sit back on the sofa with a second cup of tea. As I sip on my Earl Grey, I admire Aunt Gorawen's painting of my mom over the sofa. She got the imagery right. What a storm we weathered, and it's not ended. With all the recent drama—the cougar killings, the police investigating me, Cordelia's shenanigans—the possibility of Nuada's family coming after me hasn't entered my mind since I killed him. Silver lining?

A notification vibrates my phone. I set my tea on the steamer trunk and enter my code.

Tyler: *Don't forget to bring your paintbrushes on Saturday.*

Me: *I won't. Should Archie bring some, too?*

Tyler: *Yup. We need everyone to paint to finish this reno in two weeks.*

Me: *Are the appliances scheduled to be delivered?*

Tyler: *I know what I'm doing, Mom. You don't have to check on me.*

Me: *I'm sorry. I trust you. It's an old habit. Good luck getting Spence there.*

Tyler: *LOL. He's already grumbling, but Tanner will get him there on time.*

Me: *Looking forward to seeing you and Zoe.*

Tyler: *See ya Saturday bright and early, Mom.*

It's difficult to let go of a mom's instinct. But I shouldn't worry about Tyler. He has his shit together more than I do. He jumped into this supernatural world with both feet solidly on the ground when he discovered he was a witch. My son grabbed the reins and hasn't looked back. I think Zoe had a lot to do with that, but I'm so proud of the man he's become—no thanks to his philandering father.

I stand and shuffle toward the fireplace to examine the picture, paying closer attention to my aunt's delicate paint strokes. It occurs to me they're similar to the ones in the clouds on Seamus's morbid painting in his bathroom. I lift my phone and snap a photo. The floor creaks behind me.

"You're sneaking up on me again," I scold. "You know I hate that."

Archie wraps his arms around my torso and kisses the side of my neck. "Aye. But then I wouldn't get to admire you from behind."

I chuckle. "Flattery will get you everything."

He squeezes a butt cheek. "That's the plan. What are you doing?"

"The clouds in Aunt Gorawen's painting are a lot like the ones in Seamus's artwork in his bathroom. Weird, isn't it?"

"I'm sure lots of amateur artists resemble one another. Art classes teach the basics."

"I suppose, but I should check it out."

Archie turns me around. "How do you plan on doing that?"

"Well..." My eyes fall to the wooden floor.

"Never mind," he says in a thicker Scottish brogue. "I don't want to know. Only...remember I work with the man, Gwyn."

I kiss him. "Don't worry. I'll be discreet."

He snickers. "You and discreet are never in the same room."

"Not funny," I say, scowling.

He laughs again. "Who were you texting?"

"Tyler. He wants us to remember to bring paintbrushes with us on Saturday and any tools you think we might need."

"You have a brilliant son, Gwyn. A born leader and a talented ancestral witch. You should feel blessed."

"I do," I say, hugging him. "Did you contact Trinity and Elijah?"

"Aye. They're none too happy about Cordelia's blatant refusal to abide by our rules. Trinity flipped out when I told her about the entity she pulled from the portal."

"I'm sure. What do you think it is?"

"No fawking idea. But I doubt it's only a ritual. We'll need to keep a close watch on her."

"That'll be tough. Unless one of us stalks her."

Archie cocks his head, and his eyebrows leap.

"Don't look at me that way. I'm not gonna follow her around. She's likely to sense my presence. I've been lucky so far."

"You already have practice with Seamus. Put your new skills to good use where they're warranted."

"But you're forgetting something. He's not a witch." I blink twice.

"A pesky minor detail. We'll have to meet and discuss a covert plan. We don't want Shane to discover we're investigating her. I assume you'll sleep in your bed tonight?"

"Yeah. Please, don't worry. I'm going to add the crystals one at a time. At that rate, the dream should complete its sequence in five years."

Archie checks the time on my phone. "You should get a move on, witch. You don't want to piss off your new boss."

"I don't think there's anything that would anger Jeff, especially now that he's in love." I break from his embrace and walk toward the staircase. "Join me in the shower?"

Archie smiles and saunters after me. "Absolutely."

Archie and I wake up so early on Saturday, we catch the sunrise painting the skies with strokes of pink and orange hues. We eat breakfast and get dressed for a dirty day of kitchen renovations. I stare out the window of Archie's Tesla as we drive to Agnes's house, discouraged by the lack of progress on my dreams. They're stuck in repeat mode after adding two more crystals to the grid—a tiger's eye and a moonstone. He lays a hand on mine.

"Don't fret over the visions, Gwyn. You may have to accept they're merely dreams—your mind's fears of an unknown future."

"I guess," I say, exhaling. "I'm just disappointed, but I can't expect to excel at every area of witchcraft, especially since I gained my skills so late in life. Although, I seem to do better when I sleep in my own bed. I'll try tonight."

"Have you spoken to your mum and dad about how you feel?"

"No. Why upset them? They're dead. They aren't responsible for me now."

He chuckles. "True enough." He squeezes my hand. "I have to tell you something, and I'd rather say it now before we get to the house."

"Your expression tells me what you're going to say is not good news. Spit it out."

He presses his lips together. "Detective Schmidt came by yesterday. He had already stopped to talk to Seamus when he questioned me."

"About what?" I ask, my heart fluttering.

"He asked about our relationship—if there was a time we weren't together. He asked whether you could have been seeing Nick...romantically."

I hyperventilate and rub my chest. "What did you tell him?"

"I stretched the truth. I told him it wasn't my job to keep track of your social life when we were apart. But he said he had a witness who observed you standing in the street with Nick the night Thomas Hall collapsed. And that Nick was shirtless."

"Fuck. Fuck, fuck." I bite my thumbnail. "I'm a suspect, then?"

"Don't panic. There's no body to examine, Gwyn. No proof at all. Only suspicions."

"And Seamus? What do you think he said?"

"No clue. But he came to your defense before. I expect he told him nothing new. I know you still don't trust him. Have you—"

"No. I've been too busy with that damn useless crystal grid. But I need to make plans." Like another visit to his house, except this time, I need to go inside and inspect the premises. He's hiding something. My witch sense says so.

Archie parks his Tesla. The outside of the farmhouse needs as much work as the inside, but the kitchen is the most important. We grab our painting tools and enter the dusty house. Boisterous chatter trickles into the hallway. Tyler shouts from the kitchen.

"Is that you, Mom? We're in here sanding the cabinets."

"Good morning, everyone," I say, strolling in.

We're met with a chorus of greetings.

"Zach helps his dad paint all the time," Skye says, rotating a screwdriver. "So, I dragged him along."

Her boyfriend glares at her as he removes a cabinet door. "Pfft. You bribed me with promises of chocolate cake later."

Archie laughs and sets his toolbox on the kitchen table. "You've been productive. With all of us sanding and painting, we should get the cabinets done in a jiff."

All the young witches are here: Tyler, Zoe, Tanner, Spence, Skye, and her boyfriend, Zach. They're already busy as bees removing the cabinet doors. We're wearing our dingiest, oldest clothes to paint in. Ronnie isn't coming, because she's been so fatigued. Menopause hits you like a truck, unfortunately.

I set my purse on the table and clip my hair up. I'm so glad we have this project to take my mind off Archie's news bomb. My hands shake as I pick up a sanding block, and I wipe sweat from my face. Tyler walks over to me.

"Are you OK, Mom? You're flushed."

Spence stops sanding and darts to me. "You're one step from the grave, Gwyn. You should go home and rest." He lays a hand on my temple.

"Stop fussing," I say, fanning my face. "I'm fine. It's just a hot flash."

Archie rubs my back. "We should tell them, Gwyn. Your mum is worried the detective investigating Nick Evans's disappearance suspects she's involved. He's been asking questions about their relationship."

Spence snickers. "Well, he's good at his job, because he's right."

"I don't think you need to confirm that with Gwyn," Tanner says as he sands.

I frown at Spence. "Oh, let him ask. Nuada's corpse is halfway to California by now. And even if he found the body, it looks nothing like Nick now. He can't prove anything."

Zoe stacks a couple of cabinet doors on the table. "No. Nuada resembled a dead alien from outer space."

"Can we change the subject?" Tyler asks, hugging me. "Once we remove all the doors, we can sand and paint. We won't get much done today. Too much prep."

Tanner grabs a damp rag and wipes down the surface of the wall cabinet he's working on. "We should pull up this retro vinyl flooring today, too. Find out what's hiding underneath."

Spence bursts out laughing. "There's probably pot in the floorboards from the '60s."

"Or dead bodies." Zoe chuckles as she examines the flooring. "It's so gross. We should wear masks."

"I brought large putty knives," Zach says on the way to the door. "They're in my car."

Archie gestures to his toolbox. "There are a couple in my bag as well."

As Zach exits, familiar voices echo in the hallway.

"Who could that be?" I ask.

"It's Jeff and Kate," Skye says. "She really wanted to help. A way to thank us for all the support we've given her."

Archie stops sanding. "We should limit our conversations while they're here."

"Shh," Tyler whispers. "Here they come."

Jeff walks in with Kate following him. "Hey, everyone. We're here to help. Skye said you could use as many bodies as possible."

Tyler waves to them. "Thanks for coming. We have less than two weeks to finish this before Agnes and Leslie return from the UK for the Summer Solstice Celebration."

When Kate appears from behind Jeff, I gasp under my breath. The peachy color is gone from her skin, and her cheeks appear sunken, almost skeleton-like, as if she's not eaten for days. Her hair is thin and stringy. Spence thought *I* looked like death.

"I'm so happy I could help," she says, shyly. "I want to share my thanks in any way I can."

Archie carries a couple of sanding blocks to her and Jeff. "We're delighted you could help us. Have you ever painted cabinets?"

She laughs. "No. Never. But I'm a quick learner."

"I'll show you how to sand," Jeff says, motioning her to follow him. "Why don't I set up a drop cloth in the hallway, and we can work on the floor?"

"Awesome idea." Zoe grabs an old sheet. "I'll help you lay the cloth. There's too many people in here, anyway."

"Are you complaining about moi?" Spence asks.

Zoe rolls her eyes. "I would never do that."

Tanner chuckles. "He does have a way of spreading out and taking over a space, doesn't he?"

"Keep up the complaining, hun," Spence chides. "See if you get any nooky later."

Kate laughs as she moves toward the door. "I love how you all joke with each other. I can't remember, but I don't think my other family laughed much. Well, we better get to work, Jeff." She walks into the hallway with Zoe.

"Thank you so much for accepting Kate into your circle," Jeff says. "She's so happy, despite not knowing who she is. We're helping her to become a new person."

I pat his shoulder. "We like her a lot, too. I hope she keeps healing."

Jeff smiles. "Me, too." He turns and enters the hallway.

I dart to Skye, whispering so Kate doesn't hear me. "She looks worn out. Has she been working extra shifts at the Raven Pub? Or are they demanding too much of her when she's there?"

"I don't think so," Skye says. "But I've been working extra hours, too."

The others shuffle to us and huddle as we continue the discussion.

"What could have happened at the Raven to affect her so badly?" Tanner asks, his brow wrinkling.

Tyler grimaces. "He could be working her too hard because she gets paid under the table."

The mom in me comes out. "Maybe she shouldn't be bussing tables. I know Elijah and the counselor at the shelter believed it would be good for her to work. But she's had obvious trauma. She should concentrate on healing."

"We should alert Elijah and let him handle this," Archie whispers. "I've known the manager of the Raven Pub since I moved here. He's a kind soul. We shouldn't be making accusations without merit."

Zach ambles into the kitchen with the putty knives. "Sorry it took me so long. What are you doing? Please, tell me this isn't some kind of witchy spiritual football huddle before the final countdown."

Skye cracks up. "I'll tell you later when we're eating cake."

"That I can sign onto," he replies.

For the rest of the day, we sand the cabinets and rip up the vinyl flooring. We're pleasantly surprised to find old pine floors, but that presents another problem. We'll have to sand the wood and apply a finish before the hedge witch returns. I'm thinking two weeks wasn't enough time to complete this quick renovation.

At lunch, Kate picks at her sandwich, consuming a small bite and forcing it down her throat with a drink of water. What happened to you, Kate?

Chapter Twenty-One

TRUTH IN THE CLOUDS

Archie walks through the gate, meandering through the Celestial Gardens under the brilliance of the moon. Strips of fog block his view as he turns his head to the left. He falls to the ground, struggling to fight off something or someone. A distinctive warped growl, almost like the distorted cry of a woman mourning, fills the air. Instantly, the dream jumps to the cat sith fairy roaring deeply and standing on his hind legs. Nearby, a blue entity floats below billowy gray clouds, like the stormy swirls in Seamus's macabre painting.

I wake, gasping, to a hint of sunlight peeking through the curtains and grab my upper chest. The labradorite crystals worked. I can barely move my legs, and my back hurts like a bitch. I pull my legs into my chest in a fetal position and wrap my arms tightly around them, summoning my magic with a healing intention. Breath in. Hold. Breathe out. Repeat.

As I wait for my legs to regain their strength, I recall the vision. This is the first time the blue entity has appeared. Is this the cat sith's alternate presentation? And why did the strokes of the painting appear? Since Archie has pledged not to go into the gardens until I've solved this riddle, shouldn't his image disappear?

Sleeping on my back helped increase the intensity of my vision, but now the pain is so bad, I probably can't stand up straight. I roll out of bed, moaning, and walk to the bathroom bent over like my Aunt Gorawen. While I sit on the toilet, I realize I haven't spoken with her since right after Ostara. I should arrange a time with Tyler.

On the way back to my bedroom, Mr. Yeats circles around my feet. "Good morning. Only ten more days, and Dr. Hughes and Ms. Pritchard return."

I try to straighten my back, but moan like a....sick cat. The familiar transforms into his human persona and grabs my elbow.

"Ms. Crowther, can I assist you in any way? You appear to be in severe pain."

I frown at the feline. "You think? At least I didn't fall on the floor this time."

He scowls at me as he helps me walk back to my bed. "If you insist on continuing to add crystals to the grid, especially labradorite, the side effects will increase. You don't possess the years of training other seasoned witches have accumulated. Perhaps you should stop."

"Not when I'm having success." I push his arm away as I sit on the bed. "Only a few more should complete the dream sequence. At least, I hope that's all I need."

Mr. Yeats becomes sullen. "I worry about you, Ms. Crowther. If anything happened to you, Dr. Hughes and Dr. Cockburn would—"

"I'll make a deal with you. The next time, you can stay in my room overnight. In case I have trouble waking. Deal?"

He straightens the vest of his suit. "I would be honored to assist you."

"Just don't sleep at the bottom of my bed. It's creepy."

"Deal." He adjusts his spectacles and ambles toward the doorway. "If you need me, I'll be in the magic room tidying up."

As he makes his way down the hallway, I ruminate over the appearance of Seamus's painting in my dream. Time to snoop. I check the time on my cell phone. It's nearly nine. I search for the DUB Summer Session schedule. It's Monday, so he has a class at ten. I have enough time to get cleaned up and dressed.

I dress in a T-shirt and shorts because the temperature is supposed to hit the upper-70s. But it's raining. So, I lock up the house and stroll up Drummond Lane, pulling my sweatshirt hood over my head. Since I don't want Seamus to see me, I turn onto Sussex Way and walk up Douglas Street to Kent. I tiptoe in my sneakers to the backyard gate and sneak in. My phone reads 10:00 a.m. He must be gone by now, but I peek into the back windows to confirm.

I scan the surrounding properties to make sure no one is standing in their windows or outside in their yards, which is unlikely because of the rain. Then I dart up the back porch steps and stare at the doorknob. Even if I'm using magic to unlock the door, it's still breaking and entering. But once you've committed murder, it hardly seems like a big deal to add another crime to the list. So, I summon my witch energy and wave my hand across the knob. The lock clicks, and I enter, removing my wet sneakers to avoid leaving a trail of drips throughout the house. First stop? The bathroom.

I dash inside and close the door to examine the painting of the Dearg Due. The strokes used to paint the clouds seem similar, but Archie could be right. Amateur painters can resemble each other because of basic instructions. I open the photo of Archie's painting on my phone and compare the two. They could be the same, but it proves nothing. And I couldn't imagine Aunt Gorawen painting such a grotesque image. I shove my phone back into my pocket.

The next stop is his bedroom. I rummage through the drawers of his nightstand again, but find the usual: reading glasses, books on Irish folklore, nail clippers, an extra phone charger, and a flashlight. The large closet on one side of the room contains shirts, slacks, shoes, and ties, along with a couple of baskets holding gloves and hats. I'm wasting my time.

Suddenly, the front door creaks open, and I panic. What am I going to do? Hiding under the bed is the only solution, so I slide underneath to the center. My heart pounds against the wooden floor while perspiration dampens the surface. Why is he back here? Did he forget something? When Seamus limps into the bedroom, I hold my breath as he retrieves a few items from a drawer. He walks back toward the doorway but stops for a moment and turns. My chest is so tight, the pain spreads throughout my torso. He chuckles and leaves the room, slamming the front door shut when he leaves.

My lungs explode with a burst of air, and I gasp. I peek out to make sure he's gone. As I slide out from underneath the bed, I recall his faint laughter. What an oddball he is. I dust off my shirt and scan the room. Nothing left in here, but then I remember I haven't checked the narrow closet in the corner, the one that was locked when I snooped before. I jiggle the knob, but it's still locked. With a slight wave, the lock clicks.

When I open the door, I discover several boxes in a stack. Most are empty or have loose unused items of little consequence. A couple of framed pictures are resting between the pyramid of cardboard and a wall. The first one I pull out is an old oil canvas of fairies dancing near a stream in the woods. I guess he had no room to hang these last two paintings and stored them in here, but why lock the closet? Are they expensive pieces of art? I slide the creatures of the forest back and pull out the other halfway.

Swirling clouds with strokes of gray suggest a storm, and below is a field of wildflowers. I slide the painting out further. My jaw drops. I'm staring at the image of my mom in a rust-colored dress, and she's reaching toward the impending storm. Strands of her brown hair hook on to tufts of wind. I push the painting back.

WHAT THE FUCK?

I close the closet door, set the lock, and dart to the back to put on my sneakers. *My sneakers.* Fuck. Did he see them? No. He didn't come back here. I exit, locking the door behind me with a wave of magic, and I run all the way to Archie's house in the pouring rain.

When I arrive at his house on Duncan, I push on the front door and enter, yelling, "Archie!" I kick off my shoes.

"In here, my love," he replies from the kitchen. "I have a class at 11:30 a.m., so I'm making lunch early. Have you eaten?"

I stroll through the doorway, still panting from my run and drenched from the rain.

He turns around when I don't answer. "What's wrong, Gwyn? You're soaked."

"I just came from Seamus's house. I snuck in there."

"For fawk's sake, Gwynedd. He could have caught you, and what excuse would you have had for being there?"

"He must have cut his first class short, because he came back for something. I hid under the bed."

Archie brings me a tea towel. "Here. Wipe your face with this. So, you found nothing, I assume."

"Oh, I discovered something. Holy crystals. I found a painting hidden in his locked closet."

"Of what? What was in the picture that would upset you like this?"

"A duplicate painting of my mom." I point toward the living room. "Like yours over the fireplace."

Archie's eyes bulge out. "One of your aunt's paintings?"

"A slightly different color of dress, but yes. It's one of Aunt Gorawen's paintings. This is too fucking weird, even for me."

"Your aunt said she painted hundreds of them and spread them all over. He must be under the spell that was cast on the picture. It explains a lot of things, doesn't it?"

"I suppose. I'm gonna have to tell Leslie when she returns. And I should ask Aunt Gorawen if there's anything I can do to cancel her spell. Or he'll follow me around for life."

Archie chuckles. "You believed he had some kind of sinister secret? Turns out, he's only acting under the charm of the painting."

"I guess so." I pull off my sopping hoodie and sit down in a chair.

He places a plate with a spinach and hummus wrap in front of me and a sandwich for himself. "Iced tea or water? Have you heard the news?"

"Iced tea. No," I say, taking a bite. "What now?"

"Don't spit out your food, but this will really make your morning." He sets the glasses of tea on the table and sits down across from me. "Someone reported the sighting of a cougar behind the Raven Pub. When Animal Rescue arrived, the elusive cat was feasting on the dead body of another young male student."

I stop chewing mid-bite. "Shit." I swallow. "And was the body missing blood?"

"Aye. Strange that a cougar would lap up the blood, but it is a cat."

"Stop. I don't wanna hear anymore, or I won't be able to finish my hummus wrap."

He chuckles. "I didn't think anything bothered you now. You can read the report online if you want the rest of the details."

"I can't believe it. My dreams are filtering the stress and worry. Seamus's gross painting was in them last night. It's why I went to his house to snoop."

He caresses my arm. "Well, now you have your answer. He's only a victim of your Aunt Gorawen's protection spell."

"I suppose. Thank you for lunch, honey." I squeeze his hand and stare into his icy blues. "You pamper me."

"You can return the pampering later tonight in bed." He bends over to kiss me. "Now that you know they've caught the cougar, you don't need to enhance your visions. So, you can sleep here."

I smile coyly and rub my nose on his. "I can't wait."

While I sit in the booth seat at the Sunshine Garden Café, I recall last night's lovemaking and chuckle. It's amazing how satisfying sex is without the worry of your lover getting jumped by a cat sith...or a cougar. A slumber devoid of those frightful visions has left me refreshed for the first time in weeks. These forty-eight hours have completely changed my outlook, except Detective Schmidt still suspects me in Nick's death. I have to say this for the Bearsden Police Department. They have a competent investigation division.

You can sense the relief in the townies, too. Several people around me babble about the capture of the cougar but are so saddened by the death it left in its path. Five young men, all students at DUB, lost their lives to the prowling cat. At least the town can get back to some kind of normalcy—aside from the portal to the Otherworld hiding in its midst.

My tank top and jean shorts aren't warm enough for the chill of the café. Goosebumps rise on my arms, and I rub my skin. Ronnie bangs through the double doors of the kitchen and approaches me, a glum look contorting her face. She plops into the seat across from me and runs her fingers through the white stripe in her wavy crimson hair.

"What's wrong?" I ask, frowning. "Did Derek dump you?"

She grimaces. "What? No. We're fine. I got upsetting news this morning at my doctor's appointment, and I don't know how I feel about it."

"Oh, Ronnie. I'm so sorry." I reach for my best friend's hand. "So, it's definitely early menopause?"

She lifts her eyebrows and cackles. "Fuck no. I'm pregnant."

"Whaaat?" A grin slowly spreads my lips. "That's fantastic. Why aren't you happy? It's what you wanted?"

"The doctor says it's probably a change of life baby, and I'm high risk. Derek wants a baby, but he doesn't want the pregnancy to ruin my health either. He's so torn. I need your advice. What should I do, Gwyn? You've always had a good head on your shoulders, and I trust your judgment."

I laugh. "Really? I married the most worthless man. He cheated on me and cared more about his girlfriend than me—even asked about her first from the Otherworld. Then I fall in love with another man who turns out to be a womanizer, too. OK. So, maybe that one turned out all right. But how about Nick? Got involved and slept with the very supernatural being who was going to snatch me away to the Otherworld to fulfill a prophecy."

She snickers and waves at her waiter, Andrew, to come to our table.

"And you know how *that* turned out." I exhale and peruse the menu. "I'm the last person you should ask for advice."

"But look at you now. All this shit you've been through, and you're moving along just fine. Devoted boyfriend. Successful son." She leans over the table and whispers. "Badass ancestral witch." She falls back against her seat. "Yeah. I trust your judgment, because you're a survivor."

I grin at my friend. "OK. Here's what I think. You wanted a baby. Well, you're getting one. Is there a risk? Sure. There's always a risk with any pregnancy. But you're so healthy, Ronnie. And…" I bend over the table. "You're a witch. I'm sure there are some spells we can cast to help nurture the growth of this future Fellowship member." I pat her hand and lean back. "You'll be fine, and the baby will be healthy. My witch sense tells me so."

She grins. "Thanks, Gwyn. I already feel so much better about it. Maybe you can give that pep talk to lover boy to quell his nerves."

"I'd be happy to. I'm gonna be an aunt. Well, the closest I'll ever come to being one."

"You'll be great," Ronnie says, grinning. "Leave that calendar open for some babysitting."

Andrew arrives at the table, and we give him our orders.

"You didn't say when the baby is due?"

"It's gonna be a Yule baby. Can you believe it?"

"That's wonderful. Except you know the kid will complain about getting a Yule present for his birthday every year. Tyler whined about it growing up when we celebrated Christmas. I used to lie and tell him he was special because he was born on Pearl Harbor Day. He didn't appreciate that when he got older and found out it's not a holiday."

She cackles. "Let the kidney bean complain. They'll get nothing. Enough about me. You seem in good spirits. Is it a relief to know the cat on the prowl was actually that cougar instead of a cat sith fairy?"

"Yeah. Such a weight lifted. So much so, last night's frolicking lasted half the night." I yawn and cover my mouth. "Sorry. It's not the company."

"I wish I could stay up that long and get some. Pregnancy has knocked me on my ass."

"It will improve in the second trimester. I promise." I crouch over the table again and whisper. "The only thing I'm still unsure of is Detective Schmidt's investigation. He has suspicions but nothing else. Even if he figures out I slept with Nick, he can't tie me to his...disappearance. The only person I think can do that is Seamus, and he won't tell Jack anything. I figured out why I imagined he was stalking me, because he was."

"Oh," Ronnie says, tilting her head. "Spill the tea."

"I snuck into his house and found something."

She cracks up. "For fuck's sake, Gwyn. You took a chance. Well, what did you find?"

"He came back to the house, and I had to hide under the bed. But after he left, I got into the locked closet in his bedroom. He had one of Aunt Gorawen's paintings in there. He's under the spell of the picture, so I'll have to chat with her and see if there's a way to cancel its effects on him. It's not fair. He should be leading a normal life in Northern Ireland instead of following a middle-aged woman around in the US."

"That's unbelievable. I hope she has some kind of antidote for his sake."

Our food arrives, and I salivate over my Pad Thai noodles and tofu. Ronnie lifts her water glass.

"To a positive future. I've gotta use this, because I can't drink alcohol or caffeine now. I'm so glad I had a dry spell during my first trimester. A witch's intuition?"

I clink my glass against hers. "Absolutely. To a healthy pregnancy."

"Here, here." She drinks half the glass. "And to a strong bladder."

CHAPTER TWENTY-TWO

A LIKELY SUSPECT

By Tuesday morning, the doom and gloom of the storm has moved north, leaving sunny skies and a temperature in the low 80s, which my chilly skin welcomes after the arctic environment of Ronnie's café at lunch. As I cross the street to Mystic Sage, I receive a group text from her announcing her miraculous news to the Fellowship. A plethora of congratulation replies ensue. I grin like a grandma. Now that the worry over Archie's demise is gone, we can spend more time at Agnes's and finish the kitchen renovation. The Elder and the hedge witch return on June 19th, only eight days away.

When I enter the store, Jeff is bagging a customer's wares. He waves as I walk around the counter to stash my purse underneath.

"Thank you for shopping at Mystic Sage," he says, handing the attractive young woman her items.

She bats her eyes. "Thank you for helping me find the perfect puzzle for my younger brother. He'll love it."

"You're welcome," he replies. "We aim to satisfy our customers one hundred percent."

"I'll have to remember that." She smiles at Jeff and exits the store.

I chuckle. "You're so oblivious. That girl was flirting with you, and it flew over your head like a bat heading for the rafters."

"Really?" he asks, his eyes darting back and forth. "I didn't notice."

"That's because your heart belongs to another," I say, pointing to the glass door.

Kate enters, displaying a sweet, cheerful grin. She appears more refreshed than the last time I saw her. Her face is fuller, if a bit tired. Elijah must have spoken to her boss at the Raven Pub, because she's a whole new person today.

"Hi, Gwyn," she says, waving. "Are you ready for our late lunch, Jeff? I have to work after, so I'd like to get there as soon as possible."

He checks his phone. "Do you mind if I take off for lunch a little early?"

"You're the boss, Jeff. Remember?" I ask.

"Oh, yeah. I should probably practice." He clears his throat and speaks in a lower voice. "Ms. Crowther, mind the store. I'm off to lunch."

I snicker. "Sure, Mr. Williams."

"That was ridiculous. It's not me. I sounded like a stiff older than Shane."

Kate laughs in a girlish voice and reaches for Jeff's hand. "Let's go. I'll see you on Saturday, Gwyn."

"Thank you for helping. We have so much to finish, and an extra pair of hands will get the project completed in time for Agnes to return. She'll be so happy."

"I don't know. Does anything put a smile on Ms. Pritchards's face?" Jeff asks.

"One or two things. Have a scrumptious lunch," I say, waving.

A steady stream of shoppers flows in and out of the store, the door dinging and clanking for the next two hours. Since Jeff got the website set up online, we've been busier than ever. Diversifying the merchandise to include unique jewelry and pottery by local artists has brought in customers who would have never browsed the occult items. Although I love working for this young man fresh out of college, I miss Shane. It will be great to see him when he arrives at four.

I hope to rest for a few minutes, but a familiar face enters the store just as the last customer exits. It's Detective Jack Schmidt. I stand tall behind the counter, as tall as my short frame can fake standing in sneakers, and present him with a confident smile.

"Good afternoon, detective. Are you here to finish your questioning? The store is busy today, so get them in before another shopper strolls in." I won't cower at his accusations. He can't tie me to Nick's disappearance. Unless...

"Not exactly." He scans the merchandise in the store and gestures to the occult items. "Do you really believe in any of this hocus-pocus?"

A mischievous grin erupts on my face, recalling the time I asked Shane the same question, and I remember his words. "Many things exist in this world beyond our basic understanding, Jack. The mind is a powerful entity. Who's to say what is and isn't real?"

"You got that right. Lots of strange shit happens in this town, and I hear talk...unbelievable stuff."

I swallow. "What have you heard?"

"Aww, forget about it. It's only conspiracy bullshit. But catching a cougar that drinks the blood of its victims? That's some real shit I never imagined I'd see."

"Me neither, but I don't think you came here to discuss the cougar, did you?"

He cocks his head. "Nah. I left you the other day at the house in a pretty irate state. It's not your fault the cat bit me. I stopped to apologize. So, I'm sorry, and I hope you won't report my behavior to my superiors."

"Oh, of course not. Never crossed my mind." He's not asking about Nick? "I expected you to ask me more questions about Dr. Evans." The minute the words trickle out of my mouth, I regret mentioning him. What was I thinking?

"Well, since you brought it up. I have heard rumors about you and the professor. That you may have been a little closer than just friends."

My body stiffens. Oh, tell him the fucking truth, Gwyn. He can't connect me to his disappearance. "Are you asking me or telling me, detective?"

"Were you romantically involved with Dr. Nicholas Evans?"

I clench my teeth. "Yes. I dated him a few times. Archie and I weren't together. Well...I was kinda seeing them at the same time, actually."

"Playing the field, were you?" he asks in a snarky tone.

"It was complicated. But I stopped seeing him...like *that*. But we remained friends."

"And the last time you saw him was..." He checks his notepad. "Was on the night of that concert Dr. Seamus Duffy mentioned."

I can't lie to him. He'll know. I wring my hands under the counter. When I was with him last, he wasn't Nick. He was Nuada. "Yes."

He presses his lips together. "I'm done for now, but you should know, former lovers are often suspects in a missing person case like this."

"Should I get a lawyer, detective?" I ask, gritting my teeth.

He stares into my eyes without blinking. "Do you need one?"

"No. I don't." I cross my arms.

He shoves his notepad back into his pocket. "Enjoy the rest of your afternoon, Ms. Crowther. I may have more questions for you later...at the precinct."

I glare at Jack as he exits the store. If ever I needed to learn how to hex, now was the time. Screw that whole "do no harm" bullshit. I text Archie and fill him in, but tell him I'm not crawling under a rock. Telling the truth was the best thing I could do. As far as Jack knows, I had no motive to get rid of Nick. Unless he asks me the question directly, of course. And then I'm fucked.

Shane arrives, and I share what happened with Jack Schmidt while we work on the new pottery display. I wish I could talk to him about Cordelia. He really needs to know she's messing with the portal. But we still don't know what she's doing, and the four of us—Elijah, Trinity, Archie, and me—haven't caught her doing anything else.

"He hasn't come to me to dig up any dirt on you, darling," Shane says. "Not yet, anyway. But be assured. I'd lie through my old, yellow teeth for you."

"You're the best, Shane, but I don't expect you to lie to protect me."

"I know you don't, but I would." He kisses me on the top of my head. "I'm so excited for Ronnie. Derek must be elated."

"He is, but he's concerned about her, too. I told him we'll all be there for her."

"He doesn't need to worry. We'll make sure she sails through this pregnancy." He twists strands of his beard. "Thank you for eating dinner with Cordelia and me the other night. She can be a handful, and I realize you all may not take to her like I do. I see how the two of you throw glares back and forth. Strong women don't always see eye to eye. No need to hide your feelings from me."

"I'm sorry. I hoped I did a better job of covering that up." My face flushes. "I'm so embarrassed."

"Don't be. You don't have to take a shine to Cordelia. You're not sleeping with her." My boss bursts out laughing and pats his bit of a pouch. "But I hope you can tolerate her, because she's brought immense joy back into my life."

My gut churns. "I'll do my best. What if down the road you discover she's not the witch you remember? People change, and sometimes not for the better?"

He shoves his hands in his pockets. "I'll cross that bridge when I get to it."

If only he knew the bridge was already on his doorstep.

A cool breeze sends a chill up my spine on the way to Mitchell Hall, so I slip on my hoodie. As I pass the front iron fence, I catch Amnesia Kate walking out of the Celestial Gardens. It's not a good idea for her to be going in there late at night. She could see the Seelie Fae children playing. I dart to her. "Kate!"

She flinches and turns around, looking peaked. "Oh, Gwyn."

"Let me catch my breath," I say, panting. "I know they've caught the cougar, but you probably shouldn't go into the Celestial Gardens at night. You don't know what or who could be in there." Like fairy children and a rule-breaking witch.

"No one was in there. I always check before I go in."

"Oh, that's good," I reply, relieved. "Why did you go in there, anyway?"

"Jeff told me about the couple who lived in this mansion. He said they really loved each other. Even carved their names on a bench in the right corner. I like to sit there and dream about a love like that."

"You mean the bench under the hawthorn tree? Yeah, I hear Rose and Alistair were a devoted couple. You could have the same special relationship, Kate. Sooner than you realize."

"Do you think so? Although I have no memory of my life before, I get sad when thinking about loving anyone. I believe someone hurt me badly in my other life."

"I know so. Your old life doesn't define your future, and Jeff cares about you very much."

She blushes. "I like him a lot, too. But whenever I get close to him—kiss him—a horrible feeling seizes my body. It frightens me. I can't talk to Jeff about it. It could scare him away."

"Oh, Kate," I say, hugging her. "Have you spoken with the counselor at the shelter? Or Elijah Jackson?"

"I told my counselor. She says it must be past trauma. We're working on it."

"If you ever need another ear to bend, you can trust me to keep our conversations private."

"Thanks, Gwyn. I may do that. Well, I need to get back to work. The manager let me take a break."

"OK. I'll see you on Saturday."

"Bye, Gwyn. And thanks for listening."

Kate rushes back to the Raven Pub, only a few buildings away, and I enter the gardens to play with Shailagh and Aonghas. But when I get to the back of the building, I discover an amazing sight—the blue apparition is twirling in the air, flying back and forth, as if it's pacing and waiting for someone or something. The iron gate swings open and footsteps approach. I jump behind the shrubs to hide, masking my magic. When enough time has passed, I tiptoe back.

Cordelia stands in front of the portal, absorbing energy of some sort from the entity into her amulet. Is she banking extra power to enhance her magic? For what purpose? She snaps her fingers, and the apparition swirls around, entering the portal with a rush of air. I run back to my hiding place behind the inkberry and wait for the clicking of her high heels to pass me by. To be sure she's gone, I wait a few more minutes.

I dart to the mound and call for the Seelie Fae. Within seconds, they emerge and skip to me.

"Aunt Gwyn! You've come to play?"

"Yes, but I have a question for you. I observed a blue being floating around the portal, and then it passed through. Have you seen it on the other side?"

"Yes, Aunt Gwyn," Shailagh says. "She's very sad and cries all the time."

"It's a she?" I ask. "How do you know?"

Aonghas pouts. "She told us."

"Did she say why she's so sad?"

"No," Shailagh replies. "I didn't think we should ask."

"One more question, and we'll play. Did she say why she crosses over to a witch here?"

"No. We didn't know she did that." Aonghas pulls on my hand. "Come on, Aunt Gwyn. Let's go play. We missed you."

The Seelie Fae drag me around the gardens playing "catch me" until I stop to rest. I stare back at the portal. I don't know what the Wicked Witch of the South was doing, but it must be nefarious if her actions are causing the entity to cry. Even an apparition deserves peace.

Chapter Twenty-Three

THE WITHERING OF KATE

Trinity stamps the heel of her purple stiletto on the wooden floor as she leans against her desk. Elijah has joined Archie and me in her office at Mitchell Hall to discuss Cordelia's latest antics. It's not as warm as yesterday, but our coven leader stands and opens the window a few inches. A warm breeze plays with her long burgundy hair as I tell her about the prior night's activities.

"It's too pretty a day to turn on the AC. We can all use some fresh air." She shakes her head. "Good thing we don't have to worry about that cougar now, so we can concentrate on this matter."

Elijah rubs his jaw as he theorizes. "Let me get this straight. Cordelia is sucking the essence, energy, life—whatever you want to call it—out of this being. And she's doing it regularly. What is her endgame?"

"I don't know. But the entity isn't happy about it. She's abusing it somehow. What are we gonna do? This being may not be after anyone now, but I worry the abuse could trigger it somehow. So far, it only picked me up one time, and I fell to the ground. But who knows what it will do if provoked? At the very least, we have to tell Shane."

"Shane can find out with the others. We should convene the coven for a special summer meeting," Archie says. "We made a promise to the young witches we wouldn't keep secrets from them when it concerns supernatural beings."

Trinity puts a hand on her hip. "You don't need to remind me of the new coven rules. I just don't think we should call a meeting with Leslie and Agnes gone. The Elder is supposed to be in attendance."

"When do the ladies return from the UK?" Elijah asks. "We should schedule it then."

I roll my eyes. "That will make their day. Agnes will be jet-lagged and bitchy."

Trinity snickers. "So, like any other day for her. Am I right?"

We all laugh, but we know she's not wrong. Leslie and Agnes won't be in any shape to attend a meeting. But what choice do we have?

"They return on the nineteenth," Archie says, scratching his goatee. "I doubt much can escalate in only a week's time."

"I don't know," I reply. "A lot of shit can happen in seven days. I could end up in jail charged with Nick's murder."

"What?" Trinity asks. "What the hell are you going on about, lady?"

Archie rubs my back. "We think Detective Schmidt suspects Gwyn in his disappearance."

"Oh, Gwyn," Elijah says. "Don't you worry. We've got your back. You remember that."

I squeeze his hand. "Thanks. I'm not that worried. He has no proof."

"And he'll never find it." Trinity grabs my chin. "Nuada's body is long gone, Gwyn. And there's no other evidence. Except for your suspicions about Seamus, of course."

Archie glances at me and chuckles. "We don't need to worry about him. Apparently, he's under the spell of one of Gwyn's aunt's paintings, like the one on my fireplace mantel."

Elijah's deep laughter fills the room. "So, that explains why you think he's been following you around. Because he is."

"It's not OK," I say, frowning. "I've been trying to set up a video chat with Aunt Gorawen. I'm hoping she has a spell to counteract the one in the painting, so Seamus can get on with his life. Her caretaker, Ellie, hasn't gotten back to me yet. She takes care of the farm, and it's a busy time of the year."

Trinity snickers and slaps the desk. "Doesn't that take the cake?"

"I'm glad you all think having a benevolent stalker is so funny. I feel terrible. He must have changed his entire future to find me. I'm just going to avoid him until I chat with my aunt."

"Let's hope she has a solution or we'll be searching Agnes's library for another spell."

Elijah motions toward the door. "I best get back to the shelter to help with lunch. I hear the renovations are going well in Agnes's kitchen. Do you think you'll finish in time? I'd help on Saturday, but we're short-staffed."

"No worries," Archie says. "We have plenty of bodies."

Trinity walks behind her desk. "I should return to work, too. The four of us should keep an eye out when we visit the Seelie Fae in the gardens. Let me know if either of you catches Cordelia in there again. Otherwise, I'll schedule a special circle for the day Leslie and Agnes get back. I'll say we're having a last-minute meeting for the Summer Solstice Celebration."

"Sounds good," Elijah says. "Have a great day, all."

The gentle giant exits, and we follow him out of the building. Archie and I stop to chat on the walkway in front of Mitchell Hall as occasional Summer Session students pass by on the way to the Raven Pub.

"I have to get to work," I say. "I don't like that we're waiting for Leslie and Agnes to return to schedule a meeting. They're gonna be pissed we didn't tell them right away about Cordelia messing with this unknown being. I'm worried it will blow up in our faces."

Archie squeezes my hand. "As you said, it's only seven days. For all we know, Leslie might remember this blue entity from her younger days when the portal first opened. It is disturbing not knowing what Cordelia is gaining from this being. I'll begin my shift in the gardens again, keeping the pranksters busy. If the apparition presents itself, I'll attempt to communicate with it."

"I don't think that's a good idea. You don't know how it will react after Cordelia has been draining it of its essence. At least tell me when your shift is once you arrange it. OK?"

"Of course, my love." He kisses me. "And you must promise me you won't get snippy with Detective Schmidt if he stops by again. Your sarcastic responses did little to remove you as a suspect."

"Well, he pissed me off. I only wish he weren't so good at his job. He knows I killed Nick. I can sense it."

"You can't fault him for being competent. Will I see you later tonight?"

A naughty smile sneaks on my face. "Yes. Fluff up the pillows for me."

He winks. "I'll do more than that, my love."

Customers roll in and out of Mystic Sage like a gerbil on a running wheel as I ring them up. Wednesday afternoons were always the busiest day of the work week, but with the new website up, all three of us have to work. Jeff checks on the inventory in the back while Shane adds new arrivals to the jewelry display. When we get a lull in activity, he stops to admire a pagan necklace with a blue celestial moon.

"This is pretty as a picture. Or a bright crescent moon. Do you think Cordelia would like this, Gwyn?"

"It's a beautiful necklace, but I doubt she'd wear it. She never removes the amulet from around her neck." I suck in my lower lip. "Don't you think that's odd?"

He rubs the bald spot on his head. "I have asked her about the amulet. She even wears it during...our private time." He grins and places the necklace back on the display. "She says it's an old family heirloom that provides her strength in her old years. I'll think on this necklace for a while. I wouldn't want to pressure her to remove such a cherished item from her daily attire."

"Personally, I would give her the necklace. She can always wear both."

"Fabulous advice. Thank you, Gwyn."

"You're welcome, boss." And I'd love to see if she removes that amulet.

The door dings, and I turn my head. The Wicked Witch herself has stopped by, dressed for a night on the town, but it's the middle of the afternoon. And she appears refreshed.

"A blessed afternoon, sweetheart," Shane says, kissing her on the cheek. "Were your ears burning? Gwyn and I were just talking about you."

Cordelia squints at me. "Is that right? What about, honeybun?"

"Nothing much," I say, because she's nothing much to talk about. "Shane wondered if you would like any of the new jewelry the store is stocking. I'm sure you'll have an opinion." Of course she will.

She shimmies over to the display case in her tight pencil skirt and examines the contents. "Who chose the selections?"

"Gwyn did, sweetheart," Shane says. "Didn't she make some marvelous choices?"

Cordelia rolls her eyes. "They are adequate, but you should have asked me, honeybun. I would have found much better options for you. These trinkets aren't worthy of your store."

What a bitch she is. Surely, Shane observes how rude she is now. How can he let this pass? I stand behind the counter, blinking.

"Well, now...I believe Gwyn did a wonderful job choosing outstanding pieces," he says, flashing me a supportive grin. "She has been a wonderful help to me and my store for two years. And I'll tell you what, sweetheart. She's been the best thing to happen to Mystic Sage and the Fellowship."

The Wicked Witch of the South pinches her lips and turns from the jewelry display case. "Well, I can see my opinion doesn't matter to a hill of beans."

"Oh, sweetheart," Shane says, hugging her. "I value your opinion greatly. Gwyn just has more experience with retail. Now when it comes to crystal use, you win on your years of practice."

"I'm sure of that, honeybun." She sends me a side-eye.

I grind my teeth and offer her a compliment. "I didn't know it was a competition, but I'm sure you do." Holy crystals. I sure hope the sex is worth it, Shane.

"What can I do for you?" he asks. "I didn't expect you to stop by."

"Oh, I only wanted to invite you to dinner at my apartment. I have something special prepared for you. Please, say you can come?"

My boss glances at me. "The store is packed like sardines on Wednesdays. I'm not sure I'll be able to slip away."

For whatever reason, he loves this witch, so I suck it up and offer. "Jeff and I can handle the shoppers. The two of you enjoy dinner." And dessert. I suppress my need to snicker.

"Are you sure, Gwyn?" Shane asks.

"Yes. I mean, I haven't asked the other boss, but he's a softy, anyway. Just like you. I see why Cordelia likes you so much." I glance at her and force a smile.

"That's very, very kind of you, Gwyn," Cordelia says. "I...I appreciate your willingness to take on the extra work."

I nod and press my lips together to stop the explosion of laughter. Thanking me must have torn tendons in her face. A few customers enter the store with a ding.

"We better get back to work, but I thank you for stopping by, sweetheart," Shane says. "Come by at five, like usual?"

"That's perfect, honeybun." She kisses him on the cheek and exits the store.

And I think I'm going to vomit. June 19th won't get here soon enough.

By Saturday, the town activity has returned to normal. Follow-up stories about the young men who lost their lives to the cougar crops up in the local news occasionally. Mostly, people have stopped talking about it. But I bet the families of those students haven't forgotten. It's easy for the townies to put the deaths behind them when the funerals are out of town. How sad for all of them.

The skies don't have a cloud in sight, and it's already 70 degrees when Archie and I arrive at Agnes's house dressed in our painting clothes. Jeff and Kate are working in the garden outside, and we find the young witches hard at work. The kitchen stinks of fresh paint, and it's in shambles. They've almost finished painting the cabinets except for the doors. The wooden floor remains rough and unvarnished. In addition, the counter and sink are missing. Zoe and Skye are in the hallway, checking the cabinet doors. Tanner, Spence, and Tyler's elevated voices resound in the kitchen.

"What's going on?" I ask as I enter. "Something happen? What are you pissed about?"

My son wipes his face with his hands. "We're not mad at each other. The home improvement store we ordered the countertop and sink from was supposed to install them tomorrow."

"And now they aren't," Spence says, picking at the paint in his hair. "A delay in the shipment. So, the countertop won't get installed for three weeks. But the appliances will arrive. So, there's that."

"That's not OK. Agnes will flip out without her kitchen counter and sink."

"No worries," Archie says. "We'll put the old counter and sink back temporarily until the other comes in."

Tanner grimaces. "Uhh...we can't do that."

The three of them eyeball each other.

"Why not?" I ask with a raise of my eyebrows.

Tyler clenches his teeth. "We threw it out, Mom."

"What?" I gape at them.

"Is it still out back?" Archie asks. "We can clean it up."

Zoe walks into the kitchen with a cabinet door in her hands. "Nope. They took it to the landfill. I told them they should wait, but no one ever listens to me."

"We can put some boards on top of the base cabinets while she waits," Skye says, ambling in. "But she'll have to live without a sink."

"This is not working out how I planned." I puff air through my lips. "She'll be a bitch to live with when she sees this."

Spence snickers. "Like we'll notice a difference."

"It was optimistic to think you could pull this off in the two weeks they were gone," Archie says, opening a paint can. "Agnes will survive. We may need to bring her dinner for a couple of weeks." He stirs the paint.

I stare at the floors. "When are these getting done?"

"I'm applying polyurethane in the evenings this week after work," Tanner replies. "Tyler and Spence are going to help."

Tyler frowns. "I'm really sorry, Mom. I thought we could reno this kitchen fast with everyone chipping in to help."

"You can't control contractors, son. Don't worry about it. Worse things could have happened." Like an out-of-town witch abusing an apparition in the Celestial Gardens. I've got to keep things in perspective.

Jeff walks in from outside. "Kate and I finished weeding. She's still watering the garden."

"Did you make sure not to pull out her *money* plants?" Spence asks, pretending to count the bills. "Agnes would turn you into a frog or one of her gnomes if you even did it by accident."

Jeff laughs. "Yeah. But I didn't tell Kate what they were. Better she not know. She really enjoyed the gardening. She whistled and sang the entire time—old Irish tunes. I asked her how she knew them, but she couldn't remember that either." He peers into the hallway. "Before she comes in, I wanted you to know how worried I am. Her health has taken a nosedive again, and I don't get it. She seems happier than ever."

"Jeff already spoke to me about it," Skye says while she screws in a cabinet door. "She's been eating in front of me, so it doesn't make sense. I mean, she could eat more, but it seems like enough."

Zoe picks up a screwdriver. "Unless she's barfing it up."

"That's really blunt," Tyler says. "Sorry, Jeff."

She cringes. "I'm sorry. Sometimes the words just pour out of my mouth. I don't have a filter."

Tyler laughs. "Sometimes?"

"I thought you loved that about me?" she says.

He hugs her. "I do. But should we buy you one?"

"Good luck finding one that works." Spence hands Tanner a few sanding blocks.

She nudges Tyler and chuckles. "What he said."

"It's all right," Jeff says. "The fact is, I'm worried that's exactly what she's doing, and I'm afraid to confront her about it. We've only been dating a short time, and I don't want to create more stress and affect her healing process."

"But Zoe may be right." A crease forms between my eyes. "Has anyone told Elijah?"

"I have," Skye says. "But I inspected her bedroom when she was at work. No evidence of that, and I've never heard her throwing up in the bathroom. I just don't think she eats enough."

Tanner sweeps the floor with a broom. "If she has past trauma to work through like we think, she's gonna have these ups and downs. We need to provide her with steady support."

"No doubt," Archie says. "We should alert Elijah and the counselor at the shelter. They're responsible for her treatment. I'll be in there painting a door if you need me." He walks into the hallway, carrying the paint can and a brush.

Spence grabs a paintbrush and follows him out. "Right behind you, Archie."

The screen door slams, echoing in the foyer. Soon after, Kate shuffles in. Holy crystals. The last time I saw her, she seemed fatigued, but now she's absolutely gaunt. Her T-shirt hangs like a bag on her skinny frame. But she's grinning as if she's the happiest girl in the world.

"Hi, everyone," she says, waving. "I finished watering Ms. Pritchard's garden. I love all the flowers, even the ones that aren't so pretty—the ones with seven leaves."

Tyler quashes a smile. "Yeah. Those are Agnes's favorite."

"Are you feeling OK, Kate?" I ask tentatively.

"Yes. Why do you ask? I'm full of energy and love being around all of you, especially working outside."

I smile at Kate, hoping it's only the hard work outdoors that has her appearing so withered.

"Since you feel so great, can you help me hang this door?" Zoe asks, displaying her signature grin.

"I'd love to help." Kate walks over to her and supports the bottom of the cabinet door.

"We need to stop chatting and get back to work." Tyler shoves a paintbrush in my hands. "That includes you, Mom."

I blink at him. "You're giving orders?"

"Someone has to stop you from talking." He joins Tanner on the floor to sand the wood.

I scowl at him, and my young friends chuckle at my expense. I flip them the bird as I walk out of the kitchen with my paintbrush.

A storm rolls in after lunch, darkening the kitchen in a blanket of gloom. The rain pelts the roof all afternoon, and we work nonstop until the dinner hour. By the time my stomach growls, I'm too beat to eat. I glance at Kate while she folds the drop cloths. Could this happen to her, too? Does she get tired and forget?

"Bye, everyone," I say, getting into the passenger seat of Archie's Tesla. "We'll see you tomorrow to finish up what we can."

Tyler waves. "Bye, Mom. Bye, Archie."

"See ya tomorrow, you guys," Zoe says.

While Archie backs up the Tesla to turn around, Jeff and Kate get into his car. She falls into the passenger seat, almost disappearing into the fabric. Oh, withering Kate. What happened to you?

CHAPTER TWENTY-FOUR

SELF-FULFILLING PROPHECY

ON THE WAY TO Archie's house, the sun peeks through the clouds, sparking a rainbow. If I weren't so tired, I'd smile. Trinity sent out a group text inviting everyone to a special summer circle for June 19th, the day Leslie and Agnes arrive from the UK.

"The young witches are going to be miffed we didn't tell them about Cordelia and the apparition in the gardens."

"We're not keeping it a secret. Only choosing to wait a few days until we've informed the Elder before we meet. We can't forfeit all the rules, or why have them? Trinity will take the fall."

I exhale. "I understand, but I'm dreading it. Ronnie won't be happy about it either."

"She's preoccupied with baby thoughts," Archie says as he parks in Leslie's driveway. "I'm sure she won't care. I spoke to Derek to wish them well. He's already making plans for a nursery. Why don't you let me fix you something to eat?"

I yawn, opening the car door. "Thanks for the offer, but I have to take a nap or I won't have the stamina or the libido for tonight."

"In that case, get plenty of rest." He kisses me, offering his tongue, and a sensation twitches between my legs. "But don't rush over. I forgot it's my shift with the Seelie Fae tonight."

"What time will you go? I'll set an alarm."

"I'm going early. Around nine. The city will lock the gate by then. I should be back by 9:45."

"Don't let them wear you out. I have plans," I say, wiggling my eyebrows.

"Well, then. Get to bed, my love."

I wave goodbye, and Archie drives off as I push in on the red side door to the kitchen. After I kick off my shoes, I grab a chunk of cheddar cheese from the fridge and head to my bedroom. Mr. Yeats scuttles down the hallway and stops at my doorway.

"Yes. You can come in," I say, hopping on the bed.

He jumps up on my bed and sits, his black and ginger tail wagging back and forth while I pet his head.

"We worked diligently on Ms. Pritchard's kitchen renovation today. I'm pooped. Wouldn't it be great if we could just use magic? But no. Our coven only uses witch energy when necessary." I rub my lower back. "My back would like to have a discussion about changing those rules."

I bite into the block of cheese and chew, going through the motions but not really enjoying its nourishment. I glance at the crystal grid on my nightstand, now collecting dust. It felt like a dis when Shane said Cordelia would win out on crystal expertise. I shouldn't take the comment personally, because he's accurate. She's got decades of experience, and I can't even use a full grid to enhance my dreams. Or can I?

"Mr. Yeats, I'm going to take a long nap. If I'm not up by 8:30 p.m., pounce on the bed and wake me up."

He nods and jumps onto the floor, heading to the doorway. I dart to my family's steamer trunk and lift the lid, collecting all the small crystals I can find. There aren't enough of them left to fill the grid, but only a few spaces are empty. The familiar stops before leaving the room and transforms into his human persona.

"You're going to use the grid, Ms. Crowther? I expected you would postpone your crystal practice since they discovered the cougar was killing those unfortunate young men."

"I did. But I'm only sleeping for a couple of hours to see what happens with a few more crystals on the grid."

He examines my collection on the nightstand. "That's more than a few, Ms. Crowther. It's nearly filled."

"I'll be fine. Now, shoo. Don't forget to wake me."

Mr. Yeats crosses his arms and sighs. "When you wake and can't walk on your own two feet, don't say I didn't tell you so."

"Shoo." I chuckle and push him into the hallway, shutting the door behind him.

I hop on the bed and lie back on my pillow, channeling my intention and pulling on the energy of the crystals as I fade into slumber. Watch me, you Wicked Witch of the South. I'll be neck and neck with you after this nap.

Archie enters the Celestial Gardens, lit by a partial moon. He ambles toward the mound through streaks of fog but stops and scans the right side of the backyard. The warped cry of a woman, almost animalistic, catches his attention, and he turns his head toward the portal. The blue apparition flies around him, and he gets caught in the mini tornado and falls to the ground. He grimaces and shoves his hands at the attacker, summoning his witch energy. The vision cuts to the cat sith jumping on him, but he's already unconscious. The enormous black cat rises on its hind legs and roars at the indigo sky.

I wake, gasping for breath, and blink repeatedly to re-wet my contact lenses. But everything remains blurry, and the smell of singed hair permeates the room. I check the ends of my locks and confirm I've lost an inch of my brown tresses. When I attempt to lift my head off the pillow, I can barely raise it an inch. My skull has the weight of an anvil. I touch my legs, but they're like rocks.

A muffled voice yells, "Ms. Crowther! Snap out of it! Wake up!"

Hands clap together in front of my face, and a visage comes into focus.

"Ms. Crowther! Wake up!" Mr. Yeats shouts.

With a final thunderclap of his hands, his voice becomes clear. "Can you hear me, Gwynedd?"

"Yeah," I say, moaning. "Don't shout. My head will explode."

"I wasn't going to tell you, but I told you so. You weren't ready for so many crystals in that grid. I have a mind to—"

"Shut the fuck up. I don't have time for this. What time is it?"

He checks his pocket watch. "It's 8:40 p.m. You don't have to be so vulgar."

"I said to wake me at 8:30." I sit up and summon my witch energy, applying the amber glow to my legs, but my magic is weak.

Mr. Yeats purses his lips. "I've been shaking you for ten minutes. You were in a deep sleep."

"Oh, my gods. Where is my phone?"

I find my cell under the covers and call Archie. "Pick up, pick up." It goes to voicemail. "Fuck. Fuck. Fuck." I leave a message. "Archie, I just woke up from my nap, and I had a vision. Don't go into the gardens." But I realize he's probably on the way and shove my cell into my pocket.

"Why shouldn't Dr. Cockburn enter the Celestial Gardens? Is he in danger again?"

"He always was. You need to help me get out of this bed. I have to get there and stop the attack."

I slide out of bed and fall onto the familiar. He props me up as I hobble quickly to the mudroom and put on my sneakers.

"Ms. Crowther, you cannot go alone in this state. You need help. Unfortunately, I can't go with you. I'm not permitted to leave the house while I'm Dr. Hughes's familiar."

"No. You can't." I slip on my hoodie and throw my crossbody bag over my shoulder. "Light a red candle for strength and courage. And wish me luck."

"Will do, Ms. Crowther. Good luck," he says, straightening his vest.

I rush down the steps, running as fast as I can toward Main Street, and call Spence's phone. "Answer, Spence." I should call Tyler, too, but he's farther away.

"Hey, Gwyn. What's up?" he asks.

"Archie is in danger," I say, panting. "It appeared in a dream while I was napping. His phone went to voicemail. You and Tanner need to meet me at the Celestial Gardens as quickly as you can. The cat sith is going to kill him!"

"We're on the way, sis! Tanner, we need to go. I'll tell you in the car. See you in five minutes, Gwyn."

Five minutes. Five. Long. Minutes. He's not going to make it. I call my son.

"Hey, Mom. Please don't tell me you're mad about this afternoon. I was messing with you."

"No. I need your help. Archie's in danger. I had another vision. He's on the way to the gardens to do his shift playing with the Seelie Fae, and he won't answer his phone."

"I'm grabbing my keys. He'll be all right, Mom. See you in a few minutes."

Patrons shout profanities at me as I push through them on the paver walkways on Main Street. Still groggy from the overuse of crystal energy, I tumble to the ground several times. I brush off the scrapes and continue on.

When I arrive at Mitchell Hall, I rush to the gate, but it's locked. With a wave of my amber magic, the latch opens freely, and I run to the backyard. The air smells of wet earth and dried blood. It's too dark to find him. Remnants of clouds from the afternoon storm mask the moon, only allowing a sliver of light, but I see the black cat sith on its hind legs, roaring at the moon. Archie is lying on the ground next to him, blood seeping out of his neck. He's growing pale.

A rage overwhelms me. "Archie!"

I scream like a banshee as I summon my magic and hurl it at the cat sith. It yelps and runs toward the left side of the gardens, disappearing when it jumps the fence. I dart to the love of my life and crush my hand against his neck, casting a healing intention as I apply my amber magic. But the blood continues to ooze from his neck, only partially torn. My magic isn't back to full capacity yet.

"Don't you fucking die on me, Archie Cock-burn."

In the distance, car doors slam and footsteps approach. Tanner, Spence, Tyler, and Zoe have arrived. Their angsty voices overlap.

"Mom?" "Gwyn?" "Where are you?" "I think I see her."

"Over here!" I shout. "Near the mound!"

Spence shrieks. "Oh, my gods. What happened? The police said they caught the cougar?"

"Fuck! Is he alive, Mom?" Tyler asks as he kneels next to me.

Tanner and Spence drop to the ground and examine his neck.

"What can we do, Gwyn?" Tanner asks. "Should we call 911?"

"He looks terrible." Zoe plops down and touches his forehead. "He's still warm."

I stare at them, sweat rolling down my face. "I don't know. We can't call an ambulance. It wasn't a cougar. My healing intention is barely working."

I stroke Archie's face with my other hand as the color continues to dissipate from his skin. My son raises his hand and summons his witch energy.

"Maybe it's not enough. We need to add to Mom's intention."

All four of them place their hands on mine, combining their amber glow, and we chant a healing incantation together, repeating the final phrase. "Ancient moon, I call on your strength and might. Heal our loved one with this light." After a few uninterrupted minutes of chanting, the skin fuses, and we remove our magical hands from his body. But he's not moving.

"Why can't we call an ambulance?" Tyler asks. "He needs a blood transfusion."

"Because a cat sith fairy did this. YES. It was real, and I won't be able to explain what happened to him or why I was here. I'm already a suspect in Nick's disappearance."

"Why would the cat sith show itself now? After hiding all this time?"

"Contrary to popular opinion, I'm not a crystal ball. In fact, I'm not great at reading one either. I only know we need to get him back to the house."

Tanner scratches his head. "We def have to remove him before someone catches us in here."

"Zoe, go check out front and see if anyone is around," Spence says. "We have to move him to Tyler's hatchback."

"Gotcha. I'll wave when it's clear. I'll open the back of the car, too." She runs out through the gate.

"Well, let's do this, guys," Tanner says.

They slide their hands under Archie's limp body and lift him off the ground.

Spence grunts. "Ugh. His muscles weigh more than I thought."

"Don't drop him," Tyler says, straining his voice. "Mom will ground me."

Zoe waves to us from the sidewalk, and the young male witches lay Archie in the back with the seats down. I crawl in beside him and set my ear against his firm chest. His heart is beating steadily. We drive to Duncan Street, and Tyler pulls up to the garage. I unlock the back door, and they carry him into the house. Zoe follows the men in. The stairs present a challenge.

"Oh, fuck this," Spence says. "I think Trinity and Dr. Hughes would approve of us using magic to get him to bed so he can recuperate."

Tanner nods. "I agree. Let's do it."

"Mom. Zoe," Tyler says. "You should help."

"Yes. Of course." I take off my hoodie and move closer to Archie.

The five of us summon our magic, and Archie floats above our combined amber glow as we slowly ascend the stairs carrying his body. While he hovers over the bed, I remove one of my hands and pull back the bed linens. We lower his injured body to the bed. A faint line remains where the cat sith tore his skin.

"Help me get his clothes off," I say, catching my breath.

They all stand there gaping at me, frozen in place.

"What are you waiting for? Help me get Archie naked."

Spence talks with his hands. "Uhhh...are you really going to take advantage of him while he's incapacitated? I thought more highly of you, sis."

"That's just...not OK," Zoe says, clenching her teeth.

"What the fuck?" I yell. "I'm not going to have sex with him! He needs more healing. I'm going to connect my body with his and hope it rejuvenates his blood."

Tyler approaches the bed. "Exactly what I was thinking all along."

The others laugh as the anxiety of the situation catches up with us.

I chuckle at my offspring. "Sure, dear. And how about you, Tanner?"

"Never crossed my mind," he replies, chuckling.

After we remove Archie's shirt, pants, and socks, we stare at him, lying on the bed in his underpants. The room becomes silent as our nervous laughter fades. My eyes well up with tears, and Tyler hugs me.

"He's gonna be OK, Mom. My witch sense tells me he's going to make it."

I sniff and strip off my T-shirt. "Damn straight, he is." I unbutton my shorts and pull the zipper down. "Well, if you don't want a strip show, you need to get out of here."

They all amble out the door except for Spence. He turns around and blows me a kiss. "For luck, sis."

"Thank you," I say, shoving my shorts to the floor. "But it's not luck. It's magic."

He smiles as he leaves, shutting the door behind him. After I remove my bra, panties, and socks, I hop onto the bed. I yank his boxer briefs off and lie on top of him, pulling the sheet over us. I summon my witch energy and cast another healing intention—this time, calling on my magic to encompass our bodies. Heat builds in my torso and spreads throughout my extremities, triggering a hot flash. I wrap my arms and legs around him as droplets of sweat trickle down my face, dampening the bottom sheet.

"Don't you fucking die on me, Archie Cock-burn. You promised to love me forever. And forever doesn't end tonight."

Chapter Twenty-Five

KITTY, MY ASS

A HAND LIGHTLY STROKES my hair, waking me. Archie's heart beats a slow, steady rhythm beneath my ear. I squeeze his shoulders and lift my head. His sparkling icy blues are staring at me, a slight smile curling his lips. I slide up and kiss him.

"I thought I lost you," I say, tearing up.

"Apparently, not." He smacks his lips. "I'm dreadfully thirsty."

"I'll get you some water. Don't go anywhere."

I dash to the bathroom and fill a bathroom cup. When I return, he's pushed up against the headboard and running fingers across his healed wound. I straddle him and bring the water to his mouth. He gulps down every drop.

"Would you like more?" I ask, stroking his face.

"In a wee bit." He touches the injury again. "The last I remember, I felt the skin tearing from my neck. I blacked out after that."

"And what about before? Did you catch a glimpse of the cat sith fairy before it attacked you?"

Archie cocks his head. "It wasn't the black cat, Gwyn. The blue apparition attacked me."

"That makes no sense. The soul-eating fairy was there, right next to your body like it appeared in my dreams—upright with a white spot on its chest and roaring at the moon. I didn't imagine it. I shot a blast of magic at the being. It ran off and jumped the fence."

"Could the fairy present as the blue entity initially and transform into the cat, waiting for its victim to die?"

"Possibly? Did you see Cordelia in there?"

"Naw. I heard a faint growl and turned my head. If she was in the gardens, she was hiding."

"We can decipher this later." I lay my forehead against his. "I'm so relieved you're alive. You seem OK?"

"I think I am." He caresses my bare back. "I vaguely remember waking through the night engulfed in a bubble of magic."

I chuckle. "That's why we're naked. If putting naked bodies together works for hypothermia, I hoped it might work to rejuvenate you."

"Aye. I think it worked extremely well." He kisses me and becomes rigid underneath me.

I run my fingers through his wavy locks. "I guess so. But we shouldn't. You almost died last night. Conserve your strength."

"There's nothing wrong with me. Your healing magic worked wonders. I've never felt so alive." He swells more and rubs against me. "You may need to do more of the work, though."

I know he's still healing, but I want him. So, I guide him in. "I love you so much."

He places wet kisses on my neck while I move up and down, rocking the Victorian walnut bed. Only last night, I expected to bury him, and now I'm enjoying the expression of his love. Or at least lust. The headboard knocks against the wall, banging in closer intervals while we pant and moan. He takes a nipple in his mouth, and I can't hold back. I shriek as I reach my peak, and Archie follows right after.

I collapse against his chest, quivering. "Are you OK?"

"Aye," he says, stroking my back. "I'm so glad you saved my life."

I rub my nose on his. "Me, too. If I hadn't filled the crystal grid, I might not have made it in time."

"You added more crystals? What were you thinking?"

"Does it matter now? It made me groggy, but I recovered with Mr. Yeats's help."

"What made you try? You said you were done with the grid."

"Cordelia. Shane made a comment about her crystal skills being better than mine. It pissed me off, so…"

His brow crinkles. "That was foolish, Gwynedd."

"Yeah, well… If I hadn't done it, you'd be lying dead in the Celestial Gardens."

He raises a corner of his mouth. "Fair enough. All this dying and fawking has given me an appetite."

"I'll put on some clothes and go make breakfast. You stay here, and I'll bring it up to you." I kiss him and slide off the bed.

"I don't want to stay here. You can fill me in on the rest of what happened, and I can sit in the kitchen while you cook, in case you need pointers."

"You don't trust me to cook you breakfast?" I ask, pursing my lips.

"I want to videotape it for the archives." He laughs as he gets out of bed and staggers on his feet.

"Very. Funny. I've cooked you breakfast before. Can you walk?"

"I'm only messing with you, my love. I'll be fine. But I better cover up my nakedness. I wouldn't want to flash the neighbors."

I throw on my clothes and help Archie slip on his robe. He's not one hundred percent yet, so I steady him on the stairs as we take each step. The ticking from the mantel clock echoes in the living room and dings the first of nine. Halfway down, movement catches my attention, and I stop. The young witches, including my son, are standing in the foyer.

"You slept here?" I scan their gaping faces.

Tanner stretches his arms. "Yeah. We wanted to make sure Archie was OK."

"I'm doing well, considering," Archie replies, taking another step.

Spence snickers. "We figured that out already."

"You all stayed?" Holy crystals. They heard us. "I'm sorry, Tyler."

"It's OK, Mom. It's not like this is the first time." He chuckles and slaps a hand over his mouth.

"That was the first time we met," Archie says. "I cooked you breakfast."

Zoe snorts. "I remember Gwyn telling us what happened. It was the morning after you guys...you know."

They all laugh uncontrollably. Archie and I step onto the floor when we reach the bottom of the stairs.

"Ok. I've had enough embarrassment for the day," I say, my face flushing. "I'm going to get some food into Archie. All of you can go home. I'll call if we need you."

They take turns hugging him and grab their hoodies from the hall tree.

"We need to alert the others," Tanner says. "I know Trinity called a meeting for the night Dr. Hughes and Agnes return, but I think we should meet immediately."

I look away. They don't even know why we're meeting yet.

Archie nods. "I'll contact Trinity after I've eaten. It appears Gwyn was right all along. An apparition attacked me, but Gwyn saw the cat sith standing over me. We think it may transition while waiting for its victim to die." He hugs me. "But Gwyn hit the fairy with magic and sent it running. Saved my life."

Zoe sniffs. "That's so romantic."

Spence bursts out laughing. "And explains what happened in the bedroom this morning."

I scowl at him and point to the front door.

"Let's go, fam," Tyler says, rubbing my arm. "I'll call you later and see how Archie is doing."

Tanner opens the door. "Call us if you need anything."

"Wait." Archie's gaze bounces from one young witch to the other. "Thank you. All of you. I wouldn't be here without your devotion."

Tears well up in Spence's eyes. "Bro…" He hugs Archie again.

"I'm all right, friend. All of you, go home and get some rest. All of us will need our strength if we have to force a cat sith fairy back across the portal."

"Come on. We're really going this time." Tyler walks to the door. "Love you, Mom. Rest, Archie."

"Will do," he replies, adjusting his robe.

Zoe is the last one out. "Bye. Don't do anything I wouldn't do." She snickers and shuts the door.

Archie leans on me as we walk into the kitchen, and I help him into a chair. I put water in the kettle and set it on the stove.

"I really wanted to tell them about Cordelia. If the apparition and the cat sith fairy are one and the same, what is she doing with it? Is she sucking the souls of the dead from its being to build her energy?"

"I don't know, but I'll call Trinity and fill her in after I eat."

"Hmph. I better send Ronnie a text. She's gonna freak out if she hears about this from one of the young witches. We'll have to confront Cordelia about it. You know that. I don't think Shane will respond favorably." I type a message into my phone, updating her on what we discovered about Cordelia, the apparition, and Archie, and click send.

"Aye. An accurate assessment. We'll deal with that when we have to."

My phone vibrates. "It's Ronnie. She's freaking out, anyway. She's glad you're OK. I need to call in and say I'm not coming to work today. I should be here in case you need me."

Archie lifts a corner of his mouth. "Nonsense. We had sex. If that didn't kill me, I think I'm good."

"Well, I'm calling in," I say, taking out the frying pan. "Nothing will take me from you today."

"I won't argue with you, stubborn woman." His cell phone vibrates, and he reads the notification.

"Who's that? Other Fellowship members checking on you?"

"Naw." His brow wrinkles. "It's Seamus. He wanted me to know he's canceling class tomorrow morning. Says he got hit by something powerful last night and needs two days to recover."

I chuckle. "That's an odd way to refer to a virus. Now that I know he's under the influence of my aunt's painting, I'm warming up to the oddball professor."

"Not so creepy after all, is he?" He motions to me. "Come here."

I shimmy over to him, and he wraps his arms around my torso.

"So much has happened to you in the past few months. I worried about you after you killed Nuada. What the experience did to you? But you're such a resilient woman. I believe it made you a more powerful witch. Killing Nick gave you the strength to fight off the cat sith and save my life. And if any of Nuada's family should come across the portal, you'll be ready."

I cup his face. "My life would have been empty without you in it. I love you, Dr. Cock-burn."

He chuckles, pulls my mouth to his, and kisses me. "My heart is yours forever, my love."

Monday morning, I wake to a barrage of texts from my witch family. Trinity's group text alert triggers my phone to vibrate nonstop. I hate group texts. Buzz, buzz, buzz...

Archie sleeps late, so I cook us a hearty brunch of eggs and veggies when he wakes. After we eat, I reluctantly shower and dress for work. He waits at the mudroom door in a T-shirt and lounge pants while I tie my sneakers. I peer up at him, frowning.

"I wish you would let me stay and wait on you. How am I supposed to work knowing you're back here recuperating?"

"As soon as you leave, I'm meditating and heading back to bed, my love. Not much you can do if I'm sleeping. As much as I love having you around, you're..."

"Suffocating you?" I ask. "You don't need to throw a brick at me." I stand and kiss him. "I'll get out of your hair. Please, call me if you need anything?"

He wraps his arms around me and snickers. "The only thing I may need would require you to strip naked."

I slap him playfully and turn toward the door. "I guess you are getting better. See you tonight after work, honey."

A wave of hot air has invaded Bearsden, bringing us summer a few days early. There's not enough AC in the world to stop these hot flashes. My tank top and shorts are even too much. Would Jeff and Shane let me wear a bikini at work? I clip my hair and stroll to Mystic Sage through the Green.

When I enter Mystic Sage, Shane rushes over to hug me. "Oh, darling. I hope you received my text. I'm so sorry about Archie. Why in Sam Hill did you come to work today?"

"Archie is sleeping most of the time. Not much I can do, really. I would have made him mad, checking on him every five minutes."

He shoves his hands in the back pockets of his cargo pants. "So, you were right about the cat sith fairy. Trinity doesn't want to wait for Leslie and Agnes to return to discuss a plan to push the being back through the portal. We're meeting tomorrow night. That gives Archie time to recuperate."

"Yeah. We have to figure out a solution quickly before it attacks someone else." And we need to stop your Wicked Witch girlfriend from antagonizing the cat sith.

"Is Jeff working today?" I peer into the crystals room.

"He's in the back." Folds crease in his brow. "He was under the weather when he opened the store this morning."

"If he's sick, why didn't he stay home?" I ask, setting my purse behind the counter.

"He has an illness of the heart, I'm afraid. He said Kate broke things off with him."

Jeff drags his feet into the front of the store. "You're talking about me."

Someone yanked the smile right off of his face, leaving skid marks on his chin.

"We're worried about you, Jeff," I say. "Shane said Kate doesn't want to see you anymore. What happened?"

"Hell if I know. Her health hasn't improved since Saturday. Maybe she's depressed, and her cheery disposition was a facade. She said she didn't want to hurt me. But she did. So, I don't get it."

Shane hugs Jeff. "Give her time. She'll come around. I don't think her affection for you was disingenuous. She cares for you."

"I hope you're right. I'm gonna take a late lunch now that Gwyn's here." He ambles toward the door. "I'll be at the Sunshine Garden Café." He exits with a ding.

"I'm doubtful about this relationship, Shane," I say. "It was a mistake for me to encourage it. Amnesia Kate has too much unknown trauma to work through."

He strokes his beard. "Darling, we're all damaged. We must forge ahead to overcome the veiled wounds."

Mystic Sage has fewer customers on Mondays, so we spend the afternoon restocking the shelves and straightening up. Jeff wanders around the store, moping. After I take my dinner break, I send the bosses home. Shane walks up the street to visit Cordelia above Roots to the Earth, and Jeff goes home to an empty apartment.

I missed my shift with the Seelie Fae on Sunday, and Archie didn't get to play with them because of the attack. The last place I want to go is Mitchell Hall, but we can't afford to have Shailagh and Aonghas causing mischief on top of dealing with a cat sith fairy. So, I lock up the store and head down the street to the gardens. The night skies turn evil, with rolling mushroom clouds threatening to combust. Lightning flashes all around, and thunderclaps echo in the distance. I call Archie on the way.

"Hello, my love. It's after nine. Where are you?" he asks.

"I'm on Main Street. Passing the opening to the Green. How are you, honey?"

"Cracking. I slept all afternoon, ate dinner, and meditated with a healing intention. Why are you walking in that direction?"

"I have to stop by to play with the Seelie Fae. I'll be home as soon as I can. A storm is coming, anyway. They don't like the thunder."

"Forget the children. You shouldn't go in there after what happened to me last night."

"If I don't, they may get itchy and go into the house. We know what happened the last time they went in there during the renovations. You didn't expect the attack. The cat sith caught you off guard. I'll be ready for it."

"Stubborn woman," he mutters under his breath. "Please, text me when you're on the way home."

"I will. See ya soon, honey." I swipe the red circle on my cell.

When I arrive at Mitchell Hall, a young man staggers toward the garden gate like he's intoxicated, holding Amnesia Kate's hand. Oh, my gods. She's down to skin and bones. It's disheartening to see her with another man, and he appears to be drunk. She should have told Jeff the truth. But they shouldn't go in there. Not after last night. I'll have to make up a story to get them to leave. I run in my sneakers up the paver walkway and through the gate to the gardens.

Thunder rumbles as ominous clouds move in, and I scan the darkness. A bolt of lightning strikes nearby, and I spot Kate and the young man kissing on the grassy area in front of the mound. He passes out, and she pushes off the ground. I tiptoe to the side of the house to avoid being seen while she approaches the mound.

The portal lights up. Holy crystals. Kate's going to discover we have fairies. I walk toward the mound, and the apparition appears. Oh, my gods. I have to save her! I take one step and stop. The entity swirls around her, then seems to melt into her. It takes me a moment to realize it's hijacked her body. Radiating within a blue glow, she walks back to the drunken young man who's as limp as a wet rag and kneels next to him. What the fuck is the entity doing with Kate's body?

The possessed young woman raises her arms, and her body morphs into a hideous alternate form—a distorted mouth with unusually large, sharp teeth and hands with claw-like fingers. Her warped growl fills the gardens as the burgeoning clouds explode with pelting rain and ice chips. I stand frozen in my spot, shocked by the image, while the downpour soaks my hair and clothes. Kate, or whatever the fuck she is now, leans over her victim and places a hand near his neck.

"Kate! Nooo!" I shout. "This isn't who you are. Fight this demonic fairy."

The entity lifts its head when a bolt of lightning strikes near us and speaks in a feminine Irish accent. "There is no Kate."

The being lifts her monstrous hand to attack. I must stop her from killing another innocent victim. I chant and hurl a ball of magic at her, and she runs at me, snarling, with her claws extended. Well, that was stupid! I scream as she shoves me to the ground and swipes her claw-like fingers at me, scraping the sides of my face. The ice chips sting my skin as they beat down on me.

"Kate! I know you're inside there. Don't let this cat sith fairy force you to kill!"

While I wait for the apparition to transform into the fairy that eats the souls of the dead, a deafening roar approaches from behind. Abruptly, a humongous black cat pounces onto Kate's altered form, walloping her with its paws. The cat sith? Now I'm *very* confused.

She fights back, slicing into the enormous cat's hind leg—the one not already marred by a deep scar—prompting it to let out a high-pitched meow. Then something unusual occurs. The cat sith shoots amber magic from its sea-green eyes, and the blue apparition separates from Kate's body. The emaciated young woman falls to the ground while the entity floats nearby. She stands slowly and stares at me with sorrowful eyes while the rain continues to saturate us. The black cat paces back and forth beside me.

"I'm sorry, but I couldn't stop myself, and I don't know why," Kate says. "I know it's bad to take blood from these nice men, but eating food made me sick. One night I got the urge to drink blood, and...I got better. At least for a while. Then I'd get weak again, and I didn't know why. I lasted as long as I could this time. I broke up with Jeff because I was afraid I'd hurt him." She approaches the young man again, still passed out on the grass, and the blue entity follows her. "I have to do this."

"No, Kate. You can't." I try to get up, but my back aches. When the enormous cat jumps at her again, she darts out of the gardens. The apparition zooms into the portal and disappears.

The rain changes to a drizzle as the feline fairy approaches me, and I raise my hand, trembling. Was it fighting for the right to the soul of the young man...and mine?

"I don't know what you are, but stay back. Or I'll strike you like I did last night."

My jaw drops as the enormous cat sith stands on its hind legs and morphs into a human form—Dr. Seamus Duffy.

WHAT. THE. FUCK.

Chapter Twenty-Six

HIDDEN PROTECTOR

THE GLOOMY GRAY CLOUDS dissipate, revealing the illuminated full moon. Seamus stands a few feet away, naked as the day he was born, and his long, wet black hair glimmers in the moonlight. He's rather lean and toned underneath all those drab academic clothes he wears, except for the leg with the scar and missing muscle. He rushes to me.

"You're injured, Gwynedd. Let me heal you." He raises his hand.

"No. We don't have time. They're only scratches, anyway." I examine the wound on his right leg. "But you're injured badly. And we need to get this drunken young man out of here before the apparition crosses over again."

"Of course. I'll get dressed, and we can wake him."

"All this time, I believed there was a fairy." I shake my head. "You're actually a cat sith witch."

"Yes. I can explain later, but we should move quickly."

I roll over and push myself up while Seamus gathers his clothes where they lay strewn near the gate. He wakes the drunken man, and we send him on his way. The professor limps as we walk back through the Green, trying to avoid the light of the lampposts, and I help him into his house.

"Why don't you sit on the sofa? Where do you keep your first aid box?"

"In the bathroom storage cabinet, but you don't have to do this."

I cross my arms. "You just saved my life from that…whatever it was. I'm going to tend to your wound."

"If you insist." He props his injured leg on the coffee table.

"I'll be right back." I dash to the bathroom and pull out the first aid materials, glimpsing the morbid painting. After snatching two towels, I return to the living room.

"Dearg Due," Seamus says. "Kate is a Dearg Due."

I hand him a towel. "Like the image in the bathroom painting? The demonic ghost that sucks blood? Holy crystals. The night the first man died, I found her covered in blood in the Raven Pub restroom. She said it was her period. I don't understand. You said the Dearg Due was a vengeful woman."

"Yes. The folklore says she fell in love with a local peasant farmer. She and the young man talked of getting married and raising a family together, but her greedy father had other plans. He made the proposal of marriage to the chieftain of the village, despite the chieftain's known violent behavior, knowing the chieftain would reward him with many riches. Of course, the young couple were devastated, but she had no choice in the matter." He presses the towel on his dripping ponytail.

"Heartbreaking times for women." I wrap the towel over my head and towel dry my hair a bit.

"Yes, a wretched period. As expected, the chieftain was brutal. Locked her away for days on end. Eventually, she stopped eating and drinking and died. Legend states she was so enraged, she emerged from the grave with a thirst for revenge. First, she killed her father, and the chieftain after. And this is where the tale becomes most interesting. She drank the blood from his corpse and discovered it invigorated her so much, she couldn't quench her desire. After that, she would lure men with her beauty and the promise of love, only to sink her teeth into them and empty their bodies of their blood."

"No wonder Kate was avoiding Jeff," I say, opening the first aid kit.

"I suspected she had crossed over and evolved into a human form, separating from her spirit. I don't believe the ghost knows what she is when she becomes the human Kate. This new witch who moved to Bearsden, Cordelia Davenport. She's behind it, but I don't know what her purpose was in bringing the Dearg Due from the Otherworld."

"It has something to do with that amulet she wears around her neck. I watched her suck energy from the apparition into that glass vial. It may explain why Kate became emaciated and had to keep feeding on the young men. My guess is it was angry when it attacked Archie. Why didn't you warn us about all of this? You should have told us who you are?"

He smiles faintly. "I couldn't protect you efficiently if you knew I was following you."

"Yeah...well...there's a reason you do that." I pull out a cotton ball and the bottle of alcohol. "I'll explain after I treat your wound. Take off your pants."

The professor's eyebrows jump, and he shifts on the sofa. "I'd prefer not to strip in front of you, Gwynedd."

"Seamus, I've seen your dick. I think I can handle the sight of you in your underwear."

"Good point." He removes his pants and sets them next to him on the cushion. "You may proceed." He opens his legs to expose the injury on his inner thigh.

"This will sting a little." I wipe the wound clean with alcohol and set a cotton pad across the gash, placing a large adhesive bandage on top. "That should heal well without magic."

He smiles affectionately at me. "I'm forever indebted to your kindness. You have a tender touch, Gwynedd."

"Better than the magic blast I threw at you on Saturday night?" I ask, arching my eyebrows.

He laughs. "That was a powerful blow you sent me. I had to rest for two days."

"Why don't you fight as a witch? Why transform into a cat to fight?"

"I have more power in my animal state. I reserve the transformations for dire circumstances."

That explains why I only saw him twice. "Seamus, there is a reason you're compelled to protect me. I'm gonna confess something. I snuck into your house and did some snooping."

He laughs as he pulls up his pants. "I'm aware. I'm a witch, so I sensed you were under the bed."

"Fuck. Of course. And the day I fell in..." I shut my eyes.

"The rain barrel? Yes. I knew you were out there."

I peer back at him. "So, all this time, you were using a masking spell. But I felt your presence early on. And what about the buzzing that scared the shit out of me that day on the Green?"

"I had to make a personal connection at least once, so I would always know when danger was near you. That was the electrical charge you felt. The masking spell worked for everyone except you. It took some time before I discovered the flaw and corrected it. I couldn't protect you if you could sense my presence."

"Well, that brings us back to my...break-in. That painting in your closet? The one of a woman standing in a field of wildflowers, reaching toward an impending storm? That's the reason you have the compulsion to protect me. My Aunt Gorawen charmed hundreds of those paintings. Even witches respond to them. It's why Archie came to the US. You shouldn't be here. That painting brought you to Bearsden."

"Gwynedd, I'm a cat sith witch. Charmed paintings don't affect me."

I grimace. "Then I don't understand. Why do you have one of her paintings in your closet?"

"Because she gave it to me. I asked for a copy of the painting depicting your mother years ago, because I always admired her beauty."

My mouth falls open, and I squint. The first time he appeared to me was in Buckley. He said he was visiting a friend. "For fuck's sake. When I brought up your name in a video chat with Aunt Gorawen, she got off really quick. I guess I'll be having a talk with her soon. If I can get Ellie to respond to my fucking emails."

"Don't be angry with her." He lays a hand on mine—warm and comforting. "I wasn't lying when I said I was visiting a dear friend. I've known your aunt for many years. It was a mere coincidence that you showed up when I was visiting her. When you appeared on her doorstep, she called me. Asked if I would protect her grand-niece."

I avert my eyes, trying to soak in all the revelations. "It wasn't fair of her to ask you to give up your entire life to follow me across the Atlantic Ocean."

"She asked, yes. But ultimately, it was my decision to cross the pond. When Dr. Hughes asked me to fill in for one year, I pounced on the offer." He leans in toward me, a slight smile curling his mouth. "Pun intended."

I frown. "So, the painting of the cat sith in your office?"

"Yes. Gorawen painted that picture of me one summer when I was stuck in my transformation. I'd been hexed after making an abysmal decision."

"Was the scar on your leg a result of that incident as well?"

He nods. "Yes. Since then, I've been more careful."

"Archie's brother Quinn said a cat sith witch can only transform nine times, and the last transition is final. How many do you have left?"

He pushes off the sofa. "That's not your affair. It's extremely personal information that my kind doesn't share with anyone."

My phone plays *Don't Stop Believin'*, and I swipe the red icon. I send a quick text, telling Archie I'm on the way.

"You should get going. If I were Archie, I'd be rather concerned by now." He peers at the front door.

"Seamus, I can't notify any of the Fellowship members about what happened tonight without spilling the tea on you, too. But will you come with me to Archie's and tell him? Is your leg OK to walk?"

He stares at me, devotion shining in his sea-green eyes. "I will go wherever you ask, Gwynedd. Let me put on some dry clothes."

The professor changes and puts on his shoes. As we amble toward the front door, the memory of Ostara returns to me. I gaze into his eyes.

"You were there when I killed Nick. You saved me that night, too."

Seamus clasps my hand. "You did what was necessary, Gwynedd. Never let your mind think different."

We walk in awkward silence to Archie's house, and I recall all of our interactions from the beginning, including the time he stopped me from entering the mound in Buckley. Suddenly, a warm aura rushes over me, but I don't think it's a hot flash. This man has committed his life to me, and I don't feel worthy of it.

When we arrive at the small cottage, I push the front door in, and he runs to me.

"Where the fawk have you been? I've been tearing my hair out, and it doesn't need help at my age. You're soaked to the skin."

"I'm sorry. There's a lot to explain," I say, hugging him.

Dr. Duffy steps into the foyer, and the screen door shuts with a clap.

Archie cocks his head. "Seamus? Why are you here? Are you feeling better?"

"Yes. I am, thank you. Gwynedd asked me to come."

"Is something wrong?" Archie's icy blues flip back and forth between us. "What the fawk happened tonight?"

"We should sit down," I say. "Seamus has a lot to say. You may want to get the Scotch whisky out."

Tuesday morning, I drive to Ronnie's house and allow Archie his requested healing space. The summer heat continues as I stand at my best friend's front door, fanning my face with a lawn service flyer I snatched from her mailbox. When I enter, she lunges at me, wrapping my upper body in her boa constrictor arms.

"Oh, my gods, Gwyn. I can't believe what you've been through the last two days. Your witch sense was correct all along. How is Archie today?"

"He's sleeping a lot. Kicked me out. He said I was making him nervous." I follow her into the kitchen.

Ronnie cackles. "I bet. No offense, but sometimes your tender loving care can drive a person bananas. I'm speaking from experience."

"Well, I don't want to look back on my life and say I didn't do enough. Like when I didn't visit you in the hospital after the Sluagh attacked you." I sit down and rest my tired arms on the table.

"I know. But I wasn't even awake, so I didn't give a shit. I'll get you some tea." She shuffles over to the counter to prepare a cup of Earl Grey for me and an herbal tea for herself. "I received the text calling for a circle tomorrow night. Everyone knows about the cat sith now—the apparition in the gardens. But Trinity is going to spill the tea on Cordelia, isn't she?"

"Yeah. Thanks for not being mad I kept that from you. Trinity wanted to wait until Leslie and Agnes got back, but now we can't. I'm worried about how Shane will respond."

Ronnie sets my tea on the table in front of me and sits in a chair next to me. "No biggie. You've avoided telling him for too long. He needs to know she put the town in danger. Five young men gone. She should answer for it."

"Yeah. But I don't think he'll believe us." I wave a finger, and the spoon stirs the stevia in my teacup. "Cordelia will just deny everything. Frankly, I'm anxious about what she'll do."

"Leslie and Agnes can't return soon enough. We need their power to fight off whatever Cordelia is bottling up inside of her."

"Enough about the Wicked Witch. How are you feeling?" I ask, sipping my tea.

"Oh, I'm great. Eating everything in sight. Derek is clearing out the small bedroom for a nursery. You'll have to go shopping with me for a crib."

"I can't wait. I'm so excited for you. But don't you think you should sit out any circle we form to address what Cordelia is doing in the gardens?"

"Hey, don't become a helicopter mom on me. I'm only pregnant and feeling fabulous."

"OK. But please, take it easy. You shouldn't take unnecessary risks."

"Derek won't let me, anyway." Ronnie sips her herbal tea. "This stuff blows."

I chuckle. "Good. You'll acquire a taste for it."

"When the Otherworld implodes." She sticks her tongue out at me.

I sip my Earl Grey and swallow. "I have more to tell you. The apparition isn't a fairy."

Ronnie squints at me. "I'm confused. You said the cat sith attacked Archie."

"I was wrong. The apparition attacked him, not the fairy. And she attacked me last night, too—the scratches on my face are the proof."

"What do you mean, she? And what about the humongous black cat? You're making me dizzy."

"Ronnie, I'm gonna tell you what happened before everyone else hears the news at the circle tonight. But you're gonna need something stronger than herbal tea..."

CHAPTER TWENTY-SEVEN

A COVEN'S DILEMMA

THE OPPRESSIVE HEAT AND humidity continue with the Summer Solstice Celebration only days away, and fresh-cut grass irritates my nostrils and my eyes. My contact lenses grate like sandpaper on my corneas, and the hot flashes dampen my shirt. Archie, Seamus, and I stroll to the Pumpkin House on Victorian Row to attend the emergency meeting, occasionally wiping the sweat from our brows.

Seamus's cane clicks on the pavement as he walks, reminding me of his weakness in witch form. "Archie, thank you again for being so understanding. You had justification to demand my immediate resignation after learning of my deception."

"Under the circumstances, I understand," Archie says. "But I'm not so sure the coven will appreciate the secrets you kept under your hat when so many Unremarkables were dying in our town."

"We'll find out soon, won't we?" I say. "Seamus, you should wait back a bit. Give the meeting about ten minutes before you present yourself to the Fellowship. Trinity knows you're coming, but no one else does. Be prepared for some backlash, especially from Shane. He won't like you accusing his old love of wrongdoings."

Seamus bears down on his cane. "I'm prepared to accept whatever sanctions the coven may place upon me. But first, we must address the immediate issue of the Dearg Due and how Cordelia is involved in her presence here."

"Aye," Archie replies. "We must figure out how she crossed over into a human form, and Cordelia has those answers. We'll see you in a few minutes inside."

When we enter the parlor, the Fellowship is showering Ronnie with hugs and kisses. But they see Archie and rush to him, smothering him with a family embrace. We take our seats in the circle and fan our bodies with loose paper. The air conditioner hums more like a small jet engine as it strains to keep up with the unexpected heat. Trinity stamps her stiletto heel on the floor three times.

"Sorry about the foot pounding. I wouldn't dare start a meeting with the Elder's staff. By now, you've all heard about the attack on Archie in the Celestial Gardens, and we're all relieved Gwyn arrived in time to save him. We will meet again tomorrow night when Leslie and Agnes return to make final plans on how to deal with this supernatural aggressor before it kills again."

"At least the cougar was a suitable cover," Skye says. "But if it attacks again, the Unremarkables will become suspicious. Now I'm worried. Kate didn't come back to the apartment last night. I hope she's not a victim."

Archie locks eyes with me but says nothing.

Spence shoots his hands in the air. "How do we make plans when we don't even know how to fight a cat sith?"

"He has a fair point," Shane says. "We don't know enough about the being."

"Actually, we do," Archie replies. "There is an apparition in the gardens that has crossed over. It's what attacked me on Sunday night. We've known about it for a while. And it's not a cat sith."

Trinity puts her hands on her hips. "And before you young witches start screaming about breaking the new coven rules, I made the decision to shove the earlier sightings under the rug for a few days while we looked into the situation."

"And I agreed," Elijah says. "We only started to investigate, so there was nothing much to share."

"But that was before the entity attacked Archie." Trinity glances at me. "And Gwyn last night."

"This is getting fucking old, Mom," Tyler says, scowling. "You not telling me when you're in danger? Why didn't you call me?"

"She must have had a good reason." Zoe grins at me and rubs Tyler's arm.

Ronnie nudges me. "For fuck's sake, Gwyn. You didn't tell me about the prior incidents either."

"You know what? None of you are my keepers. I can take care of myself. And there were extenuating circumstances. Trinity had a reason to wait until tonight. We're telling you now that we have some answers."

"We all asked your mum to remain quiet on this, as well as another matter," Archie says. "Soon, you'll know and will understand why."

My son sinks in his seat. "Sorry, Mom. I care about you and don't like being kept out of the loop."

"None of us do," Tanner says. "And something tells me there's more to this story."

Trinity nods. "As always, you're perceptive, Tanner."

My fellow witches shift in their metal chairs as the room becomes quiet, waiting for the coven leader to continue. But before she can, the front door opens in the foyer, followed by the clicking of a cane hitting the wooden floor. Seamus enters the parlor in his summer academic attire, a black short-sleeved shirt and khaki pants.

Zoe sits up straight. "Dr. Duffy? What are you doing here?"

Skye and Spence glance at each other and shrug. Trinity motions for me to stand.

"I asked the professor to attend our circle tonight. Yes. I said circle. He knows we're a coven, because he's a witch—a cat sith witch who's been hiding for reasons you don't need to understand. He's the enormous black cat with the white spot I've seen twice...now four times."

Spence talks with his hands as his brain deciphers the disclosure. "So, all this time, you knew you had witches in your classes, and you kept your identity a secret from us?" He crosses his arms. "That was rude, Dr. Duffy. And deserving of a change in my grade from an A minus to an A."

"Good grief, Spence," Skye says. "He doesn't owe you anything, and it's too fucking late, anyway."

He scowls. "That blows. It was my only imperfect grade."

"Stop interrupting," our coven leader says. "We have a lot to discuss tonight."

I interject. "Dr. Duffy is going to share what happened when Archie and I were attacked."

Without divulging what brought him to Bearsden, he explains how he's been watching over us—me actually, but he doesn't tell the coven that. Only Archie and Aunt Gorawen are privy to his true motive. He describes the legend of the Dearg Due and how she lured the young men to feed off their blood to fulfill her urges of revenge. The young witches have questions.

"So, let me get this straight," Spence says. "The blue ghost is the Dearg Due, and Kate is, too? I don't know about the rest of you, but I'm confused."

Skye shakes her head. "That would explain why she didn't sleep in her bed last night. But Kate isn't a ghost. She's a real live woman. How can they both be this ghoul?"

"Kate is aware of her need to feed on blood," Seamus replies. "But she doesn't know what she is. Her spirit side crosses over and searches for her human presentation. Once the blue apparition connects with her, she finds a young man to feed on."

Zoe grimaces. "Eww. That's disgusting."

"Don't be hard on her," Elijah says. "She doesn't understand why she's compelled to drink their blood. She only knows she gets sick when she doesn't."

"I think I'm gonna barf." Ronnie covers her mouth.

"Ohhh...it's why she lost weight, even though she was eating food." Skye's eyes grow big. "Oh, shit. Does Jeff know?"

"No, he doesn't," Shane replies. "But it explains why Kate broke it off with him."

"She told me she cared too much for Jeff to hurt him," I say. "Then she ran off, and the apparition crossed through the portal."

Tanner throws a blue-eyed glare at the cat sith witch. "Personally, I'm pissed you didn't come forth with this information sooner. Five Unremarkables died because of your negligence."

"I agree," Shane says. "Why did you wait so long to divulge your true identity, professor?"

Because he had to figure out what your wicked girlfriend was up to, boss.

The other young witches join Tanner and Shane, shouting accusations at Seamus. "You had no right to hide your magic." "You could have saved those young men." "Why should we trust you now?"

"Enough!" Trinity shouts. "We can deal with your questions later."

Archie stands and rubs my back while he waits for the babble to die down. "I understand your reactions, and we will address Seamus's deceptions in the future. But he saved Gwyn's life last night. We owe him gratitude, not derision."

"You have every right to ask my motive for remaining silent for so long," Seamus says, scanning the circle. "And I have a right to my privacy. Cat sith witches are solitary beings who live their lives according to their own rules. I only agreed to divulge my secret because Gwynedd asked me to. But know this. I only recently discovered who Kate was. I could not have saved the young men.

But we can avoid any future killings by sending the Dearg Due back through the portal."

Shane nods. "Thank you for your clarification, professor. Do we know how the ghoulish demon separated, creating Kate?"

"Yeah," Tanner says. "How do we do that when there are two of them, and we don't even know where Kate is?"

Seamus scans the circle. "We know how to summon Kate. Someone pulled the Dearg Due through the portal using an incantation. Once she passed into our world, the spell created a human form, separating the spirit from her. We haven't figured out the rationale for the creation. We only know the person is accessing the energy from the ghoul following the feedings."

"And how do we find the person who summoned her?" Shane asks.

Archie glances at me. "We know who it is."

"Well?" Spence throws a hand up. "Are you going to tell us?"

The young witches lean forward in their seats while the rest of us hesitate. How can we tell Shane his beloved is responsible? I glance at Archie and Trinity, grimacing. I can't do it. The news will crush him. I catch Seamus staring at me, and he steps into the circle.

"The person is a witch who recently moved to Bearsden. Her name is Cordelia Davenport."

The young witches gape at each other and stare at the old hippie.

Shane huffs and shakes his head. "You're wrong! Cordelia would never do any such thing."

"Do you remember me telling you she was performing rituals in the Celestial Gardens?" I ask.

"That does not prove she's guilty of summoning a Dearg Due. Do you have proof?"

"Yes, I do. I watched her call on the apparition, and she sucked the essence out of it, pulling the energy into the amulet she wears. Trinity, Elijah, Archie, and I decided we should wait to tell anyone, because we didn't understand what was happening."

"For what purpose would she do this? You've never liked her, Gwyn. You're reading into this. There has to be some logical reason she did it, and I will ask her."

"No, Shane," Archie says. "You can't discuss this with her. Yes. We all have our opinions about Cordelia's personality. But we don't choose who other people love. This concerns the loss of five young students who would still be here if it weren't for the Dearg Due."

Tanner interjects. "Then what is he supposed to do? What are we going to do?"

"We'll have to devise a plan as we go," Trinity says. "Because we need Leslie and Agnes's input. May the gods help us when they find out the shit that's been going on. Shane, I'm asking you not to discuss any of this with Cordelia. You may have to use the Summer Solstice Celebration as a ruse to get her to the gardens. We'll have to confront her about all of this and hope she'll summon Kate and her spirit so the two can reunite and return to the Otherworld through the portal. And I promise you, if we find we were wrong about her, we'll apologize out our asses. Deal?"

Shane pinches his lips together, scowling, and his eyes hop around the circle. The witches nod at him, confirming their commitment.

"She'll prove you wrong. I will invite her to the solstice, and you'll see. There is a reasonable explanation. I bet she doesn't even know it happened. That's right. It was probably a mistake."

"Thank you for your cooperation, Shane," Trinity says. "Elijah, I'm gonna rely on you to alert our city council allies. We need them to keep the community away from the celebration. Tell the Unremarkbles it has to be a private affair this year."

"Will do," Elijah replies. "And I'll keep a lookout for Kate at the shelter. Let's hope she doesn't have the opportunity to attack another man."

Seamus taps his cane. "May I make a suggestion? If you can, Shane, keep Cordelia away from the gardens until the solstice. We don't need her draining the spirit again, prompting Kate to feed on an unsuspecting young man."

My boss twists his beard. "I'll do what I can. But I'm not making any promises."

"I'll text everyone with a time to meet once Leslie and Agnes are picked up at the airport," Trinity says. "Go in peace, my friends. And be careful."

I stand on the porch, watching Shane plod up the street while the rest of the witches chat with Seamus and Archie. Ronnie breaks off from the group and ambles over to me.

"Do you think he'll tell Cordelia we know about her and the Dearg Due?"

"I don't think so. He's angry, but he's loyal."

My fellow witches shake hands with Seamus and depart, leaving him with Archie. Tyler and Zoe shuffle over to us.

"I'm sorry I snapped at you, Mom," my son says. "But why didn't you text me after Kate attacked you?"

"A lot happened. I tended to Seamus's injury, and then he went with me to Archie's. By the time we finished talking, you were already asleep. I decided it was better to let you hear the news with everyone else."

"I don't know why you worry," Zoe says. "Your mom banished a Sluagh, helped stop the Kenilworths' from destroying the coven, killed a Tuatha Dé...and now she's fought a Dearg Due." Her mouth spreads into her signature grin. "She's a badass."

Ronnie cackles. "She sure is. I better get me and this growing little witch home and into bed. Derek has some milk waiting for me." She grimaces and smacks her lips. "Yum."

"We're gonna go, too," Tyler says. "See ya tomorrow night."

"Goodnight, you two," I reply.

Zoe waves as the two of them follow Ronnie off the porch. I walk over to Archie and Seamus.

"Can we go?" I ask, fanning my face. "That was a tough circle to get through. I need sleep and working air conditioning."

Seamus gestures with a hand. "After you, Gwynedd. Archie."

The two men, my protectors, follow me down the porch steps. We take our time walking up Main Street toward the opening at the Green in silence, accommodating Seamus's slower pace. The full moon glows brightly like an alabaster globe in the midnight-blue sky, signaling another night of poor sleep for me. It will test my patience when we pick up the Elder and the hedge witch tomorrow.

"Thank you again for attending the circle," Archie says. "Their anger appears to have subsided. But you will have to build their trust from this point on."

"It will be a challenge, but I aim to. However, I never intended for anyone to discover my presence. I'm here for a different purpose." Seamus peers at me out of the corner of his eye.

I glance back and forth at the professors. "If I'm such a badass, why do you think I need either of you as protectors? I can take care of myself, which I have proven more than once."

"She certainly has." Archie clasps my hand.

"Noted," Seamus says with a nod.

We arrive at Seamus's house on Drummond Lane and stop to say our goodnights.

"I will contact you tomorrow with the time to meet us in the Celestial Gardens," Archie says. "Our schedule may be tight picking up Leslie and Agnes."

"And we have to fill them in on everything they've missed. Sparks may fly." I raise my hands and mimic a fake explosion.

Seamus smiles. "Undoubtedly. I suspect Dr. Hughes will want a private meeting at the department when this is all over."

"You'll work it out, but you may want to plan on an extra class next semester."

"With that, I bid you both a good night's slumber." He gazes up at the full moon. "Despite our obstacles."

The professor limps to his front door, and we continue on to Archie's house. I glance back at Seamus.

"I don't know what to do about him. He's not here because of my aunt's charmed painting. Not because of the spell, anyway. I think he became infatuated with my mom's image. I'm worried he's obsessed with me and not only because Aunt Gorawen asked him to watch over me. He shouldn't stay here. It's not fair."

"You can't choose his life for him, my love—misguided or not. When the solstice is over, talk with him. I'm certain he'll be receptive."

I stare up at the full moon, appearing to swell and tug at my inner soul. My witch sense tells me this solstice is going to suck balls.

CHAPTER TWENTY-EIGHT

WHO'S THAT CAT?

ARCHIE AND I GRAB Leslie and Agnes's suitcases and throw them in the trunk of the Tesla. The women collapse in the backseat and exhale. The hedge witch complains immediately.

"Who let the demons out? Turn on the fucking AC. We left a cool fifty-nine degrees for this disgusting, sticky heat? I hope someone thought to turn my air conditioning on at the house. I wanna go straight there before you take Leslie home."

Leslie rolls her eyes. "Agnes, I told you to wear a short-sleeved blouse and layer."

Archie raises his eyebrows, and I turn around the best I can in this seatbelt that's strangling me.

"This is Delaware, Agnes, and the solstice is in two days," I say. "What did you expect?"

"Thankfully, we only have an hour to Bearsden," Leslie says. "I was smart to book our return flight to Philly."

I can't blurt out everything that happened in the first few minutes they're back. So small talk it is. "How was the trip? Did you have a good time?"

"The vacation was lovely. I showed Agnes some of my favorite places in Wales, and we finished up in London. She met a few British academic witches I've known for years."

And there's one more you don't even know about yet waiting in Bearsden.

Agnes purses her lips. "Those hoity-toity professors? They wouldn't know how to cast a spell on the fly if their lives depended on it."

"Yes, dear." Leslie pushes her silver bangs off her face. "We all know you don't like to follow rules or directions in a grimoire."

Archie motions to me to get on with it, and I prepare for the backlash.

"A few things happened while you were gone," I say. "And I need to update you."

Leslie lifts her chin. "Ah, yes. I read the Bearsden local news. Animal Control finally caught the cougar. So sad five young students lost their lives before they found it."

I glance at Archie and continue. "Yeah. But the town still isn't safe."

Agnes pushes her sleeves up. "What the hell do you mean? They captured the cougar. Are there two of them?"

"Not exactly," I say. "Hold on to your panties and let me finish explaining before you say anything. So, about Cordelia Davenport..."

I spend the next thirty minutes telling the Elder and the hedge witch about Cordelia's rituals with her amulet, the blue apparition, the appearance of the cat sith, and the recent attacks on Archie and me, leaving Seamus out of the equation for now. But I tell them about Kate being a Dearg Due and that we met in a circle the night before to make preliminary plans to lure her into a trap during the Summer Solstice Celebration. The two old women stare at me, expressionless, until I finish. Then they blow a gasket.

"That was entirely out of order!" Leslie shouts. "No circle should ever be convened without the Elder in attendance."

Agnes scowls. "There were ways to communicate, you know. Couldn't you have sent a fucking email?"

I frown at her. "You don't even have an email."

"Well, Leslie has one!" She throws her hands up.

The Elder glares at me and shakes her head. "What's done is done. Let's move on. So, it wasn't the cat sith, but your sightings weren't hallucinations. Cordelia called on this Dearg Due for a reason unknown to us yet. Has Trinity scheduled another circle to finalize the plans?"

"Yes," Archie replies. "Tonight at the Pumpkin House. Shane agreed to invite Cordelia to the celebration. We will confront her about her actions with the hope she will confess what she did to the Dearg Due. The plan is to reunite her two forms and send her back through the portal before she kills again."

Agnes grimaces. "I'm confused. Gwyn, you and the others saved Archie from the attack. But I missed the part that explained how you got out alive. Who saved you?"

"And what became of the cat sith? Why was it there?"

"Uhhh…" I stare at Archie, and he nods. "It's not a fairy. It's a…he's a—witch. And he helped me fight off the Dearg Due."

Leslie gapes at me. "You said he. Who has been hiding among us here in Bearsden? It was highly irregular and rude not to register their presence with the local coven."

Agnes cracks up and slaps the seat. "Sweetie, you've got to give up on your outdated rules. No one gives a flying fuck. Who is this witch, Gwyn? Anyone we know?"

"I…uh…" The Elder is going to lose her shit. "Yes. He works in the Celtic Studies department with you."

"What?" Leslie's eyes bulge out. "Dr. Seamus Duffy?"

"Before you flip out," Archie says. "He came here at the request of Gwyn's Aunt Gorawen to protect her from the Tuatha Dé Danann."

Agnes laughs like a hyena. "You can't trust those fucking academics, can you?"

"But all these years I've known him, he never divulged his identity, and I never sensed he was a witch." The Elder stares out the window.

"He used a masking spell," I say. "Except when he needed to form a connection with me."

"Obviously, I am relieved he was there to help you repel the Dearg Due, but he will need to answer for his deception."

"He understands the coven will expect his cooperation," Archie says. "He will participate on the solstice and help return the ghoulish demon to her rightful place in the Otherworld."

Leslie exhales. "I don't know how I will address him. He has lied to me all these years."

"Oh, who gives a fuck?" Agnes asks. "Witches aren't perfect. They each have their path to follow. Seamus had his and divulging his truth didn't mesh with yours. Get over it."

We turn onto the gravel road that leads to Agnes's house, and Archie parks the Tesla.

"About fucking time," Agnes says. "I wanna see my kitchen."

"Yeah. About that," I say, getting out of the car. "There are a few things to finish."

"What?" She shuts the car door and marches up the porch. "You said it would be done."

Leslie and I follow Agnes into the house while Archie retrieves her luggage. The hedge witch stares at her unfinished kitchen, her face wrinkling like a prune.

"We worked very hard while you were gone, but...shit happened," I say. "The countertops couldn't be delivered on time, but the appliances are in—just not installed. With the attacks on Archie and me and the discovery of the Dearg Due, we told Tanner not to worry about finishing the floors until after the solstice. We have more important shit to conquer."

She crosses her arms. "How the fuck am I supposed to cook my meals?"

"We'll make sure you're fed," Archie says, putting her bag on the floor. "We'll take turns bringing you food."

Leslie puts her arm around Agnes. "Nonsense. That's a waste of time and gas. You can come and stay with me while they finish your kitchen."

"What? Won't it get a little crowded?" I ask. "There's only one bathroom."

"You can always stay with me, my love," Archie says.

Leslie raises her head, grinning. "Splendid. Unpack and get settled, dear. I'll be back later to pick you up. I must go home and see Mr. Yeats."

"Mr. Yeats," I say. "I haven't been back to the house since all these attacks happened."

"More reason to leave immediately." Leslie heads toward the door. "He's probably rearranged the books in the office several times by now. See you tonight, Agnes."

"Yeah. Yeah," she replies, waving her hand.

We hop back into the Tesla, and Archie drops us off at Leslie's. I drag her luggage up the steps. What does she have in here? A dead body? Holy crystals. Books. She bought more books. She nudges the red side door open, and the familiar darts to her.

"Dr. Hughes, I'm so happy to see you. Ms. Crowther hasn't been home for..." He sees me carrying her bag and scowls. "Where have you been, Gwynedd? It's been days since you left. Have the decency to report to a familiar when you're going to disappear."

"I'm sorry," I say. "It's a long story."

He crosses his arms. "I have all day, so you can begin now."

"She doesn't have time for that, Mr. Yeats," Leslie says. "I'll explain later. If you want to help, you can roll my bag into the bedroom."

"As you wish, Dr. Hughes." He lugs the bag down the hallway.

"Gwynedd, I am relieved you are safe. Can I assume you had no time to catalogue new spells into the database?"

"No. I confess I've been a bit distracted with all this. But if Cordelia could come to Bearsden and pull a Dearg Due through the portal, what else can cross over? We have to continue our search for a spell to close it, even if it takes years."

Leslie pats my hand. "You shouldn't be burdened by this worry. I'm to blame for the mound. We will find one, eventually. Meanwhile, we have a spirit to contend with."

Archie, Leslie, and I pick up Agnes, eat a quick dinner, and make the trek to the Pumpkin House. The old women drag their exhausted bodies up the porch steps and enter the parlor. My fellow witches shower them with hugs and welcome them back to the circle.

Leslie avoids speaking directly with Seamus and starts the meeting with three taps of her staff. "Thank you all for your salutations. Agnes and I appreciate the warm reception. But we are weary from the plane ride and desperately need sleep. It appears the plan for the solstice has been finalized. Without our presence, I may add. We will address that offense in a future circle. Trinity will address the coven now."

"I'm sorry, Leslie," Trinity says, frowning. "I made the decision to address this immediately to avoid more killings. So far, no one has seen Kate anywhere."

Elijah interjects. "She hasn't been to the shelter or Skye's apartment since Gwyn discovered her identity. Who knows where she is?"

"If there have been no new killings, the Dearg Due is fucking hungry," Agnes says. "She's gonna need to feed soon."

"And she goes after young men," Tyler says. "There are a few of us in this coven."

Spence flings his hands up. "It's fucking scary. What if she comes after one of us?"

"So, the plan is we're gonna wing it?" Tanner asks.

My fellow witches chatter among themselves. The chairs squeak as the air conditioner whines, adding to the angst in the room.

Zoe hugs my son while I wring my hands, considering Tyler's worrisome remarks. A scowl has taken up permanent residence on Shane's face. Ronnie rubs her swelling belly while Skye twists her fire-red curls.

Archie leans forward in his chair. "What else can we do, friends? Until Cordelia shows up, we don't know what spell she's used or how to undo it. She has to call on the Dearg Due."

"May I offer a suggestion?" Seamus asks. "I am not a member of your coven. Allow me to confront Cordelia initially. It will put her off balance, permitting you more time to assess the situation."

Leslie finally addresses her deceitful colleague. "I appreciate your offer, Dr. Duffy. I believe we will accept your suggestion under the circumstances. We will meet after dark in the Celestial Gardens, everyone."

"I need to say something before we disband the circle," Shane says. "You sound as if you've already convicted Cordelia when we don't really know if she caused this Dearg Due separation intentionally. I only want to remind you to give her the benefit of the doubt as you promised."

Trinity nods. "We keep our promises, Shane."

"Oh, one more thing. I believe we should tell Jeff Williams about Kate's true identity."

I hop out of my seat. "That's a terrible idea. He won't believe it, and he may go searching for her with some foolish wish to prove she isn't what she is. We can't tell him until after the solstice. Once she's gone."

"And with that," Leslie says with a tap of her staff. "You are dismissed. We will convene Friday night in the gardens. Go in peace and be careful."

My boss glares at me, resentment burning in his emerald-green eyes. Oh, where did the twinkle go, Shane?

Chapter Twenty-Nine

SUMMER SOLSTICE

I stare at my mother in Archie's painting on the fireplace mantel. She will blame herself for the deaths of the young men, too, having created the mound with Leslie and Agnes. I'm not conferencing with her again until this is over. The mantel clock dings one time, signaling the half hour.

"Are you ready?" Archie asks. "It's 8:30 p.m. We should get there before Shane arrives with Cordelia. Seamus didn't want to hold us back, so he got a head start."

"Leslie and Agnes left a half hour ago. They wanted to feel out the space to prepare." I glance at my cell and register the date—June 21. No turning back now. I gape at him. "Shit."

"What? Did they find another body? Or has someone found Kate?"

"No. I didn't receive a text. Today is the solstice, which means..." I grimace, and he ambles toward me, smiling.

"No worries, my love. Yesterday was a busy day for you."

"What kind of girlfriend am I? One who forgot your birthday. That's what I get for not entering it into my calendar. Menopause sucks. I'm lucky I remember to put on my pants. Forgive me?"

"It was only another day in my blessed life with you, Gwyn. As long as you're in it, every day is worth celebrating. You were a wee bit encumbered helping Agnes move into Leslie's house."

"Yeah. Not looking forward to the next few weeks while the kitchen is finished. Three witches and a familiar are too many bodies in one tiny place. But it gave me a good excuse to take off work and avoid Shane. I was going to buy you something, but all this shit went down. I'll have to owe you a present."

He wraps his arms around me. "I have everything I want right here." He kisses me.

"We'll celebrate properly when we've sent the Dearg Due back." I swipe a finger across his lips.

We make the trek through the Green under cloudy skies and the hazy glow of the lampposts. The ghoul could be hiding in the alleyways between the Georgian red-brick buildings. She killed there before, and she's hungry. Seamus said she sought the young men to fill her bloodlust. But Kate has no memory of her spirit side unless they join. What the hell did Cordelia do to the Dearg Due, and why?

When we enter the Celestial Gardens, everyone has arrived, except for Ronnie, Shane, Cordelia—and Kate. Seamus stands with Trinity, chatting. We gather near the mound. The portal lights up and the Seelie Fae cross over.

"Yay!" they yell. "Aunt Gwyn, we missed you, but you brought everyone to play tonight!"

I dart to the children. "Shailagh and Aonghas, you can't stay. There's a scary being we need to send back through the portal, so we can't play with you now. But I promise I'll make time another night. Now go on—"

"But you've missed our playtime and the others, too. We want to play!" They run off toward the hawthorn tree.

Trinity puts a hand on her hip. "We can't deal with those pranksters tonight. Can you do something, Gwyn?"

"I don't think so. When they act like this, I do what they want and hope for the best the next time."

"And that's why they aren't listening to you, Mom," Tyler says. "Why do you think I got away with procrastinating at bedtime by saying one more book?"

Archie lifts a corner of his mouth. "Why does that not surprise me?"

My fellow witches laugh, and I frown at my son. Shailagh and Aonghas play tag, dashing around the shrubs on the right side of the gardens. If I scold them, they will dig in their heels, or should I say pointy shoes.

"I could play with them for a few minutes and try to tire them out," Zoe says.

"Never mind them," Leslie says. "They're only a distraction from our objective. Once Seamus confronts Cordelia with our knowledge of her secretive transgressions, she may try to flee. We must be prepared to act. What if Shane refuses to cooperate?"

"We'll have to proceed without his help," Archie replies. "It may require us to fight against one of our own."

Trinity ties her hair behind her head. "Archie is absolutely right. If Cordelia is responsible, we can't let Shane's relationship stop us from righting this wrong."

"He's a smart man," Agnes says. "When he sees how she responds, he'll come around."

Ronnie rushes through the gate to us. "I'm sorry. I had to pee, and every time I went to the door, the urge came over me like a long-lost ex who wouldn't let go. What did I miss?"

"You should have stayed home for this," I say. "You don't need to take the risk."

"Stop treating me like I'm dying. I'm pregnant. The teensy-weensy witch will be fine in there." She rubs her belly.

"If you feel bad at all," Trinity says. "You must move from the circle. And that's an order. Skye, any evidence Kate returned to the apartment?"

"No," she replies. "And she still has a key."

Elijah shakes his head. "She's not shown at the shelter and hasn't contacted the counselor, either."

Leslie lifts her chin. "Seamus, after a few pleasantries, you must confront Cordelia. Explain your theory to her, and we'll see how she responds."

Agnes snickers. "She's gonna be fucking pissed. Prepare for magic sparks to fly."

"I will hide behind Tanner and Archie." Seamus says. "I may scare her off."

Tanner rubs his hands together. "Good idea, because here they come."

"Does she ever wear pants?" Spence asks.

Shane and the Wicked Witch of the South stroll back to us, Cordelia hanging on his arm. As she approaches, I glimpse her face in the moonlight. Her face is haggard, unlike her usual appearance. The overdone makeup is all there, but I sense something weakened about her. She's not connected with the Dearg Due. Apprehension clutches at my boss's face.

"Hello, y'all. It's so good to see you again. Thank you so much for inviting me to your private Summer Solstice Celebration. We should play with our magic and have some real fun." A faux grin decorates Cordelia's already painted face until Seamus steps from behind Archie, and she gapes at him. "I'm so sorry." She glances at us, panicking. "I swear I didn't know there was an Unremarkable in our midst."

Seamus limps on his cane toward her, and Shane puts his arm around his love.

"I am not an Unremarkable, as those who aren't *in the knowing* are referred to here," Seamus says. "I am a solitary cat sith witch."

She slaps a hand on her upper chest, exhaling. "I am sooo relieved and trying so hard to follow your rules. But it is curious. I've never sensed you were a witch." She squints at him and smiles. "You must use a masking spell, one I've not had experience with."

"Yes," Seamus replies. "There are many reasons for that. I am here at the request of the Bearsden Coven to ask you questions. Questions regarding—the existence of a Dearg Due in Bearsden."

Cordelia's eyes grow big, and she fiddles with her clothes as we condense our circle, the young witches falling in behind her and Shane.

"I don't know what you're talking about." She stammers over her words. "I...I've never heard of a..."

"Dearg Due," Seamus says. "You may not know her by that name. But you are very aware of what and who she is. There have been witnesses to your interactions with this demon spirit. You have been siphoning the energy from her. The Bearsden Coven is also aware you have split the ghoul into two entities using a spell."

Archie signals to the coven to join our magic, creating an amber fence around her. The Seelie Fae stop playing and dart to the mound, observing our magic. Cordelia clutches her amulet as her gaze travels around the circle.

"Shane, are you going to just stand there and let your coven accuse me of such falsehoods?"

He glares at us. "No, I am not. Cordelia is emphatic about her knowledge of the Dearg Due. She doesn't know who she is. That's enough for me. If you make me choose sides, I will."

"And we won't stop you," Leslie says. "But your decision will be final. You will no longer belong to this circle."

Agnes scowls. "Well, that's just fucking great. So much for commitment to the coven, which I'll remind you I joined under pressure. But I'm still here. One solitary witch from your past shouldn't overrule the coven you've made your family. Fuck the ties that bind?"

"When that family fails to support the person you love, they're no longer worthy of my devotion." My boss shoves his hands in his back pockets as his eyes narrow.

"Wow, she's really got you wrapped around her finger," Spence says.

Tanner nudges his partner. "That really hurts, Shane. You know we care about you."

Elijah steps forward. "Man, I've known you for a long time. I consider you a brother. We've worked together to better this town, and you've come to my aid more than my fingers can count. You don't mean what you're saying."

"I think he does," Trinity says. "You better think hard on this, friend. We've known each other for many years. Is this really what you want?"

The young witches blurt out heartfelt reactions of support. "We love you!" "You've been like a grandfather to us!" "We'll keep an open mind!" "Don't leave us!"

I peer at my boss, tears building in my eyes. "Don't do this, Shane."

"He's entitled to his feelings, everyone," Archie says. "He must make his own informed decision. But make sure it's an educated one, my friend. Before you make a mistake you'll regret."

"For fuck's sake," Ronnie says. "I'll admit, Cordelia rubs me the wrong way, too. If she's innocent, I'll name my baby after her, even if it's a boy. But she's hiding something. Can't you tell?"

Shane scans the circle and ends at Cordelia's amulet. "What is the vial for? I've never asked, but they've seen you in the gardens performing rituals with it. If you only explained what you were doing, it would clear all this up. Just tell them, sweetheart."

She scowls at us as she turns her head left and right. "No. It's none of their concern." The amulet radiates, and she lays a hand over it. "I need to go."

She turns around, but the amber fence is too strong to break through. The portal lights up, and the bluish ghoul swirls in the sky, directly over Cordelia. Seamus addresses her again.

"The Dearg Due is waiting for you, Ms. Davenport. I learned many years ago it's better to admit one's mistakes and move on. Your time is now. Don't spoil the opportunity."

Shane smiles at his love. "I'll still love you. No matter what you tell me."

"Rumors had traveled on the witch vine about a portal in Bearsden." Cordelia peers at him, barely catching his gaze. "I'd been searching for a portal to access the Dearg Due because of its rejuvenating powers."

While we continue to power the magical fence, we listen intently to the Wicked Witch of the South, hanging onto each word. Shane's face remains expressionless as she continues with her confession, and the blue apparition floats around her. A gentle breeze blows as the moon plays hide and seek in the clouds above. The Seelie Fae hug each other, trembling, as they watch the drama unfold.

"I arrived long before I contacted you. I'd made contact with the Dearg Due, and we came to an agreement. She wanted to be human again. So, I concocted a new spell that would give her what she wanted, and I would get what I needed."

I interrupt her. "And what was that, exactly?"

Cordelia glares at me. "You. This is your fault. If you hadn't spied on me and stuck your nose in my business, no one would have ever known."

"Answer the question, Cordelia Davenport," Seamus demands.

"Yes, sweetheart," Shane says. "What was the purpose of the agreement?"

"All the spells of youth are fleeting." She lowers her eyes, continuing to grasp the amulet. "I wanted something that would last for days on end. I missed you all these years and decided this was the perfect solution, so I'd be beautiful like I was when we were together."

Shane glowers at his love. "So, you were perfectly fine with the ghoul killing all those young men?"

"Honeybun, don't think they're all innocent. When Kate lured those men, they were after one thing. They deserved what they got."

Shane's eyes well up with tears. "I was wrong. Oh, so wrong. You haven't changed one iota."

"I'm sorry, but we must do something about the Dearg Due," Trinity says, gesturing above.

Leslie glares at Cordelia. "Summon Kate to the gardens. So we can unite her with her spirit and send her back to the Otherworld."

"I won't," Cordelia says. "You can't force me to call on her."

Agnes raises her palm at the Wicked Witch. "Wanna fucking try me?"

A male voice speaks from behind her. "That won't be necessary."

Jeff Williams approaches the circle, and Kate is with him. She's deteriorated into skin and bones, resembling a walking corpse.

"I'm so sorry, everyone," Kate says. "I had no memory of what I was before I became human again. The urges compelled me to go after the men. I tried to stop, but I couldn't."

Jeff rubs her bony back. "It's not your fault, Kate."

Tears roll down her face. "I ran away and hid, so Cordelia couldn't call on me again and force me to feed."

"I told Jeff about Kate—her being a Dearg Due," Shane says. "Somehow, I imagined she was at fault, but I didn't tell Jeff that. He only wanted to stop her pain. I'm sorry, son."

"I don't want to say goodbye to you," Jeff says, tearing up.

Kate lays a hand on his face. "I will always remember you...fondly."

She turns around and approaches the blue apparition. She extends her arms upward but cannot join with her spirit. Seamus moves closer to Cordelia.

"Release the essence of the Dearg Due from the amulet, Cordelia Davenport. So Kate can unite with her spirit."

"I won't give it up, and you can't make me." The Wicked Witch of the South raises her arm to summon her magic, and an amber glow radiates from her hand. Shane clasps his fingers around her fist.

"No, darling. You will not hurt my family."

Shane grabs Cordelia's wrist, yanks her arm down, and pulls the necklace from her neck.

As soon as the amulet's leather tears, her hands and face wither, wrinkling in seconds and returning her to the old woman she was masking. She cries out.

"Look what you have done. I'm ugly. You'll never love me now."

"Yes, darling," Shane says. "You're ugly, but not because of your face. It's the detestable woman inside you that made you hideous. I would have loved every wrinkle of your true self."

Seamus takes the amulet and limps to Kate. When he removes the cork from the vial, an explosion of sparkling blue magic escapes into the air, swirling like a tornado around her. The essence engulfs her and swoops her up into the hovering entity. With a gust of wind, the Dearg Due flies through the portal, disappearing with a clap. Shailagh and Aonghas jump and run back to the hawthorn tree. The coven lowers the magic barrier, and our amber fence dissipates.

Leslie approaches Cordelia Davenport, who is cowering and covering her face with her hands. "Your actions contributed to the deaths of five young men whose lives were only beginning. You put our community in harm's way, all for your own narcissistic reasons. Unfortunately, you will not pay for your wretched choices in the courts of the Unremarkables. But this coven can decide on your fate within the town of Bearsden. Trinity?"

"Cordelia Davenport," our coven leader says. "Due to your use of fatal magic, you are banned from the city of Bearsden. You have one week to pack and get the fuck out of our town. That's not much time, so I suggest you get a move on."

Cordelia pouts as she peers up at Shane. "I love you, honeybun. I promise to mend my ways. Please come with me. I don't want to lose you."

"I'll have to think on that, Cordelia," he replies. "Come by the store tomorrow, and we'll talk."

"I'm sorry, everyone. I really am." She leaves the circle and walks through the iron gate.

Agnes scowls. "Sorry, my ass. She's only apologizing because we caught her. No offense, Shane. But you let your love for that woman blind you."

"I'm very aware of my poor decisions," he says. "But I still love her. Even with all her imperfections."

Elijah pats him on the back. "Well, I hope you'll stay here in Bearsden. It would be a lot less jovial without your southern humor...and your friendship."

We each raise a hand and summon our magic in respect, as the coven did for me. Shane is hurting and needs our support more now than ever.

"I appreciate all of you giving Cordelia the benefit of the doubt, but you were right. I'm so conflicted right now, my stomach is full of knots. The remainder of my night will include plenty of serious thinking." Shane wraps an arm around Jeff. "Son, why don't you stay at my house tonight? I believe we both could use the company."

"Thanks," Jeff replies. "I'd like that."

They head out through the gate, and the rest of us stand silently, gazing at the brilliant moon. My heart aches for the old hippie, and part of me feels responsible. But what choice did I have? Archie is the first to speak.

"We must respect whatever decision Shane makes. Inevitably, the heart chooses our path." He smiles at me. "If he decides to leave with Cordelia, we should wish him well."

"I'd be so sad if he left," Zoe says.

Tyler hugs her. "None of us will be happy about it, but we don't get to choose for him."

"No, we don't," Skye says. "But he'd be a fool to follow her back to North Carolina, or wherever she's headed."

"I think he may surprise us all." Tanner glances at the gate. "But he thought he'd found love again."

Spence hugs his partner. "And love can make you do stupid shit."

"Well, that was the worst Summer Solstice Celebration I've ever attended," Skye says. "I'm glad Zach wasn't here. He'd never attend another holiday event with me, ever."

Agnes starts walking out. "Enough with the fucking sullen faces. We did what we came here to do. Let's disband this circle and go home."

Trinity waves her hand. "I second that. Let's go, all."

"Then we're dismissed," the Elder says. "Seamus, please check your schedule for Monday. I request a meeting to discuss—everything."

Seamus nods. "As you wish, Dr. Hughes."

Leslie grabs Agnes's hand, and they stroll out of the gardens. Trinity, Ronnie, and Elijah follow them right after. As the rest of us inch toward the gate, the Seelie Fae wave goodbye. Even Shailagh and Aonghas have lost their cheery disposition and cross over into their world. We lock the gate and say goodnight to the young witches. I hug my son and Zoe before they head to his sedan.

Seamus, Archie, and I walk home through the Green, slowing our pace to accommodate his limp. When we arrive at the bungalow on Douglas Street, the cat sith witch pauses in front of his house.

"I am sorry all of this has caused so much distress for your coven," he says. "But I am happy to have helped tonight. The Bearsden community can rest well without the threat of further injury. Now that my identity has been revealed, please don't hesitate to ask for my help in the future. But I must remain a solitary practitioner. Sleep well." He walks up the walkway to his front door.

"I have to have a serious talk with him. How am I supposed to live here knowing he's watching over me all the time? I should have a say."

Archie squeezes my hand. "You should. But I don't think you will. You may need to make peace with his protection."

I glance back at the cat sith witch. That kind of devotion may be the death of him.

Chapter Thirty

SAYING GOODBYE

"When would you like to celebrate your birthday?" I ask, finishing the last bite of my veggie wrap.

Archie sips his iced tea and sets the glass on the kitchen table. "After last night, I'm not in the mood. We'll celebrate later this week."

"I know what you mean," I say, clinking my nails on my glass.

"Are you nervous about going to work today?"

"Yeah. There's so much I want to say to Shane to stop him from making the biggest blunder of his life, and I don't want him to leave."

Archie lays a hand on mine. "All you can do is share with him how much you care, Gwyn."

"Thanks for eating lunch early. My shift starts at 11:30, so they can take lunch breaks. I'm thinking they'll need to hire new staff when the fall semester begins, because I'll have to cut back my hours. The store is so busy. But who knows what will happen if Shane leaves?"

"Stop stressing over what-ifs. You'll find out shortly. Speaking of work, I need to catch up on this summer class and get started on my syllabi for the fall semester. I want that out of the way before our visit to the UK in August."

I get up from the kitchen table and take my dishes to the sink. "The visit will do us both a lot of good. That reminds me I should conference with my parents and chat with Aunt Gorawen. Ellie finally got back to me."

"To be a fly on the wall for that conversation," he says, scratching his goatee.

I put on my sneakers and grab my purse. "I'll sleep at Leslie's tonight, so I can conference with my parents. If Shane says anything about leaving, I'll text you."

"Cracking." He kisses me. "Let's hope for the best."

As I stroll toward Main Street, I relish the near-perfect day. It's in the low 80s, with plenty of sunshine and no humidity. We don't get many of these in Delaware. If only there wasn't a cloud of heartache hanging over it—the unnecessary death of five students, Jeff losing Kate, and Shane's inevitable decision. He fell in love with Cordelia again, and she appears to truly return those affections. Despite her irresponsible choices, he can't turn off his love like a light switch. He may decide to leave with her in a few days, and there's nothing I can or should do to change his mind.

When I arrive at Mystic Sage, Shane and Jeff are talking behind the sales counter. The last shopper exits with a ding.

"Good morning, bosses." I set my purse on the counter. "Can you put this underneath?"

Shane smiles and grabs it. "Of course, darling."

"How are you, Jeff? I wish things hadn't turned out the way they did."

"It's not your fault, Gwyn," he says. "Or yours, Shane. I only wish I hadn't liked her so much." He gestures with his thumb. "I'll be in the back checking the stock."

Jeff meanders around the counter and enters the crystals room. Shane walks around and gives me a fatherly hug.

"I'm sorry, darling. My love for Cordelia cast a fog over me, blocking out all rational thought. I see her clearly now, but I still love her."

"I should have told you she was connecting with an apparition, but Trinity said I should wait until we knew more. And then it spiraled from there."

His brow crinkles. "I was too caught up in the moment. I wouldn't have believed you."

"Have you decided what you're going to do? Before you answer, I want you to know I'll respect whatever decision you make. You deserve to be happy."

He shoves his hands in his back pockets and takes a breath. "I have chosen to..."

The door dings, and Cordelia walks in, dressed in more casual clothing—a blouse and cotton pants. The cocky air about her has disappeared, and she looks worn down. But it's not the wrinkles that make her appear haggard. She ambles toward us, her head hanging low.

"Hello. I came as you asked. Could we go in the back and discuss this privately?"

My boss glances at me and raises his head. "Gwyn is family. Whatever we discuss can be said in front of her."

"No, I'll go help Jeff." I take a step.

"Gwyn, I want you here. Please stay?"

"OK. Tell me to leave if you change your mind." I cross my arms and wait for the words I can't bear to hear.

"Cordelia, I love you with every ounce of my being. I considered my options all night. Didn't sleep a wink. I imagined spending the end of my days with you. What did I see? I envisioned a life with a woman who cared more about appearances than the lives of innocent Unremarkables."

"Honeybun, I was wrong. I know that now. Please give me a second chance? I want to spend the rest of my life with you."

She appears sincere, but how can Shane be sure? He moves toward her and wraps his arms around her, squeezing as if this is the last time.

"This *was* your second chance, darling. Goodbye, Cordelia. I wish you well."

My heart sinks for Shane. I'm overjoyed he's staying, but I ache for his loss. He steps back, and she pulls a tissue from her purse.

"I understand," she says, sniffing. "Gwyn, I'm sorry for how I treated you. I truly regret my deception."

I swallow. "Well, there's a lot of that going around in Bearsden. Goodbye."

She exits the store, and Shane stares out the door until she fades into the crowds. I lay a hand on his arm.

"Don't be sorry for me, Gwyn. As much as I loved her, she hadn't really changed. If I went back to North Carolina with her, I'd be lying to myself."

"Everyone will be so happy you're staying. We don't make up for an empty bed, but we love you."

He grins widely. "There are other fish in the sea. I guess I need to get out my fishing pole. But not for a couple of months. I'm gonna go home for lunch now, and I think I'll take the rest of the day off."

"OK, boss." I peer at the doorway to the back of the store. "Jeff has been through so much. I hope this doesn't set him back."

"He's stronger than any of us. He'll do just fine."

Shane checks his pocket for his phone and heads out to lunch. Shoppers come and go all afternoon, distracting me so I don't have to think about everything that has transpired—the Dearg Due, the dead young men, Cordelia Davenport, Shane and Jeff's breaking hearts. My dilemma about Seamus. Jeff walks into the front of the store.

"I need a break and interaction with humans. How would you like to restock the crystals?"

"Sounds like a plan," I say. "Call me if the store gets overrun with consumers."

For the next few minutes, I pull out crystal wands and place price tags on the bottoms. When I raise my head, Detective Schmidt is standing in the doorway.

"Mr. Williams said I could find you back here." He moves next to me, lifts a large rose crystal from the shelf, and checks the price on the bottom. "That's highway robbery. Are they really worth this much?"

I stand and cross my arms. "Depends on who's holding it, and what they want from it." With the events of the past week, I'd forgotten about our last interaction. "You said you were going to ask me to come to the precinct for more questions. Am I not a suspect anymore?" Better to rip the bandage off all at once.

"No. Not now, but I had many questions." His eyes narrow. "For a while, I wasn't convinced a wild animal was responsible for these murders. I surmised these young men were the victims of something—or someone more sinister."

Holy crystals. My heart lunges toward my chest. "And now?"

"We found the cougar." He stares at me and clutches his belt. "We believe Dr. Evans suffered the same fate as the other young men. We can't find any family. It's like he appeared out of thin air."

Not thin air—from the Otherworld.

"We're closing the case. No reason to keep it open now. But I am curious, and you're not obligated to answer. I suspected you, because you weren't as upset as I'd expected you to be."

I hesitate but tell him, anyway. "We weren't on good terms the last time I was with him. He was extremely upset I chose another man over him. But...I am sad about what might have happened to him." It's cleansing to speak the truth, and tears wet my eyes. "He had been a good friend, and it hurt to see that friendship end so badly."

Detective Schmidt nods. "Love triangles never have a happy ending for anyone. Well, at least you can put this behind you now. I'm sorry I ever suspected you. Take care, Ms. Crowther."

Detective Schmidt walks out, and I collapse on the floor. Running footsteps approach.

"He came straight back here," Jeff says. "I couldn't stop him. I was ringing up a customer. Are you OK?"

I take a cleansing breath. "Absolutely. I think we're all gonna be fine."

"I'm not happy with your choice to pursue crystal use without adequate training." My mom's golden image glimmers as she scowls. "It was irresponsible."

"Your mother is right, Gwynedd," Dad says, glittering in gold. "Your mind could have suffered irreparable damage."

"Well, if you hadn't raised me as an Unremarkable, we wouldn't be having this discussion, would we?" I ask in a sarcastic tone. My laptop screen lights up with a chat call from Aunt Gorawen. "I have to go. Aunt Gorawen is calling. I'll conference again when I have time. Stop worrying about me. Have confidence in my witchcraft skills. I learn more and more every day."

I wave my hand, and my parents' images fade. With a tap of the green icon, my great-aunt appears on the screen.

"Hi, Aunt Gorawen. It's been a while since we spoke last."

"So wonderful to see your face, niece. How is Tyler?"

"He's fine, but he's busy today working on the renovation of a fellow witch's kitchen. I've wanted to chat for so long, but some horrific things happened. A Dearg Due came across the portal, and we had to send her back. She killed five young men before we figured out she was responsible."

"Oh, Gwynedd, that is dreadful. I'm so sorry your town had to suffer so. But all of you are doing well? None of you were hurt?"

"No. We had a couple of very close calls. The Dearg Due attacked Archie and me." I bite my lip. "But we got help from a cat sith witch. Here's a shocker. Turned out to be Dr. Seamus Duffy. And he has one of your charmed paintings of Mom. Why do you think that is?"

I squint at her, and she gapes at the screen.

CHAPTER THIRTY-ONE

MY PROTECTOR

A WEEK HAS PASSED, and it's hotter than a bucket of lava by 6:00 a.m. I could have slept in the buff at Archie's, but I don't dare try it at home with the familiar scuttling around. There's nothing worse than continuous night sweats in an old house with inadequate air conditioning. I shuffle into the kitchen wearing my cami and shorts sleepwear and get bombarded by a smoky haze.

"For fuck's sake, Agnes. Do you have to smoke pot at the breakfast table?"

"I wouldn't be here if your crew had finished my kitchen," she says, scowling.

The hedge witch is dressed in a black, knee-length cotton nightgown. She takes a puff on her joint and blows smoke in my direction. I hack and cough as I wave my hand in front of my face. Leslie ambles in wearing her summer cotton robe.

"Good morning, Leslie," I say, hacking. "I think I'll stay at Archie's until the renovation is completed. This house isn't big enough for all of us."

"Indeed." Leslie frowns at her girlfriend. "Why didn't you open a window like I asked?"

"You've got the AC on. You don't want to air condition the outside and let the heat in, do you?"

Leslie opens a window a crack. "At least, try to blow it out. It smells like rotten mugwort in here now."

Mr. Yeats enters the kitchen in his chimeric cat form and hisses at the hedge witch. She summons her magic and throws a tiny ball of amber at him. He meows loudly and scurries back into the hallway.

"Don't tease him, Agnes," Leslie says. "I depend on his assistance, and you're high."

Agnes cracks up and strikes the tabletop. "The best way to start the day."

The Elder sits down at the table with her coffee. "Gwynedd, how is Shane adjusting?"

"You know how he is," I say, pouring hot water into my teacup. "He wears a grin and moves on to the next day, always the optimist. But my witch sense tells me he misses her."

Agnes puts out the joint. "Cordelia's transgressions had to be addressed by the coven. I'm all for breaking rules, but she wouldn't have changed. She only repented 'cause she got caught."

"Well, we'll never really know, will we?" I wave a hint of magic at my cup, and the spoon spins.

Leslie's eyebrows fall in disapproval. "Are the young witches meeting at the farmhouse today to work on the floors?"

"Yeah. The appliances will be hooked up, too. Next week, the countertops will be installed."

"About fucking time." Agnes pushes up from her chair and waddles. "Woooh. I better go back to bed and sleep this off." She wiggles her eyebrows at the Elder. "Care to join me, sweetheart?"

"It's morning, Agnes," Leslie replies. "I have much to do today."

"Suit yourself." Agnes belches and staggers down the hallway.

I laugh and take a sip of my Earl Grey. "What did you ever see in her, Leslie?"

"She has her redeeming qualities." A mischievous smile slips slowly onto her face.

I snicker. "I bet. If you don't mind, I'm going to take my shower and drive over to Agnes's. While Tanner and Spence work on the floors, the rest of us are going to return to the witchcraft database. Even if the Tuatha Dé Danann don't come searching for Nuada, we have to close that mound. Other beings may stumble across it and invade our town. We need to continue our search for a spell."

"Indeed," she says. "Gwynedd, I've not spoken with you about Dr. Duffy. I had a discussion with him, and he told me everything. I, too, was appalled he had kept his cat sith witch status hidden from me all these years. But they are solitary witches who make decisions without the input of a coven. I can't fault him for his reasons. But I imagine you do."

"Aunt Gorawen should have never asked him to follow me here. He gave up his life in Great Britain to protect a woman he'd never met—only from afar."

"What are you going to do about it?"

"I don't know. I've been avoiding him since the solstice. But I'll have to have a heart-to-heart with him, eventually."

"Indeed."

The young witches stand in the hallway, peering into the kitchen at the gleaming pine floors. Tanner, Spence, and Tyler did a fantastic job on them.

"I can't thank you guys enough for spending so much time on this kitchen. Agnes will love it when the countertops are installed."

"No, she won't," Skye says. "She'll complain about how long it took and ask us what project we're starting next."

Tyler chuckles. "You're probably right."

"I dare her to get snarky with us," Spence says. "We don't have to do shit."

Zoe nudges him. "But you will. Because she's family."

"Absolutely," Tanner says, hugging his partner.

Archie comes down the steps and joins us in the foyer. "I powered down the desktop and turned out the lights. That's enough spell search for today. The floors are smashing."

Tanner grins widely. "Thank you. Isn't it amazing what we can accomplish together?"

"Now, if we could only find a portal-closing spell," Skye says. "Then we'd be up for the witch's hall of fame."

"Is there a witch's hall of fame?" I ask, tilting my head.

"I don't fucking know," she replies.

We all burst out laughing as we admire our work. I would have never made it this far without the humor of my witch family. We turn out the lights and lock up the house. As we drive down the gravel road, I take comfort in knowing life is nearly back to normal. As normal as it will ever be for an ancestral witch in a town with an open portal.

"Whenever you get this quiet, I worry. What's floating around in that head of yours?" Archie asks.

"Wondering what I should do about Seamus. I can't report him to the Bearsden Police. What do I say? Hey, there's a cat sith witch who feels obligated to protect me. Can I file a restraining order against a protector? I finally got the detective off my ass. I don't want to give him any reason to come knocking at my door again."

He strokes my arm. "To be honest, I'm glad Seamus is here to help you and the town. Talk to him. He's a kind soul and surely reasonable."

"When the appropriate time presents itself. I convinced Aunt Gorawen to release him from her request. That should convince him to return to Britain. But enough of that. I don't want anything to spoil this evening."

"I'm so looking forward to tonight, my love. Now that I'm back at full capacity."

"I can't wait. Oh, I almost forgot. After dinner, I have to go play with the pranksters. With all the mess surrounding the Dearg Due, I don't dare skip playtime tonight. But I'll be quick."

"I don't know how you can go there in this heat and humidity."

"Yeah. It's like a sauna outside. Running around with the pranksters will leave me sweaty as a construction worker. I'll need a shower before we...celebrate."

He smiles. "Then I might as well wait and join you. Let's wash away all this talk of Dearg Due and fairy revenge."

"Sounds like a plan, professor." I blow him a kiss.

After I wave goodnight to the Seelie Fae children, I wipe the sweat from my face and neck. If it's like this in June, what fresh hell will August bring? I make my way out through the gate and head to Archie's house to celebrate a belated birthday with him. I receive a text notification.

Ronnie: *Hey, are you going baby shopping with me tomorrow?*
Me: *Yup. I'm so excited to pick out baby clothes.*
Ronnie: *Have fun with Archie tonight. Wink. Wink.*
Me: *Thanks. Get some rest, mama.*
Ronnie: *Night. Zzzzz.*

When I look up from my phone, Seamus Duffy is standing under the lamppost in front of Mitchell Mansion, appearing as eerie as ever. But I no longer find him frightening or weird. His presence provides a level of comfort I could get accustomed to, but shouldn't.

"Hello, Seamus," I say, shoving my cell into my pocket.

"Good evening, Gwynedd. Before you say anything, I was leaving the Raven Pub and saw you enter the gardens. I thought you might want company on your walk home. If not, I'll be on my way."

I smile affectionately. "That would be silly, don't you think? I'd be two steps behind you."

"And then *you'd* be following *me*." Seamus leans into me. "Should I alert the Bearsden Police?"

I chuckle. "Please don't. Detective Schmidt removed me as a suspect in the disappearance of Nick Evans only a week ago. I'd like to remain out of his radar."

"Understandable. Then, shall we?" He gestures toward East Main Street.

As we stroll through the Green on this muggy night, the temperature is oppressive. I can't wait to get to Archie's and strip—one for the nasty heat, and two for the celebratory birthday sex. When we approach the Old Men oak trees, I catch the professor staring at me.

"Seamus, I'm not comfortable with you devoting your life to being my protector. Aunt Gorawen was wrong to ask you. I don't suppose you'd consider looking for a permanent academic post back in the UK?"

Folds form in his brow. "What if I want to stay? I love teaching at DUB. The students are wonderful. My colleagues are amiable and supportive...and witches, I might add. I love Delaware."

"Really?" I ask, doubting his sincerity. "Because sticky summer humidity and heat,"—I swat at a mosquito—"and annoying insects are lovable?"

"There's more to Bearsden than the weather. It's full of kind, supportive witches and Unremarkables."

"But I don't want you following me everywhere. Don't I have a choice?"

We arrive at his bungalow on Drummond Lane and stop at the bottom of his walkway. He moves closer, his sea-green eyes shining under the streetlight like glass.

"I've grown fond of you, Gwynedd, and it's in my nature to follow through with a commitment once it's made."

A longing appears in his eyes, and I turn my head. "I spoke to Aunt Gorawen about you. She's going to release you from that commitment." I peer back at him.

"Gorawen may have requested the protection initially, but I choose where I go and who I serve." He lowers his eyes briefly. "Gwynedd, the threat of the Tuatha Dé Danann remains. They may not cross through the portal for years, but eventually, they will come. And they will arrive en masse. You are a powerful ancestral witch, as is Archie. Your son will be a force in his own right. But even with a strong full coven, you will need protection."

"But I didn't ask you for it."

"I offer you a proposal. I promise only to track you when I sense you're in danger. Could you live with that?"

I squint at him. "And if I can't?"

He smiles at me and remains silent.

I exhale. "Thank you for walking with me. Archie is waiting for me. We're going to celebrate his birthday belatedly. Goodnight, Seamus."

He gazes at me, and for the first time, I sense a sadness in his eyes mixed with the longing. Is he harboring romantic feelings for me?

"Enjoy your evening with Dr. Cockburn, Gwynedd."

Seamus limps up the walkway to his front door and smiles at me before entering his house. I continue on to Archie's. After a few steps, I stare back at the bungalow. He's watching me through the front window.

Suddenly, a strange aura overwhelms me, building from my gut and spreading throughout my body. The surrounding homes spin, and a foul stench permeates. I quell the urge to throw up. I must be dehydrated. This is the weirdest hot flash ever. I rub my temples and turn back around, walking toward Duncan Street.

But I stop when an obnoxious buzzing fills my ears and a vision seizes my brain. I hold my breath.

The portal in the Celestial Gardens lights up as steam rises from the musty, damp earth. Wavering moonbeams spotlight the mound as a dark figure emerges. As the unknown entity reveals itself, the hideous being grows larger until it's fully visible—a monstrous giant with gray skin, dark hair, and deformed bulging muscles. The mas-

culine monster pounds the wet earth with heavy boots and trudges forward two steps into the light of the moon. His facial features are severe, marred as if he's spent years warring. One eye appears permanently disfigured and closed. The other is black as obsidian crystal. He cocks his head and makes eye contact with me.

I gasp and snap back to reality. My heart is pounding against my ribcage. I run the rest of the way to Archie's, shoving the front door open with a bang.

"What the fawk, Gwynedd?" Archie asks, rushing in from the kitchen. "You could have damaged the wall."

He examines the plaster while I stand in the foyer, speechless and panting. Sweat slides down my face and chest, soaking my bangs and tank top. The chill of the AC prompts goosebumps on my arms. I swallow and try to speak, but the words get trapped in my throat.

Archie grabs my arm. "Are you all right?"

I stare back at him, breathing through my mouth.

"No. You're not. What happened?"

I close my mouth and swallow again. "I had a vision."

ACKNOWLEDGMENTS

Thank you to my daughter for the brainstorming sessions. There's always a part of you in my books.

To my book cover designer Charles Clark. My books would be naked without you.

Special thanks to my editor Sarah Faeth Sanders. You made my book shine!

To my ARC Team. I can't thank you enough for your devotion to my books.

About the Author

J.C. YEAMANS is an author of PWF Urban Fantasy and other paranormal fiction. A former public school teacher based in Lewes, Delaware, she writes about all things witchy to find the inherent magic in life's journey of discovery and love—all while making blunders along the way. As the owner of Reed Shore Press, she also publishes fiction and nonfiction works for others. Her prior career revolved around the performing arts. She is married and has two adult children. When she's not putting pen to paper (or more aptly, fingertips to keys), she spends time biking, hiking, and weightlifting.

Sign up for J.C. Yeamans's newsletter at jcyeamans.com to download A Trinity of Witches, a free backstory to The Bearsden Witch Series.

OTHER BOOKS

The Bearsden Witch Series

Secrets of a Midlife Witch
Schooling of a Midlife Witch
Stalking of a Midlife Witch
Trials of a Midlife Witch
TBD of a Midlife Witch
(Spring 2024)

9 798886 520125